BEYOND THE MIST

Also available:

Beyond the Mist – Book 1
Beyond the Mist – Book 2

and as an "e-book"

Beyond the Mist

Books One and Two

R FERGUS MCGHEE

First published in Great Britain in 2006 by

Lulu.com

Copyright © 2006

Cover Illustrations by www.mindlandgraphics.com

FIRST EDITION

Printed and bound in Great Britain
by Lightning Source UK Ltd.

ISBN 978-1-4303-0045-8

Prologue

The ice-cold wind beat across Sharon's face, sending a cool chill down her trembling spine. She had been wandering the icy wilderness for hours now after losing the tourist party a few miles back. She sat stiffly on a jagged rock of ice, her body weight slowly compressing the natural mound. It was sheltered by a high turret of sleet guarding her from the fiercest of blasts and harsh frost of the Icelandic climate. No fear flowed from her glassy blue eyes; she was not one to let fear overcome her. No, it was worry that crept upon the fibres of her mind, etching out a menacingly bleak future.

Her mother, now lost amid the snow, was born in France and her late father in Norway. Through all the events of her life - moving to Germany then Britain, her father's death and the deep mourning she had for him and now her loss of the party, Sharon never changed for the worse; she became stronger and somehow, she could not only see light at the end of the tunnel: she could feel its warm glow even from a distance. She did not grow in pain and sorrow. Her unique sense of hope kept her going.

The ice beneath her was suddenly shattering; breaking into small sections quickly, each splitting into a now vast network of tiny streams absorbing the ice faster and faster. Sharon grabbed hold of her travelling bag and darted away from the collapsing ground beneath her. She ran with all the energy she had left, and finally the quiet but so piercing cracking noises ceased and the land was still. Her bag, however, was not. It was shaking steadily when Sharon opened it to find her mobile phone vibrating rhythmically inside.

Sharon's mother Sacha was a few dozen miles north of her as part of a search party organised to look for Sharon. So far they had had no successes, until finally Sacha could hear a ringing tone at the receiver's end, which was answered after about a minute of anxious waiting.

"Bonjour... mamon?" Sharon's voice responded to the monophonic beeping.

"Sharon? C'est moi," Sacha replied. The pair always spoke with each other in Sacha's native language French, but English was Sharon's first language and confusion had to be avoided at all costs.

"Mamon! Je suis... eh..."

"Please, speak English. Where are you? We're looking for you," said Sacha anxiously.

"I don't know. Somewhere near the coast; I can see it, but only on the horizon. The ground, it broke up in front of me... I almost fell. Come quick!" Sharon replied.

"We're trying, darling. Keep in contact."

"Yes, it's freezing. Can't you..." But the connection broke off and the line went dead. Sharon took the phone away from her ear to inspect it, but the handset was blown off by a sudden gust of wind. Sharon herself was even blown back by the power of this blast and found herself instantly covered in sharp ice. She had fallen towards the ground, her sense of hope completely shattered, and was waiting to die. The bleak freeze concealed her body with a blanket of snow while she sat inert, ready to decompose under a deadly covering of coldness. An ominous mist of sure fatality shrouded the area, and Sharon fell slowly into a deep sleep.

CHAPTER ONE

The Slave of Ignorance

Sharon awoke after a long night's sleep in which she had expected to die. However, when she unveiled her face, previously hidden by her waterproof coat, it was not a golden paradise, a fiery pit, or even an icy wilderness she beheld, but a corn field in the middle of no-where. Was she still in a dream? Sharon pinched herself: it hurt. The skies were a pale but pleasant blue and the odd tree here and there housed choruses of birds singing randomly yet in what seemed to be a perfect harmony. Maybe this *was* heaven; then again, thought Sharon, maybe not. To the south of where she stood, a few hundred feet away, was a little farmhouse of a most unusual shape: it consisted of a long narrow block joined onto a peculiar-looking pyramid-shaped tower. On this tower block there was a large brick chimney, a gentle and steady flow of smoke billowing from its top. To the right of the house there was what looked like a barn and stables, and to the left for about a mile there was nothing but countryside. Then there was a little church, and to the left of that, beyond a few houses and a little shop, was a shabby medieval-looking public house. It had a small sign dangling from above the door lintel, which swung violently with the wind.

After several further unsuccessful attempts at convincing herself she was no longer in the realm of reality, she decided to walk into the village, nursing a terrible brew of fear inside her. As she approached the farmhouse she caught sight of a lazy river which flowed round the back of the village, meandering smoothly, a few of its tributaries apparently irrigating the fields nearby and providing a water supply to the residences littered across the nearer bank.

As Sharon got closer to the house she saw a little wall guarding the grounds from the fields and a lop-sided black iron gate giving way to a rough path. The coarse grass either side gradually gave way to a finely kept lawn with beautiful perennial borders. The enclosed front garden was simple but elegant, and rather appealing. Another gate, this time standing upright, was the final entrance to the garden. A large bay window came into view, and as Sharon walked on a door appeared on the east-facing wall. Above it, in a facing of stone, were engraved with gold the words 'Shanklot Stead', worn away slightly by many years of wear. Underneath was a large oak door with a brass handle and knocker. There were two steps up, and Sharon climbed them each with a deep breath. Her resolve was strong and she had just taken hold of the knocker when a plump, middle-aged woman came plodding hurriedly along to the door from the back garden holding a wicker basket of clothes. She was wearing a little cap and apron, both blue and white, and called over to Sharon before she could lay the knocker to the door.

"Hullo?! Who be you then, eh? From the village are we? No, it's not Anna is it?"

Before Sharon could answer her the woman opened the door and led her in, still talking.

"Of course it is. Why Anna, how you've grown! How is life in the city then?" she kept on. "It'll be a right ol' adventure, eh, working in a big city like Sulla! Wow, what a life, eh? What a life!" All these questions went unanswered as Sharon struggled to get a word in the conversation.

"Come now, girl. You're awful quiet today! Ah … ye'll be tired, o' course. Tired o' all that work, eh? How are ye lass? How are ye?" Sharon was by now sitting in the leather-bound wooden bench in the main sitting room overlooking the fields she had just come from, and watching the blazing fire crackle in the corner.

"Excuse me: I'm not Anna, and I've not come from the city either. I'm Sharon Jarls from Britain. I was in Iceland and…" But it was no use explaining - she was cut off by yet more speech.

"You're not Anna, eh? You're a Sharrin from a Britten, are you? Tell me, lass; what's a Sharrin and where's this Britten? Not in this country? Near Westclock, no, or Yriad, or are you one o' those Arvadians. Or further away? Fording per'aps, or Muirstone?"

"I'm sorry, but I've never heard of any of those places. I'm from Cheltenham in England, Britain. My mother's from France and my father is… was Norwegian. I used to live in Ger…" Again she was cut off by the woman. Her life story seemed to flow out of her mouth quite naturally and unrestrainedly, but it was too much for the poor old woman to stomach.

"Wooooooh, lass. Slow down. Ye're off yer trolley, lass. These places I ain't ne'er 'eard of. Ye're geography's pretty bad if ye've ne'er 'eard o' the places I mentioned. There ain't many more places in this world, my dear."

"I don't think I'm from this world, you see. That's just it. Now, can you tell me where I am and who you are, please? I need to get back quickly."

"Why, you're in the Gleddock Bank by the Shanklot corridor, the little river that runs just past here. This is the stead and we're just south o' the border. Don't go a-crossin' there though, my love. Dangerous business, crossin' that. We're west o' Mount Gleddock, that steep slope up there, ye see."

She pointed to the window and Sharon saw a distant mountain centred in the left pane of glass.

"I'm Mrs. Bugle-Thom, and I be the keeper of this 'ere house and farm. My husband's the real head though. He's the worker. Now, from another world are we? Come through the portal, did we?" Her friendly tone seemed to merge into one of curiosity mingled with suspicion.

Suddenly, a little wooden door no bigger than a foot square opened into the room from the opposite wall, revealing a man's head popping almost instantly out of the hole. He had a dark, rough beard and a brown moustache and wore a pair of worn-out spectacles which had perfectly clear lenses, but grimy casing.

"Let's not confuse the girl, Martha. Who is this young one?" He turned his stare to Sharon. "Don't be listening to her baffling wives' tales. They mean nothing."

"They ain't any ol' wives' tales Jock; they're pure legend, truth maybe," Mrs. Bugle-Thom retorted.

"Anyway, where did you come from and what are you doing in my house?" Mr. Bugle-Thom asked the girl.

"That's Jarls. She's a Sharrin from a Britten, apparently. Her mother's a French and her father likes a wee gin, eh lass?"

Sharon could tell this was not going to be easy.

After a lot of time and countless explanations Mr. and Mrs. Bugle-Thom, or Jock and Martha as they let Sharon call them, took Sharon on a tour of the village to meet the locals to see if they could help in any way.

Martha led Sharon out the back door, down a few little steps and onto some rough ground which led as a path around the back lawn towards another matching blue gate. This gate was larger and as Martha pushed it open Sharon saw it provided a route through some sparse woodland. Past this, which only lasted for around twenty yards, was a brick arch in a wall surrounding the small forest. Through the arch was a cobble path with tall black lampposts which had unlit candles inside. This narrow path turned right abruptly and became a wide road, with the river (the 'Shanklot Corridor') on one side, and a row of pretty houses on the other. Sharon and her leader waited patiently on the housed side at a bronze sundial. It had peculiar markings engraved into it, but Sharon could tell from the shadow it was about three o'clock in the afternoon.

"The transport comes round 'ere thrice a day. Just wait an angle or two and he'll be round."

Mrs. Bugle-Thom was referring to the angles marked on the sundial, Sharon noticed, and sure enough within three marked angles came a man wearing a long, green velvet robe and a squat little matching hat. He was riding a most peculiar form of bicycle and when he saw Martha and Sharon he stopped and let them sit on the back two seats.

"Mrs. B-T! How nice to see you. Out for your shopping are we? And who's your little friend, eh?"

He had a lively, jocose spirit which appealed to Sharon. She was drawn to his personality straight away; he reminded her of her father.

"Good reflex, Mr. Tolliery. This 'ere is Sharrin from Britten and..." Martha continued to explain Sharon's purpose for being there and asked to go to the 'P.H'.

When they drew up to a halt outside an old ramshackle building Martha opened her leather purse and dug around in it. When the bicycle came to a halt she drew out a little green leaf and tore it in half.

"Here. Half a Forden-leaf do?" she asked. This was more than enough.

"Oh, you're too kind. Have this one for free, Mrs. B-T, seeing as you've got a guest. Have a nice day." With that last remark the man cycled off down the road to his next destination, not noticing the piece of leaf cleverly attached to one of the handlebars.

As the pair approached the building Sharon posed a few questions to Martha.

"Why did you want to pay him with a leaf, Martha?"

"My dear, a leaf from the tree of Forden is worth half an hour's pay. It can buy a couple of drinks of good spirits in 'ere, or a good book maybe. If someone offers you one, take it, lass. If you learn nothin' else from me, let you remember that!"

"So it's your currency?" Sharon asked.

"Yes, it is. I got a whole branch for my birthday once. Come on, let's go in," she replied kindly.

The faint ringing of folk music became louder as the pub door opened, acting almost as if it were a giant anti-mute button. There was a pleasant enough reception hall with a deep red carpet and light, saffron walls. There were also a few paintings hung on either wall and the lights suspended from the ceiling drooped all the way down to Sharon's head level.

Two corridors led off to the left and right from the reception and straight on were two glass doors encrusted with precious stones in each of the panes, each stone shining brightly in the artificial light.

On entering the main lounge Sharon noticed windows which revealed many of the picturesque settings captured on the canvases of the paintings in the reception. Several round tables with short tubby chairs placed around them were attended by huge flocks of men and women. A chorus of greetings went up as the current drinkers recognised Martha had entered. She and Sharon walked up to the bar and Martha ordered two lemonades with blackcurrant and chatted about the weather to the kindly woman serving. The pair accepted the drinks and went to speak with a man apparently known as Sophios, 'the knowledgeable one'. He had served at the Court of the Emperor of Sulla and had been private counsellor and adviser to the City Burgomaster. He had many contacts and was reputed to be the wisest man in the village.

"Sophios, how are you? Good to see ye in fine health. A friend of mine has a few questions to ask you. Ye won't be mindin' if you spare your time for a while, eh?" she asked with the fullest charm she could muster.

"Not at all Martha; I'd be happy to assist at any time, you know that. Now, who are we, miss? How old would you be then, and where might you be from?" he asked. He too had positively wonderful, and slightly nauseating, charm.

"I'm Sharon. I'm from Britain and I was on a holiday in Iceland when..." She continued her hurried explanation and to her surprise Sophios asked no questions afterwards. He seemed to understand everything perfectly clearly.

"So you want to know how to get out of here, yes?" he replied, his gaze still firmly positioned on his glass tumbler which had only a trickle of some beverage left in it, swirling like a never-ending whirlpool as he turned the glass round and round in his hand.

"Yes, please," Sharon replied nervously.

"I see." He paused and then made a perfect right angle turn towards Sharon. "A mind works best on a full stomach, my dear. Order another '22', will you please?"

"Of course ... sir," she said rather hesitantly, eager to get on Sophios's right side, but not quite sure how much politeness was called for in this new 'world'. She passed the other tables quickly to the bar; she received one particularly nasty look from a young woman who reminded Sharon of her most annoying cousin, Demerara, a vain and pompous girl whose haughtiness was guaranteed to outshine that of anyone in her company. Her odd name might not have been so comical had her mother not married a factory-owning Englishman, Mr. Sugar.

"Hello. Can Sophios have another '22' please?" she asked politely.

"He can indeed." The woman made shuffled movements to her right to pour some lustrous liquid from a small green bottle labelled '22' in elaborate writing.

"Here it is. Two Forden-leaves, please. Or will I put it on his tab?"

"Oh!" Sharon was lost for words. "He, eh.... didn't say. Just put it on his tab; I don't have any leaves, sorry. I'm sure he won't mind. Thank you."

The barmaid smiled and with that Sharon wandered back to the table, clasping the heavy glass in her right hand and supporting it with the other. It was incredibly heavy. The drink's tempting odour allured Sharon to taste the sweet flavours of the '22'. She stepped behind one of the square pillars supporting the building, which were dotted around the room, and raised the cup to her mouth. She tipped it towards her and as soon as the liquor touched her lips she fell instantly to the ground.

When she never showed up with (or for that matter without) the drink after a while, Martha of course decided to go looking for her, eventually finding the poor girl unconscious behind her hiding spot. She concluded correctly what had happened and took her to Sophios and his circle of friends to wish them goodbye. Sophios said it must have been 'an element in the drink that reacted with her unaccustomed body fluids and knocked her out'.

"She'll come round soon," he said. "Send a cat to fetch for milk and trust goes to sleep. And curiosity killed the cat, didn't it?!"

"Wise words," Mrs. Bugle-Thom remarked. "Wise words indeed."

CHAPTER TWO

Sophios's House

Sharon awoke cooped up in a small wooden bed. It had a simple design which was echoed by the plain blanket laid over her. It was coarse sackcloth, but better than nothing. Pure, unspoilt sunshine gleamed through the little square window beaming glorious hazy rays on to the bed. There was a pair of yellow floral curtains suspended from an old wooden pole. The window's frame was meant to be white but like so many other things in the house was not in excellent condition. Some of the paint was rubbed off, revealing coarse brown pine beneath. The room was, however, clean. The brown carpet was spotless, the patterned wallpapered walls were in perfect condition and there was no dust to be seen on the small quantities of furniture. The few items of furniture in the room were plain and old, but Sharon suspected this guest bedroom was not used often and so gratefully accepted her accommodation.

She placed her hand on the little bedside cabinet to stable herself and rose from the bed to approach the wardrobe. It consisted of a red velvet curtain draped across a small space with a wall to the left, right and back and with a pole for hanging clothes on. In it was a small dressing gown which Sharon put on immediately. Down the little creaky stairs from a tiny landing she realised she must have been on the second storey of the block on the right of the house, but that was all she realised; she had no idea of what she had done to herself the previous night. It was evident to her it was morning and so she presumed she was put to bed the night before after hearing from Sophios how to return to Earth, but it seemed peculiar that this great secret she had been waiting to hear had escaped her for the time being.

In the main room Mr. and Mrs. Bugle-Thom were silently relaxing, pondering over a mug of some hot drink each, gentle wisps of steam rising from each of them. The fire was blazing as usual and as Sharon entered the room the pair turned to her with questioning glares.

"Good obtuse, my love. What an ordeal last night, eh?" Martha said.

"Sorry?" Sharon replied, not understanding what Martha was referring to.

"I said, what an ordeal it was..." She was broken off by a quick, sly look from Jock. They had agreed not to remind her of the incident.

"I mean ... you must be tired, dear. Come, sit and have a rest. We shall go and speak with Mr. Sophios this reflex and hear what he has to say about how you can go about leavin' 'ere," she continued.

"But, didn't we see him yesterday? And what's with the 'reflex' and 'obtuse'?" Sharon asked impatiently.

"We were going to see him yesterday but you went an' knocked yerself out, didn't ye? Now, reflex is after midday, obtuse is between the end of acute and midday and acute is between dawn and obtuse. Don't you measure time?" she said.

"Yes, but not in 360 degrees; just sixty," Sharon tried to explain.

"Gosh. That can't be too accurate then, can it?" Martha replied.

"Well, it is. We have two sundial markers, you see. One shows the hour and one the minute. We also have a 'second' hand that goes quickly," Sharon rushed.

"A second hand? Shouldn't it be called a third hand? That's complicated. No; one 'and does us, eh Jock?" She turned to her husband, chuckling.

"Oh.. eh.. yes. Just the 360," he responded, not paying attention.

"Let's not get ourselves sucked into the details, though. I'll go and make lunch. There're a few books in the cabinet in your room, Sharrin. There's also a little one-man game upstairs. Try them; we used to like them. Then after lunch we can go and see Sophios. All right, run along then, eh?" Martha turned abruptly and marched, out of step, into the corridor to the kitchen.

Sharon walked back upstairs and opened the cabinet to find four dusty and thick books in a kind of leather covering. The first of these was entitled:

The Heroine of Achbar,

and on the spines of the others read:

In the Forest Past the Border,

The Heroine of Achbar - Volume II,

and finally, in a dark red velvety cover bound with golden straps that glittered in the sunlight:

Beyond the Mist

The authors of the first two were Trachid Veston and Leopold Jharnaux, but the last book was anonymous. According to Martha all of them were hundreds of postins old (apparently a 'postin' was 400 days). Sharon began reading *The Heroine of Achbar*, but she soon grew tired of it and lay gazing out of the window. By this time it was lunch and the appetising spread of refection laid out for her was not disappointing. The table was huge and had spread out on it not only several fish on silver platters, all sorts of fruits, a few bowls of thick bread and countless glass goblets, but a fully grown pig! The starter was fresh chicken soup with chopped coriander and mussels. A strange combination, Sharon thought, but equally filling and tantalising. It appeared that Mrs. Bugle-Thom was a truly great cook and a fabulous housewife. The second course, dessert, after-course, preliminary afters, afters, seconds, thirds, mints and finally tea and biscuits with crumpets composed what was the most fantastic and huge meal Sharon had ever experienced.

Afterwards Sharon thanked Martha for the meal and Jock for his wonderful company. Sharon had never expected to find such humour in a man so serious.

Martha encouraged Sharon to put on her raincoat because it looked as though a storm was brewing. And indeed, as Mrs. Bugle-Thom struggled to slam the back door shut the heavens burst open with an almighty crash of thunder and flood of rainfall. An endless supply of fresh rainwater seemed to spill onto the cobble stones, filling the little cracks between each one as Martha and Sharon waited on the 'transport', operated by one Mr. Tolliery, to arrive. The little gold-plated sundial did not show the time, but the bicycle came wheeling down the road within what seemed a minute.

"Awful day, Mrs. B-T, awful! Where to now, then?" the rider asked politely.

"We'd like to go to 3 Halsworth Square, please," Martha responded.

"To Sophios, I presume?"

"Yes, that's right."

"Hop aboard. Reflex, lass!"

"Good reflex," Sharon replied quickly while the man goggled at her, a wide smile spreading across his face. He looked friendly enough, but a sense of fear in Sharon could not help thinking he was somewhat devious.

Along the way Mr. Tolliery made conversation by warning the pair that he was not too keen on Sophios and his ideas, or at least he implied as much.

"The Government aren't too keen on Sophios. Say he stirs up trouble. I can't say I could blame them, honestly. He could do plenty harm if he wanted; maybe even destroy the whole system."

"Don't be ridiculous," Mrs. Bugle-Thom retorted immediately. "Sophios is a kind man. Anyway, what trouble could an old wizard like him do to a fly, let alone the system? It's been in place for postins. It'd take a lot of evidence to convince me o' his power o'er *that* lot."

"I'm just saying, Mrs. B-T, that if this man has the ability to access important documents, files an' all that, I don't see why he wouldn't be using them. I've heard he was expelled from the Private Office to the Ruler because he plotted against 'em."

"I won't hear of such things. Although if he did, but I'm sure he didn't, he would be a hero for us all. Things were so much better under the King." Martha was instantly cut off by Mr. Tolliery who interrupted her at the sound of her last word.

"This is a democracy! How can you criticise the nobility of this nation!" He now sounded increasingly heated. "Sorry," the steaming cyclist hastily added, "I'm sorry. It's just… my father's mother was born into the New Aristocracy. They were a great and influential power, until she married. Awful things happened, then. The Old Nobles tried to kill her, but for that they were all stoned to death and so the manor's in ruins now. Of course, the New Aristos are back in power now, but not my branch. Ever heard of the Carrs?" he asked slyly, knowing the answer he was to receive.

"You know the Carrs of Felicity Manor?" she asked, utterly bewildered at the thought of the local bus driver being related to one of the most noble (and infamous) families of all time.

"Yes; Sybil Balton-Halcrow, seventh Countess of Carr and Basilshire. She was my grandmother. Had an awful father, though: Sir Roderick Balton-Halcrow of Carr and Basilshire and ninth Earl Tubolton. That name was dropped after he had a son, though. Now, when Sybil left the family she became poor, and us alike of course. She accepted Lady Sybil Tolliery of nowhere and that's how we come to me, her grandson."

"So you're Lord Tolliery?" asked Martha, still utterly bemused. Her facial expression was timeless.

"Well, I suppose so. But call me Roland." There was a pause. "I suppose you're wondering where I found this information, are you?" But he had perplexed the poor woman, still trying to come to terms with the fact that the person who had taken her to the market to get her vegetables and come to clean her windows at the weekend was a Lord.

"Erm... yes. Where did you-"

Lord T. answered her before she could finish her sentence.

"Found it in the library under 'Family History'. There's an updated tree and everything. Traced back to the Dark days. Amazing, really!" He sounded cheerier than ever. At least this study in genealogy had replaced their disagreeable debate on society, Martha thought. Sharon was listening intently, but strived not to show it in case a new argument erupted and she was dragged in; thankfully it did not.

The cyclist took them to a very small square; the ground was largely yellow paved with slabs and with a house on every side except the entrance. The three buildings were identical in design, coming into clearer vision as the bicycle passed through the small white stone arch serving as an entrance to the square. They looked rather Viennese with their pointed roofs and elaborate decoration. Each house had three floors and the inhabitants of each were listed outside their respective residences:

'Phoebos Little

Baron Brockton of Gleddock

The Honourable Sophios of Sulla'

"That's fine, thanks," said Martha.

"All right then. Have a nice day!" replied Roland smugly as he drifted away out of sight in the fresh summer breeze. There were several mature trees beside and behind the houses and green leaves wafted their own respective paths down through the mild air, resting gently on the hard surface of the cobbled square. The harsh rain that had plagued them before was beginning to ease as black clouds were pushed aside to make room for blue sky. Martha walked over to Sophios's house, climbed the long narrow steps to the front door and rang the brass bell. It made a loud gonging noise as its peals echoed in the large belfry above. Almost at once Sophios emerged from behind the huge oak door and pleasantly asked, his eyes beaming down in admiration,

"Who can it be today? Ah, Mrs. Bugle-Thom and her little acquaintance; Sharon is it?"

"Yes," Sharon replied.

"These questions Sharrin has… can we come in and ask you them?" Martha pleaded with puppy-dog eyes widening by the minute (or indeed angle).

"Yes, yes of course. Do come in." His voice became lower and thinner. "We must be quiet, you see. The government doesn't like me discussing such matters with anyone except them; especially not foreigners. But do come in, I say. They can't stop me. Anyway, the police guard that usually mans this place is away just now for some reason. Sick, most likely."

Sophios opened the door wide for them to enter his 'humble abode' and checked right and left before closing it, locking it with an army of automatic bolts that pelted shut as soon as the door was shut. He then walked slowly behind Sharon and Martha, ushering them in the correct direction.

The magnificent hallway rose up three grand storeys and at the top was a long thin row of little square stained glass windows. There was a large staircase that branched off in two directions after rising forward for five steps. At this landing a tall arched stained glass window stood tall, right to the ceiling, which was vaulted. These branches of stairs led onto two separate narrow landings with three doors off each. The elaborate white balustrade continued along these landings to prevent anyone from falling.

"Just through that door," instructed Sophios in his usual easy tones of calmness.

Martha led the way into a beautiful drawing room with a very high ceiling and elaborate cornicing. There was a large white fireplace with logs burning ferociously inside it. Above it hung a gilt mirror with carved designs of flowers and wildlife. The room was lit magnificently by a huge bay window that reached the ceiling and streamed in masses of light directed through its colossal panes. There was a large golden chandelier hung elegantly from the ceiling that had twelve candles inserted into each of its gold stems. The floor was covered by a large carpet-rug that was cut thin and had fanciful floral designs and wild deer in rings designed in perfect symmetry. This carpet covered most of the room's hard oak floorboards but a border about a foot wide stretched out to the wall's high skirting from the rug. The walls themselves consisted of three feet of hard oak panelling painted white with decorative Regency wallpaper above to the coving. These were laden with stags' heads, again in perfect symmetry, passing concerned glances at each other and looking down haughtily at Sharon.

"How vile," whispered one head under its breath, looking at its partner across the room.

"Foreign vermin; a disgrace to the household," said another.

"If Lady Brockton were alive today…" continued the first deer.

At this final remark Sophios made a distinct gyration towards the stags with his head and gave them a collective look of sincere disapproval of their comments. At once the chattering ceased, though they retained their disgusted looks.

"Do take a seat, my dear," he instructed Martha. She did so on a long elaborate sofa and gestured to Sharon to sit with her.

"Well," said Sophios sitting down on his large green leather chair. "What is it I must answer? Nothing too hard, I hope?" he said jovially.

"Sharrin - what is it you want to ask Sophios?" asked Martha looking slightly concerned at the way Sharon was sitting. Sharon was looking straight down at the floor, trying to look away from the stags which were making disgruntled looks at her.

"Yes," said Sharon sitting up straight, looking into Sophios's great and ancient beaming blue eyes. "Erm... you heard how I got here-" she began.

"Yes, yes," replied Sophios looking as eager as ever to answer her questions.

"Well, I want to know how to get back to my world," she asked. Sophios gave her a peculiar look of inquisitiveness. His puzzled expression changed into a quizzical glare.

"You want to know how to get back, eh? Well, how did you come to get here? Exactly?" he asked.

"I... well..." she stumbled. "I just woke up."

"Woke up, eh ... in the field. I see." Sophios fixed his eyes on a large bare section of the wall and moved his hand over to the little side-table set beside him. He picked up a sort of pipe, although it looked like several pipes all joined together, and puffed great bellows of smoke from the four tiers of pipe-ends. He appeared to be in deep thought and after a moment or two turned his eyes back to Sharon. Martha, in her usual blithe way, was admiring the stags.

"Well, I wouldn't want to subject you to the harsh climates of our nights here and make you sleep in the field again, but that's about the only solution I can think of."

Sharon sank into her seat.

"However," he said again, "there is the Oracle at Sulla." At the sound of these words Mrs. Bugle-Thom looked straight at Sophios's bold face.

"It is kept deep underground in the caves below the Tower in Sulla. It's a long way but you'll get a right answer, for sure... if you try hard enough. You see, the Oracle is in a great torpor and is not easy to awaken. If your question is important enough, or if you show enough determination to get to her, I suspect she may awake and answer you. There are some other problems, of course. The Tower is heavily guarded, you know. The government would never allow a foreigner anywhere near it." Sophios paused suddenly. "It could end in death." He turned a solitary pale colour and relit his pipe after it had puffed out.

"But it's worth a try?" said Sharon.

"Oh yes, indeed. But you couldn't go on your own. You'll need someone to help guide you through Sulla. It's like a different country altogether down there. Customs, culture-" Sophios stopped dead in his tracks as Martha let out an uncontrollable "Ha!" at the word culture. It was true; Sulla was devoid of culture: very little art, music, literature… but plenty of shops.

"Hem hem," interrupted Sophios. "Different people, strange streets, and plenty of criminals waiting eagerly to take advantage of you kind of people without any knowledge of the city. But who to take?"

Sophios regained his thinking mood and moved his thumb and forefinger down in an arch towards his beard and puffed away. Then, suddenly, he said, "I'm far too old. Can barely get my essentials from the shop, eh Martha? And Mrs. Bugle-Thom's not acquainted with the city. But who is? I can't think. Give me a moment."

Sophios lurched out of his chair and placed his quadro-pipe on the mantelpiece. He then left the room swiftly and clambered through the hall. Sharon heard him murmuring to himself as he climbed the staircase and disappeared upstairs.

Sophios had in fact entered the library of the house and by this time was searching rapidly for a particular book. He sieved his way through what seemed like mountains of dusty old leather-bound novels and reference books. He drove his finger along the middle shelf of an old bookcase marked, with a brass plaque, 'Directories, etc.' Finally he stopped abruptly and extracted a large and thick book entitled: 'Private Ministry to the Ruler; List of Commanding Officers and Members of the Most High Order of the Knight-Nobles in Council, Honourable Gentlemen Enrolment List, Founding - Present'. Sophios opened the book for a second as if to check if it were really what it said in the title: it was and he withdrew from the room and clambered down the stairs again. The book was just a huge list outlining every respectable squire in the land. He opened the page to "Son-Spa" in which he found his name on the third column from the foot of the page. It read:

'The Most Honourable Sophios of Sulla, MHOKN, Noble Advisor to the Ruler, Royal Counsellor, Chancellor of Sulla, Lord Protector of the Baronage of Sulla City, Keeper of the Keys, Royal Employer, Secretary of State.

'Awarded medal: 1702189344315/1874 J.C. for Services to the Crown and State'

Sophios felt himself ooze with pride and he felt, as he had not felt for a long while, good about himself and content as the words flowed along the pale white page, guiding his eyes along his long title.

When he re-entered the drawing room Martha was gazing in silence at the ceiling, trying to work out if there was a pattern to the cornice, and Sharon sat bored but anxious inspecting the plasterwork of the fireplace.

"Here we are," Sophios mumbled to himself.

"Ah… well?" said Mrs. Bugle-Thom.

"Well, hold on. I've got a list here of all the great and good in Sulla who can help you on your way round." He scanned the sunned pages quickly and eventually stopped at a page with the letters "Nja-Nop" listed at the top as a guide to the noble occupants of the page.

He seemed to have found a suitable representative when he stated quite plainly, without looking up from the book, "I see there's a man here that might be suitable; I don't know if he would do it, though. He's a bit old. Lives in Sulla and has achieved quite a barrage of decoration from the Ruler. I'll send him a message – hold on." He placed the book onto a long wooden table with a glass surface and scrambled out of the room to rummage around for a strange instrument he found in the hall cupboard. It was silver and had a small tapper like those used in sending Morse code. It also had a little back like a typewriter into which Sophios inserted a small roll of parchment, marred slightly by years of dust-collecting. He lifted the book again and tapped away happily at the instrument. He was tapping in a long code written to the right of all the lists of names. It read: SULLA 702/7:02//7:02. At each of the forward slashes he held the tapper down for a long space of time and at each colon he held it for a shorter length. Then each number was tapped in according to its size. The letters 'SULLA' were also typed but Sharon could not tell how these were done. After inserting the code Sharon could hear a long beeping noise from the receiver as if it were trying to connect to the other end. Eventually the beep stopped and was replaced by a pleasant woman's voice: "The number is now connected. Please continue."

Then Sophios began tapping wildly, and as he did so figures appeared on the parchment and then disappeared under the silver bar as it was fed through like a facsimile.

After he had finished the woman's voice instructed him as follows, after the beep: "Thank you. This message is filtering through now. Please wait..."

There was a pause.

"A reply message is being sent now. Please wait..." Again a short pause followed. "Please wait, message received." The parchment filtered through and was emerging from the top of the silver bar, littered with strange lettering and mountains of incomprehensible punctuation.

"Ah; he must have been sitting beside his machine. It's come through quickly," said Sophios cheerily.

"Yes," both of the others replied in agreement.

Sophios read out the message in English as it appeared.

"Erm... Dear Honourable Sophios, Thanking you from the noble household of d'Arrawor for your message. I - am - afraid - that - in - my - old - age - I - cannot - accept - your - offer."

All three sighed in disappointment, but the paper now emerged completely from the top and the receiver beeped loudly then finished:

"Message received. Thank you." A little green light on the machine ceased flashing and the instrument appeared to have switched itself off. Sophios could now read the whole message without pauses for the machine to write it out.

"However, I am sure that my son Apnar-Séab would be interested in guiding the girl. He is twenty and two years of age and lives with me in Arrawor Hall on the banks of the river here in Sulla. He is also currently working for the Government. Call back if you would like to go forth with my proposal. Many gracious blessings, Noggard d'Arrawor, M.H.O.K.N., Loyal Master to the Crown, Commander of the Empire Gold Class."

Sophios then turned his bulging eyes on Sharon. "Well?" he said.

"Yes. That would be great. When can I leave?" Sharon responded keenly.

"Well, I shall have to notify him of your acceptance. Then we can arrange dates and so on."

"Good, good. You're on your way now, Sharrin," said Martha encouragingly. As a matter of fact Sharon was not encouraged one iota. She was afraid, but ready.

Sophios pressed a little button on the machine and began tapping away again after replacing the tattered parchment with some new blue paper that shined in the sunlight. The message was carried (as the operator again stated) and the message-sending ritual completed. The trio awaited a reply with finalised dates.

The blue parchment furled out of the top of the machine bearing a shorter but still important message confirming the dates and times proposed by Sophios on the last message. It read:

'189000000/3, yes? By the Marquis Entrance in the west. My son will be waiting. If you ever return, drop by.'

Sophios read the message aloud indicating that he would take Sharon to Sulla to meet Apnar-Séab and then the young noble would take over from there.

"When have I to meet him?" Sharon asked, confused at the long string of numbers that appeared to be the proposed date in the message.

"Why, later today, of course! Can't you tell the time? Don't they learn in your world?"

"Eh…" Sharon hesitated, "We learn; it's just we measure time a little differently."

"We've had this discussion already, Sophios," Martha chipped in.

"I see."

"So we will leave later this evening?" inquired Martha.

"Oh, no! We must depart immediately, Martha. We'll never get to Sulla in time if we leave tonight!" he replied, unaware of Martha's crude understanding of travel.

"Very well. How shall we leave?" she further inquired.

"By the Tunnels, of course. It's the only direct route to Sulla from here."

CHAPTER THREE

The Tunnelled Network

The trio left the beautiful Viennese square and departed, in the unrelenting rain, to the Shanklot Stead. Martha explained the situation to Mr. Bugle-Thom and he hesitantly agreed to let Martha travel beyond the Gleddock bank to the first station that Sophios and Sharon were to leave from. It was hundreds of miles to Sulla; 'dangerous miles' as Sophios kindly prophesied in a dark and gloomy voice. This was not the encouragement Sharon needed.

Sophios led Sharon and Martha to the church where there was a narrow path, battered by postins of precipitation, leading to the river. A small picket fence bordered its much worn ground and guided it towards the other side of the village. The crops in the field were being blown wildly from side to side as a gale whipped the delicate sheaves. Sharon and Martha followed Sophios, who was wearing a thick and long green cloak and tweed cap. He had decorated himself with a long and hefty-looking gold pendant with a large round gold seal hanging from it. It was engraved with an emblem of an oval shield surrounded by two falcons facing each other, their bodies encircling the shield. It was a fantastical heraldic design which looked as ancient as Sophios. The pendant swung to and fro ahead of Sophios.

The path led to an opening in the rocks to a grassy bank where there were a few trees swaying in the breeze. The party marched on for a while until they came to a large stone bridge leading across the river. The bridge bore a small memorial plaque inscribed:

JOHN HAROLDER

Died here waiting for the downpour to cease

Alas, his patient mood but caught him out

And killed him here to rest in peace.

This bridge constructed here will serve

A reminder to cross in haste.

Do not wait as John did, no!

Cross now, travellers, go, go, go!

"What-" Sharon began as they crossed the bridge. She doubted if she had ever read worse poetry in her life.

"Shh! I think we're getting closer. Follow me," Sophios instructed.

The pair followed suit and, like sheep, crossed the bridge and said no more. The rain was gone, but there were no traces of it ever having fallen on either side. Not a drop existed on the beaten grass. Sharon was puzzled: the grass on the other side was a lush velvet green but the patches on which she now stood were beaten and coarse. Yet, when she had looked across before, the grass blades on the side she now stood had a perfect appearance while the grass on her side was patchy and worn. She shrugged and moved on – there was so much in this world she simply could not understand or see the point of. The twittering of birds resounded in the delicate blue skies and the trees swayed elegantly in time to the songs. At one tree sat a small, bandy-legged man playing the lyre which echoed across the valleys. He seemed oblivious to anything around him and continued playing even as the three travellers passed him, his eyelids firmly closed.

Sophios led the way to a tall and mature Chestnut tree nearby. The overhanging branches drooped as low as his head and the party had to clamber their way through these; typically, Sophios failed to notice the unending torrent of chestnuts falling on the two females' heads.

"Here," Sophios announced proudly. "Just stay with me."

He prodded around to find a specific area of the trunk, which he evidently found as when he impressed his medallion into a hollowed space in the tree trunk, a little door, much like the one in Martha's main room, flung open, and rebounded off the trunk itself.

"Yes?" cried a small goblin-like creature with long pointed ears and a curled tail who had emerged from the doorway behind a little desk. His voice was hoarse, but fairly pleasant.

"Sulla, please," asked Sophios. The elf sifted through a small mountain of paperwork and scanned each paper quickly.

"You may make your way to the principal tunnel yourself; otherwise, the first chute arrives in three angles. I'll let them know to stop if you would prefer," said the creature, his bespectacled head lunging forwards to inform the potential passengers.

"Yes, do so. Where can we wait?" Sophios asked.

"Hold on, sir!" The creature disappeared beneath the counter and popped up again brandishing a quill and several multi-coloured papers.

"Fill these in please." He turned to the women. "You too."

It handed them three papers: one white, one pink and one blue. They were all exactly the same and Sophios was told to fill in only the top leaf: the rest would complete themselves. Martha, Sharon and Sophios each completed their respective sheets and passed them back. Sharon had some difficulty in filling in hers (the questions used a whole range of terminology she had never before encountered) so Sophios proposed he should complete Sharon's, which he kindly did. The form had the same emblem as its letterhead as Sophios had on his medallion. The creature behind the desk ripped off the white forms and filed them away in a hidden cabinet beneath the counter. It posted the pink forms in a chute that, when switched on, blew the forms up a tube and along a complex system that supposedly led to some sort of bureaucratic office hundreds of miles away. The third and final forms were stamped with bright red ink and returned to the applicants along with a set of three pale orange tickets with the same ensign as the forms. They read: "Sullarian Government, Department of Transport, Tunnelled Network. Thank you for travelling with Μοτορτρανσπο." The last word was, as Sharon noticed, written in Greek. She, however, had chosen not to study the subject the year before in favour of Latin, and therefore had no idea what it said. As she was pondering this notice Sophios interrupted her line of thought by suddenly inquiring,

"Where is the waiting room?"

"If you would hold on to all your belongings I will permit your entry into our executive waiting room. Please wait. Thank you once again for travelling with Motortranspo," the elf replied just before shutting the door in the trunk and disappearing altogether. Just as Sharon was beginning to suspect that there might not even be any alternative companies to travel with, the ground gave way beneath her, just like the time when she narrowly escaped her peril in Iceland. This time she was not so quick to act and dodge it. The three fell abruptly through the ground, until they landed in a glass lift carrying them down slowly to the platform. Before any of them could speak, a woman's soft voice illuminated the capsule:

"Good reflex, ladies and gentlemen, wizards and wizardesses, warlocks and witches etc. etc. You have arrived at Rastinun Tunnel Station. Please vacate the elevator and await your capsule on the platform. Thank you."

Sophios led the way as usual across the platform in through a door marked 'Executive Waiting Lounge'. There were large comfy seats bound in leather that responded to your every need. Once sitting on them they could massage your back, lift your feet, make you a drink and much more. The three sat down and looked up at the ever-changing notice board detailing the arrivals and cancellations of different capsules. There were plaques yellowed with age moving independently, labelling the destinations and times. Sophios scanned the board for an update of their capsule. He found it - it read:

SULLA

via ACHNABAR and ST. OGILVIE

212°

ON TIME

{currently at Thomslinne}

Sophios checked his watch; his was apparently digital and read: '210 degrees'. He slouched back in his recliner and held a copy of *The Wizarding Scholar* in his hands that had just appeared, bearing the headline 'Parliament called to discuss whereabouts of Casper Leighton'. Sophios muttered at the monthly political review's articles and tutted where appropriate. Sharon noticed Martha had received a large pillow for her head as well as an incredibly tasteless patchwork quilted duvet with pictures of geese covering her outstretched body; she was asleep. Sharon lay back to think when she noticed a huge lemon sorbet drink had appeared by her side on one armrest of the great leather chair. It had a silver straw which Sharon gleefully drank from, downing the whole concoction before realising the board had changed. It now read:

SULLA

via ACHNABAR and ST. OGILVIE

216°

LATE DUE TO TUNNEL WORKS

{currently at Barkanzet}

"Dear, oh dear! When will we arrive?! My goodness, we shall have to apologise to Apnar-Séab when we get there. Unreliable, I tell you," Sophios raged calmly.

Suddenly the boards rearranged themselves:

SULLA

via ACHNABAR AND ST. OGILVIE

213°

LATE

AT PLATFORM I NOW

"Ah, here we are! Quick delay, it must have been. Come now Martha, Sharon." The elderly man roused Martha from her sleep.

"Oh? Oh, yes indeed. I'll see you off at the platform," Martha replied, confused and tired.

Sophios swung open the black door to the platform and walked over to a small metal capsule, followed by Sharon and Mrs. Bugle-Thom. The capsules available were two small metal boxes, each heavily riveted and thoroughly rusty. The door of one slid open and Sophios ushered Sharon in before him. Inside was a surprisingly spacious room heavily furnished with comfortable light-grey leather sofas and a small screen flickering above the doorway. Sharon could see Martha waving them goodbye through the small window and almost shed a tear for the dear woman. It would have been a rare occasion - but it did not happen. She held her straight face and tried to look happy. The capsule suddenly jerked forward and continued along the rails bumping up and down at high speed. Though the capsule was four feet square it seemed luxurious compared to what Sharon had imagined it to be like when she first saw it clattering along the platform. The screen now displayed a man wearing a pointed hat and sitting behind a desk. He announced in an obviously well-practised and perfected tone,

"Welcome aboard. We hope you enjoy your ride to Sulla. We shall be interchanging at Achnabar and re-railing at St. Ogilvie. In the unlikely event of an emergency please stay within the capsule and do not perform any magic whatsoever. Enjoy your trip and have a good day; apologies for the short delay. Thank you." The man then flickered and was wiped off the screen by a message in black and white:

'*SULLA* via ACHNABAR and ST. OGILVIE'.

Another message flashed up underneath this:

'Refreshments available'.

Sophios suddenly conjured a table and a thick drink appeared on it, along with another copy of *The Wizarding Scholar* which had disappeared since leaving the waiting room. Sharon wished something would show up on her table to keep her occupied. Suddenly, twenty different newspapers and magazines appeared beside her. Included in the pile were *The Educationalist, The Comet, Daily Wisdom, The Chronicle, The Sunday Cauldron, The Operatic, The Squall, The Proud Crier, Sulla Herald, The Achnabar Times, The Thomslinne Star, Astronomical Monthly, The Gleddock Press* and many more beside.

Sophios exclaimed in great delight, "You'll be there for a while reading those, eh?" and then giggled to himself rather disturbingly.

Sharon picked up the publications in turn: *The Educationalist* reported that the hunt for notorious killer Sireel Thomps was about to begin, *The Comet* featured an interesting article on the functions of the brains of different creatures, *Daily Wisdom* sported a confusing piece entitled 'Why do we endeavour to find life elsewhere?', *Astronomical Monthly* ('a periodical for budding as well as established astronomers') had black-and-white pictures (all the publications were black-and-white) of a new comet sighted just above the Crailow Ridge and, finally, *The Gleddock Press* had up-to-date pictures of the Village Ball the previous month, in which Sharon noticed Mr. and Mrs. Bugle-Thom dancing away cheerfully.

"We should be changing over to a new capsule at Achnabar from this old rusty thing, my dear. Then we can live in luxury for a few angles!" Sophios commented from behind his magazine.

"How long will it take to get to Sulla?" Sharon asked unknowingly.

"Well... I would say no longer than forty angles."

"Hmm," Sharon mused. It was impossible to extract a simple answer from this affable fellow.

She turned to pick up *The Proud Crier* when the capsule came to an abrupt and obvious halt and Sophios made a small gyration towards the window where he glanced at the sign on the wall of the platform they had just arrived at. Sharon could see it read:

'Thrasymachus Station

Bishopshire

Felworth'

Sophios considered it his duty to announce for her, "Thrasymachus Station. We're in Bishopshire now."

"Oh." Sharon strived in vain to find a reply to such a statement.

"But we're still in Felworth, see."

Sophios pulled out a tattered copy of *The Geographer's Journal.*

'What an original name,' Sharon thought to herself.

On the inside front page was a map of the whole country and its surrounding national neighbours.

"Have this. It will be an invaluable source for you, believe me. You can't be without a map..." he paused, "ever."

"Thank you," she responded.

"This here," he instructed, "is Felworth. All the area from the border line in the north to the valley at Achnabar. That's where the area changes to Achbaria."

"Like states?" Sharon enquired.

"I suppose so. Yes, states or counties," Sophios answered, slightly flustered; these two words were rarely used in Sullaria.

"Now, Achbaria ends here." He pointed to a mountain range. "And this is the beginning of Kuznetjirs, which surrounds Sulla by the north, east and west. Then we have Sulla, and then all the rest is a vast space of land called Eliatia which covers the rest of the country. That's all of Sullaria, for now anyway. The Empire's expanding all the time, you know."

Sophios handed the torn page to Sharon who studied it thereafter. Sophios seemed utterly oblivious to the man who had just appeared on the capsule behind him, whom Sharon could see in the reflection on the mirror above Sophios's head. It gave a direct line of vision through the window above Sharon. While pretending to examine the map, Sharon really inspected the man in the next capsule from behind her strategically-placed magazine. She could see he was wearing a black suit with tails and a black bowler hat, which Sharon found an odd combination. He carried a type of umbrella with a lion's head on the top and a black leather case whose handles opened independently to hand the man several papers. The man suddenly looked through the window as if sensing someone had been watching him, and Sharon ducked under her magazine and tried to look absorbed in the front cover article on Casper Leighton, though she didn't understand a word, and didn't try to understand one for that matter. The man conjured his umbrella to come to him and with a slight flick of his right hand motioned to it to close the shutters on the window above Sharon's head. The lion growled and a few small sparks flew from its mouth and zoomed towards the blinds, closing them quite sternly, reflecting the expression on the face of its owner.

Again another face flashed up on the screen in the capsule. This time Sophios turned to look at it eagerly and with a little more fervour than before when he had completely ignored the announcer.

"We have arrived at Achnabar. Here we will change over capsules. Please retain all your luggage and hold tightly while we come to a halt. Please do not stand until the vehicle has come to a complete stop. If you follow the signs to 'St. Ogilvie' and await the capsules marked 'Sulla' you will be on your way. There will be many individual capsules down the next tunnel to Sulla and therefore please wait until the line of capsules comes to a complete stop, at which time you can board one of the vacant end capsules. Thank you again for travelling with Motortranspo. The High Council of Felworth thanks you for not smoking."

With that last remark the image disappeared and a new message flickered on the old and well-used screen: 'Μοτορτρανσπο'. The two capsules then shuddered to a halt after a gradual deceleration. Achnabar, it seemed, had a large station and many staircases led off the platform labelled 'Rural In'. This platform was adjacent to one labelled 'Rural Out', wich had been vandalised to read 'Keep Rurals Out!' It seemed the countryside was not popular and the city was considered a much better place to live. As the little door slid open Sharon stepped out onto the platform followed by Sophios. The magazines and newspapers had disappeared and Sharon saw the man in the other carriage's umbrella give her a cold look; the man flicked it sharply, and its expression became placid once more. Sophios drew her away from this distraction by offering her a drink in one of the cafés in the station, but after Sharon had inspected them (even from a distance) she declined quite decidedly, but sweetly. So, with this idea forgotten, Sophios led Sharon up and down many corridors all bustling with people and then finally rose up eleven flights of stairs to the platform marked 'St. Ogilvie and Hoodchess' and Sophios waited with Sharon on one of the many wooden benches scattered across the platform against the wall. After a short wait, a great stream of light approached, pelting up the dark tunnel from the right. It appeared that the lanterns on the walls of the tunnels were only lit as capsules went by and then dimmed themselves when the nearest capsule had passed. A huge amount of sound filled the confined area as the clunkety-clunks of the capsule wheels on the iron rails echoed around the platform. Sharon made to stand up and go towards the capsules to board but Sophios restrained her. There was an endless amount of capsules coming along, each filled with people. Sharon began counting and reached about forty when she lost count completely. Still more and more came for what seemed like an age until the carriages finally slowed down and came to a halt. There were about seventeen capsules free, eight of which were taken by people standing at the platform in Achnabar. Sulla was clearly the most popular destination. Sophios and Sharon boarded the ninth capsule freely and awaited movement. The inside of this carriage was very different to that of the other one. This was designed for long-haul journeys. It was much more spacious and there were again two light-grey leather seats on each edge which collapsed into beds either side of which were small lamps. A drinks cabinet pulled out of a compartment under each chair and again a screen was positioned in the corner. The windows were larger and there was another, smaller screen in the cabin that occasionally read, in bold red LCD letters:

'SULLA via ACHNABAR, ST.OGLILVIE- t h i s t r a i n t e r m i n a t e s a t S u l l a'

The words streamed across a ticker and then changed to permit a large white light to glow in radiance and illuminate the cabin. There were black curtains on the windows and coat hooks above them.

Suddenly, the capsules sped to life and began to rocket down the tunnel. After just a few seconds, the tunnel lifted up at a slant and came out into the open where Sharon could see the city of Achnabar all around her. She took out the folded map from her pocket to refer to and stared out of the window, listening intently to Sophios's commentary. It was a beautiful and cultured city with many Gothic buildings and spires, but it also had multitudes of very-high-rise skyscrapers that really did scrape the sky. These more modern architectural marvels disappeared into the clouds because of their vast height.

"There is the Great Tower," began Sophios. "Every respectable settlement granted the title of 'City' has a 'great tower', you see. The one here, eh … I think it's called Achbar's Tower. And over yonder there is Achbar Falls, and nearer to us on the right there is the Palace of Achbar. You can see the great castle on the hill, yes?" he asked in a flurry of delight. Sharon looked slightly sullen at this influx of information, but instead of nodding respectfully she suggested a name for the building.

"Let me guess… Achbar Castle?"

"Castle Achbar, actually." Sophios looked both disgruntled and indignant at the same time.

"Well, why is everything called Achbar's this or Achbar's that? What *is* Achbar?" Sharon demanded.

"Achbar? *What* is Achbar?" Sophios looked shocked as the train of capsules entered the tunnel, and his hilarious but fond image was captured in the contrasting light and dark of the two worlds. "Achbar was one of the most prominent and influential Wizards of all time!"

Sophios lay back.

"Achnabarum est quod Achbar erat! That's what they say. He saved this city from complete and utter destruction!" He looked excited now: "He would surely have been Ruler of the whole Empire had it not been for the corrupted oligarchy that still governs today."

Sharon looked aghast. "But you worked for the government. You were the adviser!"

"I," announced Sophios profoundly, "was employed by an uncorrupted government long ago, if you do not mind. When the Emfisc came to power, I resigned in protest!"

"What's the Emfisc or whatever it's called?" Sharon was no longer addressing Sophios with her usual respectful tone.

"The Emfisc (I mean the M – F – I – S – C) was the Movement for Imperial and Social Change. It's an evil organisation formed by a group of graduate university students seventy postins ago. They forced their way into power by storming Parliament and capturing Sulla. They are a dictatorship, giving most power to their 'New Aristos', but they are very free market – that's about all they got right. The Emperor, a distant cousin of the King, took over total control and appointed himself Ruler. The position of Ruler is the more practical side of ruling the country, and it used to be separate from the King. The Ruler would carry out the day-to-day ruling of the country, and the King would officiate and make decisions. When the Emfisc came to power everything became the property of the Emperor, who is supposed to be so benevolent that he lets us all use it for free. Nonsene, I say! All they want to do is expand, expand, expand! They're not interested in anyone but themselves. A bunch of good-for-nothing-but-firewoods, if you ask me." He was now in extreme rage and looked very flustered.

Sharon interrupted him:

"I thought you said Apnar-Séab and his family were noble?" Sharon said, somewhat confused.

"The d'Arrawors are a cross between the Old Nobles and the New Aristos – that's the only reason they have some power now. But I know they're ONs at heart!"

At the end of his sentence a message burst onto the modern screen accompanied by a rather angry voice exclaiming:

"Would Capsule 196 please keep the noise level to a minimum? Thank you."

Both passengers swivelled their heads to the window and looked over to see their number. Their capsule was labelled, in bold red lettering contrasting to the blue fascia of the capsule, 196. Sharon gulped.

"Don't worry," Sophios said calmly. "These warnings are routine. They go through every capsule warning each one to hush up just to keep everything calm.'

"Why did you look, then?" Sharon asked.

"Well, because I wasn't sure if they had changed the system, my dear."

Sharon could tell he was only trying to preserve his pride.

Sophios smiled smugly and settled back into *The Wizarding Scholar*'s magical crossword that changed every angle to make it harder for the magazine's opponent. Sharon did not venture further in asking questions. Though she was impudent and could be rash at times, she knew when to stop; especially when the man sitting opposite her was an acclaimed wizard.

"Sixty-five degrees south-west. Hmm," Sophios muttered to himself, "I just don't get it."

The crossword filled the back page with columns and rows moving occasionally in every direction, and there were hundreds of them.

"Can I help?" Sharon asked kindly, trying to mend the previously frosty relationship the last angle had created; but Sophios was calm and relaxed and had no hard feelings against Sharon. She could tell it would be a pleasurable journey from now on.

"Hmm?" he replied. "Well, if you understand this cryptic clue: 'When the tide is low and the drift comes in, they're all shipped off to the big sin bin.'"

"Criminals, maybe? Is there a prison somewhere, on an island or something?" she suggested casually.

"Ah, yes of course! You've done it my girl! The Isle of Yriad, it is! Well done, well done!"

Sharon smiled contentedly. The rest of the journey to St. Ogilvie was spent bearing Sophios's wild mutterings:

"She did it!"

"Of course!"

"Why did I not see it before?"

"Unbelievable!"

The string of capsules slid slowly to a halt at the gleaming silver-walled St. Ogilvie platform. A look of awe spread across Sharon's beaming and excited but tired-looking face.

"We'll stay on here," said Sophios as capsule doors opened and businessmen walked out onto the shiny platinum platform. This station was very chic and sophisticated, very unlike the others; diamond candelabra illuminated the platform which had on its wall a bright silver plaque with emerald-encrusted lettering spelling out the words: 'TO SULLA'. Two golden staircases wound up from the platform, but before Sharon could catch a glimpse of where they led to, the capsule began speeding up the tunnel again.

"Plenty of money in St. Ogilvie," Sophios observed. "A whole forest of Forden trees was planted there as a gift from the saint."

"So there's an unlimited supply of cash?" Sharon asked.

"You could say so, yes. Because in those days the banks couldn't cap the amount of leaves you got from a forest. Nowadays they do – so the forest owned by the city is worth hundreds of times that of what a normal forest is worth today," Sophios explained.

"But wouldn't it be easy to steal some?"

"Steal?" Sophios appeared to be highly alarmed at this comment. "No-one but Nemo would steal anything here! Anyway, it's all heavily guarded."

Sharon was taken aback by this statement, but restrained from asking anything more except one small question about Sophios's choice of vocabulary:

"If you don't mind me asking, who's Nemo?" said Sharon, trying to be more polite. Sophios laughed heartily, then said:

"Nemo? Don't you know your Latin, my dear? It's become an old saying here, that if one wants to refer to nobody, one says 'Nemo'."

The capsule continued to chug along the rails in the damp tunnels and eventually a new message flickered onto the screen.

'Approximately IX miles to Sulla. Please gather all your belongings together for arrival. These capsules terminate here. Thank you.'

Within less than an angle the capsule slowed to the platform for the last time. There was a cheap-looking plastic sign on the brick tunnel wall which read: 'To the South'. On the opposite wall a large glossy poster in a glass display case read: 'Welcome to Sulla City Station'.

This platform was wide and long, and scores of businessmen like the one that left in Achnabar were waiting patiently for the next train of capsules, either sitting on one of the uncomfortable-looking dark wooden benches lining the cold walls or standing wearily on the threadbare carpeted platform, yawning. Above each bench were plaques of some very dull metal engraved in dedication to some great or good citizen of the city, or a very conceited inhabitant leaving money to insist everyone remember him forever, immortalised on a dusty plaque in a derelict and abandoned-looking station platform. According to Sophios, this type of self-dedication was only permitted if you had no living family, defeating any meaning it might have otherwise had. Sharon read each one in turn as the capsule slowly passed:

Augustine Franciscine

a native of this parish of Sulla

Mervyn Wogsall

a distinguished merchant who led a prominent political life

Prunella Absentia-Crania

a noble fighter for peace and freedom who died confused

Dennis Callidus

an accomplished musician and distinguished court official

Renée of Achnabar

a most prolific artisan

Constance de Walden

a torch-bearer of peace and justice

Cyril Valentine

a most generous merchant

St. Benedict

we are blessed because of him

St. Ogilvie

a miracle-doer who gave a deprived area endless finance

St. Claude of Dalmatia

founder of the monastery which bears his name

St. Josef III Rex

the greatest King to ever rule

"I must say, I didn't expect to see that last one again," commented Sophios. "The government must have overlooked it – I suppose not many officials come by this way often."

Finally, the huge locomotive slowed to a halt yet again and the capsule doors slid open to reveal a full view of Sulla City Station rather than a postage stamp-sized peak from a condensated little window. A few strip lights flickered to brighten up the gloomy platform, but Sharon decided they just added to the melancholy effect.

Sophios offered Sharon the first foot forward onto the platform and she accepted the proposition. Sophios followed her out and the pair shuffled through the crowd of people awaiting a journey south. They arrived at a staircase numbered '65' on a small round copper seal above the arched entry. Though this station was derelict, it did possess all the charm of an old building.

Out of the gloomy platform, the sight of a high-ceilinged dome supported by very bright walls of red and yellow was a welcome one, however questionable as a matter of taste. Stairways led down all around the circular dome that was the centre of the city station.

"Lovely, eh?" Sophios said. "Newly refurbished, too! Jolly good show at last from the council."

Sharon was not stirred by this unexpected comment - she hardly even noticed it at all. She was absorbed in embracing the full quality of craftsmanship in the station. Large stone pillars surrounded the hall, above which were circular windows. The pillars were painted red and gargoyles overlooked the whole building from their peaks, their eyes moving constantly, surveying each passenger in turn. Four huge doorways at the main compass points rose to the ceiling from the cold black-and-white tiled floor. Each one of the doorways bore a different message, all in Greek (which perplexed Sharon): SULLA NORTH, SULLA SOUTH, OUT, LA RUE ROYALE.

People were scrambling across the huge atrium, emerging from and descending the steps from the numbered doors all around. Sophios guided Sharon to the doorway marked 'SULLA NORTH' and the pair walked through it to discover a long tunnel filled with beggars wearing those idiosyncratic caps taken off to any passer-by for leaves. Sophios gave the first a stern look of disgust and utter disapproval at their idleness and then walked on brusquely past the others, Sharon following closely at his heel. He never spoke a word down the corridor until they came to ticket machines, which were much like the examples Sharon could remember existed in the London underground. Sophios handed her the ticket and said,

"Insert that into the slot and then push hard through these barriers."

She did so and the machine spat out her ticket, now stamped and punched with the perforated section at the bottom gone, replaced by a simple sticker that read 'THANK YOU FOR VISITING SULLA'. Up ahead there were glass doors that led onto a busy city street. They passed by the queue at the customer services desk of complaining travellers (which was customarily long) and Sophios pushed aside the glass door in front of him and stopped to take in the 'fresh air' he had been used to for such a long time. The air was slightly contaminated with fumes which could be seen swirling up into the sky in the distance in the industrial part of the city, but it was all rather unexplainable, a very unusual fragrance. High-rising department stores lined the fashionable street facing the dominant symbol of power and authority that protected the city: the great stone walls as high, and sometimes higher, than the department stores. Sharon was so interested in the buildings all around her she hardly noticed Sophios saying,

"We shall go into Wilfred and Wilfred's and get ourselves a street map for you, eh?" He seemed happy to be back in his home town, but a little sad to know he would be leaving it shortly.

"Oh, eh ... yes," Sharon said as she struggled to recollect what the question was.

After passing *Seymour & Seymour, Aphra Perfume &c., Warren Lazare and Company, Maurice and Sons* and *Orlando's Technical* Sophios and Sharon arrived opposite *Wilfred and Wilfred Bookstores* which Sophios indicated was the shop they were going to enter. Having weaved their way through the stationary and congested traffic they came to the grand ebony doors of W&W, as the huge circular sign read above. They entered a massive hall quietly buzzing with the chatter of voices discussing the latest publications, or even reading them aloud. Two staircases led to a landing on either side of the huge room, which was completely lined with books from floor to ceiling, and was what looked like eight storeys high at the very least. The upper floors contained other library resources, such as maps. The two sifted through the small collective groups of people to the staircase on the right-hand side, which they climbed. In the centre of the bookstore was a large statue of a young man wearing ancient attire, accompanied by a small but faithful dog. He was resting on a rock writing a book. On the memorial stone beneath it read: 'Multignosis Kudos, deliverer of language who visited Sullaria to give the gift of written word and the alphabet. Died many years ago writing his last unfinished work, *The Storm Cries*, when he slipped on a rock and fell to his death off a cliff.'

Sophios walked quickly along the landing; it had small leather seats dotted all over and bookshelves of the latest bestsellers. He opened a door marked 'REFERENCE' and Sharon followed him into another large room lined with many bookcases with a large stained glass window of 'Wilfred Wilfred; First Duke of Wilfredshire.' This window was black-and-white of a tall man with little round spectacles peering down at his bookshop. Signs were hung from the intricately decorated ceiling intimating the sections of reference to be found below them. This was evidently the oldest part of the bookshop. Sophios ushered Sharon across with him to the 'MAPS-Street' section, where street maps of most cities and towns could be found, not just of Sullaria but of many other nations as well. Sharon scanned the 'S' section and pointed to a map. It was simple; just a sheet of hard, thick paper with a simple street map of Sulla with directions to other places near the sides. It looked quite old (but then all the maps looked old) and a small rectangular sticker with cut-off edges showed three simple symbols of leaves, followed by a decimal point and half a leaf and a stalk. Underneath this price guide was the logo of the store: two crossed Ws in black.

"Yes! This will do nicely. Come," Sophios said as he brushed passed other customers on his way to the till desk. A woman in turquoise stood behind it, ready for her next customer.

Sophios handed over the map to the woman, who took out a small bag with the 'WW' logo and placed it inside. Then she took hold of a stamp, rubbed it in a small circular red ink pad and stamped a hand-written receipt with it.

"Would you like to make a donation to our sponsored Charity of the Month, the St. Ogilvie Foundation?" The woman's droning but high-pitched voice pierced Sharon's ears almost as much as her turquoise plumage would have put off any customer from going within a hundred-metre radius of her desk.

"Let's see. Take these and put the change to the fund, all right?" Sophios said nicely.

"Of course." She sounded more cheery now, but expectant as Sophios placed five Forden leaves in her hand.

"Here." Sophios handed her a stalk as a tip.

"Thank you, sir," she replied, the transformation from gloominess to happiness now complete.

They left, Sharon clutching the bag tightly in her fist, and proceeded down the stairs and out the ebony doors. Sharon thought it might seem rude to open the map now and start gazing at it intently, so she kept it safe inside the bag while they crossed the busy road, now bustling with moving traffic advancing in an extremely unorganised fashion – it was even worse than French traffic, Sharon observed. Sophios looked over to a small clock-tower, which simply read the time as a figure, taking its reading from the sundial on the top of the tower. It was made of many cards that changed as they clocked up the time. It read: 188999997/3.

"We have three angles to go. We're early," he said.

The pair walked up the street, watched all the time by guards dressed in black patrolling the wall. Finally, Sophios and Sharon came to the grand Marquis Gate where they found a handsome, tidy and smart young man awaiting them beside the sentry.

CHAPTER FOUR

Apnar and His House

A high stone arch greeted them ahead. Two black boxes with golden filigree decoration were home to two sentries, standing like statues in their gleaming white uniforms and golden helmets. They carried an elaborate spear each and bore swords strapped to them by their sides. On their uniforms a large navy blue badge with gold lettering read: '195th Armoured Regiment, Sullarian Army' and underneath this was the military motto: 'Rule Sullaria'. Enraptured by these stunning costumes Sharon turned her gaze upon the man she had spotted earlier. He too, like Sophios, was wearing a long cloak, but in black. His hair was perfectly manicured and inside his cloak a golden sundial pocket-watch peered out from behind a neat three-piece suit. He was clean shaven and had his hands clutched together behind his back. He looked about twenty, Sharon thought. He looked at Sophios and then turned to Sharon who quickly averted her gaze and then re-positioned it back to the man, just in time to catch and replicate a small smile.

"Good Apnar-Séab! It must be you. How is the household, my son?" Sophios asked loudly, beaming at the man.

"Very well thank you, sir. We're prospering from that tree in Forden we bought fifty postins ago more than ever! A sound investment, sir," he replied.

"Oh, my boy… Call me Sophios, please!" Sophios said kindly.

"Yes, and you can call me Apnar, sir. I mean ... Sophios."

"Indeed."

"I see your guest is in good health," Apnar commented.

"Yes, yes. She's fine. Tell Apnar a little about yourself, Sharon."

"Well," she began, "I just found myself here a couple of days ago..." and so the story continued, the guards at their posts shooting wary glances at each other all the while.

"Come back to the house for a rest, Sophios!" asked Apnar.

"Oh, no!" Sophios replied. "I mean..." he hastily added to prevent Apnar from interpreting this statement wrongly. "I'd be delighted, but I have to be back soon. I said I would be."

"Yes. Good to see you well," Apnar added finally.

"And you dear boy. Farewell!"

With this final valediction Sophios swept his cloak behind him and walked away, his medallion swinging effortlessly ahead of him as much as ever. Sharon was sure she heard another "Take care!" call from behind her.

"This way, Sharon," Apnar said patronisingly. "I thought we could go back to the house, so I invited you to meet me at the Marquis Gate. However, things have come up and..." Sharon waited for the catch. "I'm afraid I'll have to do a few things at the G.O."

"The 'G.O.'?" Sharon said, puzzled.

"You know, Government Offices?" Apnar responded with a look of disgust at her ignorance. Sharon despised his know-it-all character, but decided to try and get along. It was he, after all, who was helping her.

Apnar led the way by turning right up a street which stretched the whole length of the shiny black department store on the right, with many tiny derelict houses barely managing to stand up on the left.

"Dingys. That's what we tend to call *those*." Apnar gestured towards the houses. They resembled some sort of South American favela. The contrast between rich and poor was sharp here. Both lived together in harmony, which was positive, but they bore striking differences. There simply was no middle class. 'You're either in-service or with-service!' as Apnar put it. Sharon found this a little odd, but decided not to comment.

At the end of the road were two other streets leading off the one they had just come along: a crossroads. One street forked off at forty-five degrees to a huge estate on the right with more township residences on the left, and the other street was almost identical, demonstrating the simple symmetry the city was based on. The second street led to huge black and gold gates, through which Sharon could see a huge white chateau with white and blue oriflamme flags fluttering from its many turrets, surrounded in perfected gardens and mature woodland, which occupied at least a twelfth of the whole city.

"That's the Emperor's palace. The supreme Ruler of the Empire lives there. Nobody but Nemo ever enters that gate. They say it's just for show. They say officials go through tunnels deep underground," Apnar commented. Sharon gave him a look indicating her interest.

Taking the street to the left, Sharon could see a long portion of land which formed the storage and delivery areas at the backs of the department stores they had seen earlier, and on the opposite side of the street was the fence of a large manor house situated in grounds as large as 'W&W's, if not larger. This fence was lined with mature trees at the edges of the gardens, so as to afford the viewer only the occasional view of the private house.

Apnar and Sharon turned left again, down a long street of houses facing the backs of office blocks on the other side. These residences were huge buildings. The first three were ancient picturesque castles, and the other houses following them were lavish stone homes with at least four floors and countless windows. One of them reminded Sharon of her school back in England. At the end of the six houses was the iron fence of the palace Sharon had seen earlier, giving another glimpse of the most fashionable residence in town. After this a very wide river cut through the whole street diagonally.

"That's L'Attler. The river comes down from the north, there." Apnar pointed in a random direction. "We'll have to board a sailing boat and cross that to get to the Main Street."

"I see," Sharon lied.

A little shack of a boathouse which reeked of a foul and unwelcoming fish smell came into view, beyond which several small fishing boats could be seen tied up at the pier. Tall galleys and quinqueremes were lined up along the river, boarded with luxurious goods to be traded abroad. Several schooners provided ample transportation to foreign shores and Sharon noticed a small rowing boat bobbing up and down on the glimmering water just ahead of her.

"This is a boat," Apnar said in the most refined yet state of platitude.

"I can see that, thank you," Sharon said in response.

"Do I have to stand and accept your unfriendly remarks or may I continue to instruct you properly?" Apnar said coldly.

"Go on," Sharon replied before mumbling a derogatory comment under her breath.

Apnar climbed aboard the unmanned little wooden craft, pulled up the pair of oars and was already moving gradually away from the city shore when Sharon tried to board it with him. They crossed the river quickly and were soon confronted by a large man laden with golden jewellery, an avaricious look of contentment written across his bulldog-like face.

"Two Forden leaves, please," he demanded of rather than asked Apnar in his grizzly voice.

"Two?" Apnar replied. "Isn't that a little extortionate? Say a leaf without stalk, or one and a half? Be reasonable!" Apnar pleaded confidently.

"Two or sink!" the man commanded, withdrawing a large staff from his black cloak pocket. Apnar handed him two full leaves and remained silent, terrified.

"Thank you," the man said, waving his staff to life and conjuring the leopard's head at the top of it to open its mouth and roar noisily in the boat's direction, sending it straight back to the other side.

Apnar and Sharon walked on silently to the huge road that was Main Street. It was even wider than the river and was buzzing with all sorts of cycles, carriages, hovering vehicles and so much more creating a disturbing muffle of horns and skidding. On the side of the street nearest to the river a large enclosure sealed off what looked like a great cathedral with accompanying grounds. It was situated by a substantial palatial house, made of red brick. The house had mullioned and oriole windows on all of the many floors, and looked quite magnificent. A clock tower rose up from the top floor bearing an ebony sundial with gold markings. Though the house was right on the pavement, it had vast gardens behind and around it to give it a real presence.

At this point the pair fashioned out a twisted path across the road through the stentorian commotion to the wider pavement which welcomed them to the 'G.O.' The building was an awkward shape: a wide front protruded nearest to them, where the main entrance of modern glass doors became apparent, followed by an inward dent preceding a further lurch out in stone and then a final cantilever jutting out. The building was right next to a gargantuan palace which Sharon could not imagine as a house to be lived in. Great gates of gold presented themselves proudly with valid distinction. Behind these a short path led to the eight-storied mansion, again in red brick. The house was very wide and rectangular with scores of windows peering out onto the immaculate lawns and mature trees protecting it from intruders, and, more generally, the horrible outside world. On the two gateposts were gold plaques engraved with 'BURGOMASTER'S HOUSE' and, on the left post, '17'. A large blue and gold flag fluttered from a high turret of the house, symbolising the city's pride and glory. And as they embarked across to the Government Offices the image of this flag, and of the flamboyant mansion it fluttered from, became evanescent behind the trees.

Apnar swung the great glass doors aside, and they remained open for Sharon to walk through behind. A huge hall with light marble floors was inside. It had a huge dome decorated lavishly and ornately which greeted the outsider into the Offices. In the centre of the great and bright room a huge bell decorated with the four animals of Empire – Aquila, Agnus, Pelicanus, and Leo – was placed for viewing. Each Latin inscription was accompanied by an engraving of its corresponding beast. In front of the great monument cast in pure gold, a small sign in a glass case informed the viewer: 'THE IMPERIAL BELL, taken from the Cathedral of the Holy Rude during the 19th Reformation.'

Beside the bell a large statue of a serpent stood snobbishly above the floor beneath it. It was decorated in chryselephantine and peering out of the serpent's aristocratic head was a gold sceptre, adding to the absurdity of the sculpture. Along the snake's twisting body a message in Latin was inscribed eloquently in silky gold, unlike the bell which was coarse and dirtier.

A tall woman dressed in uniform was standing behind a mahogany reception desk at the far end of the hall. Apnar walked past her, lifting a little blue identification badge, at which the woman made no objection and sat down to her paperwork. Apnar could see she was still observing them from the corner of her eye, and so let his great and hefty medals bound in the air then return to his chest ostentatiously. The woman scowled and stared back at her papers.

Apnar proceeded to walk towards a large steel door, obviously replaced since the building's opening. It split in half vertically and slid into the wall making way for Apnar, for whom conversation was not a forte. He walked through without batting an eyelid at Sharon. She followed him to the door but the two panels slammed shut and barred her entry.

"Hem...hem," came the gentle whimper from the receptionist's tiny voice box.

"Sorry?" Sharon said, not daring to turn to face the woman for fear of revealing her perspiring face glowing with sweat in the intense light of the hall.

"Identification?" the woman inquired, peering over her desk.

"Eh... I'm afraid..." Sharon tried to muster an acceptable response.

"Yes?" the receptionist said amplifying her tone of voice upwardly in a swooping thrust of muliebrity.

"I was with that man. I'm his... guest," she panicked.

"Do you have appropriate identification?" the woman said strikingly.

"Well... no," Sharon answered honestly.

"Then I cannot be permitted to authorise your entry into the offices. You may wait patiently here or in the tarry lounge."

"I'll just wait here, thank you," Sharon replied.

"Indeed," the woman continued in a rather irksome tone. "However, a court dignitary will be touring the premises in a few angles. Do you know how long your 'host' will be?"

"I'm not sure. Not long, I don't think." Sharon lowered her voice. "I hope not anyway."

"I see. Please take a seat here, then. Shortly before His Excellency arrives you will be ushered to the tarry lounge."

The woman pointed over to a small bench near the door, at the same time attempting to operate some bureaucratic task, which failed miserably when the papers in her hand drifted feather-like to the glossy floor. She picked them up furiously and stuffed them unceremoniously into a small filing cabinet already open for its meal, never again glancing back at Sharon for the remainder of the period, for a reason Sharon considered to be embarrassment at having been chagrined.

Sharon trotted over to the bench allocated to her. It was green in colour and had a plastic touch. Sharon slumped into the bench's cold structure and almost fell asleep (certainly not because of the seat's comfort qualities, but rather of the tiring day and all-night travelling she had endured the evening before). Her eyelids slowly drew to a close and the now blurry image of the hall became hidden behind two dark shutters.

A corridor of panelled walls led straight down forwards. The floor was a blur, yet everything seemed utterly realistic. At the end of the hall bright white light glowed fantastically through an arch, such radiant and awesome, hurtful light. It was blindingly powerful and painful, yet Sharon looked on. Swirls of brightly coloured beams of light surrounded the arch but the focal point of this vision was in the arch's centre. Sharon's parents stood smiling at her, their warm faces beaming at hers. Fear played no part in this dreamy episode; calm, tranquillity and peace were the expressive qualities of the scene. Sharon moved forwards to approach her parents who were still smiling at her.

"Sharon," said her dead father, "Sharon?"

The voice of her father became gradually colder and stern as his image drifted away into oblivion and a light room with parched threadbare floors came into focus.

"Sharon?" the now louder voice of Apnar bellowed impatiently. Sharon now realised she had fallen asleep and had been ushered to the tarry lounge while still in a slumber.

"A-Apnar?" Sharon questioned, still in a daze.

"Come on! We must get back to the house. You'll have a nice big room tonight and we shall have our meal in your honour. Let's go!" Apnar was in an unusually happy and talkative mood as if he had just received good news.

"Yes," Sharon said, graciously accepting his more joyous nature. "Let's go."

Apnar gave his hand to Sharon to help her up and proceeded towards the large oak door of the tarry lounge, this time holding it open for her. Once more Sharon entered the huge entrance hall where Apnar's little round spectacles glinted in their diamond-encrusted frame of gold. He drifted across the gleaming tiles to the huge front door which he opened to let Sharon out before him.

The street was a bright muddle of vehicles flashing all over the place. The sky was a clouded mist of bleak grey and, though the sun had managed to peep round a cloud, it was with only great difficulty. The pair crossed the busy road and, from behind the towering government blocks the street was home to, the authoritative magnitude and splendour of the Grand Tower (or simply 'the Tower' as it was more commonly known these days) could be seen peeping over the cityscape, somewhat overwhelmed by the vastness of the other buildings cluttering the citadel.

Apnar and Sharon boarded a small boat which took them upstream to Apnar's home. The boat ploughed through the gleaming silvery water of L'Attler with ease. To the right, the huge four-towered oval stadium containing the cathedral-like structure rose up from the banks of the river. A colossal entrance arch with a trefoil frame acted as the grand way into the massive building. Above the arch was engraved a shield with the same emblem on Sophios's medallion. Above that, a pair of scales was etched into the stone.

Having observed Sharon's interest in the building, Apnar commented, "Those are the law courts. There are also a few cells in there. We'd best avoid those, though, eh?"

"Yes," Sharon replied cheerily.

Opposite the courts the vast gardens of the Palace gave the viewer a charming view of the Imperial residence and its enclosure. The flapping flags presented a marvellous indication of the power and authority that the 'corrupt oligarchy' stood for, ever since the debacle of the 'righteous government' (if there is such a thing) of Sullaria.

As the vessel proceeded up the river, houses of immense capacity lined the left-hand side while extensive and exclusive department stores and boutiques on the opposite side dazzled onlookers. The first of these stores was a large square building with fifteen or more floors and large red lettering above its several swing-doors reading 'CLEMENT MAURICE, *Exclusive Bespoke Furnishings*'. The next building was tall and narrower than its neighbour and a large sign above its showroom read 'LAURIEN, *Carmakers of Luxury and Prestige*'. Another square building, much like the first but red in colour, dominated the riverbank. The notice on its great walls intimated 'MARCEL'S, *Proficient Specialists in Habiliments and Comestibles*'.

These three stores took up the space of only two of the stately homes opposite them, however. Sharon had noticed by now that each house or shop had its own pier for docking boats for guests or merchandise. The next store was entitled 'HERMAN LAZARE & SAMUEL TALLIS, *the store for all your needs, incorporating* THE CHOCOLATE EMPORIUM, TRAVELTODAY and LANCELOT REFECTIONS'. Opposite this fourth store was sited a large domed and customarily palatial mansion, at which the boat turned to approach.

"Here we are!" exclaimed Apnar.

Sharon was still taking in the ornateness of 'Arrawor Hall'. The boat tied up at the stone port, which had several thick turned legs, battered and bruised with wear which gave it exceptional character. Engraved into the stonework an inscription in Latin read: *VILLA ARRAWOR*. Apnar walked onto the platform, on which a red velvet carpet had been placed for him by a manservant dressed in a black suit of top hat and tails with an orange tartan waistcoat. He had a silver tray with champagne flutes filled to the brim. He approached the boat to help Sharon out, but Apnar gestured to him not to and put his bony hand out for Sharon instead. Sharon was deeply comforted by this and excited at the prospect of inhabiting such a mansion and being waited on hand and foot for a while.

Apnar perambulated towards the mansion house across the deep-red velvet carpet that led to his front door, Sharon by his side, drinks in hands. Apnar took a polite swig from his flute of sparkling liquid and Sharon almost copied him before she remembered her previous unfortunate incident with an other-worldly beverage.

"Do have a drink, Sharon," Apnar offered.

"No, thank you. I'm afraid I get a bit drowsy and sick when I drink these other-wordly liquids," Sharon replied.

"Surely you have water where you come from? It's just sparkling!" Apnar said merrily, laughing to himself. Sharon giggled and sipped the cool refreshment which was indeed water.

Two sentries stood at the front door, rapiers by their sides, helmets down. They wore bright blue uniforms with gold buttons and polished black leather shoes. The house was white stone with gold decoration. It had a domed facade and renaissance windows and the front door was a dark mahogany with a gold knocker. Around the arched door beautiful carvings protruded majestically and Apnar moved towards them. The huge door opened and Apnar stepped in. A butler dressed in black welcomed them in.

"Good obtuse, sir…" He turned to Sharon, "madam."

The entrance hall was fifty feet high and mainly white. The intricate plasterwork had ebony inlay which was arranged in small squares on the huge domed ceiling, laden with ivory decoration. Steps led down into the large square area with doors to other rooms leading off it. The red carpet continued down these steps to the area and two pillared corridors led off each side from the front door.

"We'll have our meal through here." Apnar pointed at the large door directly opposite them and walked forwards with Sharon.

The double-doors swung open to receive Apnar and his guest. Inside, a table set for three was laid out and heavily panelled walls shouted their magnificence at the observer ostentatiously. The ceiling was again very high and coned three times with ornate plasterwork. A grand chandelier was hung from the centre and the red carpet continued along the room to the table. It was made of rosewood with green velvet upholstery on the chairs. Sitting at the head was Apnar's father, looking resplendent in his long purple robes. Apnar later explained he had been attending the Imperial Court, for which the robes were compulsory.

"Apnar-Séab, my son!" he bellowed.

"Hello, father," Apnar said and he bowed.

"And our charming visitant lady; welcome, child!"

"Thank you," Sharon said.

"Sit and eat," commanded Apnar's father.

"Thank you," Sharon repeated.

Suddenly three plates of soup appeared at each setting.

"Apnar, I told you not to use magic anymore! We pay the servants to do a job; let them do it," Apnar's father said, slightly annoyed.

"Sorry," Apnar apologised.

The soup was a brown-green colour and soggy-looking. Apnar's father bowed his head and clasped his hands together and Apnar (and therefore Sharon) followed.

"For what we are about to receive, for the rich gifts bestowed on us, for family and amicable interaction, and for our guest today, may the Lord our God make us truly thankful. His will be done. Amen." Apnar's father had conducted the grace.

Once again Sharon was in a trio; one of kindness and togetherness, and once again she restrained herself from shedding tears. She lifted her white napkin and placed it gracefully on her lap of sodden clothes. Sharon dipped her silver spoon into the liquid and devoured a full spoonful of the mixture. It was surprisingly delicious and salty.

After the first course was fully devoured, Apnar's father clicked his fingers and three servants removed the bowls and replaced them with warm dinner plates. Then, one other servant poured some spirits from a small decanter and left the room.

"May I?" inquired Apnar, smiling.

"Go on, then," his father complied reluctantly.

A roast pheasant instantly appeared on the table in the place of the silver punch bowl, and the dazzling candelabra above the party glittered brightly, illuminating the table and its occupants. Serving staff marched ceremoniously and automatically to the table, serving hot vegetables and seasonings. They carved the pheasant and divided it among the three diners and also provided new napkins, each one white with the letters 'AH' embossed in gold. A young parlour-maid poured water when accepted and then dismissed herself. Finally, all the servants returned in silence to their previous positions either side of the doors, directly opposite each other.

"Dismissed!" Apnar's father bellowed in a disgruntled manner.

The servants immediately departed and manned the same doors on the other side of the incredibly thick walls.

"Pheasant is always a favourite of ours, is it not my boy?" Apnar's father commented warmly.

"It is indeed, father. Sharon," Apnar paused, "your verdict?"

"Lovely! Very appealing, yes. Now, on the matter of tomorrow's business..." She paused to invoke one of the others to carry the conversation. Apnar's father, however, looked quite utterly bemused.

"Eh,... we are not accustomed to speaking at the dinner table, Sharon. It usually simply isnt... done, I suppose," Apnar explained.

Sharon fumbled an "Oh," but Apnar's father cut in.

"Come come now, boy! If our guest wishes to converse at this time, so be it. After all, we would never be where we are today if we never advanced in anything, never changed."

Apnar's father turned to Sharon, "Tomorrow? I suppose tomorrow will come in due time. Let's not worry. Apnar sorts these kinds of things out. Enjoy your meal, my dear. Eat up!"

Sharon was warmed by Apnar's father's kind politeness and so did not pursue the matter further. After this course Apnar summoned a waiter to clear the table and prepare the next course. Sharon commented by-the-by that she was full, which the two gentlemen took profoundly seriously.

"If Sharon is elegantly sufficed, I think it right for us all to adjourn our meal here. What do you say, father?" said Apnar.

"Jolly good, my boy. Arise! Apnar: show our guest where she will be sleeping this evening," his father replied accordingly.

Sharon was offered the first exit from the room and as Apnar's father followed, he instructed the doorman, "That will be all."

Apnar's father then vacated the entrance hall to enter a large drawing room, puffing a strange sort of pipe, while Apnar himself led Sharon up to a large bedchamber on the first floor. A doorman opened the panelled mahogany door which opened into a high-ceilinged, heavily-ornamented room with a huge oak four-poster bed complete with red velvety curtains with gold tassels. Two windows the full height of the room let light flood onto the wooden floor. Three gold beams held up the domed ceiling, each one bearing a lantern drooped by chains yet still metres up, which crowned the room in glory. Fancifully decorated wardrobes, a commode, a dressing table, writing desk, bureau, bookcase and several French-looking chairs were present, to name but some of the many precious furniture pieces within the room.

After Sharon had gazed around at the room for a few moments, observing the beautiful mirrors and portraits, Apnar asked pointedly, "Do you like it?"

"Yes!" Sharon exclaimed. "It's wonderful. Thank you!"

"I'm very glad you like it. Have a nice sleep. A nightgown and new clothes for the morning are in that wardrobe. Good night."

"Thank you, good night," Sharon replied as Apnar closed the door.

She drew the huge curtains and sat on the duvet, testing the mattress quality. It was indeed high, like everything else in the house. Then she pulled off her soggy and baggy clothes and slipped into the decorative nightgown in the large wardrobe. Sharon lifted a book at random and settled herself into bed, snuggling into the heavy duvet over her. Opposite her was a large oil portrait of a decidely devious-looking man – Sharon knew she would not be able to sleep with this image facing her, so she drew the curtains around the bed and turned to her book. The dusty volume was about the history of L'Attler in the city. Its highly uninteresting facts drifted into Sharon's mind unconsciously while the silent fire in the cast-iron fireplace beside her dwindled and blurred softly into a hazy mist. Sharon was, once again, dormant.

CHAPTER FIVE

The Tower

Sharon rose early and dressed herself in the plain black dress hanging in the wardrobe. She then put on a small, tight jacket that matched the whole suit. Inside the wardrobe were a long, silk black cloak and a hat. And in the umbrella rack a dainty parasol was laid, again in black. Sharon examined herself in the tall looking glass inside the wardrobe. Although the outfit looked rather gloomy, it was not unattractive, she thought.

The newly-dressed girl moved over to the curtains, drew them, and sat down at the dressing table. Sharon opened the middle drawer: a maze of different make-ups sparkled in their bottles in the sunlight. But Sharon dared not use them: she could not make sense of what they all were. So, in the light of this, she opened the drawers to the left and right of the long centre one. Inside these, glittering jewellery shone up at her. In spite of the temptation, Sharon did not adorn herself in the jewels, but closed the drawers and sat on the little green chair by the window, thinking.

She was now in a dilemma: should she go down to breakfast or wait for Apnar? She decided it best to wait in her room because it was so early. Remembered facts from the previous night's reading now flashed in her mind.

'The river was formed in a deep valley millions of postins ago between two great mountain ranges and was originally just a stream of water from the peak of an extinct volcano where the city of Lambdasia now stands.'

'It takes thirty times the volume of space inside Sulla's city walls to fill just half the river.'

'The origins of the name 'L'attler' are uncertain, though it is thought to have been a misspelling of the Arvadian term for 'landing place', probably the landing place of either rainwater, or foreign invaders, probably the Arvadians themselves.'

Sharon looked out across the small estate she was on, and then out into the busy streets, observing the busy world go by. Before she could settle down, however, a few rapid knocks on the door suddenly echoed around the room, followed by Apnar's call of:

"Sharon? Are you hungry? I'm afraid we'll have to be leaving quite early so there's only time for a small bite of toast."

Sharon opened the door. "Just a drink for me, thank you. I'm still digesting last night's meal!" she said.

"I see. Come down, then."

Sharon walked out of the bedroom and followed Apnar through the high-ceilinged corridors of 'Arrawor Hall' and into the breakfast room. Apnar pushed aside the door and the pair entered the large room. It had three huge windows and much decoration on the ceiling; the intricate patterns were of astounding craftsmanship. In the centre of the ceiling was a large coat of arms – the shield was a dark shade of red with a single gold leopard's head, and two red dragons were supporting it. The motto underneath read 'Felicitas Perpetua': Sharon read it aloud and translated the phrase in her head. Her hours of Latin *had* come in useful, she thought. The room was heated by several candles in glass frames glowing brightly on the walls. In the centre of the room a large square table was set with red and gold mats, coasters, tablecloth, runner, double candelabra, table-napkins, flowers and bread baskets.

"We shan't bother the staff. Here," Apnar said as he conjured a tall, thin glass which had a gold rim and the letters 'AH' embossed onto it in red.

"What would you like to drink?" Apnar asked.

"Anything not too strong," Sharon replied.

"We'll make one ourselves, shall we?" suggested Apnar.

Instantly, an orange liquid filled about a quarter of the glass followed by some blue powder and some red liquid. This was followed up by the appearance of a kiwi fruit squeezing itself, the juice filling the glass to the brim. Then, Apnar waved his finger in a circular motion and the concoction whirled round making a spiral in the liquid. The end result was a white and very luminous liquid which sparkled as bubbles whizzed into place to create the two letters 'AH'. After this display, ice cold foam erupted from the glass, chilling the air all around it. This gradually disappeared and all that was left were two solid cubes of the foam dissolving in the drink. Apnar then caused a warm red glow to appear inside the solution. The cubes melted instantly in the heat and a straw appeared in the mixture, followed by a tiny but dainty wooden parasol with the letters 'AH' on its wings.

"Enjoy," said Apnar happily.

Sharon lent forwards to devour the sweet-smelling refreshment. It was beautiful. It was smooth yet very fizzy and cool. The drink was the perfect way to start an exciting day. Once Sharon had completely extricated the liquid from its container, and while Apnar was munching his toast, she asked if Apnar's father was coming down to breakfast.

"Oh, but it's too early for him! He doesn't rise till midday!" Apnar explained.

"I see," said Sharon. She knew the type – her mother rarely experienced morning if she could avoid it.

"Sharon… you're probably wondering about my mother, Sylvia. She passed away last year. We were so heart-broken, but I still treasure her memory. She was so generous; she donated so much to good causes."

"I'm so sorry, Apnar," Sharon said comfortingly.

"Thank you, thank you. She was a victim of Act 22."

"Sorry?"

"I know you are - you just told me. Please, Sharon, don't persist with me. It is difficult enough…"

"No. I mean, as in 'pardon'?"

"Oh!" Apnar chuckled to himself.

"Act 22 is the law passed that activates the immediate execution of any peeress of the realm who 'squanders' her money on others 'in any manner or means'," Apnar continued. "Sometimes it works well, but in some cases, well…"

Sharon gasped. "That's terrible!" she declared.

"It was without trial."

Sharon gasped again and remained silent. She almost could not believe Apnar's mother could have been executed for doing good, especially in her social position.

"Let's go now, shall we?" Apnar proposed, wishing to end the awkwardness as soon as possible.

"Yes," Sharon replied.

Apnar summoned the cloak from Sharon's wardrobe and it floated down the staircase to the hall where he and Sharon were now standing. It wrapped itself around Sharon and fastened tightly at the collar.

"All right?" Apnar asked Sharon.

"Fine," she replied.

"Then let's go!" he commanded, and the front doors blew open in a gust of powerful wind that seemed to emanate from Apnar's fingertips, almost knocking the vast doors off their hinges.

Sharon followed Apnar into the blazing heat that met them outside. Though midday was at least a couple of hours away, waves of superbly strong heat wafted towards the mansion. Apnar summoned two menservants to prepare a coach quickly, which duly arrived within the next thirty seconds. The pair boarded the black and gold coach and moved swiftly down the pathway to the pier. They hovered above the ground as the coach glided in the air a few inches above the path.

Eventually, as the stone, lichen-ridden pier drew ever closer, the coach halted and opened its doors wide while ejecting two rows of steps for the passengers to leave by. One small hovercraft was floating by the pier, which Sharon and Apnar boarded. Apnar waved his hand and the boat immediately rose above the surface of the water and skimmed over the waves beneath it. Sharon sat on the hard painted wood which was chipped and battered. It was not the most pleasurable experience. Therefore, Apnar replaced the bench with a throne of gold with red velvet upholstery and a silk cushion. The two eagles' heads on either arm had their mouths opened wide, their diamond-encrusted teeth shining in the sunlight. This was certainly more comfortable, though Sharon could not explain how the vessel did not immediately sink under the weight. She sat back in her chair and enjoyed the fresh breeze and scenery while Apnar did the same in his green leather throne. Gentle zephyrs passed over Sharon's cool face and the clouds separated further to enhance the scorching sunbeams, occasionally dampened by a breeze.

The craft glided over the shimmering glassy river and past the department stores and towering mansions. The obvious dominancy of the Palace then covered the scene on the north bank, opposite the courts of justice. The river bustled with life, full of ships and galleys, tows and rowing-boats, down to brave swimmers risking their necks in the busy river. The boat now approached the huge bridge that joined the two sections of Main Street. The massive scope of the arched water-crossing amazed Sharon as she marvelled at its architectural brilliance. It was painted green and was decorated with ornate designs of lions and serpents. As the hovercraft passed under the bridge everything became dark. It took at least a quarter of an angle to get to the other side, this at full speed.

Emerging from under the bridge, however, the sight of blue skies and the feel of a fresh breeze were very much welcome.

The Tower was now in sight: a huge structure dominating the complex landscape of the city. Its lancet windows and castellated peak were a visible sign of the power and authority of government, such a presence immediately conjuring visions of emperors and fairy-tail castles in Sharon's mind. On the right, much more modern buildings jutted out onto the riverside. The ultra-modern, hi-tech doors were very sleek and the glistening signs above these added to the fashionable, chic look. One read: 'PRENTICE'S OF SULLA, 178 L'Attler, 64 Kingsmarket Parade, *Master Tailer*'. Another sign: 'HUTT AND LESTRANGE, 180 L'Attler, *Specialists in Polo and Other Sports*'. The third said: 'TELFER'S, 182-184 L'Attler, 72 Fabula Row, 47½ Mandebule Circus. Based in Sulla, Achnabar & Sémento. *Building, decorating and furnishing taken care of by a professional*'.

The small hovering craft slowed down as it approached the Tower's large pier, bigger than that of any other building on the waterfront. Apnar stepped onto the stone platform as did Sharon, and the pair made their way to the pillared main entrance of the Tower that stood before them magnificently. The grand doors were flung open wide for anyone with the nerve to enter.

"What's it used for, the Tower?" Sharon asked.

"Partly a prison, a few courts, a few offices; the parliamentary halls mostly, though. And, of course —"

"The Oracle." Sharon completed the sentence for him with ease.

"Precisely. But we must be 'hush-hush' about this. I'll say we're here to debate in the City Chambers. I'll pretend to be a City Consul — they run the city day to day, and I think I can remember a few names. You just stay silent, right?"

Sharon was enjoying all the excitement. "Sure," she replied.

"Good," Apnar said finally as he and Sharon walked into the reception. The foyer had a glossy floor and vaulted ceiling with bright, low-strung lights and a desk with glass panels. Behind this desk sat a stout man who was sneezing erratically. His name badge read 'Warren Stultson'.

"Excuse me," Apnar began. The man slowly turned to face Apnar.

"Can I help you?" he asked slowly.

"Yes, please. I am Franz Percival, Thirty-Second Viscount Ebringdon-Camworth. I've come for the debate in the City Chambers," Apnar lied.

"I'm not aware of a current debate in the City Chambers, nor of a Viscount Ebringdon-Camworth. Are you sure you have an appointment? I'll check in the book, if you would like?"

"No!" Apnar said hastily. "I'll sign on my way out. Thank you."

"No you will not!" Mr. Stultson retorted as Apnar tried to start for the door. "And who is this?" he further inquired.

"Oh, just my, eh... maid-servant. She always comes with me, of course."

"Rather well-dressed for a maid, isn't she?"

"Well, I *am* Viscount Ebring-"

"Yes, so you said. But what you obviously don't know is that Viscounts were abolished sixteen postins ago, and that *Earl* Ebringdon-Camworth died last postin. Now, who did you say you were?" the receptionist asked suspiciously.

"Come on!" Apnar shouted to Sharon, grabbing her by the hand and darting out the door.

"Get some security here now! We have an intruder! Security!" Stultson bellowed.

Apnar took Sharon hurriedly round the back of the Tower, which was surrounded by a wide path. To his dismay, no other doors were apparent; only windows.

"Can't you make a door appear?" asked Sharon quickly.

"I can't easily affect what's already there, but I can create new things."

At once a heavy red brick appeared in his hand. Sharon fastened her hands tightly over her eyes as Apnar prepared to throw it at one of the windows dotted around the outside of the building. There was a loud smash and they were in. Apnar grasped Sharon and pulled her through the tight space that was the window, onto an inside ledge, and into a small side cloakroom with a winding stone staircase positioned in the corner. Apnar quickly covered Sharon's mouth as she was about to speak, overhearing voices within the Tower.

"What was that?" one high-pitched male voice said.

"A smashed window, obviously," said another.

"But which one?"

"I don't know."

Another voice was then introduced here. It said, "I don't like this, Jasper."

"Me neither," agreed the first voice.

"Quick!" Apnar exclaimed in a hushed voice as he made for the stairs, followed closely by Sharon.

Unfortunately, the sound of footsteps on the staircase echoed violently around the room, and evidently through to the passage next door.

"In here!" shouted a low voice, just before the cloakroom door swung open, letting in a fierce band of high-security guards.

By this time, Apnar and Sharon had emerged onto the next floor, where a long, narrow corridor met them, leading off left and right. They ran left, where a short flight of stairs came into view. Apnar and Sharon climbed these and turned right along another corridor, up another few steps, along a corridor to the left, down eight steps diagonally and along a further corridor, which was exceedingly long. Up one more flight of steps, turning right up a slope and then along left, up a flight of sixteen steps, down a few, turning right down ten steps and left again. The maze of stepped corridors sloping upwards this way and that never seemed to end until they came to where another long corridor leading off to the left and right met them. Apnar and Sharon turned right to a crossroads which were in the centre of all the other corridors in the complex. From this position, Sharon could see several guards running around the many corridors searching for her and Apnar below, but none of them appeared to be even nearly close. The maze was sloped as a pyramid, and from Sharon's position she could see all of it. Apnar grabbed her by the hand to continue running, hoping desperately to find a door somewhere. But as they crossed the peak of the pyramid, they both fell through the air and landed with a thud on the cold, stone floor that was the base of the pyramid into a large, deserted room lit by equally spaced lanterns of burning wax, crackling unrelentingly against the eerie backdrop.

Suddenly a woman appeared from no-where, prancing up and down the room like a confused reindeer. She resembled a kind of middle-aged jester with her tri-plumed hat with tinkling bells.

"Well!" she shrieked revoltingly. "I never thought I'd see another soul from the outside world. I expect you came through the Pyramaze, eh? We'll have a feast tonight, eh Sapientia?" The woman then cackled disgustingly as a second woman entered through a huge bronze door on the opposite wall, walking slowly down the steps from it.

"Silence yourself, Stultitia. Don't jest with our visitors." The woman turned to Sharon and Apnar. "You arrived via the trapdoor? Through the Pyramaze? But why? Why enter the Tower?" she asked in a terrifying smooth voice.

"I am Apnar-Séab. This is Sharon. She has come to us from another world and seeks to get back. Where can we find the Oracle?" Apnar asked.

"You know about the Oracle?" said Stultitia, bemused.

"The Oracle is in the chamber behind those doors," said Sapientia, pointing to the doors she had just come from.

"I am its Keeper. But the Oracle is in a great torpor and will only awake for one gift," she continued.

"What gift? We'll get it for her," Apnar proposed.

"She will only awake for the emerald star in the Temple of Onyx on the Isle of Yriad. But the Temple has been lost for millennia. You will never find it. Only one man knows, and that is… the hooded man in Sémento. The emerald was stolen from the Oracle's vast treasury and she refuses to work without it," Sapientia explained.

"Then we'll go to Sémento and the Isle of Yriad and we'll get the emerald," Apnar concluded.

"Oh, I doubt that," Sapientia rebuked, a smile widening across her pale face.

From behind Apnar and Sharon had appeared two bulky security guards ready to hoist them up and take them away. The two men in white took a hand of Sharon and Apnar whilst another fastened a great handcuff to them, binding their hands together in a tight lock.

"NOW!" called one soldier loudly to his counterpart above.

A rope ladder was let down from the trapdoor, followed by a large rope. The two men strapped Sharon and Apnar with the rope and tied a tight knot. Then one cried, "Go!" and the pair of law-breakers were hoisted to the top of the Pyramaze, followed by the two soldiers who climbed the ladder. This was the end of the road, the termination of her quest, Sharon thought. All this effort for a cold cell, or possibly worse. She feared the punishment they might use in Sullaria, her only frame of reference being Apnar's mother's execution. Apnar remained silent as the trespassers were taken through the maze of corridors once more, this time to a different door, into a tiny cell.

"You will be staying here for tonight and then will be transported to a different room where we can arrange a date for a trial. You will not be fed and will remain silent. Everything you say will be recorded and monitored and may be used in the case against you," said a tall, slim man before slamming the cell door shut and marching down the corridor to safety, away from the cold and damp cells in the dungeons of the Tower where Apnar and Sharon were, for now, reside.

CHAPTER SIX

The Trial

"What now?" Sharon asked Apnar desperately as she sat upright against the wall of her dusty prison cell.

"Keep it down!" he replied in a whisper.

"You said your mother was beheaded without trial! What if that's what we'll get?!" Sharon worried.

"We're having a hearing, didn't you listen?" Apnar said.

"But who can defend us? Oh, Apnar I've made you look a fool…"

"Don't be ridiculous," cut in Apnar. "I'll handle the case. As soon as they hear you're foreign, you'll get off."

"But what about you? Why should you get let off?"

"Just leave that to me," Apnar returned. "Now, please be quiet or else we *will* both be in for it."

Sharon silenced herself to hear nothing but the dripping of sewage waste directed through pipes above her head mingled with the ominous clanging of other cell doors along the corridor; and with this near-silence she drifted into the night's sleep.

Suddenly there was a wild ululation from along the passage, followed by loud growling and teeth-gnashing.

"Zorn! Zorn! Heel, boy, heel!" called a loud voice accompanied by the pounding of six feet on the stone-flagged floor of the corridor.

A guard appeared at the cell door's barred grill and turned the key in the lock. His accomplice was a huge, snarling dog that grimaced at both Sharon and Apnar.

"Another case finished early and so the Judge wishes to see you both now," said the guard. "You will be escorted to Court 6 in the Tower. Please verify that these are your correct details: Apnar-Séab d'Arrawor of Arrawor Hall and Sharon of Unknown." As he said this he referred to a thin sheet of paper he held in his hand.

"Those are correct," verified Apnar.

"For your records, please ensure you memorise this criminal roll number…" The guard then read the 'villains' their personal numbers (which Sharon inevitably struggled to recall after only a few seconds).

"I am now instructed to ask you several questions and to explain the course of justice to be taken forthwith," intimated the guard, again with reference to the sheet of paper.

Apnar and Sharon watched and listened intently, eager expressions on their faces.

"You may employ one defence lawyer in the trial at Court 6, but he must be registered and authorised under the Government Justice Regulator and approved by both the Judge and the Prosecution. There is no jury in such cases as these and you may be asked to give evidence as witnesses against yourself. You may be permitted to bring in witnesses for the Defence but they must also be approved by the Prosecution. If you are acting as Defence Attorney on behalf of yourselves please ensure you notify the Judge in advance. Your lawyer may not cross-examine and may submit only one report, after which he must, and you must, listen to the verdict by the Judge and adhere to its implications.

Remember that under Imperial Law you are guilty as charged until proven innocent beyond all doubt. Follow me, please."

Apnar and Sharon followed the guard out of the cell and along the passage past a whole row of other barred cells. At the end of the corridor a very large stone hall stretched up to the ceiling for many hundreds of feet. A long stone staircase wound round the oval hall up several floors. The guard took them to the staircase and led them up to the second floor of the underground complex, along a corridor with marked doors. He stopped at the door marked 'Court 6' and knocked politely. Another guard from inside opened the door.

"The next Defence is here," said the guard who had guided Apnar and Sharon.

"Good. You are dismissed," said the other.

The guard stomped off with his snarling pooch while his superior let Sharon and Apnar into the court vestibule. It was a pokey room with just one door with two glass panels leading into the courtroom. The guard then instructed them:

"His Honour will see you in three angles. Do you have a defending lawyer present?"

"I am acting as lawyer on our behalf," said Apnar.

"Please verify that you are..." Once again the guard repeated the numbers given to Sharon and her 'lawyer' by the previous civil servant.

"We are indeed," said Apnar.

"The charges brought against you are: 'Trespassing', 'Vandalism', 'Breach of Government Secrecy Acts', 'Breach of Security', 'Insubordination to Officiating Guard Patrols', 'Perversion of the Course of Justice', 'Impersonation Fraud', and 'Public Disrespect to the Deceased'.

"You will be told this again during the trial. I will now contact His Honour to let him know of your presence and your acting as lawyer."

The man pushed open the door and walked down the court, before disappearing into another room at the back. Apnar fiddled in his pocket for a handkerchief to blow his nose and then waited patiently with Sharon in the vestibule. Within little time the guard had reappeared at the door to guide the pair in. Through the glass panels Sharon could see a type of clock above the Judge's grand seat. It would be at a round number for the case to start, Sharon supposed. Sure enough, as the zero clocked up at the end of the number on the display, an organ began playing what Apnar knew was the Imperial Anthem. A guard stood ready at a podium at the front of the courtroom and intimated, "The Prosecution consists of: The Right Honourable Thomas Johnnes Esquire, the Member of Parliament for Bridgeton West and Hollowater Valley, registered attorney under the Act of Justice passed under Emperor Philistonia Dei Gratia, and accepted as common law under Emperor Parragon II Dei Gratia, and his Barristers-in-Waiting."

Then the guard in charge of the Defence opened the door at the back after the prosecuting lawyer had sat down at his bench on the right beside three other lawyers.

"The Defence consists of: His Most Noble Imperial Grace, Lord Apnar-Séab d'Arrawor of Arrawor Hall, Junior City Baron of Sulla, registered lawyer under the Act of Acting-Attorney & Related Justice passed under Emperor Heinemann IX Dei Gratia, and accepted under Emperor Parragon II Dei Gratia."

Apnar followed the guard to his own bench at the front, preceded by Sharon. The guard in white opened the little wooden door into the stance and then stood up at the front of the courtroom.

"Here entereth His Most Excellent Nobility, His Honour Lord Algernon Cohen-Banehurst, registered Judge of the Tower of Sulla Courts under the current legislation passed under the Emperor and Ruler of the Sullarian Empire Dei Gratia."

Hence entered, from a large door on the left, the Judge dressed in flowing green velvet robes.

"All rise," said the intimator, and everyone did, including the organist on the balcony behind who stopped playing and stood for the Judge, who now took his place on a large wooden chair between two flags.

"You may sit," said the plump Judge as he reclined in his uncomfortable-looking chair. "Will the Defendants please step up to the box," he continued.

Apnar and Sharon rose and walked to the podium. "Please place your right hand on the Book of Books and swear to tell the truth, the whole truth, and nothing but the truth."

"I do," Apnar replied, his hand firmly resting on the leather binding of the Holy Book.

"Do you, Sharon, swear to tell the truth, the whole truth, and nothing but the truth?" repeated the guard.

"I do," said Sharon.

"Are you both who we are led to be believe you to be?" the guard questioned.

"Yes," said Sharon, slightly puzzled.

"Indeed," said Apnar.

"Please resume your seats."

Apnar and Sharon sat back down and the proceedings began.

"Apnar-Séab d'Arrawor of Arrawor Hall and Sharon of unknown origins, you are charged with…" and so the judge continued to reiterate the list of evils which the guard had recited before.

"Do you confess to these?" the judge said to Apnar.

"We seek to prove ourselves not guilty of all charges," Apnar responded firmly.

"On what pretence, Lord d'Arrawor?" rebutted the Judge.   The Prosecution chuckled collectively.

"On the argument, which I assure Your Honour is *not* pretence, laid down in our report which we shall submit to Your Honour shortly in due time."

"It will surely be a great difficulty to convince this court to be able to comprehend how one can drop all charges made against you, Your Lordship," said the Judge.

"Then it will be difficult for the court, Your Honour. However, we seek to prove our case under the rightful acts of legislation cited within the report, which we are sure you will comprehend."

"We shall see if the Prosecution comprehends your report as lawful. Would the Prosecution now present their report for the case against the Defendants?"

"Thank you, Your Honour," said the MP Prosecutor. He stood up straight and walked to the front of the courtroom to begin his speech.

"I would like to analyse each charge individually, Your Honour. It will not take long…

"The first charge is trespassing. Not only did these two nefarious outcasts trespass, but they did everything in their power to do so. They entered the most off-limits part of a government-protected building. Therefore, it would be completely incorrect to deny the existence of purposeful trespass. Therefore we have established that the denial of such a charge is an open perversion of the course of justice, as well. So, what are the motives for this trespassing? We will examine those in a moment, but first I would like to rectify that the next charge, vandalism, is in fact truly and wholly correctly brought against, and that it would be fraudulent to claim that a deliberate vandalism of government property took place. The damage done to the original window in the Tower is disgusting, and the feature irreplaceable. Next, the Defendants have completely ignored Government Safety Acts. It is my belief – nay, my conviction! – that they are spies of the Republic of Arvada who wish to expose the Sullarian authorities and ridicule them. They must have made plans to destroy the Oracle in the Tower, but were caught out. If they are freed, how does one know that they will not tell the entire world about our secret phenomenon? If they are freed, how does one know that they will not report it to the Arvadians and cause all manner of trouble and unrest in this nation. They have breeched one secrecy act, they'll breach another. These two criminals have been continually uncooperative with the system in resisting warnings and chases right to the Oracle itself. I'm surprised they even showed up here today. We can't let these things run loose to terrorise the rest of the government offices. These disgusting brutes, Your Honour, posed as other people! Not only that, but they posed as the deceased. How disgusting!"

The man paused for effect.

"How disgusting! This is an utter desecration, Your Honour, of the graves of our precious aristocracy. It is only right that they be eternally punished for these unforgivable crimes. As I said, no excuse is plausible in this situation. Ignorance of the law is no defence and an insanity claim necessitates the locking of the criminal in a secure prison until death, so I would urge the Defence to choose their words carefully. 'Guilty as charged' would be their best bet, I think. Thank you, Your Honour; I rest my case."

"Thank you, Mr. Johnnes. My mind is certainly at ease after that report, and my conscience positively buzzing to punish. Lord d'Arrawor, please present your report."

"Your Honour, the defence still pleads 'not guilty' of all charges. We have reason to believe that Sharon is not of this world…"

"Insanity, Your Honour!" exclaimed the Prosecutor.

"Your Honour, my client arrived in Sullaria in the north by unknown means, and has travelled here to the city to try to get back to her home, for her own, and our own, good. I took her into my care and we arrived at the Tower yesterday to contact the Oracle. We tried to enter safely, but this came to no avail. Therefore, we attempted entry be other means, which may have been to any normal person illegal. However, my client wishes to claim diplomatic immunity, and since she is in my care, I claim this immunity from all forms of the judicial system, too. Your Honour will know that all foreign persons who originate from a country with which the Sullarian Empire is not at war are granted diplomatic immunity. In this way, no charges may be brought against us. I rest my case."

"This is absurd! He can't, I mean he just can't do that…" said Mr. Johnnes pleadingly.

"I'm afraid it would seem he can, Mr. Johnnes. However, these serious allegations have been confirmed and are of such a highly controversial status, *and* we have no full proof that this girl is truly foreign."

"So they will both be condemned immediately?" demanded the Prosecution.

"So they will both be taken to the High Courts of Justice for further trial with a High Court Magistrate and selected jury. I wash my hands with the matter. I don't know what to do," the Judge declared finally.

"But Your Honour!" shouted Mr. Johnnes.

The Judge was by now irritated, and he slammed the small wooden hammer down on his desk and shouted, "Silence in Court." Then he continued: "Sentence is deferred for further inquiry at the High Court; case adjourned."

The verdict had been given, but Mr. Johnnes persisted with an unsatisfied look of angry despair at the Judge, who simply replied thus:

"I will not be held responsible for denying diplomatic immunity to a person possibly from an entirely different galactic spectrum. I will *not* be involved in a judicial blunder."

With this final statement the Judge left the courtroom and entered his study to the sound of the organ. Sharon and Apnar were taken down the centre of the stone court and back out the door they had first come through. Their guard led them up the stone staircase to the next floor above them. Through one door was a station platform, and the guard showed them in.

"This is Sulla's Underground Tunnelled Network. We shall most certainly need a secure capsule for you two. Excuse me while I try to book one," he said, rather politely.

The guard walked over to a little desk and inquired at the ticket booth. He returned with three tickets.

"There's a security-locked capsule in storage, so the man will bring it out for you if you wait half an angle," the guard intimated.

Just moments later appeared a metal capsule, its door strongly bolted shut and inlaid with tough rivets. It had no window, but for a grill of steel bars with blinds to cover it. The capsule was very large; indeed, much larger than any capsule Sharon had ever used. The guard walked over to the capsule while the rail attendant unlocked the door.

"This is just the outer compartment," he said. "The real capsule's inside if you take a step further."

Sharon did not notice that the outside casing was just a thick shell, and this fact necessitated Sharon to take two strides simply to enter the inner capsule. It differed greatly from the example she had used earlier. Instead of comfortably-cushioning leather, the seats were just hard planks of wood. Apnar and the guard followed her in, and once the door was closed fully the capsule began to rocket off down the tunnel, swaying to and fro in an unpleasantly erratic and upsetting movement. Steadiness was not one of the Tunnelled Network's great features.

Inside was a small magazine rack, placed by Apnar's right side. In it were the day's press and the month's periodicals, updated since Sharon last saw such items.

The Sullarian Tribune, a compact-style broadsheet, was headed in bold, black ink:

'ARISTOCRAT AND ECCENTRIC RAID TOWER AS SECURITY PROVES LOW'.

The next, a common tabloid, read:

'IDIOTS BREAK INTO TOWER IN DRAMATIC CLIMAX OF EVENTS'.

Imaginably, Sharon was very offended by being branded both an 'eccentric' and an 'idiot' by some journalists. Another magazine was fronted:

'EXCLUSIVE INTERVIEW WITH TOWER BURGLARS: ALL REVEALED INSIDE'.

'Utter trash', thought Sharon. 'The amount of complete rubbish these rags print is unbelievable'.

The Chronicle's headline read:

'PANDIMONIUM BREAKS OUT AS TOWER IS STORMED IN MOST TENSE BURGLARY OF THE CENTURY'.

It seemed the press could not print a story about the Oracle, and so reported instead that Sharon and Apnar had tried to steal precious artefacts from deep within the Tower.

The Squall chose:

'MAYHEM AND MADNESS TERRORISES CITY CENTRE'.

However, the most personal headline yet was fronted by the respectable broadsheet, *The Proud Crier*.

'LORD D'ARRAWOR & ACCOMPLICE STORM BASTILLE OF THE CITY, DISGRACING THEIR NAMES'.

Inside the *Crier* were pictures of Apnar posing as the Viscount taken from video footage inside the Tower. Sharon felt her heart sink as she realised how much she had disgraced Apnar and his family; but she had already attempted apologising, and to no avail.

Slowly but surely the chugging of the tin-like capsule died away, slowing down to a halt at the platform entitled, 'Sulla Magistrates Court of Justice'. The guard opened the capsule doors and made sure that both prospective prisoners were firmly on the platform before closing them again. The dirty stone walls were like some murky mirage, setting the tone for the court's station, through which so many convicted criminals had passed. How could it be that after less than a week of being on holiday Sharon had been swept off to another world where she was to finish her episode of misery in a court battle against a corrupt government which she was completely alien to? Could it all be a nasty nightmare? The guard clamped his hand on hers and gave Sharon a strong shove forwards. This was definitely not a dream, Sharon thought; nothing had ever hurt so much in a dream.

"Turn right and go up these stairs. When you come to the top just wait there for me. I shall go and sign you in now," instructed the guard ominously.

The stairs rose for several steps, then took a dramatic turn left and up more. This pattern continued for several flights of stairs until Apnar and Sharon reached the top and emerged out of the stairwell into a huge, dark hall, poorly lit by flickering torchlight. There was an eerie atmosphere, exploding with fear; but this would not deter Sharon. It never had. To the right of the hall was a small desk, behind which a woman sat blithely thumbing the pages of a newspaper, no doubt eager to find out more about the case. Little did she know that the offenders were sitting in the very same room as her.

From one of the arches in the hall emerged the guard to whom Apnar and Sharon had become accustomed, who escorted them to an arched doorway leading onto a long and narrow corridor marked with the following notice: 'High Courts'. By this time the pair of criminals had been accompanied by a further six guard officers to lead them to the central 'Supreme High Court' at the end of the hall. A colossal architrave mounted two great double doors at least twenty feet high, each of them engraved with ornate carvings and stained glass windows, standing as the entrance to the highest court of them all: The Sullarian Empire Supreme High Court of Justice (as the glass lettering intimated).

Inside there was no vestibule – just a low-ceilinged corridor with two doors either side leading into waiting rooms, so the criminals could see right into the courtroom up ahead. This court was bulging with opulence and majesty, a far cry from the stone-walled 'Court 6' in the Tower. Sharon had no time to stand and admire all the objects, however, for she and Apnar were hurried through the right door into the 'Green Room' where they were to wait until the hearing commenced. This room was windowless, but did for some reason possess a decorative fireplace and a delicate chandelier. The walls were laden with pictures of past Supreme Judges, themselves sentenced to life imprisonment in gilt frames. The white wall-to-wall carpet was complemented by a rug positioned in front of a two-seater couch with soft red stripes, along with two easy-chairs in matching patterns. A gold mantel-clock ticked interrogatingly as Apnar and Sharon sat anxiously in their easy-chairs, together with two guards in the two-seater. After two painstaking angles of waiting, at last a knock came at the panelled door. It was followed by the appearance of a slim man with large feet and tiny spectacles. He was holding a scroll with a message inscribed on its parchment.

"The Supreme Judge's Secretary to the Courts has ordered me to read the following message on behalf of His Serene Highness:

"It would be suitably appropriate for the immediate conduct of the trial to begin. The Supreme Judge does wish to ascertain the complete safety and confidentiality of the Defence party and that the disclosure of any information given throughout the case is open only to the scrutiny of those involved with the trial directly and officially to ensure the course of justice may be carried out in the most correct fashion appropriate, apposite and fitting."

After this administrative garbage had been absorbed by Sharon, she and her lawyer were led back into the courtroom to await their calling. The intimator stood at a gold lectern at the front of the court. He said:

"The Prosecution consists of: The Most Noble and Most Reverend Lord Milton, Marquess of Shropbourne, Bishop of Strettonby, registered lawyer under the Act of Induction passed under Emperor Parragon II."

Hence entered a tall man in top hat and tails who sat at the bench without a flinch.

"...Baron Browbrint of Tombowlerley, registered Barrister under the Act of Barristers passed under Emperor Parragon II."

Another man, on this occasion stout and pompous, and wearing a red robe of office and a wig which looked inexplicably pathetic, entered the court and sat by Lord Milton.

"...The Right Noble Lord Swanham," the intimator continued. Sharon sighted yet another barrister for Apnar to contend with. "Earl of Shoeborough, registered Disdain High Barrister, Dux of the Courts, Congenial Majesty of Justice, registered under the Act of Justice passed under Emperor Parragon II."

Their time had come, thought Sharon. She was correct. After the even more obese and more pompous barrister had sat in his padded seat, the Defence team was called. Sharon and Apnar took their places at the front of the Court on green-upholstered benches with comfortable armrests. Finally, the Supreme Judge himself was called upon to enter the room. Everyone rose, including the selected jury who had arrived before Sharon, and the grand organ began to play the Imperial Anthem once more.

"His Serene Highness," the intimator bellowed over the noise of the organ, "and Most Noble Ecclesiastical Scholar of Law and Moral Justice, His Honour the Supreme Judge, Almighty Adjudicator Dei Gratia, Lord Lionelly-Chester-Seymour-Basil-Nelson-Blakenham-Chetwind-Cholmondeley,   High Libriator of All the Empire."

Through the grand door to the left of the courtroom entered the Supreme Judge, clothed in regimental garments of a deep purple gown cloaked by green velvet robes with a coronet resting on his wigged head. He descended the mahogany staircase to the front, and stood in front of his gold throne of red leather.

"You may be seated," boomed the senile voice of the ancient Judge. On sitting back on his throne, everyone else followed his example and came to order. The Judge then called upon the Prosecution to make their case once the charges had been read.

"Your Honour, the Jury," began the first lawyer. "I wish to make the case for the Prosecution by examining the charges and giving a light analysis of each, which will be covered in more detail by my counterparts further up the bench.

"The criminals in question have trespassed on government locations secured by Secrecy Laws, which have also been breached. In doing so, the defendants have vandalised an important historical and diplomatic landmark, a symbol of the Empire's authority. Surely the Empire does not wish to be mocked by neighbouring states because it cannot secure its own property. How do we know that others will not attempt to imitate these foolish and vicious villains' mad escapade? The government has been publicly humiliated by these dunces, and I would hope that Your Honour would not want to be held responsible for letting them loose. These idiots have repeatedly avoided being caught and brought to justice. They have been completely uncooperative with the system..."

"Objection!" cried Apnar. The Judge turned to face the Defence.

"Continue..." the Judge begged.

"We have cooperated fully with the system after arrest, and I am positive that many guard officers would testify as much," Apnar defended.

"Your Honour, if I may..." began the prosecuting lawyer. "If breaking into the Empire's most secure and secret political office is not uncooperative, I think one would struggle to find what is."

He then continued:

"I know not what evil thoughts flickered through their minds when they posed as a deceased nobleman. This is utter disrespect, and I hold these two people culpable of much future evil in the world. They are encouragers of felons, and they must be made an example of. Your Honour, I rest my case in begging to propose the most feared sentence of decollation for both in the Defence party."

With this final rocking statement, the lawyer sat down to tremendous applause, followed by respectful silence. The next member of the Prosecution rose to debate his argument against the Defence, and Sharon thought her doom was sealed with yet another awkward persecution.

"Your Honour, the Jury: I should like to pick up on a few of Lord Milton's righteous remarks. But for what reason did the criminals enter the crime scene? This is *my* main concern. Was it to cause havoc and disruption across the entire city, for this, Your Honour, has been achieved. Or, was it to purposely make a public show of the government and the military at a crucial turning point in the War at Pachel Lake across the ocean? I would like to call Miss Sharon to witness to give evidence."

Sharon, prompted by Apnar, left her seat to stand at the podium. She was incredibly nervous; her hands were shaking incessantly.

"Sharon, did you or did you not violate the Act of Secrecy Laws this very morning?" asked the barrister.

"If they are as you say," she replied cunningly.

"They are as I say, Miss. Did you or did you not? Yes or no?" he asked, pressing for a direct answer.

"I did, yes," Sharon was forced to reply.

"Aha!" cried the barrister with great delight. "So you are pleading guilty to this charge?"

"That would depend on how you interpret the situation, sir," said Sharon.

"How do you mean? Believe me, I know when people are playing word games with the law. Out with it: do you or do you not plead guilty?"

"I don't recall being asked to swear an oath of truth on this..." said Sharon.

"That," interposed the Judge, "is because you are in a High Court. You are bound by common uprightness to speak truthfully."

"But how do you know if I don't?" the girl responded.

The Judge appeared severely disgruntled, and the Barrister continued.

"Do you or do you not plead guilty?"

At this point it is important to note that Apnar gave a subtle nod of the head in Sharon's general direction.

"As we have said, we did commit the crimes."

"Do you plead guilty to this charge?" the barrister continued.

"I do," was the girl's solemn answer.

"Then why did you deny it in the Tower Courts? Is this not evidence of more lies?!"

"I do not remember ever saying such things," said Sharon, trying her best to sound grown-up.

"But the Defence *did* plead 'not guilty'?"

"Indeed," Sharon answered again.

"Then why do you now plead guilty?!" the Barrister roared.

"My lawyer will explain that," said Sharon, not herself fully understanding what Apnar had come up with.

"Your Honour, the Jury, it is clear to me that this child is mentally unstable and requires immediate assistance. I would suggest a secure cell, personally. I now call upon Lord Swanham to conclude the Prosecution's case."

The lawyer resumed his seat and made way for the Head Barrister to make his conclusion.

"Your Honour and His Court of Justice, it seems very transparent to me what course of action must be taken to punish these criminals, which I think we have convicted quite obviously, and to prevent further cases of this sort ever recurring in the future. Your Honour, our time is precious and so I will not dissipate it; I wish to remove the opaque cloudiness from the scene, and to make everything simpler.

"These criminals are charged with trespassing, vandalism, breach of government Secrecy Acts, insubordination, uncooperativeness, perverting the course of justice and posing as another person (deceased no less), thereby causing more grievance to his family and disrespect to His Nobility the Earl. The correct jurisdiction must be administered today, once and for all: I propose decollation for both criminals to be carried out in view of the public eye. For all the exhausting trouble these persons have caused, this is much more than fair – indeed it is mightily merciful – and I urge the jury to comply. Your Honour, the Jury, the Prosecution rests its case."

The man sat down to thunderous applause and sneers at Apnar and Sharon.

"Thank you, Prosecutors. Would the Defence now make its report?" the Judge asked.

Apnar stood confidently and made his way to the front of the courtroom.

"Your Honour, the Jury, under the reign of King Artaxerxes XVIII of Eliatia, an act was passed which allowed 'all persons of foreign nature' to be granted complete diplomatic immunity, so long as they originated from a country with which Sullaria was not at war. This Act was passed under the control of the Sullarian Empire under Emperor Parragon I. Your Honour, I think you will find it correct that my client is of 'foreign nature'. Indeed, she is from another world altogether."

"Nonsense," Sharon heard Lord Milton mutter under his breath.

"I think *you* will find, *Lord Milton*, that there are no records of registration of any person by the name of 'Sharon'. Indeed, it is a strange name we have never encountered. This girl is recognised by no-one, and there are those up north who would gladly testify that they discovered her out of no-where when she came to Sullaria. Therefore, Your Honour, my client is completely immune from all charges."

At this profoundly controversial statement, a chattering of whispers broke out across the courtroom, sending shrills of anxiety down the spines of the prosecution – shrills not as anxious as those Sharon might have been experiencing had she understood the word 'decollation'.

"But that does not free you, Lord d'Arrawor," boomed the Judge confidently.

"Actually, it does, Your Honour. You see, my client prepared a contract for me which I agreed to in order to make myself bound to her in every way as an *obligor*."

"And when was this contract made?" inquired the Judge.

"The night we spent in the Tower cell," Apnar answered.

"*That* was after you had committed the crime, Lord d'Arrawor."

"But it was *before* I was officially charged with anything," Apnar responded.

"Where is this contract?" said the Judge finally, eager not to be overruled.

"It existed only orally, Your Honour. There is no paper contract."

"Then I shall want a recording of everything that was said in that Tower cell. Which of you guards works at the Tower?" asked the Judge, turning his gaze upon a series of officers scattered across the room.

"I do, Your Honour," spoke up the guard that had been with Sharon and Apnar since their apprehension.

"Then get me a recording immediately!"

"I'm afraid that just isn't possible, Your Honour," the guard mumbled.

"And why not? I thought everything was monitored in there. Answer me, officer. Why not?" the Judge roared, his intimidating glare focusing piercingly on the guard's face alone.

"We don't monitor everything, Your Honour. That security warning is simply to intimidate the prisoners."

Gasps were let out throughout the courtroom as these words were said.

"Your Honour, if I may continue," resumed Apnar. "I propose that we, my client Sharon and I, are cleared of all charges related with this incident through common law of diplomatic immunity with an obligor, and that a private investigation or internal inquiry into security at the Tower begin at once; I rest my case," he said defiantly.

The Judge sat back in his throne and sighed weakly, before intimating kindly the following announcement:

"You have taken the words from my mouth. A jury is here unnecessary, for I regret that there is no case to decide. All charges are cleared - case dismissed."

With this verdict, warmly welcomed by Apnar and Sharon though met with a rather neutral reception on the jury's part, the Judge banged his small gavel onto the table and exited the courtroom, leaving the triumphant Defence team free to see through another day.

CHAPTER SEVEN

Another Journey

Free from the wrath of the merciless courts, Sharon found the fresh air a welcome relief and pleasant change from the stuffy hot air of the courtroom, and the barristers. However, not everything was as rosy as planned. The newspaper headlines read: 'VANDALS ESCAPE FREE WITH "DIPLOMATIC IMMUNITY"'. Sharon winced at the thought of the editorials.

Apnar, also feeling relieved and greatly in need of some sleep, led Sharon to the City Station. The large boxy building complex did not exactly match the grandeur of the architecture of the city elsewhere, but its massive and grand scale certainly imitated that of the other structures within the huge stone walls of Sulla. Through the doors of the station was the very centre of the national rail network. The whole thing was just one colossal hall, excepting the smaller services to rural areas which occupied a smaller section of the building.

The buzzing crowds, moving in a highly uncoordinated fashion, filled the stadium-like hall, where every whisper echoed in the ceiling and came back down as a booming voice. Luckily for the passengers, however, everyone's murmurs collaborated together to form nothing more than an awful clamour.

"Well, I'm certainly glad that's over," said Apnar.

"Yeah, thank you for getting us out of that," said Sharon.

"Oh, don't…"

"No! I must thank you. I might never have been able to get back to Earth if it hadn't been for you – I really am eternally grateful."

"Thank you."

Apnar took the nineteenth door on the left, which was labelled 'Sémento and surrounding villages.' He and Sharon walked down the oak staircase to platform nineteen, which seemed quite large; it had to be to accommodate the bustling streams of people travelling to and from the historic Sémento every day. The changing timetable board indicated that the next string of capsules would arrive in six angles, and was currently half-full. The board also gave a list of the stoppage points along the way: St. Ogilvie (depart), Achnabar, Sulla, Kurt, Juntreaux, Sémento, Phicellocia (terminate). There was an alternative service that left Sulla Station in nine angles and travelled round to the east side of the city and along the towns in the east of the country: Sulla (depart), Leminghurst, Wilmsley, Emelot, Port of Mansleigh, Sémento.

Apnar disregarded this service as it would take even longer to get to Sémento, where the Oracle's 'keeper' had told the pair to go.

"Well, let's have a seat in the waiting lounge, away from all this hustle and bustle. Anyway, I've got to make a call to father," said Apnar once he had arrived on the platform.

Sharon and he entered the large waiting room; hardly executive, but mildly comfortable. This was busier than the platform, but much quieter. Apnar lifted his cuff to his mouth as he sat on the blue fabric chair in the waiting room.

"Father," he said.

"Please wait while we connect you to the nearest available service," buzzed the tiny earpiece implanted in Apnar's inner ear.

Finally a connection was established, and a voice responded to the call at the other end of the line.

"Yes, Apnar. Where are you? What a mess you've got yourself into. What will the government say..."

Apnar turned the earpiece to a less audible level, thus disabling Sharon of hearing any more of what his father had to say.

"I'm at the station with Sharon. We're leaving for Sémento."

There was a short pause here followed by: "The keeper of the Oracle told us we needed to get something there. I'm in public; can't speak now. Goodbye."

During this dialogue Apnar had made sure his voice was barely audible, to protect him from anyone noticing his true identity. There was now little time left to catch the next string of capsules to Sémento, and the pair left the stench of the waiting room and stepped out onto the platform. There was already a large train of capsules marked 'Port of Mansleigh via Emelot'. Several people had already climbed aboard, and were waiting for the rails to shift them forward at high speed at any moment. The timetable now removed the blocks for Port of Mansleigh and moved the sequence for Sémento up to the top bar. The timer section read 'ON TIME', then changed with another destination to 'EARLY'.

Indeed, the sound of the rails down the tunnel could be heard screeching with the pain of the Sémento capsules dragging over them. The capsules came to a rest at Sulla within moments, and the sight of them was not what Sharon had expected. She had envisaged the flashy, modern and sleek designs of the capsules she had come in on her way to the city she was now leaving. However, these 'capsules' could not have looked more different. The first cabs were black and closely resembled London taxis, yet only smaller and more compact. The orange-lit displays above them read 'ECONOMY'. The next class of capsules were also black, but had a more prestige look about them. Their windows were one-way, but satin curtains could be seen vaguely through the tinted glass. These capsules were marked 'BUSINESS CLASS' on the doors.

The next set were first class capsules, in black with silver rims and very darkly tinted windows. Inside were cream leather seats with all the latest gadgets attached and a small chandelier light fitting hung from the white ceiling. A fireplace had a mantelpiece adorned with valuable ornaments, and beautiful plasterwork carvings could be seen on the ceiling from the inside. The next class up (which was difficult to imagine as being more lavish) was 'PRIORITY', but these resplendent transporters were not stamped with lettering, but had pure gold embossed script on the doors, which had gold handles and knockers. Everything on these capsules was gold-rimmed and the wheels were even plated in the rare commodity. Only three of these types were on the string, but the most opulent carriage was still to come.

'THE IMPERIAL CARRIAGE', which was at least twelve times longer than the others, was highly decorated with pure gold, outside and in. Large bayed windows opened out into the tunnel, each deeply tinted so that not even the grand velvet curtains could be viewed from the outside. A massive gilded Emperor-sized bed occupied half the space in the carriage, which was completely adorned with silk, satin and velvet cushions. Beautiful leather armchairs including a large throne were positioned out of line with any window, lest something dangerous happen. A pearl and crystal chess board on a matching table was centred in the living space along with a small billiard table, and a whole host of wines and spirits behind a bar at the top end. Above the carriage the imperial standard fluttered, indicating that a member of the royal household (that is to say a direct relation to the Emperor and Ruler) or the sovereign himself was present in the capsule. Sharon marvelled at its glorious grandeur, before stepping into a marvellous 'PRIORITY' cab with Apnar.

"These are for the nobility," Apnar said.

"It's very grand," said Sharon.

"Isn't it? But you should the Emperor's!"

"Have you been in it?" Sharon asked.

"Certainly. In the Royal Museum, before it was closed and became a clothing store."

"Another doing of the new government?" Sharon supposed.

"It was, but let's not place all the blame on them. I do, after all, work for them. I can't be derogatory towards them."

"True," concluded Sharon.

The capsule was grand, with opulent cornicing and a Victorian-style fireplace. Above the mantelpiece, a large gilt mirror was placed on walls of elegant patterned wallpaper. A small chandelier glistened in the centre of the 'room' while the blazing fire crackled and the carriages rocketed off down the tunnels.

"Now, what is it we're looking for, again?" said Apnar.

"Sapientia said someone in Sémento knows where the Temple of Onyx is, and knows how to get there. If we find him, we're on our way," replied Sharon.

"You're very efficient, aren't you? Why, if I didn't know you personally I'd hire you as my secretary!" exclaimed Apnar.

Sharon gave a polite giggle and realised what had just been said about her. Three important things had occurred within the last ten seconds. Apnar had described her as efficient: 'Nothing wrong with that,' thought Sharon. He said he knew her personally; it was no longer Apnar and his guest, or Apnar and his burdensome 'child' whom he was babysitting. It was Apnar and his friend; an amicable relationship had now been built upon the foundation that was teamwork and loyalty. It was here that the established duo of Apnar and Sharon had been confirmed, eventually, by one of them as one of friendship, and this felt good to hear. What had started as a frosty relationship was now a friendly partnership.

"Kurt International Capsule Station is now being approached. All passengers wishing to enter the station by de-boarding the string, please prepare yourselves now and press the red button within a quarter of an angle. Thank you."

The voice from the tannoy box in the top corner of the capsule startled Sharon, and only now did she notice the red button on the door. Once more, she was startled by the following announcement:

"Sulla Inter-City Rail Network would like to apologise for the misunderstanding now to be explained: Our passengers at Kurt have unfortunately been told that the next string of capsules would be freely available to them. However, it seems that as a result of an administrative error, we have overbooked the number of passengers to each capsule. This would mean that all those in capsules of Business Class or above are asked to make certain room for others in your capsule. Otherwise, this would undermine our policy of honesty. Each capsule will be filled from Business Class upwards to a maximum of seven per capsule. Please excuse this mishap, but we assure you that all those boarding at Kurt will be departing at the next stop. Thank you for your cooperation in this matter."

By the end of this long intimation, the capsules had drawn up at Kurt Station to a vast crowd of commuters. The large group was mainly made up of young professional businessmen and women, and as soon as the capsules slid to a halt, the customers ran like a mob to the cabs to try to find a seat where they could, though they too had been given instructions. One man knocked on Apnar and Sharon's capsule door. Apnar opened it for him. The tall, very thin and positively malnourished-looking man spoke hurriedly: "I'm only on to Juntreaux. May I share your capsule?"

"Come in," Apnar said welcomingly. Two women also stood at the door.

"May we?" they said simultaneously.

"Come in, ladies," said Apnar.

"Thank you."

"Thank you." They each spoke in turn.

There were three seats on each side. One woman sat by the opposite window on Sharon's side, the other sat opposite her. The man sat by Apnar.

"Let us introduce ourselves," said one woman in a perky, giggly tone.

"Yes, I'm Eustace," said the other.

"And I'm Patience. Pleased to meet you, Your Lordship. We're going to Juntreaux on a shopping trip, Your Lordship…"

"You know, you can call me Apnar." This was rather a large mistake to make when he had just been arrested and flashed all over the front pages. The man who had got on lowered his book to look over his spectacles at Apnar inquisitively.

"You are Apnar-Séab d'Arrawor?" he said curiously.

Apnar averted his eyes. "I am," he said quietly.

The man turned to Sharon, and with the greatest conviction in his voice, said, "…and you will be Sharon?"

"I am. What if I am?" Sharon said cautiously.

"But why did you give that interview to a tabloid? I'll tell you, my boss at the Press could have strangled you," the man blurted out.

"I gave no interview," said Sharon honestly, looking at Apnar for support.

"We were in the cells the whole time; we never said anything to anybody," Apnar said in Sharon's defence.

"Well, would you mind having a talk with me? Tell me everything, everything!" the main said excitedly.

"I want some identification proof first," said Apnar.

Sharon could not fathom why he was willing to give an interview. The journalist fiddled around in his leather work-bag for a card, while the two women looked on in anticipation. He eventually pulled out a slightly worn business card with his details written on it.

"Here… it's my card. I'm Madoc Bridges. It's so fortunate for me to be in such a position. I'll be promoted, no doubt. Now, tell me about everything," the man continued as he handed the card to Apnar.

"This is no proof. Show me something with a picture of you."

"But… I don't have… hold on…" The reporter once again delved into his bag, but by this time the capsule was fast approaching Juntreaux.

"Next stop: Juntreaux. All passengers leaving here please gather your belongings," said the voice on the tannoy.

"Looks like it'll have to be another time, Mr. Bridges," Apnar stated gleefully. The capsule drew to a halt at Juntreaux Station.

"I'll stay on to Sémento, to Phicellocia… whatever it takes," said the journalist.

"Actually, I think I'll contact you later. You'd better not miss the station."

"But I'll stay o..."

"No, you can't stay, Mr. Bridges. That's a noble order. You cannot refuse me," said Apnar cleverly, exercising his authority over commoners.

The capsule door slid open and, with a smile of wry displeasure, Madoc Bridges stepped onto the platform, followed by the two gossiping, giggling ladies, chuckling, "We shall *have* to tell Henrietta. What a novelty! Nobility *and* criminals! Oh joy, what a day!"

"And wait till we tell Faustina. Not so lucky now, is she, eh?!"

"And Eunice,"

"Eulalia,"

"Eugenia,"

"Camilla,"

"Hyacinth *will* be jealous; literally green with envy!"

The capsule doors finally closed, and the cabs began to jostle down the track again.

"What a pair!" exclaimed Sharon in disbelief, exhausted from the episode.

"What a nerve!" said Apnar loudly.

"Sorry?" said Sharon.

"Oh, I was talking of that impertinent journalist. No doubt we'll be bombarded by the paparazzi by the time we get to Sémento," Apnar sighed.

"But you were going to give him an interview," protested Sharon.

"Ha, ha! Nonsense, Sharon; I was merely stalling time to Juntreaux. Oh well, no interview for now, eh?"

"Yep."

Apnar nodded off to sleep on the way to Sémento, which could only have lasted an angle. Then, when the bright lights of Sémento City Station floodlit the capsule, Sharon shook Apnar to waken him, and he pressed the red button on the door, embarking on their next mission, to find the man in the know and successfully locate the Temple of Onyx.

CHAPTER EIGHT
Sémento

elcome to Sémento City Station. Please gather your belongings together for arrival, and once again we thank you for travelling with Motortranspo. These capsules all terminate at Phicellocia," called the voice of the tannoy.

Apnar rose from his sleep immediately and Sharon peered out of the window at the sight of the south. This station was very large, much like the one at Achnabar. The platform seemed endless as the capsules rocketed by.

"Here we are," said Apnar. "This is the second largest city in the whole Empire, after Sulla. But stay with me, by my side always, right?"

Sharon nodded.

"It's not so much like Sulla here," he continued. "People aren't as law-abiding here as they might have seemed in the capital."

Eventually the cab stopped, and having pressed the red button, the door opened onto the wide platform full to its capacity with commuters. Not one, but several arched stairways led up to the main atrium which all stations had. Each arch's panel was inscribed 'Phicellocia and Other Far-South Towns'. Apnar let Sharon step out first, following her onto the platform.

"We'll take the staircase directly in front, there," said Apnar, indicating the stairway opposite them.

Indeed, it did seem as though the people of Sémento were not as gentlemanly as the Sullagians and their families. People of all ages lay at each side of the stairs, some sleeping, some begging for help and money. Apnar gave each one a look of disgust as he brushed past them. Then, as light shone through the arch at the top of the stairwell, the large atrium became apparent, its glass dome shimmering like a heavenly kingdom.

"They call Sémento the capital of the South," commented Apnar.

A few poor people had set up stalls all around the atrium, and were selling everything from cheap food to black-market silver. Something odd had occurred to Sharon about the city: everyone wore black gowns with hoods, but none wore their hoods over their heads. And unlike Sulla Central Station, only one massive arch led out of the room into the city. The other doorways led onto platforms. Like Sulla, however, many cloaked beggars manned the archway, ready to poach passengers for their cash. As Apnar and Sharon walked through the arch, several of the beggars approached them.

"Please sir, madam," began one.

"Give me something," said another.

"Madam, let me have anything."

"Something for a poor old man?"

Apnar shrugged them all off with his umbrella, as did Sharon, though she felt a little guilty afterwards.

"Get out of my sight and be at work in the mills, the factories. Get up and work you idlers!" shouted Apnar in rage. It was true: the mills and factories offered reasonable wages, and would take anyone from the streets; the rationale of homelessness here just did not seem to make sense.

Sharon held Apnar's hand tightly as they walked through the dimly lit cavern-like structure as more cloaked men asked for help or clothing. Again and again Apnar gave them the same answers. Finally, as Sharon and her guide approached the opening of the high-ceilinged tunnel, the station opened up to a crooked street, from which many other erratically built paths and lanes led off. They all sloped up and down, and the housing and little shops also followed this unusual pattern of awkwardness. Unlike the capital of Sullaria, Sémento was strewn with thousands of tiny shops, with each owner seeking to make their fortune in the city.

"Most of Sulla's department stores started here, you know; as corner shops," said Apnar as Sharon and he both turned left along the pavement. The houses of people were on the ground level, and the shops were unusually on the upper floors of the buildings. One sign read, 'Crystal Ré Ttop-Ffinne, *Master Jeweller*'. Sharon could not imagine telling someone her jewellery was from 'Crystal Ré Ttop-Ffinne's'. The heat emanating from the next outlet was very welcoming, and sweet-smelling scents wafted down the side staircase to the shop. 'Seton's Bakery' was contained in a marvellous building, and was full of marvellous treats.

"So, we're to find the 'hooded man', are we?" said Apnar.

"It certainly looks like it," replied Sharon.

"But where in all the city can we find a hooded man?" Apnar asked again.

A bachelor whom they had just passed suddenly pricked his ears up and withdrew his hood to listen in on the conversation taking place in front of him. He nimbly shuffled along the house walls to keep up with Apnar and Sharon as they strolled briskly up the street.

"I've not seen anyone with his hood up yet," said Apnar.

"Well, we'd better keep our eyes peeled if we want to find that emerald and get a message out of that Oracle thing."

At this moment, the hooded man's suspicions were confirmed. It was he they were trying to locate, he whom they had just passed unknowingly.

"I think you are looking for me," said the hooded man coarsely.

"We are?" said Apnar, bemused.

"He *is* hooded," said Sharon quietly.

Apnar was still rather suspicious, but he agreed to inquire further into the man's business.

"And why is that?" he said.

"That is because I know the precise location of the Temple of Onyx."

Apnar's curious suspicions faded away at once at these words.

"So, where…" began Sharon.

"We shan't speak out here. There are too many ears. Follow me; I know a place," said the man in hushed tones.

"By the way, who might you be exactly?" asked Apnar.

"I'm Aylwin Marmaduke Lucaleo," replied the man.

"Aylwin Marmaduke Lu-" repeated Sharon.

"Just call me Aylwin. I'm not from Sémento, I'm from Yriad. My family have long been established there. We have the maps to the whole island and all its fantastical treasures and secrets. It's Lord d'Arrawor I presume, and Sharon?"

"That's correct," confirmed Apnar.

"But how did you kno-" began Sharon again.

"Know? How did I know? Your names are household by now. They've been flashed on the news, exploited by the press, and ridiculed by the government."

"Ridiculed by the government?" said Apnar, shaken.

"Don't worry, your cosy job's safe," said Aylwin.

"How do you kn—" began Apnar.

"I've told you, everyone knows. Didn't you read *The Witness*? You know, that interview you had with Madoc Bridges?"

"But we didn't give him an interview!" squealed Sharon.

"Keep your voice down, Sharon," worried Apnar.

"Well, Madoc's fairly boasting about it. He said in his article he met you on the capsules."

"He did," Apnar confirmed.

"And that's when you gave him the interview. It didn't look very exciting, but it was an interview none-the-less."

"But Apnar held him off by asking for I.D.," interrupted Sharon.

"Yep, that was about it, and something else about coming here."

"And that idiot called it an interview," said Apnar, disgusted.

"It did occupy a double-spread of the paper. Maybe he broadened the language."

"Broadened the language? Made it up, more like," said Sharon.

"Here," said Aylwin as they paused below a little coffee shop. "Just stick with me and don't say a word until I tell you it's all right to speak, got me?"

Sharon and Apnar nodded and proceeded up the wrought iron staircase, close behind Aylwin. Aylwin entered the busy room, overcrowded with people sitting at tables which practically touched each other. To the right there was a bar, and straight ahead a few steps which led onto a back lounge which the three climbed. From there, Aylwin led them up a spiral staircase to the next floor and into the upper room. The large barren chamber was windowless but for one particularly small example, desolate but for a worn table and chairs in the centre. Aylwin closed the door into the room and locked it with a key already in the lock. Then he bolted the door several times before even uttering a single word. He said:

"Sit down at the table," and he joined them.

Sharon opened her mouth to speak, but was silenced by Aylwin's powerful stare indicating that she could not. Aylwin tapped the table three times and the wall to the right of the door slid back to reveal another barren room. The table then glided over to the room, and the wall repositioned itself. Aylwin again tapped the table three times, but this time nothing happened.

"You may speak now," he said.

"What was the point of those last taps?" asked Sharon, fighting in vain against her insatiable curiosity.

"Can't you see? Probably not," replied Aylwin.

"What?"

"The room has just turned upside-down," Aylwin explained.

"But it's..." began Apnar.

"Exactly the same. I know. But now we are safe to talk; since we are on the ceiling, nobody beneath us can hear our voices. If we were to sit on the floor, anyone with an ear in the right place could easily hear every word we said, if they were directly beneath us."

"What is directly be—" said Sharon.

"Paternoster's the funeral directors," replied Aylwin, once again cutting off Sharon's sentence endings.

"And above?" inquired Apnar.

"Let's see, shall we? Can't be too careful."

Aylwin tapped the table three times and the table fell through the floor, or rather, it rose through the ceiling, and made the next floor's ceiling its floor. It was all a little confusing.

"Now no-one can possibly hear us," said Aylwin, his husky voice echoing around the new barren room.

"No-one but Nemo!" said Apnar.

"Indeed," said Aylwin. "Now, the whereabouts of the emerald. It is inside the Temple of Onyx on Yriad. The Temple can be found quite easily with the correct maps."

"Which we presume you possess," said Sharon.

"Naturally," replied Aylwin.

"May we see them now?" asked Apnar.

Aylwin chuckled in much the same manner as Sapientia had done, which was not a good sign.

"You may see them as soon as you bring me a map of Gwendolyn Vashti's tomb, the tomb of the Empress of Yriad."

"You're joking?" said Apnar.

"Sadly, I am. It would have been a nice addition to my collection," replied Aylwin.

All three of them laughed for a moment, but then an eerie silence filled the space as Aylwin prepared to speak again.

"But you will not receive this knowledge for nothing. I want five million Forden leaves tax-free, and the map back again."

"You're jo–" began Apnar again.

"I most certainly am not. Now, I demand my pay now, and you may receive the map."

"Four million?" Apnar proposed.

"Five million or nothing and I slit your throats!" Aylwin shouted, withdrawing a dagger from within his cloak.

"Yes," agreed Apnar.

"I'm sorry, Apnar. I'll have to pay you back someway," offered Sharon.

"Don't talk nonsense, girl. There's nothing you can do to pay me back. Now, just sit and hush and do stop apologising."

Sharon stopped speaking while Apnar signed a sort of I.O.U. that apparently acted as a cheque.

"Now may we have the map, please?" said Sharon, carefully speaking as politely as possible.

"Believe me, girl, I'm no double-crosser. I may be mean and greedy and heartless, but I'm honest," responded Aylwin.

Instantly, a tightly bound scroll labelled 'Mapp of the Tempolle of Onyxe' appeared on the table in front of Apnar.

"It's hundreds of postins old," said Aylwin. "I want it returned within one hundred days, you hear me? Just show up outside this café and I'll be waiting. You may not recognise me at first, but I'll show myself. Now, it is time to leave."

CHAPTER NINE

Port of Mansleigh

Apnar grasped the map in his hand and, breaking the wax seal, unfurled the scroll of parchment to reveal a complicated map. Sharon bent over to observe the page. It was headed 'North' and showed a district of the island named 'Nyxia'. In the top right hand corner of the page a little inset box showed the whole island, with Nyxia shaded in red. This district was in the far north of the island, occupying the peninsula on the east.

"You can examine the map later, but now we must go," said Aylwin. "Someone'll think we're up to something up here."

'And they'd be right,' thought Sharon.

Aylwin tapped the table nine times, and the whole room (or rooms) jostled up and down until they were back in the original Upper Room. Of course, it was really they who were moving most, though it didn't appear so. Aylwin then left the table and, having unlocked the many bolts on the door, opened it with a piercing creak to reveal the dingy coffee parlour below. He then gestured to Apnar and Sharon to follow him, which they did. He led them back down the spiral staircase and into the café once more. Aylwin marched confidently through the shop and out of the main door, Sharon and Apnar following on, all three wearing distinctly serious countenances. He then walked down the iron-wrought staircase to the city street in silence. Re-cloaking his head with his black hood, Aylwin settled back down outside, saying not a word more.

"Thank you," Sharon mumbled, but there was no reply; not even a flinch of acknowledgment.

Apnar and Sharon turned the street corner before speaking, as they had already discovered Aylwin's attribute of super-sharp hearing.

"We'll have to go back to the station, then?" said Sharon.

"We will indeed," Apnar replied.

"Then shouldn't we be going back that way?" Sharon suggested, gesturing towards the way she had just come.

"If you want to end up back in Sulla," returned Apnar.

"What d'you mean?"

"We need to get to Sémento Central Station; it should take us east."

"To Yriad?" said Sharon.

"No, no! To Port of Mansleigh, where we can get a boat to Yriad. It's about six angles to the Port from here, so not much longer than the capsules from Sulla to Sémento."

"Okay," agreed Sharon.

Apnar walked up a steep street lined with little shops, at the top of which was a box of a building which served as Sémento Central Station. From its main entrance, Sharon could see the whole city. The city was, like Sulla, walled, but there were many towers positioned around these walls, in clear contrast to Sulla's four. The city was very busy, and teeming with activity. It was a sort of circular shape, but the edges were all straight. Evidently, Sémento was not built to precision. It could, perhaps, be best described as an 'irregular undecagon'.

Apnar entered the station with Sharon into a damp lobby. He then walked to the reception desk to book a ticket. There was no queue and the receptionist was sitting on her swivel chair half-asleep, and looking incredibly bored. Apnar approached the woman quietly and banged the brass bell on the table down with the resolute aim of shocking the receptionist into waking up. The woman shuddered with the undulations of the resounding sound waves.

"Y-y-yes? How can I help you?" the receptionist asked.

"We'd like to book tickets to Port of Mansleigh, please," said Apnar.

"Indeed; there are two services available: the regular midday or the earlier 165 angles. Which would you prefer?"

"The 165 would be fine, thank you," Apnar replied.

"Certainly. We'll have to be quick, then; it leaves in a semi-angle. So, details, details. Blue sheet, pink sheet, white sheet, green sheet. Names please?"

"Names?" repeated Apnar.

"Names," the receptionist reiterated.

"Names?" Apnar said resolutely once more.

"Yes, your names, *please*?"

Apnar quickly looked over through the glass doors on the left, which led to the platform. A poster on the wall there advertised a new fashion line: Tyler Roberts. Underneath that was another advertisement inviting the reader to buy tickets for a new concert starring, amongst others, Elizabeth Marion.

"I'm Robert Tyler, and this is Marion Elizabetha," was Apnar's final answer.

"I'll just look you up. Erm… oh, this machine doesn't recognise you. Hold on… what's your NR number?"

"My NR number is 027947334222," replied Apnar, before covering his mouth as he gasped at letting out his real national registration number.

"Ah, yes: Apnar-Séab d'Arrawor?! What in the name of Nemo's going on here?" the receptionist screeched.

"Must have just been a mist…" Apnar mumbled.

"Oh, hallo! I recognise you from the newspaper! It is you; hold on, can I get an autograph?"

Apnar darted to the left through the glass doors, followed closely by Sharon. Once on the platform, Apnar quickly locked the door by securing two bolts. The capsules were just arriving, and Apnar and Sharon slipped on one without having bought a ticket. It was a regular and modern capsule, and Sharon sat by Apnar on the leather seat, waiting for the capsules to take off.

"Wha…" Sharon began, but she soon realised that Apnar was already asleep by the window. Another law was broken, but it was either that or a flock of autograph-hunters.

The train of capsules was a direct line, so it did not allow for anyone getting on or off until termination at Port of Mansleigh, which of course did not bother Sharon or Apnar, who continued to sleep all through the journey. Eventually, after a little waiting of about two or three angles, the capsules slid to a halt at the large Port of Mansleigh Station. The screen was broken, and so buzzed annoyingly when the capsules stopped moving, but the message was predictable. They had arrived at their destination, and had to get out.

The platform was bustling; many commuters and businessmen stepped out of their capsules into the hive of activity that was the station of Mansleigh. Apnar and Sharon ascended the wide stone staircase which led up to the central block, from which many streets of the city could be accessed. All around were signs above the many doors leading to the outside world, and Apnar's careful

deliberation (closing his eyes and pointing randomly at a door) resulted in a choice on the far side of the hall.

Apnar chose the way: 'Stokechapel Square to Simmsdon and Almswood by Too Close and the Port'. So the duo ascended to the outside streets of Mansleigh. It was a fine day, and but for the city's gloomy boxy buildings it looked cheerful. It seemed that Mansleigh was really just a collaboration of many small towns built near to the bay. Stokechapel Square appeared to be a jumbled collection of offices and other administrative complexes. On the opposite sides were what looked like banks and company headquarters, many of the fishing or sailing industries. Of course, Stoke Chapel also existed on the top side of the Square in the centre of the outer row of buildings. It was pleasantly grand, but not too ornate. Part of this Church formed an arched alley onto the next street, Too Close. This way was as its name described: it was very narrow. Rows of *olde worlde* bookshops and public houses lined the Close, above which were several storeys of housing. At the end of this street was at last the harbour. 'Welcome to Port of Mansleigh Harbour', read the sign.

But the harbour was not just a small port. Many sailing offices were situated along Navemvia Street, which Apnar and Sharon surveyed closely for openings.

'No sail today' read one sign. 'Closed' read another. Almost every business was either fully booked or shut for the day, until Sharon sighted a small, unsuspecting outlet by the name of 'H.A. Starver & Co.'

Sharon let Apnar enter first into the cold and bare room of Starver's Ships. Apnar approached a small and very worn desk at the back of the shop and rang the service bell.

"Indeed, I come!" called the far off-sounding voice from behind the opposite wall. From the right emerged a grubby, short and stout man dressed (rather badly and scruffily) in a red sailor's uniform.

"Which of my services may I offer such a gentleman and young maiden?" asked the man in a wretched voice, making a revolting grimace at the pair.

"Do you offer a service to the Isle of Yriad today?" asked Sharon boldly.

"Yriad?! Not today, lass, not today. Today's Review Day for the island ships. All vessels to Yriad are inspected this day every postin, child. Kind gentleman, what may I do for thee?" The man turned to Apnar and twisted his horrible face into another frightful grimace.

"I'm in guardianship of the girl," said Apnar. "Is there anyone who might offer a service to Yriad today?" he asked hopefully.

"If there is, I don't know of 'em; and I shouldn't like to neither, running a banned service. Here, come back on the morrow, and I'll sort you out. Starver's the name, transport's the game, eh? In fact, just for your inquirin', I'll give you the journey for just a hundred Forden leaves. How does that sound?" returned the sailor.

"Thank you. We'll see how things work out," said Apnar.

"You do that, sir, you do that. Be back soon, now; come again!"

With this final jovial remark, Sharon and Apnar departed from the shop and strolled back out to the pier.

Indeed, most of the other shipmerchants were closed for the day. So with the proposition offered by the ship owner looking better all the time, the pair entered a decent-looking tavern, of a somewhat respectable nature, but certainly nothing extravagant. The shop consisted of a few wooden tables, in reasonable condition, with menus on each. Sharon sat at one with Apnar, but was startled when the boar's head on the wall to the left of her began to speak in a hushed tone.

"I beg your pardon, ma'am," began the boar in a whisper. Sharon felt like using a similar reply.

"You were inquiring about boats in town, to Yriad?" continued the boar, still quietly.

"And what business is it of yours?" said Apnar prudently.

"Well, sir, I know of a service running today."

"You do?" asked Sharon curiously, but Apnar gave her a look clearly intended to shut her up.

"I do indeed, ma'am. But you must be quiet about it, indeed."

"You mean smugglers' boats?!" exclaimed Apnar in fury.

"Surely you are not prejudiced against men just going about their business? They are just proprietors of a shipping business," repeated the boar.

"*Surely* I am prejudiced against criminals!" said Apnar.

"But you are one yourself, are you not, Lord d'Arrawor?" spoke the boar.

Apnar fell silent.

"And I could easily make that fact known to all in this town quite quickly, Lord d'Arrawor. Owing to this, I suggest you comply," the animal continued. "I want you to meet with an associate of mine. He can be found in room AB17 of the Wagstaff Hotel, down by the Plaza. Ask for Mr. Kettlefisk, and when you get to his door, knock thrice *very clearly*. Then when he answers, cough loudly and repeat the words: 'What a fine day, to be sure, Mr. Tomlinson.' Is that quite clear? It has been made so cryptic for security reasons. The man will direct you to a free boat. Any questions?" said the boar.

"Yes, one," said Sharon. "How did you know Apnar's name?"

"And yours, Sharon Jarls. Let me keep that to myself, shall I? I know, and that's that. Now go."

Sharon was overwhelmed by the amount of intelligence the silly boar had accessed. She had never told anyone her full name, but for the Bugle-Thoms

in the Shanklot Corridor, and that was hundreds of miles away. Nevertheless, she accepted the boar's amazing knowledge and let it be. What did it matter if one more being knew her name? As soon as she would be out of Sullaria and the world she was presently in, it would be of no concern whatsoever how many people knew her name.

Without ordering anything to eat, Apnar and Sharon departed from the coffee parlour and set on their mission to the Wagstaff Hotel. This was an unfortunate hotel to have been chosen as the mysterious man's residence, as Apnar remarked, because of its location being so far from theirs. However, it seemed necessary for them to comply and obey. A small carriage taxi, hovering above the hot ground, was passing by, and Apnar signalled for it to stop.

"Wagstaff Hotel, please. Two seats," Apnar requested of the driver of the vehicle.

"There are two seats in the back, sir, madam," replied the coachman.

Certainly there were two comfortable red leather-upholstered seats in the back compartment of the cab, which was black externally, with scarlet and gold livery. The coach hovered slowly along the many streets and lanes of Mansleigh to Central Plaza, where the Wagstaff Hotel towered majestically above the other buildings.

"Here sir, madam? We are at the Plaza," proposed the coachman.

"Very well, thank you," replied Apnar.

When the coach door was opened it was evident that they had reached the hotel, with its innumerable storeys, the peak made visible by the glittering golden 'W' positioned at the building's summit. Apnar and Sharon thanked the driver, paid him, and walked over to the tall hotel. The reception area was elaborately grand, complete with expensive patterned wallpaper and gigantic chandeliers. The reception desk was made of teak and behind it stood a neatly-uniformed, well-spoken receptionist of small stature, delicate complexion and charming nature, awaiting the arrival of a guest who would make an inquiry.

"We're here to see Mr. Kettlefisk," said Apnar. "I believe he knows we are coming. Room AB17, please."

The receptionist burst open a filing cabinet drawer which had been elegantly labelled 'K'.

"Is Mr. Kettlefisk a permanent guest?" asked the receptionist.

"I'm not sure," answered Apnar.

"I see; here we are. I'll just notify him of your arrival," the woman replied, thrusting a grotty file out of the drawer and laying it flat on the tabletop. She typed a strange code into a little machine by her side, and spoke to 'Mr. Kettlefisk'.

"Good reflex, Mr. Kettlefisk. This is reception; your guests are waiting here..." she began. There was a muffled reply from the other end of the line, followed by:

"Very good, sir. They will be with you shortly." A final muffled piece of conversation which vaguely resembled a 'thank you' came through the machine, and the receptionist gently pushed a red button which turned the device off and then slammed the filing cabinet drawer shut, turning to speak to Apnar and Sharon.

"I'll have an attendant take you to Mr. Kettlefisk's room. Enjoy your visit," said the girl softly. "Andreas? Andreas, show the guests to apartment AB17 in the North Wing."

As the woman said this, a well-dressed attendant standing by one of the side walls approached the desk. "Haave you any baags?" he asked Sharon and Apnar.

"We haven't," Apnar replied.

"Andreas is from Corscía, sir," remarked the receptionist. Apnar acknowledged this comment with a nod of the head.

"Pleasa follow me," said the foreign employee in his Corscían accent.

Sharon and her companion followed the attendant through a beautifully decorated arch to another grand but narrow room with a huge oak staircase leading to the North Wing. The hall's elaborate chandeliers sent beams of light across the room that glowed on the scarlet wallpaper. The wide staircase led up to a large stained-glass window on which an image of 'Horatio Shahn, 13me Vicomte Sylvestre d'Arvada, Founder of St. Paul's Chapel in the Plaza' was depicted, or so the inscription read. It was in vibrant colour, and turned the red velvet carpet leading up the staircase into a labyrinth of luminescence. After this landing, the stairs turned right up to the first floor. The attendant marched through many corridors closely followed by Apnar and Sharon, now becoming rightfully frightened of the events which might follow.

"Room AB17, Mr. P.Q. Kettlefisk," announced the attendant finally, standing outside a frosted glass-panelled door. He then knocked twice very distinctly, and stood back.

Remembering his precise instructions, Apnar added another knock to the door, making sure of its clarity. Then he urged Sharon to speak with a nudge. She coughed.

"What a fine day to be sure, Mr. Tomlinson," repeated Sharon without an ounce of hesitation.

The panelled door was unlocked and opened widely by a stout man wearing a tweed blazer, white shirt, green cravat and green socks.

"Mr. Tomlinson, I presume," said the middle-aged man in a soft, soothing tone.

"It is," returned Apnar, unsure of what response would be most appropriate under the circumstances.

"Enjoy your visit," said the porter before swiftly wandering off in an entirely random direction.

"Come in," instructed 'Mr. Kettlefisk' with a suspicious glare from his beady green eyes. Apnar and Sharon followed this instruction and took a seat at the beckoning of the mysterious man.

The gentleman walked steadily over to the blazing, roaring fire which was built into one wall, making a grand ten-feet wide hearth. He stood in silence for a few seconds, carefully examining the two travellers, as if waiting for some sort of communication.

"Sir," began Sharon timidly. "I don't think there was anything else to tell you. The boar in…"

She was suddenly cut off by a loud grunt of acknowledgment made by the gentleman, now smoking a peculiar pipe with serious vigour.

"And what did this boar tell you?" he inquired.

"He simply told us to leave at once, come here and address you as we have," replied Apnar.

"But what for? What for? That's the true test, my guests. I warn you now, if you speak falsely I'll have your skin and bones roasted in that fire as soon as you can say Curate Quippelminster." Yet again, another example of a common saying in Sullaria, whose origins remain completely unknown, had slipped into conversation.

"But it was the *boar* who spoke to *us*," interposed Sharon fearlessly.

"Of course it was! Who ever heard of a gentleman and his lady freely engaging in colloquy with a beast, a dirty creature?" boomed the man.

"If it doesn't bother you (though I expect it will), you are very fastidious," returned Apnar indignantly.

"And if you don't mind, I am not *his lady*," Sharon corrected.

"Oh, I do apologise for my evidently impolite and ignorant manner, but I trust there will be unanimous consensus from now on." With these gentle but firm words, the mysterious gentleman extracted a small (but convincing enough) knife from his left trouser-leg pocket, which was sufficient to quell Sharon's uproar.

"Now, what I want to know is what brought you to this town, and what the boar assumed I might be able to assist you with?"

"We are here in search of a boat to Yriad on personal business. However, seeing as none of the ship-merchants are offering any services today, I assumed you could help us find a place for the night. After all, this is a hotel;

and, with you a permanent tenant, I suppose some discounts could be arranged?" explained Apnar.

"I'm quite sure I can find you a place to stay, *and* a boat to Yriad - tonight," answered the man.

"Great!" shouted Sharon. Apnar shot a suspicious glance at the man to keep Sharon wary.

"We were under the impression that it was illegal to sail this evening," said Apnar coolly.

The man ignored Apnar's comment.

"Ah! Lo, my introduction is not yet made. Sir, you do not know who I am?" bellowed the man. "Let me reveal my identity. I am a Baron!"

"Oh, a Baron!" Apnar exclaimed excitedly, but stupidly. "How delightful it is to be in the presence of another nobleman. I am Apnar-Séab d'Arrawor of Sulla." Apnar outstretched his aristocratic hand awaiting a handshake, and then sense returned to him. He had just blurted out his own identity yet again.

"So we are indeed alike!" exclaimed the man, leaving Apnar's hand hanging in the air, before it was quickly withdrawn. Apnar and Sharon stood silent. "But possibly not in the way you interpreted. You see, you are both criminals." Sharon and Apnar greatly disapproved of this assertion, as they had both been proved not guilty in a court of law (though of course they were guilty.) "And I am a Smuggling Baron!"

"A what?!" Apnar yelled.

"A Smuggling Baron!" repeated the 'noble'. "I lead international operations of smugglers, and am setting out for Yriad tonight. I'll transport you, for a small fee…"

"Of?" interposed Sharon.

"Of your honesty," replied the man cunningly.

"What good is our honesty to you?" asked Sharon.

"If you two speak not a word against my name, not a word of my name, and not a word of tonight's practices, you may be transported free of further charge."

'Fair enough,' thought Sharon, 'considering we don't even know your name.'

"We'd rather just wait, thank you," said Apnar, frustrated.

"Oh? But I thought we were on agreeable terms," replied the man. He brandished the knife and struck a porcelain vase on his mantelpiece with it, smashing it to pieces. Sharon let out a small shout of shock, and almost fainted. Apnar answered the 'Baron', this time quite sure of what to agree to:

"When do we sail?"

CHAPTER TEN

The Emerald Isle

"As soon as the lamps fade," said the man in response to Apnar's question. He smiled and looked out the window.

"And when is that?" asked Sharon.

"Have you never seen the lamps fade? As soon as the darkness is too dense to be penetrated is the time."

"How can darkness become too thick?" Sharon asked again.

"Pollution, child, pollution…" The man jostled over to the window, where he drew open the great curtains with enthusiastic flare, revealing the bleak city beyond. Many buildings were packed tightly together, each one illuminated by internal light. However, most of the beams of light came from the flickering street-lamps, of which there were thousands littered all across the bay town. In the distance, a huge hill towered over the city, forming the south half of the crescent-shaped land which surrounded the bay. Up it were small settlements of housing, but the number of these grew gradually thinner further up the hill. It was dark, but the light of boats could still be seen glimmering on the horizon. The scene really was picturesque, and provided a superb spot on which to build a hotel. But the Baron drew Sharon's attention to another feature of the area, somewhat less attractive.

"See, over yonder to the north, d'you see it?" he said. "See the twists of black foggy smoke rising? Pollution!" he exclaimed.

Indeed, further north, masses of factories were piled high on the hill, causing infinite amounts of smoke to rise into the air.

"See the problem! Those man-oo-factories produce the light for these lamps by burning all the waste products of the city."

Sharon nodded.

"But because of their quotidian churns of pollution, the darkness has become denser than *ever*! So, the lights can't penetrate the darkness' density, though it is the origin of the power that causes it!!! See, child, see!! Bah! and Nonsense!" the man roared. "But ne'ermind, Lord d'Arrawor," he said, turning to Apnar. "It is this very process that keeps me in business! Ha ha!" The man laughed heartily, roaring until his bulging eyes watered.

"It's not so much the darkness that's dense, but the government!" Apnar joked. The man roared once more, but Sharon was not at all amused by the situation. The aging man then offered his guests a seat by the fire in his lavish apartment.

"What is your name?" asked Sharon.

"My name is, eh... well, you can just call me Baron. I'm not bad at heart you know, just out there making money like everybody else in this wretched town. Now, I have a question for *you.*"

Sharon gasped as Baron lent forward, causing his spectacles to slip down his nose like skis on a slippery Alpine slope.

"What was it you were doing in the Tower? What business would you want there?" Baron asked out of curiosity.

"Does it matter?" Apnar cut in quickly, disallowing Sharon to explain.

"It matters if I say so, and I do," replied Baron firmly.

"Very well," Apnar began. "We were, eh, seeking a treasure. It was something stolen from my household centuries ago. We went back to reclaim it."

"So, the government doesn't want the public to know that they stole from you, because people wouldn't trust them if they knew?"

Sharon thought she distinctly heard Apnar mumble, "They don't anyway," but clearly heard him pronounce:

"Precisely."

"I see. And what is this 'treasure', and what does the girl have to do with it? Where does she fit in?"

Sharon was growing indignant at being referred to as 'the girl', but kept quiet.

"I'm looking after her, so I took her to be a look-out," Apnar lied.

"Not a very good 'un, was she?" shouted Baron, again roaring fervently with laughter.

"She served her purpose, as far as I'm concerned," returned Apnar. At least someone was on her side.

The gilt mantel-clock above the fireplace chimed a very rapid succession of three hundred chimes, and its delicate hand turned to the same number on the dial.

"My, my, the time is come. Look, the lamps have dimmed. We go, my friends; we go! Pack up, now. I'll show you where to get to."

Baron again walked over to the window and pointed out a small cove where he and his comrades did 'business'.

"Meet me there within four angles. I'll take only one, I should think. Drink this, and jump out after me. I'll be long gone, just keep to north-west and you'll get to us soon. If you're questioned just answer: 'But Mr. Pilkington sent us.' Hurry now; if you're not there within four angles, I'll have my dogs come after you. Follow a north-west course, and come."

Baron leapt from his window ledge after gulping down a peculiar solution taken from a glass decanter on a table by the window. Apnar drank a glass and followed on, waiting for Sharon. Sharon lifted the tiny bottle and gently poured a few centilitres of the liquid into the glass. The liquid began to effervesce, but the fizzing died down within a few seconds.

She grasped the glass and lifted it to her mouth to drink. The liquid was soft, but tasteless. Everything was suddenly greatly illuminated. Dark corners of the room became beaming with light, and the central candelabrum became brighter still. Sharon clambered onto the window sill and jumped straight down, worried of the outcome. However, her concerns were unfounded. Sharon had landed upright on top of the roof of the floor below. The roof was flat but solid, and Sharon could see Apnar clearly standing on the ground below, silently beckoning her to him. Sharon searched around for some sort of way down, but Apnar motioned to her to jump. She walked slowly to the edge of the hotel roof and jumped off, falling into a cushion-like bush which immediately broke her fall. Sharon was convinced many people had heard and seen her tumble down, but Apnar quickly reminded her that it was pitch black outside to those within, even though he and Sharon saw everything as clear as day, or clearer.

"Well, that wasn't very ladylike, Sharon! But you did show stamina. Come on, let's get down to the cove," said Apnar quietly as he helped Sharon to her feet.

From outside, Sharon could see directly into the rooms of the hotel, though they had no lights on inside in reality. They were all, of course, decorated ornately and beautifully, but not a soul inhabited them now; all the guests were gathered in the large lounge awaiting the results of the annual pigeon race, their eyes glued to a large screen on the wall.

'How dull,' thought Sharon.

"Apnar?" she said. "What do you think about... about all this?"

"I think that it would be best if we didn't talk about 'all this' for the moment, because if I am not mistaken we are being watched," Apnar replied.

"We are?" Sharon gasped.

"We are."

"By whom?" asked Sharon emphatically.

"*I* don't know. But you know how it is; one can never be sure of privacy these days."

"Oh," returned Sharon, confused.

The pair continued to perambulate down the road, before turning right down a back street to follow the bearing north-west given them by Baron. The street was long and narrow, lined by shop-houses on either side like those Sharon had seen in Sémento. At the end of the road was a crossroads. The road on the left's sign read, 'Trumpington - to Trumpington Hall'. To the right the sign read, 'Marque-Manor Road - to Swellbridge'. Straight ahead a sign was posted, 'Parmanderock Station - to Bayshore'. It seemed obvious which way to choose, with one sign mentioning the words 'bay' and 'shore'. Therefore, Sharon and Apnar walked forward.

But suddenly there was a shuffling, a cough, and then a grumble heard coming from nearby. Sharon heard someone running. She looked in all directions, but nothing was to be seen. Some being let out a loud cry and then fell from the top of a flat-roofed shop-house, landing upright on the stone ground, before picking itself up and scrambling straight down the road to Bayshore. A shout followed, and suddenly two great troops of soldiers descended upon the crossroads, blocking all passage as they jumped from above.

One of the troopers shouted, "Which way?" to Apnar and Sharon, at which they both pointed straight ahead.

At least fifty soldiers of the Royal Brigade, the army's special branch unit, rushed down the lane filtering through all the side roads on the way down until silence returned to the area.

"Now I think it's safe to say who was watching us," commented Apnar. Sharon nodded – it had just been a police chase.

"What now?" she asked.

"I just don't know. It can't be safe to go down there, and there's a chance that *we* might get caught by those soldiers. Let's get to Trumpington Square for a taxi. There's an abundance of theatres down there, my uncle tells me, so it's sure to be filled with taxis."

The two adventurers followed the lane on the left to Trumpington, which appeared to be a magnet for fashionable society people. Men and women dressed in full evening wear were flooding in and out of the theatres all around. Trumpington Square was in the cerntre of the *arrondissement*, and indeed there were multitudes of taxis of all shapes and sizes there. Some hovered, some bounced, and some cycled. Apnar found an apparently comfortable taxi parked outside 'The McWhirter', a highly recommended theatre, and asked the driver if he would take them to Bayshore.

"Bayshore?!" the driver replied, astounded at such a request. "This is the circular! I drive round Trumpington. Farthest I go out is to the Hall."

"What do you charge to the Hall?" inquired Apnar.

"Half a Forden leaf," replied the taxi driver.

"I'll pay you ten score Forden leaves to take us to Bayshore," Apnar proposed.

"Ten score? Let me see it!" demanded the driver.

"In cheque-form," replied Apnar.

"Aha! So it's likely to bounce!" exclaimed the driver.

"I'll give you a bundle up-front, and a cheque for ten score. How does that do you?"

"That'll do me nicely." The deal was finalised.

Apnar entered the cab and sat in the back with Sharon, trying to relax in the uncomfortable felt upholstery.

"Have you been to Bayshore?" asked Sharon.

"Never. But we'll get there, I'm sure," responded Apnar.

Sharon began to wonder how on Earth the driver could see where to go, and then she realised: she wasn't on Earth. The taxi she was in hovered slightly above the ground for about two angles, and then halted outside the 'Bayshore Village Centre' (whatever that was). By now it was easy to spot the smugglers' cove with the enlightening solution in their digestive system, and it looked just demi-semi-angles away.

Sharon ran with Apnar down the avenue after Apnar had paid the driver in full, and then bolted down a small lane which led to the shore. The towering south hill was just metres away and the smugglers' cove could be seen just at its foot. Apnar and Sharon walked over to it, where Baron stood, joking with his fellow criminals.

"Look who it be! My little comrades, my dear friends. Everyone, behold Lord d'Arrawor and Sharon Jarls, the infamous masterminds behind the Tower break-in," said Baron excitedly. The other smugglers were shocked, and stood in awe of their superior felons.

"I told you I had a surprise in store! Ha ha!" Baron roared again.

"Now, my fellow felons, a boat I suppose?" he said to Sharon and Apnar.

"I suppose," chorused the pair in perfect unison.

"Last barrel!" cried one smuggler beyond the cove.

"Yea, the time is nigh. My friends, Tote will escort you to our boats," said Baron; he turned to a short dark-haired man of a scruffy but pleasant appearance. "To 'The Ermine Crown' with them, Tote. Take care, and be helpful."

"Hmph," grunted Tote.

He led Sharon and Apnar round the protrusion of rock which formed the smugglers' cove and onto the shore where a fleet of small boats were lined, ready for departure. 'The Ermine Crown' was not as regal as its name suggested, and was in need of major attention. But then, what could one expect from a boat named after a crown made of fur? This need of major attention caused the two passengers some concern. A large white sail with black painted spots was very holey, and several cracks in the carrier's framework were beckoning the undulating waves to split the boat in one perilous swipe. However, it seemed, quite ironically, that choice was not an option! Apnar stepped into the boat, helping Sharon in with him. On the vessel were five containers: one of water, one of apples, one of stolen Forden leaves, one of 'Aspidistra Juice', and one of 'White's Full Liquor'. Room was made on a short plank dividing the boat for Sharon and Apnar.

"Alabaster Camamile and Satin Pyjamas!" cried someone loudly. Evidently, this absurd description was the signal to move out. The vessels began to speed out across the sea bound for many nations, bouncing vigorously across the water.

"'Bouncing Boatees', these ships," remarked Tote.

"I thought so," Apnar replied.

"How long to Yriad?" inquired Sharon softly.

"How long? Not long, not long. Ten or eleven angles, no more," Tote intimated.

"Look, Sharon, the island's just over there," said Apnar.

"Behold the Emerald Isle," Tote remarked, his face bright amber with the cold. "You'll be there soon. What business is it you have there?"

"Only a small quest; not an important matter," Apnar explained hesitantly.

Tote made a nimble and sudden movement to extract a small knife from his trouser pocket and aimed it towards the two passengers.

"You mean to hide out at one of the ruins until you're discovered again. You mean to wait there until those authorities, slow as they are, realise your villainy and come searching, DO YOU NOT?"

"We do not, sir. Most certainly not, no," Apnar replied sternly.

"You lie, sir. Did you not cloak your identity at Sémento, both of you? It is a fact you did, because I was there; yes, our operation has many contacts, many men of quite high disposition, men who have been in your company recently. Won't you speak?" Tote roared disturbingly.

"I'm not sure of your intentions, boatman, or where your fanciful information is being procured from. However, I do know that what you speak is a load of absolute nonsense. Steer on, you fool, and be silent in our presence," Apnar declared firmly, though without much triumph. His confidently contemptuous manner was not welcomingly accepted by Tote.

"Are we rather arrogant today, Your Lordship? At this rate I'm not forming a gracious opinion of you. Speak child, 'tis your cue. Make up for his wretchedness..."

Sharon stood to speak, her body quivering with fear. *"You* are the wretched one!"

"Well well, you little witch," the aggressive boatman returned.

"Stop, stop, stop!!" Sharon screamed indignantly.

Now the boatman was standing at the head evidently prepared for more than a verbal skirmish, his right hand gently steadying the vessel, his left clutching a knife tightly, showing off his dexterity and sinister thoughts.

"Oh, save me from your senseless alliterations! I'm not much impressed with your defence, but I can't report you, being who I am. Indeed, my kind-hearted generosity prevents me from doing so. I ought to put you both out of the certain misery you'd experience on the island when Baron's through with you."

With this final statement, Tote let the boat go from his care, causing it to swing haphazardly from side to side. He barged forward, knife in hand, swinging two blows at Apnar, knowing Sharon's defenceless position. Apnar dodged these and pushed Sharon unceremoniously into the sea, causing himself to be dragged in after her in splashes of spraying liquid, probably contaminated by centuries of pollution. Apnar held Sharon tightly, swimming in haste whilst Tote burst into the channel, pounding on the water with greater celerity than he himself had even ever witnessed. Fortunately, this was to no avail as he soon noticed his boat slowly sinking further down beneath the tumult, still loaded with smuggled valuables. This fact sufficed to quell Tote's mad desire to kill the pair, and as the rest of the fleet headed north into the distance to a secluded area of the island, where Baron could rule in villainous peace (undisturbed by the authorities), Tote steered his boat likewise to the smugglers' kingdom.

Yriad was not far at all from the boat's previous position, as the very large majority of the journey was already completed. The pair glided for a few seconds above the deep ocean, whilst Apnar's apparent powers ("really just an educated manifestation of cleverly manipulated advanced physics" so he said) supported the two until dry land became visible beneath the refugees' bodies. The shore of Yriad was dry and barren, covered by a thick layer of plant material. This Apnar noted, and upon such a consideration withdrew the pocket map given him by the man in Sémento, probably yet another of Baron's many confederates scattered across the globe (or whatever shape this world happened to be).

The parchment was crisp, and Apnar slowly untied the red ribbon around it and unfurled the map. However, a serious lack of light did not help the situation, and so Apnar extracted a small instrument from his breast pocket which glowed dimly but sufficiently. Sharon leant over to view the map, but to her utter dismay it portrayed not a single line or contour, not a single smudge of ink. All was lost; the map was erased and all hope with it. Apnar gaped in distress at the blank sheet and without speaking began to roll up the paper. His eyes were shut in shock, but Sharon noticed some ink on the facing side of parchment, and in her astonishment took the map from Apnar's hand, unfurling the outside face. The map, supposedly lost alongside hope, lay outstretched before them just as it had before in Sémento. Apnar, in his folly, had opened the map on the blank side, the other face being the actual map in complete and perfect condition.

"There," said Sharon contentedly. Apnar smiled back in embarrassment, and looked on with his companion.

"We must be somewhere on the west coast of the island. What puzzles me is that there is no port to be seen," Apnar began.

"Perhaps we landed slightly north of the port. The other ships were headed north," added Sharon.

"Perhaps. The map doesn't show the natural landscape. We'll have to work out our bearings from the shape of the coastline."

"From that tiny map?" exclaimed Sharon, pointing at the small sketch of the island at the top right corner of the page. Apnar ignored her.

"Now, a slight cut in for the bay, a slope eastward, and a ragged coastline near the northernmost point. South, what appears to be a town, and another bay. Surely we can position ourselves now; but where?"

Apnar pored over the document, his finger gliding over the sheet. Suddenly, Sharon shouted out in delight at finding their bearings.

"There! Here! Look, Apnar: a bay."

Sharon showed Apnar where a little arc curved inwardly, and where in every way the map matched reality.

"Quite correct, Sharon. Well done; what luck you're here to keep me right. And I thought I was supposed to be caring for you!" said Apnar loudly, laughing softly.

"I do try, Apnar."

"Oh, I'm sure you do."

"Well then, where to?" asked Sharon inquisitively.

"Well," began Apnar. "It seems that the area we're looking for is quite a way away. I shouldn't like to rush on, Sharon. Let's head into the town and find a hotel for the night. I have a great uncle who owns and runs a capital place, while he's not in Arvada on his estate."

"We'll have to be quick, then. I think it's dawn already," Sharon proposed.

The pair walked down a short path which led through a forest into the town. It was dimly lit by some very old lamps hung from iron fencing which closed in the path. It seemed that the air was less polluted here in this rural setting than in the ancient cities of Sullaria, as the lamps' light did faintly penetrate the thick and deep darkness. The path led into a very wet long cobbled street, lined with dozens of chalets, lit softly in the midnight glow of the stars. In many ways, this new world was so similar to Earth, Sharon thought. At the end of the road stood a pair of golden gates, closed and locked, at least twice the height of Apnar.

As the pair approached the gates, there was a gentle creak and they opened, giving way to a crossroads in the centre of the town. Between each of the roads were four small statuettes, each of separate design. All were creatures of some sort, all crowned, and each bore a shield and flag. The north shield was engraved with a rose, its flag bearing a single vertical stripe. The east shield was carved with a simple chevron with three arrowheads and its flag was plain but for a small 'V' shape in the centre. On the south side the shield bore a simple lion rampant, and this design was replicated on its flag. Finally, on Sharon's side (which was west) the shield was entirely blank and the flag bore a dove with a ribbon of simple writing beneath it: 'Pax Praevalet Armis'. This inscription also carried the name of its author: Sage Sylvin IX. Sharon, of course, knew nothing of the sages of Yriad; she even doubted if Apnar did.

Apnar led Sharon to a comfortable inn named 'THE WYCOMB', a rather expensive-looking hotel, but also rather limited in size. Sharon could see only one room from outside, though it *was* dark (the illuminating solution now beginning to wear off). Upon entering through two stately oak doors, a small reception greeted the new recipients of its hospitality. It was lavishly decorated in the rich style of Versailles, and warmly lit by a grand ornamental crystal chandelier. However, despite its appealing homeliness, there was not a soul to be seen in the building.

Apnar approached the front desk and rang the brass bell three times. Its tinkling chimes echoed smoothly throughout the reception, tickling the ornately embossed gold wallpaper. Then, there was a clatter from upstairs, followed by the booming of boots on the old mahogany staircase.

"Yes? We are closed for the season. Please leave, we shan't open again till..." called the feeble voice of an elderly man, stopping in his tracks upon seeing the two guests.

"A-Apnar-Séab?" he faltered. "It isn't ... it is! Oh, my dear boy! Where *have* you been? In the middle of the night bringing your visitor? Tell me, boy, how are we and what can I do for you?"

"Uncle Cirrus, could we bother you for a room for the night? We're awfully tired," explained Apnar pleadingly.

"But, Yriad... in the night... with the girl... and all so abruptly?" The aristocrat looked puzzled, and not without reason. Sharon and Apnar were invited into the drawing room to talk, but Apnar advised Sharon to go to bed straight away, with which she was delighted. Not a moment of rest had been granted up to then, and the girl was in desperate need of some sleep.

"You may have the second room at the back; I assume you'll find it spacious enough. I have had an en-suite fitted recently. I trust you'll soon find your way around. Second at the back, my dear girl," said Cirrus.

Sharon climbed the staircase slowly, striving to hear the hushed conversation taking place on the ground floor. She could hear Apnar's voice, then Cirrus's, and then there seemed to be a short period of astonishment for Apnar. There was silence for a moment, and then a shuffle of shoes moving towards another room. A door slammed shut, and silence resumed. Sharon assumed that Apnar was just relaying the long journey he and Sharon had taken to his uncle. But there were more pressing matters, such as where Sharon's bedroom was located.

A gallery surrounded the staircase, and several doors led into hosts of rooms, almost all private. However, at the back side of the gallery was a corridor, which led on for another twenty paces at least. On the walls were enchanting paintings, each framed in ornate gilted frames. One large window, sumptuously decorated with velvet swags and tails, was fitted on the right wall. At the end of the corridor was a single door, bolted firmly with a giant padlock. On the left wall were two doors; one half-open through which Sharon could see a library, the other closed. Sharon approached the second door (as she had been instructed) and gently turned the door-knob anti-clockwise.

Behind the door was a large room, slightly smaller than her room at Apnar's house. Once again, antique lavishness was the theme of the chamber. There was only one window, but on closer inspection Sharon found that it was only a painting of the scene outside. Of furniture there was no shortage. What can best be described as a gigantic mahogany bed, with gold ormolu mounts, veneered panels and wooden side rails was positioned in the far left corner. An ornate inlaid mahogany wardrobe stood against the opposite wall, and to complete the furnishings were several chests of drawers, a washstand, a dressing table, a work table, a small piano (or something similar), a sideboard, mirrors and chairs galore, without forgetting a huge fireplace giving heat to an assortment of armchairs. The ceiling was, as expected, very high, and was beautifully decorated in gold leaf cornicing. A battered and worn carpet, severely worn away with centuries of age, covered the floor throughout, but its rips and tears only added to the ancient character of the room.

Sharon looked around the room in search of the lavatory Apnar's uncle had mentioned. On the right wall, adjacent to the fireplace, was a large oak panelled door. Sharon walked over to it and turned the knob in desperation. Inside was a spacious bathroom, entirely fitted with expensive antique utilities. Sharon relieved herself and searched for some sort of nightgown in the wardrobe. There was not a choice: a single nightdress was hanging in the cupboard, as if it were expecting Sharon. She dressed for bed, drank a small glass of water and climbed into her bed, wondering what would be happening in her own world. However, lost in her pondering, the girl fell into a deep sleep, having aged another day, weary and helpless, fatigued and burdened, yet pursuing her impossible quest with incomparable readiness and determination.

CHAPTER ELEVEN

An Old Friend

A s pretty beams of light flooded the upper chamber, the gentle rays streaming through a window Sharon had not noticed before, the girl woke from her sleep. Her feeble knowledge of daily life in the new world did not extend to the operation of lighting equipment, and so the lamps set on tables around the room were still burning brightly and the fire continued to crackle. All this light prevented Sharon from dreaming the night before, and her mind was in any case set on other matters. She pondered for a moment on how everything in her new world was based on trust. Faith and faith alone in Apnar, his uncle, Sophios and all the other colourful characters she had met along the way had maintained her health and safety. Faith and trust in some however, is not sufficient to maintain health or safety, as Sharon had discovered the previous evening.

Sharon dressed in a made-to-measure suit found hanging in a wardrobe, which was a rosy pink colour. Once ready, Sharon awaited the call to breakfast with anticipation, filling the time by indulging in some classical literature she found in the bookcase. 'Lady Chequers' by Augustus Artemisia told the story of a flamboyant heiress to a wealth of country estates, lost in a choice between the respected suitor and a poor commoner whom she is deeply in love with. When the suitor inherits a vast estate the balance swings in his favour. But when the pauper is falsely charged with murder, it is up to Lady Chequers to prove him innocent. Sharon was arriving at the climax when a knock at the door echoed throughout the bedroom.

"Excuse me, Sharon; breakfast's ready," said the muffled voice – it was Apnar.

"Yes, I'm coming," replied Sharon, discarding the book and walking to the door. She opened the panelled door carefully and saw Apnar standing in the corridor wearing a red suit with a waistcoat and a silk cloak of the same colour.

"We're the only guests. There's a morning dining suite at the back. Are you ready?" asked Apnar.

"I think so," said Sharon.

"Then I'll lead the way," replied Apnar.

From Apnar's neck dangled a large gold medal in the shape of a rhombus, surmounted onto an ebony oval. Apnar floated down the staircase swiftly, whilst Sharon attempted to keep up.

"Apnar?" said Sharon.

"Yes, Sharon; what is it?" was the reply.

"What does the medal signify?" she asked sweetly.

"This?" Apnar held up the medal towards Sharon. She nodded.

"It's just another item of clothing. The badge isn't of much significance; just a design, I assume."

Suddenly there was a loud clatter from a room at the back of the morning dining suite, which the pair had just entered. Out of the archway and into the conservatory entered Apnar's uncle, clenching a plate in each hand.

"The eh..." he fumbled. "Plates! Plates... fell, and eh..." He was breathless and his wispy hair bounced gently up and down.

"You really should employ someone else to do that sort of thing, uncle. Whatever happened to Alfonse, the cook?" Apnar replied sympathetically.

"Alfonse? He only works when the hotel is running. I think I'm able enough to cope reasonably well without him." Apnar's uncle's strong reply was undermined at this point when, on raising his right arm to stress his point, he dropped the plate which had been in the very same hand with a great crash. Apnar looked at him unconvinced of his uncle's dexterity, and his relation stared back humbly.

"Well, do sit down. I shall join you in a moment, after I just reconfigure the heating. It's rather cold, I think you'll agree," the elderly man said. He disappeared behind a small door, and Apnar drew a leather-backed chair out for Sharon, sitting down at the table with her.

Uncle Cirrus re-entered the room, bringing with him a tray of breakfast and stepping over the remains of the smashed plate.

"Whatever happened," began Apnar, "to cousin Wilhelm?"

"Oh! He's in his seventh year at the Arvadian Conservatoire, professing music, I believe," answered Uncle Cirrus.

"I see. And Wolfgang? I haven't seen him since I began schooling!" Apnar continued.

"Wolfgang is in his final year of training at the Quentin Wooket Military Academy in Achbaria. He'll make a fine contribution to the Empire."

"I'm sure his services will be greatly appreciated by the Emperor," Apnar responded dutifully.

"If only Wilhelm would follow his elder's example, rather than waste his time with his music," retorted Uncle Cirrus, a war veteran himself of the Battle of Dubhai' Sai decades before. As Sharon recalled, the arts were not encouraged in Sullaria – winning wars was much more important. Apnar sensed tension, and so hastily changed the subject.

"My," he said, "we have a long day ahead of us, Sharon. We must fill up on this meal, eh?"

"I'd love to," Sharon concluded, eyeing the strange but tender and appealing meat on her plate with eager anticipation, the warm scent of the odd but equally delicious-looking pastry wafting towards her.

Once again, it was difficult for Sharon to avoid thinking of her mother, and dwelling on past memories. This chain of thought was snapped, however, by Apnar's remark of, "Superb breakfast, Uncle."

"Thank you, Apnar. And what is your opinion, young lady?" Uncle Cirrus turned his glare to Sharon, who only then realised that she had not even begun eating. She hastily consumed a mouthful, and replied that it tasted magnificent; an honest remark indeed.

It took no less than twenty angles to consume the three-course 'petit déjeuner' as Uncle Cirrus elegantly put it. After breakfast, Apnar extracted the map of Yriad from his pocket and unfurled the page in his hands. The page was just as before, and the map remained comprehensible. Uncle Cirrus leant over to study the map of the island.

"I say," said he, biting a crust of toast. "Here we are, here we are!"

The exclamatory tone of his voice would have suggested to anyone unfamiliar with Cirrus's nature that he had just had some amazing revelation; this, however, was not the case. Uncle Cirrus pointed his bony finger at a point on the map to show his present bearings.

"Thank you, uncle," Apnar acknowledged.

"We must go north, then?" Sharon presumed.

"It certainly appears so," answered Apnar.

"Then it *is* so!" exclaimed Uncle Cirrus, once again with a shout of triumph.

"How long will it take to reach this area?" Apnar inquired, indicating the area where the Temple was situated.

"I should say six angles, seven, eight, nine, ten? No, not ten." Uncle Cirrus paused and racked his disused brain. "Nine angles, at the longest, Apnar, my boy. Nine angles, I say, and strike me down if it be longer than such a time!"

"Then time's not an object, really. Sharon, if you're ready, we can go now. Is there anything you think we need?" Apnar continued placidly, ignoring his uncle's fits of excitement.

"I don't think so. Will we be... safe?" Sharon asked.

"Safe? It's difficult to tell, I suppose. I say, is it safe, uncle, in these parts?" Apnar again indicated the area in question.

"As safe as ever it was safe, I say! Although, how safe I don't know. I say, strike me down if I know, nephew! Strike me down if *I* was ever to know! Ha ha! However, what I do know is that such a person as will know resides in this very town! Strike me down if he didn't!"

"Who, uncle?"

"Oh, David Whittocks. David Whittocks! I should say he would be up by now, and circling the town in his daily promenade. Poor fellow! He doesn't know what's good for him, dear man. David Whittocks, I say; he knows!"

"But does he know about safety and..."

"Does he know?! David Whittocks knows all sorts! Why, he knows all about it. When does he ever stop ranting on when he comes in here for a sherry! Ranting on and on about this and that! The Temple, says he, oh the Temple! Blah, blah, blah, a load of nonsense and poppycock, if ever there was such! Strike me down..."

"Thank you, uncle," Apnar said forcefully. "It seems we should have a talk with this man, eh? Do you agree, Sharon? Let's get our coats on, then."

Sharon concurred, but was stopped mid-flight to the cloakroom by Uncle Cirrus.

"Coats? Whatever for? David comes in here every morning for a drink. Tarry a moment, good fellow, and he'll be along. Strike me down if he isn't, ha ha!"

In all the confusion, (Sharon grasping a coat half-heartedly, Apnar half-way through opening a cloakroom door, Uncle Cirrus at a table) the frosted glass of the front door became slightly darkened by a small figure standing behind it, ringing a most annoying bell incessantly. Uncle Cirrus walked forward into the vestibule, calling to the stranger, "I'm coming, David, I'm coming. Strike me down If I'm not coming, ha ha!"

The bell stopped ringing, the door was opened, the stranger stepped in, and a small cuckoo clock hanging from the ceiling chimed the round angle.

"Bang on time, as ever. Strike me down if this man has ever not been bang on time, ha ha!"

"Guests, Cirrus?" began the man, the man whom Sharon recognised instantly as the smuggling gang-leader, Baron.

"This man knows all there is to know about Yriad, and all its waters, nephew!"

"I'm quite sure he does," said Apnar, also recognising the figure who had offered transport across to the island.

The man gave the two visitors a stern look, as if meaning to silence the pair.

"My nephew was wondering whether he could have a talk with you about the Temple?" Uncle Cirrus asked unknowingly. There was a short pause before Baron, or David Whittocks, gave his answer.

"Certainly."

Uncle Cirrus led the trio into a little side room and assembled the characters around a small drop-leaf table, he himself taking the head.

"Well," said Apnar. "What is your knowledge of the Temple of Onyx? Is it safe?"

"No," answered Whittocks shortly.

"Why?" said Uncle Cirrus. "Tell them *why!*"

"There are great mysteries unsolved in the Temple. Curses and all the rest of it, you know the general score."

Apnar nodded.

"Not the kind of place *you* would want to enter. The vicinity is condemned by the provincial government, thank goodness. Why are you interested in the Temple?" Baron asked pensively.

"We must get the emerald," answered Apnar.

"The emerald is lost. It has been lost for millennia; I sincerely doubt if you will ever find it! The quest for the emerald is ancient; riddled with legend. It is said to be hidden..." Baron paused briefly. "It is said to be hidden in..." Again he paused, looking directly at Uncle Cirrus. "You are all on your oath, mind! No leaks; it is a legend, a myth some say. Truth! Over time, what is it they used to say? Truth became folklore, folklore became legend, legend became myth, or something to that effect, eh?"

The onlookers stared intently at Baron; *four* onlookers, and three is a crowd, so what must four be? For, unnoticed until now, an uninvited guest was standing behind the door, attempting to remain hidden. Baron blinked softly, and fell to the ground, off his chair, unconscious. It all happened so abruptly. Sharon looked from Baron to Apnar, from Apnar to Uncle Cirrus, and from Uncle Cirrus to the door. No-one but for the three living and one deceased was present. However, the three had all seen a shadow of a mysterious figure just moments ago; how could it be that he had vanished, and Baron was dead? Considering these questions rapidly in her mind, Sharon sat in wonder. Apnar got up immediately and, without speaking, searched the house and gardens. It was to no avail; while Cirrus nursed Baron (an equally unavailing practice) Sharon accompanied Apnar on a short walk. They decided it best not to notify anyone of the murder, if that was what it was, but to keep the matter quiet amongst themselves.

"Wh..." Sharon began as she and Apnar turned a corner on their stroll.

"It's best not to ask questions; things happen, and we must accept them. I know no more than you; Baron being who he is, should we be surprised? As for the Temple: it will have to wait."

"For how long?" Sharon asked her companion.

"So long as Baron is alive. Don't you see, Sharon? Can't you... you can't?"

"Can't what?"

"Isn't it plain? Doesn't everything fit together now? Is the clarity not pure enough, bold enough, obvious enough? Sharon, we're being followed. Someone wants to get our attention by injuring Baron. Let us make the presumption that Baron knows what's going on here. When he recovers, he will either run away from his enemy, or he will make peace with him. However, his enemy, whom we do not know, will want something from him. Baron would promise him us; the enemy wants our attention, and once he has this, he has us. He didn't mean to kill Baron, just to injure him threateningly. The enemy wants something, Sharon, and if Baron lives it'll be us he gets!"

Sharon stood in utter and complete astonishment at these words. Apnar continued to speak, however:

"If Baron is dead, we can proceed. If he survives, our quest cannot continue. We must abandon everything, and you must live here until... death. I'm sorry; you appreciate the gravity of such an issue, don't you? You *must* understand, Sharon; someone wants to get at us, for whatever reason. Have patience, and don't say a word. We'll walk back now."

Sharon walked to the hotel with Apnar in silence, considering the endless possibilities of a bleak future. Apnar seemed to understand everything perfectly, very much unlike her.

She lived with Apnar's Uncle Cirrus for the period of sixty-three days afterwards, all the time Baron apparently growing stronger. He was walking now, albeit stiffly, around his little room of confinement on the ground floor of the hotel. But, at last, fate provided a new hope.

It was the sixty-fourth day of her sojourn in Yriad, now engulfed in a deep wintry spell; so wintry, in fact, that confinement was an experience everyone in the island was now well used to. Sharon sat up in bed staring at the panes of glass which made up the window on her wall. They were entirely covered in frost and ice. Nothing could be seen beyond this thick layer of ice but the patterns of trickles of rain slowly moving across the glass. It was the first sign of thaw; the rain would turn the snow to sleet, and what Apnar called the 'orb', very similar to the sun, would do the rest. It was early morning; all was dark, and nothing stirred. However, just thirty angles into the day, Sharon heard footsteps, the noise of somebody ascending the staircase and slowly but steadily walking along the corridor to her room. Sharon became frightened; her sense of security was lost, and she lay dreading the moment when... It was too late, the door-knob turned, and the door opened.

"Sharon?" The quiet voice was Apnar's. "Are you awake?" he called from behind the door.

"Yes," Sharon responded.

"Some news; quite urgent."

"What? Tell me."

"It's Baron. He called for me just an angle ago; I entered his room a moment later, and he lay motionless in bed. Sharon: he's dead. For sure, he's dead. My Uncle Cirrus knows already, so I came up to tell you. It was a natural death. He passed away peacefully at thirty and an eighth of an angle today. We're safe. I'll go now; I'll see you at breakfast. I hope we can go north today. That's all, I'm just going to call the Imperial Records Bureau to confirm his death (as Whittock, of course.)"

"Oh – Apnar?"

"Yes?"

"Are you sure we're safe now?"

"Oh, most certainly. If the killer hears of Baron's death, he can't get at us easily, and so should leave off. Baron owned a smuggling ring, yes?"

Sharon nodded.

"So it needs a new leader. Either the killer continues to hunt us to find the way to the Temple and kill us, claiming a forest worth of Forden leaves, *or* he takes over the smuggling operation, guaranteeing him hundreds of forests of Forden leaves every postin for life! He has access to the smugglers now he knows enough about Baron. Smuggling's a risky but well-paid business. Baron died an avaricious plutocrat, but the state will claim it for the war effort. Now do you understand better?"

"Much better, thank you," replied Sharon earnestly.

"Good."

Apnar closed the door softly and went down to the ground floor, leaving Sharon in her room. The heavy rain had by now washed away the frosty layer from the window, and a bright sunny sky revealed the next sign of thaw. Sharon dressed herself in one of the many new sets of clothing which had been provided for her over her stay. She washed at the small stand in the corner, brushed her hair at the dressing table, and reached for the door. Sharon turned it gently and opened the door into the corridor. It was lit by a small light fitting which hung from the ancient ceiling. Sharon descended the staircase and entered the breakfast suite. It was morning, the sun was rising to its zenith, and Apnar was sitting at the table poring over the map of Yriad.

"Apnar?" Sharon called.

"Ah, Sharon! Look outside, the snow is practically gone! What a fine day for adventure. I've been looking at this map; we shall have to cross two rivers, clamber over a little rocky patch, and enter a forest to find the Temple."

"Oh, and Baron?"

"Quite as dead as ever. All is well, Sharon – don't fret. He'll be buried here in Yriad, no doubt, sometime within the next few days. He had a few friends here and there; honest friends, I mean. David Whittock was a well-respected member of the community here, and word spreads fast. As soon as the record of death is officiated, anyone and everyone will access it through their Auto-News devices. You know, the little machine that prints the latest news or announcements. Everyone'll know of his death now."

"And when will that be?"

"That was about ninety angles ago. The killer's bound to know now."

Sharon was amazed by the apparent speed at which information was spread. Suddenly the front door rattled loudly.

"The papers! Here they are." Apnar hurried to the front door excitedly, and extracted from a small mail box behind the door three newspapers, one journal and a magazine, to which belonged the following titles: 'The Yriad Septdaily', 'The Proud Crier', 'The Daily Citizen', 'The Journal of the Imperial Society of Hoteliers', and 'Successful Horticulture'. Apnar leafed through the pages of 'The Proud Crier' enigmatically, searching for the announcements page.

"Here: 'Deaths: It is to be announced with regret the death of Mr. D. Whittock of 7 Wigfield Close, Xavier District, Isle of Yriad, this morning at thirty angles, of peaceful natural causes. Funeral to be held this coming sept-day at St. Mark's and Wemmick's Parish Church, Little Hamling, Isle of Yriad at 150 angles. By private invitation only.'"

"Will we be going?" Sharon asked tenderly.

"Well, I suppose I should. But you – you should probably stay here that day; we don't want everyone knowing about us being here."

"I suppose so," Sharon agreed.

"Now, look here!" Apnar ruffled the pages of 'The Yriad Septdaily'.

"'David Whittock dies today, by Rufus Montgomeryson. This morning a well-respected member of the Yriad community passed away after long-suffering illness. At the Wycomb Hotel in Port au Buerre, where Mr. Whittock had been recovering after a fall on one of his familiar walks, the upstanding gentleman eventually died peacefully after suffering serious injury' and so on and so on. Anyway, what does the Citizen say? Erm... here: 'Public Intimations of Death; TODAY; Yriad; Mr. J. Cuik, Miss A. M. Gwendyline, Mr. J. P. Griffin, Mr. D. Whittock, Miss S. Black.'"

"News circulates quickly, doesn't it?" commented Sharon impulsively.

"Certainly. Now, Uncle will get you some breakfast, while I make a call to father."

Apnar wandered into a side room marked 'COMMUNICATION', and Uncle Cirrus emerged from a door behind the staircase.

"Le petit déjeuner pour ma belle visiteuse?" he asked Sharon.

"Oui, s'il vous plaît, oncle."

"You speak Arvadian?" Uncle Cirrus inquired, impressed by Sharon's knowledge of his native tongue.

"I speak French. My mother is French, from France."

"France? Arvada is the country where they speak like that."

"In my world, that's called French, or français."

"Baffling! Strike me down if that isn't baffling! Come, come. The breakfast suite awaits! So does my lovely Arvada!"

"You're returning to Arvada?"

"Of course! It's thawtime, dear, the season I always return to my estate. Sit down; Apnar should be through in just a moment."

Sharon sat at her circular table by a window and unravelled her napkin, placing it elegantly on her lap. Apnar joined her shortly afterwards, and Uncle Cirrus arrived with glorious, steaming repast. The former began plotting co-ordinates on the map of Yriad, attempting to estimate how long their peregrinations would be, both in time and distance. The latter urged him to enjoy his breakfast before beginning his calculations.

"Just a moment; that's approximately twenty-five angles on foot, just five on transport."

"Which then?" Sharon asked.

"Twenty-five angles is a long time. What transport have you here, Uncle?"

"Oh, eat first, do. Come on, here's a slice of newly-burnt toast. Eat!"

Apnar shovelled a mouthful of toast into his mouth most unceremoniously with his hands, before looking to his uncle for a reply to his inquiry.

"A cyclist runs round each district every twenty angles. Which district?"

"Nyxia."

"Nixy-what? Come, I've never heard of such a place. Repeat the name for your old uncle."

"Nyxia," Apnar slowly and loudly told his uncle.

"No, my boy. Never to be heard of. Let me see, there's Aquiveria, Donswillage, Littlaria, Manerea, Suita, Tuita, Uita, Vuita, Wopsolia, Xia and Zu. Pick one, not another, my boy."

Apnar walked over to Uncle Cirrus, showing him the map.

"That great land mass! That's Suita, Tuita, Uita and Vuita all in one. Where's the temple? Ah, in Vuita! Vuita's Ds is what we learnt in school: desolate and dangerous. Never been there, nor do I know anyone who has."

Just then, a surly servant whom Sharon had come to recognise as Uncle Cirrus's personal manservant approached the table.

"A letter for Lord d'Arrawor, dated three days ago, from Sulla."

Apnar took the yellow envelope from the servant and broke the black seal. He removed the contents carefully, and Sharon could just make out the top half of the first page. It read:

'HIS MAJESTY THE EMPEROR'S HIGHEST IMPERIAL GOVERNMENT OF THE SULLARIAN EMPIRE

'Department of Nobles-in-Council

'Lord A. d'Arrawor

'*Your Noble Lordship,*

'*His Majesty's Government is obliged to aware you of your current circumstances. At present, you are half-way through your term of absence of one postin. Enclosed is the Epistle for the Postin Beginning Twelfth in the New Reign, which contains an updated version of the Secret Services Authorities regulations. Read and retain for...*'

Here, the letter ran out of Sharon's sight. Apnar's postin off work was half-way through; the pair would have to work quickly and unhindered if Sharon was to return to Earth with his help.

"Well," said Apnar, tearing the letter in two, "we shall just have to try. Vuita's Ds can just stare us in the face. Surely nothing of this world can be more frightening than Cousin Boris and his strange collection of clock hands. Scared me out of my wits the first time I heard about it!"

Uncle Cirrus chuckled, and added, "He's my brother's son, truly; always a man for amassing useless trash."

Sharon, however, was not amused by the concept of entering a marked danger-zone. She stared at Apnar for a moment in an attempt to reveal any trace of cowardice, or at least anxiety, in Apnar – there was none. Apnar was brave through and through, a fighter whose fortitude would never end. Like Sharon? Once, she thought, but not now. Her experiences had made her, surprisingly, more gentle and lady-like, and Sharon's conduct was now more refined in the company of Apnar.

The late winter snow had settled to a reasonable level, and Sharon and her companion set out for the Temple, armed with a map, a few Forden leaves, a loaf of a fresh bread-like substance, an automatic lamplighter and sixteen 'bulleters', small hand grenades which Apnar explained exploded upon impact. The day was going to be exciting and terrifying, and the consequences of the pair's actions could ultimately determine their eventual fate.

CHAPTER TWELVE

The Dead Forest

The frost-bitten street outside extended for some time into the town centre, where Sharon and Apnar caught 'transport' which would take them to the outskirts of Vuita. A small man with bouncing and untidy curly hair drove his 'Island Transport' vehicle (a little tricycle with spaces for three passengers) around the island, bordering each district or going through them.

"Vuita, please," said Apnar quietly, in a vain attempt to be discreet about his destination. Almost everyone in possession of good hearing immediately turned to look at Apnar, and a cold silence broke out across the main street.

"I can take you to the border, if you're sure," replied the tricyclist nervously.

"Very well," Apnar replied. "How much?"

"Six Forden leaves."

Apnar paid the distressed man, and he and Sharon boarded the vehicle. Apnar's calculations were flawless; Vuita's border was met within just five angles. The rolling meadows of Yriad's countryside flew by on the way, draped in a thin blanket of ice. The coastline finally disappeared from the horizon as Vuita became closer, and as the pair moved eastward.

A stone barrier marked the border of Vuita, a high wall bearing the fairly recent inscription, 'VUITA: Unauthorised Entry Forbidden. Government Danger Zone.'

"Here?" proposed the small man.

"Here would be very satisfactory, thank you," replied Apnar. No sooner had he and Sharon dismounted from the tricycle than the little man had gone, speeding off into the distance.

"That's a mighty wall to climb," commented Apnar.

"Too mighty?" suggested Sharon.

"*I* should think so. How about the Tunnelled Network?"

Apnar walked over to a sparse patch of land and dug his leather boots' heels into the ground to reveal a brass plaque inscribed, 'TN; Station Reference Y22621. Service Withdrawn by Government Order."

"Apnar – the service is withdrawn," Sharon pointed out.

"But the tunnels are still there. Help me lift this plaque off."

Sharon lifted one side of the cover, while Apnar raised the other. A pearl-walled chute led down into the dark abyss of the Tunnelled Network. Apnar climbed down the hole, disappearing into the dark underground station. He called to Sharon:

"Come down on the ladder. It's perfectly safe. I'll light a lamp down here."

Sharon was reluctant, but eventually her fears subsided enough for her to grab hold of the metal ladders and clamber down onto the platform. It was still dark, pitch black even. Suddenly a source of light appeared as Apnar lit one of the wall lamps; its glow was dim, but bright enough to light the whole area into a semi-visible state. Apnar lit a second lamp, a third, and a fourth, until all the station was filled with glorious radiance. The place was dull and rotten; the result of many postins of closure. The walls of dazzling pearl gleamed at the boring stone ground. A track, covered in moss and overgrown plant life, was slowly rotting away. The timetable had been removed, but an angle-clock still ticked sorrowfully amid the gloom, many angles out of the real time. The date clock's mechanism had sprung out of control; it was, as Apnar calculated, well over nine thousand days out. The bleak tunnel which extended endlessly down a disused track was as dark as coal, and the walls as cold as ice.

"We shall have to make our way down then," said Apnar.

"Down?"

"The tunnel. Just until we can get out. By that time we should be in Vuita. Come on! Follow me."

Sharon followed Apnar down a large section of tunnel, clinging to the freezing walls for support. Apnar lit each wall lamp along the way with his automatic lamplighter, feeling the arched ceiling with his hands for a vent large enough to crawl through. It seemed to take much longer than either Apnar or Sharon had anticipated, but finally they found a vent of sufficient size through which to emerge out into Vuita.

Apnar pushed the vent without effort, and elevated himself out of the tunnel, followed immediately by Sharon. The snow here was thicker; darkness engulfed the landscape. The pair were in a bleak forest, blanketed by ice. The ground was hard and slippery, and only the occasional rays glimmering through the trees shed some light on the wood. But for this unknown source of light, however, darkness ensued. Apnar covered the vent and placed his gold pocket-watch over it, securing it with its chain, which he attached to one of the openings of the grill on the vent.

"We'll return here after retrieving the emerald. I've marked it so we should be safe," said Apnar positively.

"Where are we?" Sharon asked.

"Why don't we consult the map?" asked Apnar rhetorically, unrolling the crisp parchment of the ancient map.

"What are our bearings?" asked Sharon.

On the map were simple drawings of landmarks, including the Temple, of course, as well as various paths. It depicted the 'Gate of Nyxia', now replaced by the wall Apnar and Sharon had seen, a beast's lair, a fountain of 'survivale', a poisonous tree, a great city, a palace and, just beyond the 'tempolle', a very tall tower. All the more confusing to Sharon was that none of these huge structures (whose heights could be read in parentheses on the map) could be seen anywhere. Only trees filled the land right to the horizon; nothing more than a twinkling light ahead and behind could be seen, one from the artificial light of the high security wall, the other's source as yet unknown.

"Apnar, I don't understand," said Sharon.

"What?" came his reply.

"Everything! All these landmarks; where are they? If they existed, surely I could see them above these little trees."

"Sharon, would I bring you all this way to explore pure fiction? Don't ignore the geography of this place! Don't let it confuse you!"

"What do you mean?"

"Vuita lies on a steep hill; we're standing at the top of it. You cannot see the tops of these monuments because their bases are so far down. Believe me, they're there. I researched the area over all that time we were waiting for Baron to die."

"I trust you, Apnar. But where do we go from here?"

"There should be a path over to the right somewhere. If we find that, we're well on our way to the Temple."

"Just one more question…" Sharon resumed.

"Go on…"

"These trees: if they're on a hill then why are they all the same height?"

"This is, according to the map, the 'Dead Forest', because these trees have stopped growing; they're still alive, but their heights have been carefully planned. These trees may look the same height, but as you go down the hill, the trees grow taller. Do you see? It gives the illusion of a vast forest, impossible to get through. In fact, by walking down this hill, we can get through to the Temple quite easily."

"Amazing," Sharon marvelled.

"It is," Apnar agreed.

After approximately an angle of walking to their right, the pair stumbled across the remains of a path which had once led to the Temple and the other monuments. It was a rough beaten track now, but still a useful aid to finding the emerald. Ahead, Sharon could yet see the dim sparkle of a light opposite her far off in the distance, and asked Apnar what it could be.

"That, for all my research, I do not know. But let's be thankful for it; without it, we'd surely be lost," was his response.

There was a rustling in the bushes; the cold breeze blew flurries of snow across the path. Once more, the rustling resounded; the wind blew a cold and shivering screech, which echoed eerily in the mist which now surrounded them. Apnar and Sharon both stood silent and motionless at these ominous sounds. Four footsteps pounded on the hard ground. A great roar of terror swelled, and out of the darkness arose a terrifying and colossal beast, gnashing its teeth at the travellers. Causing a frightening eclipse to occur, only a small ring of light could be seen around the monstrous beast, one third boar, one third goat, one third tiger. It waved its great tail high in the air and brandished its gleaming and sharp teeth at the invaders of its territory, before leaping in one tremendous jump of energy towards them, with an almighty roar. Apnar grabbed Sharon and ran without a sense of direction into the mass of trees. The beast's heart throbbed to a horrifying beat, causing miniature earthquakes to pulsate across the ground of the forest. Apnar had entered the darkest realm of the forest; the distant light was now impossible to see, making everything invisible. Apnar dashed here and there to avoid the beast, which persevered to the very end.

Sharon's hands trembled in Apnar's grasp; the terrific excitement of the event had given her a great turn. Her eyes closed and she fainted momentarily, before awakening in the cool clutches of a relieving and soothing liquid, water. She was resting by a fountain, part of her head submerged in the water it spouted. Apnar was beside her, trying to wake her from her sleep. There was a light on the fountain which illuminated the area; was this the source of that distant light? It was not, as Sharon soon perceived. The distant glow could still be seen, but it was much brighter now. Had she come much further through the forest with Apnar? She posed him this question.

"Further?" he replied. "I wish we had, but no. I just came through the trees and ended up here. As soon as I came near the fountain, that great... thing, I suppose, just left. It gave up, thank Nemo; but we're safe now. I've had a look at the map; this is the 'Fountaine of Survivale'. We just need to follow the path, and we should come to the Temple eventually. Are you ready?"

"I'm ready. Which way?" replied Sharon.

"You really don't give up, do you?" Apnar remarked, laughing slightly.

"But why should I?"

"I like your philosophy, Sharon."

"Thank you."

Finally safe, the pair continued to descend the great hill towards the Temple. The bitter cold gnawed at Sharon's skin unrelentingly, and a fierce wind began to blow from the north. Through the great congregation of tall trees, Sharon could just make out the rising tops of many ruined ancient buildings, over to her right. These ruins formed the dynastic home of the Nyxian Governors, an ancient family line long terminated. Apnar's map, which he held commandingly in the grip of his two hands, showed this city, and gave it the name 'The City of Alfon the Great', presumably a long gone Governor of the area. Though all Apnar's evidence clearly showed the city as a forgotten ruin, Sharon could sight curious beams of light rising out of the city into the dark sky above, floodlighting the ruins in a cloak of radiance. She never once, however, even dreamt of mentioning her inclinations of suspicion to Apnar, who was permanently enthused in studying the map and investigating the course that lay ahead. He had no time for any other monument but the Temple of Onyx, and why should Sharon bother him by giving a childish commentary on her imaginative suspicions of goings-on in the City?

Apnar continued to lead his fictitious legion of soldiers down the hill, marching steadily, strictly keeping to the winding path which led to their legendary destination.

"Aha!" Apnar called out. "It's well within sight now, eh, Sharon? Straight ahead, d'you see that? Why, it's a marvel, it's so huge, so splendid, so... so... lit? What in Nemo's name... the great thing's lit, by... by... by artificial light?! What is going on *here*? Look!" The bemused navigator pointed to the Temple in reference to a few bodies, well and living, already clambering upon the rooftop, which was all that was visible from this location.

"Who are *they*?" asked Sharon, overcome by the suddenness of such a discovery.

"It's of no matter who they are, but I assure you they'll be gone by the time my bulleters and I are through with them. Step back, Sharon, I'm going to blast these intruders right out of here! How dare they enter a government-marked Danger Zone?!"

It had obviously not occurred to Apnar at this time that he too had entered, quite unofficially one might add, a government-marked Danger Zone. Yet, he *was* in the government, so was this his excuse? Sharon, for one, was not having any of it.

"Apnar!" she cried loudly in despair. "Apnar! What do you think you're doing? You don't even know these people! Put those stupid things down at once, I insist! I said, PUT THEM DOWN!"

Apnar was flustered; droplets of sweat trickled down his weary forehead, and he mopped his brow disconsolately at the outrage he had just caused.

"Oh, Sharon, I'm sorry! It's just my temper, you know, it lasts long for Nemo. What a commotion! I'm astonished those men didn't hear us, you know! Please accept my honest apologies."

"I will, but only if you control your fury next time. That was no way to act in this situation! Now, let's approach *quietly* this time, and we can think about what to do once we get closer. Agreed?"

"Agreed."

It was at this point, however, that the path became eroded, and the only way to the Temple was through the several trees that lay ahead, their branches eerily overhanging the bed of rotting leaves which covered the ground, still coated in a thin and cracking layer of fast-thawing ice. Apnar walked calmly through the sylvan mist, Sharon following on, staring around at the dark and gloomy wood which surrounded her, away from the safety of the path. The great trees suddenly cleared to leave a small space around the grounds of the Temple, which was enclosed by a thin circle of much smaller trees. These species were small enough to see over into the gardens which belonged to the Temple itself, now decayed with age.

Suddenly, as the pair emerged into this area, everything became flooded with brilliant light which dazzled Sharon's soft blue eyes, unfamiliar to the sensation of light after several angles in the darkness of the Dead Forest. The dramatic truth was then revealed to the travellers: all over the Temple of Onyx, inside and out, and all around its grounds, were dotted at least a hundred men, all operating illegally on the disused premises. To the left of the Temple were stacks upon stacks of barrels and boxes, each containing valuable quantities of smuggled goods, as was evident from their choice of location for their 'business'. The Temple was being excavated by these smugglers, hunting for relics to sell on the world market for enticing sums of Forden leaves.

The operation was quite established, too, for the Palace of Nyxia, a building to the extreme left of the Temple, appeared inhabited, and was very well lit for its guests.   Through the windows could be seen glorious rooms, medieval in design as the city was.   There were desks at the windows on which stood piles of papers detailing the most elusive of schemes to escape the government's wrath.   At these desks were sitting at least twelve secretaries, constantly filing or contacting others on their communicators.   The room which captured the attention of Sharon and Apnar most, however, was behind the front wall of the Palace, guarded by five or six tall windows, each with curtains drawn tightly, shielding the operations of the notorious ringleader, the one who had confounded the authorities by running the largest smuggling ring the world had ever seen, and the one who had taken over from that master of disguise and Wagstaff regular, Baron: the chief smuggler's nefarious murderer and the intruder at Uncle Cirrus's little hotel just south of where they were standing!

The sheer scale of the killer's masterplan was awesome, and the smugglers must have brought in a postiniary revenue of at least several forests of Forden leaves.   Their surreptitiously kept secret, however, had now been revealed to Apnar and Sharon, and the pair would have to be exasperatingly careful if they were ever to enter the Temple of Onyx alive...

End of Book the First

CHAPTER THIRTEEN

In Asher's Den

Men swarmed around the giant Temple like ants, each one carrying boxes of ill-gotten gains. It was now quite clear what Baron's intentions had been, and what those of his killer's were: Baron had wanted Sharon and Apnar to lead him to the Temple where he could conduct his operations out of the eye of the government, and where he could obtain all manner of treasures to sell on the black market. But Baron had not counted on his fellow smugglers' audacity – they had mutinied him in favour of the new ringleader, who had obviously found his own way to the Temple by now.

Sharon was annoyed she had spent two months at Uncle Cirrus's hotel in vain – she knew Apnar was being too cautious. It was impossible to say anything, though, since Apnar had been so generous to her before, and the last thing she wanted was to appear ungrateful.

"How should we try to get in?" Sharon contemplated, gazing at the vast Temple of Onyx that stood before them.

"We either make a dash for it, or make our way to the door stealthily," replied Apnar, her companion, almost sarcastically.

"What door..." Sharon began.

"Fine then, we'll make our way *through the ruins.*"

"And how do you propose we do that?"

"We could ... just walk."

"Just walk!" cried Sharon, a look of horror written across her pale face.

"We must go unnoticed, but look how absorbed they all are in their 'work'."

"Well, all right then."

Whatever had possessed Sharon at that point, causing her to agree to such a hasty and haphazard plan, one cannot tell, and we will never know. It must have been a result of that strangest of human attributes: impulsiveness.

Apnar and Sharon swallowed their fears – it was time to find the lost emerald. The time had come to act, to conquer adversity and to proceed beyond the ring of trees. Apnar went through first, making a quiet rustle, but not disturbing the nearby smugglers who were at that moment so close to them that it seemed ridiculous to continue. The cruel monster that was Fate would have to be on their side if they were to succeed in their quest; but Fate cannot be coaxed.

Sharon followed on closely, and as she stepped over the foot high fence which secured the area, she could only look ahead. At this point, there was no turning back. Straight ahead, there was a high pile of wooden boxes, mounted one on top of the other in a pyramid. Apnar looked left and right, and seeing that the smugglers were all busily engaged in their dealings, he ran softly to the nearest side of the pyramid of boxes. The nearest smugglers were just beyond these boxes, but Apnar was concealed entirely by the stack. Sharon, likewise checking both left and right just in case one or more extra smugglers were hiding nearer her than she thought, made a quick dash over to where Apnar was positioned. Luckily, there were no extras, and Fate was so far firmly on her side.

Although night had fallen, it seemed as though it were mid-day because of the great and almost blinding light given off by the many artificial lights positioned all over the grounds of the Temple, three of which stood several metres ahead of Sharon, providing a convenient hiding place for them.

"We'll go to those standing lamps over there, to the right. From there, we can get to somewhere even further right, and avoid the smugglers that way," Apnar whispered, all the time cautiously looking round him on the lookout for unwanted eavesdroppers. "Do you understand?"

Sharon nodded her head in solemn recognition of her instructions.

"Right," said Apnar, taking a deep breath. Looking carefully round the corner of the pyramid of boxes, he sighed and walked across to his new station, the farthest away light, at great speed. Then, at the silent beckoning of Apnar, Sharon copied his movements to the other lamp standing near Apnar.

Their movements so far had been unnoticed, but would they fare so well on the next leg of their journey across the weary lawn which surrounded the Temple? Apnar checked about him for onlookers, and on seeing none, made his way silently to a small tree to his right, several metres ahead. Once he had arrived safely, Sharon began to move forward, but on catching sight of a smuggler quite close to her she swiftly about-turned and hid behind the lamp Apnar had been standing at just moments before. From the corner of her eye she could see the smuggler look all around him for quite some time, even gazing straight at Sharon, but without noticing her behind the lamp. After making quite sure the vagabond had looked away, and that no other eyes were prying, Sharon darted nimbly to the tree where Apnar stood, her heart throbbing incessantly.

"Close one," she remarked quietly.

Apnar made a surreptitious run for the Temple with Sharon, daring to leap boldly through the rubble and to enter the ruined site of the legendary Temple of Onyx. But the raiders working on the Temple had spotted the pair, and as shouts went up to signal to the others that they had unwanted company, dozens of men came bounding after them in a fantastic chase. Apnar jumped here and there through the debris of rock and stone, and followed by Sharon, he found his way to an opening in the Temple wall. He and Sharon ran straight in without considering any of the implications their actions would have, and bolted down a narrow corridor to a wooden door. They shoved it open strenuously, and held it shut from the other side with a hefty piece of wood. Here, there was a choice of two directions: straight ahead, or left. A decision would have to be made instantly, however, because the weight of the many smugglers attempting to force open the barred wooden door was wearing hard on the piece of wood which secured their safety. It was beginning to splinter apart like Apnar's brain at that moment – for once he just did not know what to do.

"Come on!" screamed Sharon anxiously.

She seized Apnar, and dragging him by the arm down the left corridor, came to another obstacle. Part of the stone floor, well over a stride in length, had fallen into the weak foundations, and she and her guardian would have to take a tremendous jump if they were to get across the space.

Apnar noticed a small overhanging gargoyle of onyx overhead, and seized it with his hands, swinging across the open space to safety on the other side. Sharon was afraid to follow suit, but knew that her only chance of returning to Earth now depended on her bravery; Apnar had survived the swing, and he was certainly not the nimblest of people. She had much more of a chance of getting across, surely?

The smugglers had broken down the door and would be behind her in a few seconds; it was time to do or die, to succeed or be succeeded, to try and triumph. With memories of home drifting sweetly through her troubled mind, Sharon grabbed the piece of onyxwork and swung with all force across to the other side to safety.

Running straight ahead down a long corridor, Apnar and Sharon's hearts throbbed loudly, as if one was an echo to the other. The smugglers behind were having difficulties with the opening in the floor, and so far none had crossed the gap. Sharon was too tired to make idle conversation; she could only follow Apnar through a series of halls and corridors. Finally, at the end of one such corridor, was a dead end. The smugglers would have come over the gap by now, and even then Sharon could hear the distant clattering of footsteps rushing to catch her. Apnar rested against the wall fatigued, and kicked the stone structure with his heel in anguish.

Completely unexpectedly, the wall began to move, swivelling on a pivot in the ground. Apnar's cape was caught in the gap between the swivelling wall and the real wall to his left as he quickly moved away from the turning wall towards Sharon. Attached to the other side of the wall was a pair of ladders, leading up to the high ceiling. There was no opening above them, and so the ladders seemed superfluous. However, with no other alternative, Apnar ascended the ladders. Not thinking straight, he continued to climb to the top, bumping his head on the ceiling. But it was only Sharon who noticed that, as his head touched the ceiling, it had pushed opened a small hatch, just big enough to fit through.

"Apnar, look!" Sharon exclaimed excitedly.

"At what?" was Apnar's frustrated response.

"The ceiling! There's a hatch – look above you."

Apnar felt the ceiling with his hands, and pushed open the small hatch which led to the hidden upper floor. He stuck his head out into a small hall, and peered all around to inspect the area. Asserting its safety, he bade Sharon climb the ladders and emerge onto the next floor before him. She did this, and upon reaching the next floor, stood quietly in the hall. Apnar, not wanting to lose his property, grabbed his cape which was lodged in the opening by him, and pulled with all his might at it. At last it was dislodged, but so powerful was Apnar's pull that the wall turned back to its original position, and Apnar, cape in hand, climbed out onto the level above, sealing the hatch. He could not have imagined how puzzled the smugglers below him would be at how he and Sharon escaped their grasp.

Up above the confused criminals, Apnar and Sharon stood in awe of a great wooden door, bearing gold rivets and standing tall about three times the height of Apnar. Aside from this mysterious door, nothing else could be seen in this hall. There were bare stone walls all around, and a cold floor, but nothing of interest. Apnar pushed with all his strength against the great door; it was excruciatingly heavy to open. Eventually, after what seemed an eternity to Sharon, the door just budged wide enough for the pair to fit through the gap into the room behind it. Apnar entered first, walking calmly into the area which this great door had concealed. Sharon followed him through the space into a colossal treasury, unchanged since the Temple's construction. Great mounds of gold coins were positioned randomly around the treasury, piling up to the very heights of the ceiling, which was decorated with gold leaf. Four grand pillars stood around the room to support the roof; this truly must have been the room the entrepreneurial smugglers were searching for. Huge treasure chests lay bursting or open, littered everywhere on the ground. Jewels and precious metallic ornaments were strewn all over the marble floor. Four elaborate chandeliers hung majestically from the ceiling, surrounding one great lamp suspended from the centre.

"The emerald is bound to be here somewhere!" shouted Apnar excitedly as his voice echoed across the treasury.

"But where? Let's look, there's just so much to search through!" Sharon replied.

The intrepid tourists began to search through the vastness of the Temple treasury, inspecting each item carefully to see if it by chance disguised the emerald.

"So, why a treasury in a Temple?" Sharon asked Apnar.

"Ah! It's not that kind of Temple; it's not a place of worship. 'Temple' is just an old word for a fortress, or castle. Legend has it that Asher, an ancient miser, lives here forever. Bah!"

It took about two angles before any glimmer of hope could be sought, but finally Apnar's searching produced a result. In a corner of the room, from under a chest of elaborate jewellery, Apnar spotted the green glow of a precious stone, resembling the bright green which emanates so boldly from an emerald. Upon removing the chest, Apnar saw a huge green gem, sparkling in the dazzling light of the chandeliers above. It was as large as one of Apnar's hands, and as heavy as a whole bag of coins.

"I've got it, Sharon; I've got it!" he shouted, his face beaming with the joy of finding something so eagerly sought for.

Sharon turned to face Apnar to view this momentous discovery - the discovery which might ensure her return home, and which surely would bring her one step closer to this crossover, if it could ever happen. In his hands she saw the prized jewel whose only value was success. Sharon crossed the treasury to inspect the object more carefully, and to admire its beauty, but as she did so she was interrupted by the call of a voice overhead; had the smugglers devised a new plan to ruin hers? The voice grew louder with every syllable, each word resounding with crystal clarity:

"Listen, listen to me. Stop what you are doing and listen to me! I have important matters to discuss with you. Be silent whilst I speak. I have carefully watched you since you entered my grounds; I saw you hide behind the trees and bushes, and behind the infernal machines which you may call lights. I thought you had arrived to save me from the confounded idiots that have intruded upon my land. I thought you had come to reclaim my land back for me. So I continued to keep a close watch on you, through the Temple and to this, my Den. You insolent robbers have disappointed me gravely; however, and I am overwhelmed by your lack of respect. I refrained from speaking until now because I so wanted to give you another chance - but you have tried to steal my precious emerald. How dare you commit such a crime!" the voice bellowed terrifyingly from the roof.

Apnar and Sharon looked up silently at the ceiling in amazement – they could not see anything.

"From my position on top of the Temple I can see all that goes on in my grounds; if only I had been able to see your wicked intent. You have both, as I said, disappointed me. You have attempted to escape here with my emerald. But you will most certainly not! What have you got to say for yourselves?!"

These wounding remarks provoked Sharon into shouting indignantly at the voice.

"The emerald belongs to the Oracle in Sulla. You stole it from there! We are returning it to its rightful owner!"

"Oh, but girl," replied the voice, "I have always deserved that jewel more than that monstrous thing in the City. No-one but Nemo could deserve that emerald less! I wanted a collection to rival her hoards; I tried and tried but could never get enough. The emerald would complete my collection, you see? But you have been incredibly rude, anyway, and so I have no option other than to do away with you. How? My glare turns everything it looks at in the eye to onyx. You will not last long before I get you both. This is *my Den!*"

Suddenly, part of the ceiling split open widely, and from the level above descended a figure cloaked in a blood red cape, sitting on a grand onyx throne, but facing the opposite wall. Could it be Asher, Sharon thought?

"Asher has time for no-one who doubts his very existence!" the voice echoed loudly, as the throne slowly began to move round to face Sharon and Apnar. Doom impended like an angry monster, and Fate had changed sides.

Sat regally on the throne was a vaguely human creature robed in scarlet and gold, and wearing a small crown of silver. Asher stared intensely at Sharon's eyes, trying to fix her gaze on him to transform her into a cruel statuette.

"Look away!" Apnar called from behind a pillar. Sharon buried her head in a mound of coins, trying desperately to avoid Asher's face altogether. But he had turned his attention towards Apnar.

"You won't be able to resist! Look at me, look at me! I have eternity to play with you," the beast shrieked. It seemed that it was confined to its throne, without any sort of mobility whatsoever.

As peril loomed closer, Apnar's heart of steel began to show signs of weakness, his respiratory system almost spiralling out of control as he gasped and groaned in the agony of panic. Although signals of weakening strength and morale were plain from the outside, his peerless intuition and resourcefulness had not failed yet.

Sharon looked at Apnar intently for some sign of what to do next, carefully shielding her eyes by holding her right hand against her face in terror. Apnar gave no sign, and Asher had once again set his sights on the female foreigner. With one clear swipe of his monstrous hands he reached for Sharon's head, aiming at her shielding hand. Fortunately the attack failed, and Apnar called to Asher loudly from behind.

"Here!" he shouted to the creature, which turned to face Apnar, relishing the chance to turn Apnar into an onyx figurine.

In Apnar's two shaking hands was held the great shining emerald, dazzling as before in the glittering light which came from above. He held it up, the cut side facing him, but the flat side held out towards Asher. Apnar's head was facing the floor, and the tension all around was mounting by the second.

As soon as Asher looked towards Apnar, he saw his reflection in the emerald and gave a dismal cry of grief, which echoed piercingly throughout the treasury, his Den. There was a flash of blinding light, and Asher froze into an onyx statue, his features horrifically portrayed in the all-too-life-like image. Every light in the building blew out in one rapid swoosh of air, and the ground began to shake. Asher had been the sole lifeline of the Temple, and without him it could not stand. The structure began to fray and stones began to fall as the tremors beneath gathered pace and there were almighty jerks here and there. The ground beneath the adventurers' feet was about to break, and the building was on the verge of collapse. One battle followed directly after another, but had Sharon got her fair share of victory? Whose side was Fate on now, or was it as confused as Sharon? Terror engulfed the place, and all havoc had been set loose. Survival seemed impossible as Asher conquered even in death.

Apnar, however, moved quickly with his thoughts. His actions determined almost everything that was to occur. He jumped onto the platform on which Asher's throne was placed, and beckoned Sharon to follow him. Once Sharon had joined him on the platform, he raised his arms to the ledge above him from where the platform had descended. Apnar pulled himself up onto the ledge, and offered out his hands to help Sharon up with him. She emerged onto the next storey by Apnar, the ground beneath her breaking and splitting all the while. Above her was a metal ladder which led up to the flat roof of the ruin, fixed sturdily to the onyx wall in front of Sharon.

Apnar, still clutching the emerald, climbed onto the roof, terrified but in control of the situation. Sharon copied his movements to the rooftop, and just as she ascended the final rung of the ladder, the floor below fell through, probably crushing the smugglers which would still be searching for her and her companion even then. The bright artificial lights showed the entire district to Sharon, as if ostentatiously directing her attention towards the great structures which could be seen all around. Aside from the Temple, Vuita possessed many ancient monuments.

To the right, beyond the Temple, Sharon could see the grand tower which had been marked on the map of the area epochs ago. It ascended majestically into the sky, and towered over every other structure. It too, like the Temple, was lit well. It must have also been in the process of being excavated for treasure, relics and the like; the tower was surrounded by robbers. To Sharon's extreme right she could just make out the tops of various buildings which made up the great Nyxian city, also being looted. Finally, to her extreme left was the Palace which she and Apnar had spotted earlier. But there was no time to absorb in detail the magnificence of these buildings; the Temple beneath was on the verge of total collapse, and Sharon's life hung in the balance.

The back edifice of the Temple consisted of a pyramidal block which adjoined the rectangular building at one side. The other two sides of the true pyramid pointed outwards, and a whole sequence of steps ran down the side which divided the two. Apnar ran forward to them, but on stepping onto the first step, the entire flight sank down to form a chute. Apnar flew down bemused, and Sharon, having no other option, followed him down the great slide.

This huge structure, of quite gargantuan proportions, led right over the Temple grounds and into the Dead Forest. Sharon felt the billowing winds thrash against her face, their icy chill able to penetrate the most substantial of clothing. The frosty zephyr reminded her of the cold night she had spent long ago in the wilderness of Iceland. At the bottom of the chute was the bleakness of the forest, at least away from the dangers of the Temple. Apnar turned to face the ruins of the Temple of Onyx, and thinking of the horrors he had escaped from. When Sharon tumbled gracefully to the woodland floor, she looked round to see the remains of the Temple. To her astonishment, she saw it ravaged by fire, burning unrelentingly before her eyes. Probably ignited by the earthquake, which had caused all the lights to collapse, the fire raged on all over the grounds, destroying the smugglers' evil encampment. Deadly fumes ascended to the skies, great towers of smoke choked with perilous gases exhaled from the building, bringing in their wake death to all who caught a breath.

"We'll really have to run for it now," said Apnar, exhausted beyond description.

"Where to?" Sharon asked, desperately out of breath.

"To the tunnels which we entered by. If we can only find them, we can escape Vuita and these awful gases."

Grabbing Sharon's hand, Apnar ran with all the speed he could muster towards the path which lay ahead. Once he had reached this, he kept straight on the path back to safety. However, this fantasy was still far off. The intrepid travellers would still have to cover quite considerable ground to reach the tunnel at the far end of the Dead Forest. This journey was not without hope, though, and Apnar was running quickly. The wintry conditions had disappeared by now, and it was becoming increasingly easier to move about. Not all was favourable of course; the mysterious gas which had emanated from the burning Temple was hot on the pair's heels. Swallowing the already smoggy air, Sharon could only watch as it swirled closer and closer to her and Apnar.

Even the expeditious Apnar was growing tired, but as darkness ensued as they came further away from the monuments, the fountain which they had rested at on their way to Asher's den came just slightly into view, enhanced by the radiant glow of the burning Temple in the distance behind.

The journey continued southward, but there was no time to stop for a rest. And this final lag unearthed some unexpected finds. As Apnar pushed steadily forwards, carefully avoiding the main path which had before led him to the strange beast, he saw ahead of him a glittering accessory. Recognising the article as his pocket-watch, Apnar bent down to inspect it. However, this pocket-watch was not attached to a tunnel vent; it had blown off since, and lay abandoned on the thawed ground. Apnar picked it up in despair; his and Sharon's only chance of escape was practically ruined.

"Come on! Don't stop now… the fumes!" Sharon screamed.

Apnar took a deep breath, and without commenting, ran on even faster. At the very least he had found his watch, and in good condition too, Sharon reasoned. Tramping onward, the gases had now reached a record two metres proximity to Sharon and her guardian. The wall would have to be found quickly if their only chance of survival was to transpire, but look! The wall was in sight! With sighs of relief, the pair reached the wall without much breath. The vent was now lost, and there was certainly no time to attempt to locate it now; there was only one option left open which could lead to survival: the two would simply have to scale the wall.

Apnar began, climbing up with unparalleled determination, and Sharon followed on immediately. Now the fumes had progressed to be just about one metre behind them. The bumpy face of the wall made it easier for the pair to climb. Apnar finally jumped over the wall, with Sharon directly behind him, and she followed him to security on the other side, deadly black gases only a hair-breadth away from her skin. At long last the tension was over, and Sharon could rest. The fumes could not overcome the security wall, which had been proofed for every possibility.

When she had reached the other side, by the roadway, she found Apnar already fast asleep. He must have been utterly exhausted, and Sharon had not even realised that darkness had fallen on the 'real' world after being so used to the blackness of Vuita. Night had fallen, and a journey would have to be made to Sémento soon to return the map of Nyxia. There was no time to think on these things now, though; Sharon was tired, and so, strangely, she fell into the most comfortable position possible on a pavement, beside the empire's most famous, and one of its wealthiest, aristocrats, who was at this moment in time lying at the side of a rarely used road. Relief at last, however uncomfortable!

CHAPTER FOURTEEN

Back to the Mainland

When Sharon woke up, it was mid-morning. Apnar was still sleeping, but the birds in the trees on the other side of the road were singing sprightly tunes. It was a fine day indeed; 'orblight' flooded the area, sending beams of radiant light across the pastoral landscape. Yet, as Sharon listened to the gentle tweets of the birds, another sound entered her ear; it was the sound of a tinkling bell, and it grew louder as Sharon looked around to investigate its origin. Around the corner to her right appeared a tricycle driven by a man Sharon recognised to be in charge of the local island transport service. He was ringing his little bell infuriatingly loudly as he passed each district, and Vuita, despite its reputation, was no exception to this round-trip.

"Good obtuse! Didn't have the nerve to go in, eh? Ah, well, ne'ermind. I wouldn't either. All aboard, is it? My, you could surely have walked to the nearest village! Ne'er mind, eh? More service for me!! Ha ha!" said the driver exuberantly, dismounting his vehicle to approach Sharon and Apnar.

Apnar, by now, and it is little wonder why, was awake, if a little dazed. All his initiative and quick thinking had been drained for the time being, and he appeared really quite confused. Sharon ordered tickets back to Uncle Cirrus's house, and Apnar obediently sat on the back seat of the vehicle with Sharon. Everything now seemed topsy-turvy, upside-down, as if Sharon's position had been swapped for Apnar's; it was as if she was caring for him, and doing all the necessary arrangement-making. However, Apnar soon regained sense, and was readily and willingly able to exchange pleasant conversation with Sharon and the driver, of course restricting the topics to universally mundane and well-known subjects. Neither of them allowed themselves to talk about the Temple or what was to be the next stage of their incredible journey, and so all conversation was limited to such subjects as the government, the beautiful countryside, the weather, and the driver's aunt in Fordenia, each more loathsome than the one before.

The journey was not entirely free from enjoyment, however. Sharon took in the breathtaking scenery around her, and observing the lives of the inhabitants of the sleepy villages and hamlets. The soft breeze soothed her neck, and while hills rolled by, she was comforted by the thought of becoming ever-nearer to her destination. And at last, the journey ended, and high tea at Uncle Cirrus's beckoned. After thanking the driver, the pair walked together out of the centre of the town towards the hotel which was owned by Apnar's uncle.

"I'm glad that's over," remarked Sharon whilst walking.

"Certainly; but we've a way to go yet. Sémento, Sulla, who knows where after that? I just want a rest. It seems as though we spent an eternity in that Temple. The very word makes me shiver," replied Apnar.

"How long until our map deadline runs out?" asked Sharon.

"Twenty-something or so days; plenty of time. All will be well."

"I'm sure it will be. But how long until your uncle returns to Arvad or whatever it's called?"

"Gosh, Arvada! I completely forgot! He's away already, I should think. He always leaves at the same time each postin; I should expect he'll be on his estate this very moment. He'll have left a key, don't worry. Now, I'll tell you what: when we get back, you can contact Sophios and inform him of our 'latest developments', just as soon as my father hears from me. He'll be wanting to know the lot, you know!"

Apnar's uncle's hotel was the next building along the road, and Apnar approached the door in search of a key, hidden discreetly somewhere by the front entrance. It was just above the lintel, concealed by the front door. Apnar felt around for it with his hand outstretched above him, and, upon eventually successfully locating the key, inserted it into the silver lock on the door, and turned the great handle to open into the reception hall, which was cold and dark.

Apnar lit the lamps in the hall, and walked over to a door on his right which Sharon had come to know as an office, in which Apnar would report back to his father every other day. This was one such day, and Apnar closed the wooden door behind him softly as he went in to speak with his father. Sharon wandered upstairs to the library, where she could find solitude in her own company. There she would often ponder the latest events in her journey, and wonder how long it would be until she would meet her mother again. Today, however, a new thought, a new philosophy, entered her mind. It was a whimsical, fleeting thought, and a thought which would endanger her crossover. Sharon thought, in a bewildering fuse of desire and a flight of fancy, that she could, if she wanted to, just stay in Sullaria for the rest of her life, with Apnar and his father, or the Bugle-Thoms. But then, what would they think of that? And what about her loving mother? As before, when in doubt, ask Sophios. This resolution was decided upon, and Sharon heard Apnar's voice call on her from downstairs.

"I'm coming," she replied.

Sharon then made her way downstairs to where Apnar was standing, and saw him in new clothing; he was wearing a navy blue suit with an 'undercloak' over the top. Hung round his neck was an ebony cross, encrusted with dazzling diamonds. It seemed to Sharon that this world's elements and raw materials were similar to those of her own, lesser developed world. Just what was this place? Well, that sort of thinking was not relevant now; Sharon was about to speak with her original guardian, Sophios.

"We can contact Sophios now, Sharon. I've quite finished my business," was Apnar's introduction. "Follow me into the office; they must be aching to know about you up north."

"Strictures on safety, eh?"

"Strictures?! Me?! They trust *me*; why shouldn't they? Ha ha!"

They both laughed, and Sharon followed Apnar into the office, a smile once more playing round the corners of her gentle mouth. Walking into the office, Sharon saw for the first time in her stay the patterned wallpaper, the dark carpet, the dust-covered paintings languishing in pulveratricious dirt, the great oak desk, and a series of mechanical contraptions which were littered all over the room, which made up the room which Apnar had kept himself in for these few months. The room was not messy or untidy in any way, but the appearance of the objects around it, most of which were outwith the boundaries of Sharon's imagination, gave the area a certain look of randomness.

Apnar led her over to the desk which stood at the far side, and offered her the leather-backed chair which was positioned behind it. Sharon sat down gracefully, and Apnar gave her the operating instructions of the communications device which was on the desk, all of which would be far too complex and confusing to explain here, or in writing at all. Rather than a marvel of digital technology, however, the invention was strictly and solely mechanical, as was every working object in the world. Had this world not yet developed the use of electricity; could it be developed? Indeed, if this development was prohibited, then how could such tremendous and amazing advancements in the scientific world have been made?

These matters, of course, were of not much concern to Sharon at this time. Sharon did manage to contact Sophios, after all, and this was all that mattered. A connection was established, and Sophios could be heard, albeit faintly, on the other end of the line.

"Hello?" Sophios said.

"Hello, Sophios!" was Sharon's reply.

"Sharon, what a joy it is to hear from you! Where are you now, Mansleigh?"

"Not yet, no. I'm in Yriad, at Apnar's uncle's house."

"Well on your way to returning home, I hope."

"I hope so, too. So much has happened, I have to tell you about it all."

"Well, just wait an angle, dear. Apnar's father has kept me informed. He called just yesterday to say you were leaving for Mansleigh. I expect you'll be tired after all that action."

"Very, but do you know about the Temple of Onyx, and the oracle?"

"Everyone knows about the oracle from the media. The government is saying you were delusional, though, and that it doesn't exist. Even today's copy of *The Educationalist* has an article on you; they suppose you're in hiding with Apnar, outside the Empire. What nonsense, eh?"

Sharon laughed gracefully and resumed the conversation.

"What about Yriad? Did Apnar's father tell you all about that?"

"He did, I'm afraid, so there's no use in telling me now. But let's talk about what you're going to do from here."

"Now? Well, to Mansleigh and beyond, I suppose. Somehow we shall have to get back to the oracle, who knows how now, not even Apnar has devised a scheme for that yet."

"*Let fate decide*, eh? An old Boothcotian proverb."

"It's a good one."

"That depends on how you look at it. Remember, it was fate that brought you here, anyway."

"Well, how could I have met you or Apnar or any of the rest if I hadn't come? It's a blessing in disguise."

"A grand disguise!" Sophios chuckled.

"Then eventually we'll know what to do next, of course. There's no great masterplan; the journey should just fold out. Now, how are the Bugle-Thoms?"

"Oh, as well as ever. They're all hanging on my every word down in the village, and I'm hanging on yours. But don't worry; *The Gleddock Press* won't be publishing anything unwanted. It's old Dr. Jacoby that owns it; he won't allow any nonsense, if you know what I mean. We don't want this information in the public domain, as I'm sure *you* understand."

"Absolutely, as long as you're there, I'm fine. I can trust you."

"Well, that's comforting. I shouldn't be increasing your guardian's communication bill, it's augmented enough with calls to Lord d'Arrawor, I'm sure. It's better if we leave it at that, for now."

"Right then, I'll contact you later."

"It'll be a pleasure. Goodbye, Sharon."

"Goodbye."

Sharon stood up from the table, and walking across the room, glanced at the rows of old books on the dusty shelves lined across the wall of the study.

"So when do we leave for Port of Mansleigh?" she inquired eagerly.

"Why, as soon as the shipmerchants permit, I suppose," was the dissatisfying answer she received.

"Tomorrow?" Sharon persisted.

"Tomorrow, if you wish. The sooner the better, as long as our transport is trustworthy."

"What kind of ship will be board?"

"Most probably a passenger-carrier, although they only run every other day."

"What would be the other option?"

"Only hiring a ship, but I can't steer a vessel."

"Nor I," concluded Sharon resolutely, closing the door on such a proposition.

"Well, should I contact some of the merchants in town and check if the service runs tomorrow?"

"That sounds like a good idea," said Sharon.

Apnar walked over to the desk and seated himself behind it, calling over to Sharon:

"In the meantime, Sharon, you can relax in the garden. I'll come out as soon as I hear any news on the boat front."

"Great."

With this final monosyllable, Sharon exited the room and walked out of the building into the mature gardens at the back, just beginning to blossom in the wake of the new season. The 'orb' was at its zenith, and the day was beginning to end as the ascent of stars in the sky would appear within about fifty angles. Sharon sat on an elegant bench shaded by the overhanging tree. However, no longer had she sat down to indulge in a little well-deserved relaxation then the glass doors of the small hotel burst open to reveal Apnar, quite remarkably flushed, almost to the point of distress.

"Apnar?" Sharon mustered out of the shocked chords of her voicebox.

"Sharon! We must leave immediately, I tell you. The carrier departs in half an angle, and only crosses every ten days! Hurry up, come on! What do we need? I've got the map, now grab some clothes from your wardrobe and let's go."

Sharon, understandably dizzy from all the excitement, stood up quickly and rushed into the hotel after Apnar, pounding on the ancient staircase like an elephant, but with all the grace and composure of a delicate swan, however unaccomplishable that may sound. She hurriedly pulled some clothes out of her wardrobe and packed them away in a case which had been lying discreetly under the bed, and then running hastily, turned the door handle and proceeded down the staircase to the hall, where she was met by Apnar already aching to leave. It was true that the harbour was only a few streets away, but time was pressing on.

"Right, a demi-semi-angle to go," updated Apnar as he slammed the outside door of the building and clambered down the steps.

What followed was an incredible rush to the harbour, in which the pair of intrepid travellers did everything they could possibly do in order to reach the carrier in time. Around the corner, Sharon could see the great stern of the boat that was or was not to take them to the mainland, and as she turned she saw two naval assistants begin to lift the temporary steps onto the craft away from their position.

"Stop!" Apnar cried in demand; the two assistants raised their heads towards him, as perplexed as the passengers aboard the carrier ship.

Apnar ran over to the boat and withdrew his government pass from his inside pocket, waving it before the sailors. They let him on, of course, and Sharon, too, gained entry.

"Only for emergencies, you know," commented Apnar.

"Oh, I see," said Sharon gently, thanking the sailors as she went by.

Apnar led Sharon to the upper deck of the ship, where they both seated themselves near the balcony overlooking the sea beyond. A fresh sea breeze blew a pleasant chill down Sharon's spine, reminding her of her last day on Earth, as the Icelandic gales tickled her structure. It was a glorious radiant day, and as the carrier ship headed westward, the rough coast of Sullaria could be seen in the distance, tall stone fortresses lined irregularly along the shores. These strongholds looked mainly deserted, torn apart by the rough sea winds over centuries.

"You see those towers, over there?" Apnar asked Sharon.

"I do," she replied.

"Those are inhabited by the ancient wizards of the land, kept safe by them for all eternity. Many are wise, all are cunning, but few live a comfortable life. There we can see Gamma Steeple, Beta Belfry, and just south of Mansleigh, Epsilon Tower," taught Apnar, pointing out each bastion in turn.

Sharon had to interpret Apnar's use of language with caution, of course, because she knew that the existence of magic, in the common Earthly usage of the word, was not any more common there than back home. Advanced scientific developments had fallen into the clutches of the superstitious, and so had become known as magical spells and such like as science gradually disappeared over the millennia, in language, from the face of this new-found world.

After the history lesson, Sharon stared out across the waters, waves undulating terrifically in the distance to the East. The breakers crashed, and the perilous roar of the ocean swelled. Yet these instinctively frightening sights were far away on the distant shores of Boothcotia, away from the safety of Sullaria and its deep blue shining sea, the orb's rays shimmering gently on its surface.

As Port of Mansleigh came into view, so did the old buildings of which it consisted. The town appeared like a pretty Mediterranean village, the happy villagers scurrying about in the sun. But this image was seriously flawed; the hotspot for international smuggling and fraud was not as beautiful as its picture-postcard appearance may have suggested to the unwary tourist. The haven for illegal trade was as full of the evils of the world as the Ruler himself. The dark town was an elegant and obliging home for criminals by night, an elegant and obliging home for sailors and tourists by day. Sharon was such a tourist, although her business there was rather more important than that of your average sight-seer.

The carrier ship slowly harboured at the port at Mansleigh, the Emerald Isle now a distant memory. Sulla beckoned, and success was surely near. Sharon let Apnar lead the way off the boat and onto the urban shores of the Sullarian Empire. Apnar walked out of the harbour area, showing his government pass to the assistants at the docks, as if proud to be a member of the most terrifying organisation in the world, save for the Arvadian militia forces.

"So where now?" Sharon asked hopefully.

"Well, I'd think it best if we just got the capsules to Sulla straight away. Remember that the tribe of smugglers might still have an interest in us. After all, we don't want to run the risk of having any more disasters."

Sharon sighed despairingly, desperately in want of a rest after such a tiring day, and Apnar spotted her mood almost instantly.

"Why don't we take the long capsules around the country, and you can sleep during that time."

"Oh, Apnar, I don't want to empty your pockets!" Sharon protested.

"Now, now, don't even think of that! I don't mind! Now, I really insist that we take the long capsules. You need the sleep, and so do I!"

"All right, then, if you think it's best."

CHAPTER FIFTEEN

Sémento Revisited

Apnar navigated his way through the dusty streets, until he came to the burgh capsule station. It looked in complete disrepair, but was in fact fully operational. Sharon walked beside him all the way, chatting about life on Earth, and the strange parallels that could be drawn between it and the world she now walked. The pair entered the old station through sliding glass doors, the only remotely modern facility in the amenity. There was a large vestibule, rather like Sulla's, but much older, and covered in a particularly thick layer of dust. There were benches around the main atrium, and one large desk at the end of the room opposite the entrance, at which was seated one rather uninterested stewardess.

"Excuse me?" Apnar called for her attention.

"Oh! How can I help you sir, madam?" she responded.

"When are the next round-country capsules coming in today?" Apnar inquired.

"Let me think, now there's the local, the direct line, and the national won't be in till, oh, about ten angles. It's quite a wait, don't you think?"

"Well, we do need a bit of rest. Where is the tarry lounge?"

"Just round the corner there and through that door," the woman answered, indicating the door in question.

"I see. Thank you."

Apnar walked over to the tarry lounge with Sharon, and entered the waiting area quietly, hoping not to disturb anyone already inside. He need not have worried, though, as there was no-one but Nemo, as he might have said, waiting for capsules. The room was not as unpleasant as expected, however, and there were plenty of comfortable seats to go round. Apnar seated himself in a red leather-backed chair with a copy of *The Proud Crier*, and Sharon lifted the day's edition of *The Educationalist* and sat on a beautiful carved walnut chair, standing by a window through which a shaft of light shone into the lounge.

The newspaper which Sharon had lifted was printed on yellow paper, and appeared to be a kind of compact broadsheet. The headline read, '18 held in suspicion of affiliation to Sireel Thomps', and the article ran as follows, supported by a photograph of three blurred faces in the dark of the night:

'*Eighteen men are currently being held in connection with the escape of Sireel Thomps and Casper Leighton from the high security prison encampment "ooo" on the island of da'Quina. The men, all members of the secretive criminal organisation "SAMPA", were taken into custody in the early angles of this morning after being identified by witnesses who themselves cannot be revealed at present while proceedings are ongoing. The Secret Service announced that the authorities had considerable evidence against the men captured, who will be questioned later today. It is suspected that the eighteen assisted the escape of notorious killer and fraudster Sireel Thomps, who in turn assisted the most infamous killer of our time, Casper Leighton, who is still on the loose somewhere within the Empire. Sources have indicated that Thomps and Leighton may be in hiding in the dark forests above the northern border.*

'*The ringleader of the so-called "assistance group", Phillipe Gilbert, was released ten postins ago after being acquitted over charges of manslaughter after an appeal tribunal decided his innocence. A few days after his release it was discovered that the vital evidence which freed him was flawed, and police have been searching for him and his lawyer, Jérie Auberge, ever since.*

'*The government was made aware of Gilbert's whereabouts sometime within the last thirty days, and had been monitoring his movements for this time until it was safe and most advantageous to make the arrest. Only three of the group's names are known at present: Gilbert, Auberge, and Auto-Klak, the last an expert in chemical technology and the inventor of Klak's fuel, a gaseous substance which was the cause of last postin's Pampadou attacks on the city's commuters.*

'*A government spokesperson gave this message early this morning for the media:*

' "*Eighteen men have been taken into custody, where they now remain, to be questioned and tried for suspected links to Sireel Thomps and Casper Leighton in assisting their escape from da'Quina. No further details can be released at present, but please be assured that justice will be done for the Emperor's sake, for the sake of His government, and for His Empire.*"

'A press conference is expected to be held later today to give more information on the case. Photographs on pp3-7.'

Other front-page stories included 'Government report reveals 10,000 leaders of old government still living in Empire', and 'Mother's joy as son is reunited with her after thirty postins in captivity'. The newspaper was very interesting to Sharon, and many stories captivated her interest for the next six or seven angles, before Apnar let out an exclamation of anxiety:

"My, what's the time? We'd better be going, I shan't want to miss this capsule. I can't wait for a good sleep. What's that you've got there?"

"*The Educationalist*," Sharon replied honestly.

"Oh, is it? What does it say today, then?"

"It says that eighteen of Sireel Thomps' and Casper Leighton's helpers have been captured."

"So does the *Crier*. We've a tough time getting those ones, I'll *tell* you."

"'A notorious killer and fraudster' it says."

"He's that indeed. At least it gets us off the front pages, eh? Come on, let's catch the capsules."

Sharon placed down the journal and left the tarry lounge with Apnar, walking over to the door in the atrium which led down to the central platform. Apnar led her down the cold stone staircase to the deserted platform, where they stood patiently for a moment in wait of the distant rumbling of capsules coming down the line, which came in due time. The sleepers shuddered ominously as the trail of black capsules shot down the tunnel in a thundering wave of noise. Apnar swung open the door of an unoccupied capsule and entered the cab with Sharon. The capsule was similarly furnished to those Sharon had been on earlier to Sulla, and the familiar image of an enthusiastic gentleman flickered on and off the screen in the corner.

"Sémento direct line. This train of capsules terminates at Sémento City Station. Thank you for choosing Motortranspo."

The lively tones of this sprightly young man, however, did not awaken Sharon from her slumber of boredom and fatigue, and as the journey went on a sense of even greater weariness hung about her.

"Sharon..." Apnar began not long afterwards, but this attempt at conversation was in vain. Sharon was sound asleep in a torpor of great magnitude, the result of many sleep-deprived angles. Apnar almost sank into the realms of dreams too, but he was prevented by something rather alarming. As his eyelids slowly but surely began to cover each glistening green eye, Apnar caught sight of a terrifying message on the screen of the carriage, yet it had been there for the whole journey: 'This train of capsules terminates at Sémento City Station.'

The aristocrat suddenly realised his dramatic error: he was not on a capsule bound for Sulla via the long circuit, but rather for Sémento, and on top of that it would arrive there within a single angle. Apnar waited for a little time in order to give Sharon some kind of sleep, but when the capsules approached Sémento he had no choice but to wake the girl.

"Sharon! Sharon! Wake up! We're on the wrong capsules! Wake up, we need to get off now!" Apnar exclaimed.

Sharon appeared dazed, if not altogether troubled by the scene around her, but she gladly agreed to Apnar's proposal. The pair exited the capsule and made their way up from the platform to the central atrium.

"What now, then?" Sharon asked desperately after Apnar had explained the situation.

"We have two choices, clearly; namely, that we catch the long capsules from here, buying new tickets since I seem to have left our own on that other infernal capsule, or to stay here in Sémento. If we go for the latter, we can book a hotel and rest for the day, seeking out Aylwin tomorrow."

"Oh Apnar, you decide. I honestly can't think straight just now. What's best for you is best for me."

"Well, I do think there's more sense in staying here."

"Well, if you think so, that's fine by me. Where can we stay?"

"I'm sure I'll find somewhere. We just need to wander until we find suitable accommodation. I'll not trail you round the shops this time, though. We're both tired, and I'm hungry."

"So am I," Sharon added.

"Let's have high tea at the hotel and then sleep until tomorrow. We've a busy schedule ahead of us. We must meet Aylwin soon, remember, because only about a septday remains."

"A septday?"

"Seven days, as in *The Yriad Septdaily*," Apnar educated. "As opposed to *The Fordenian Heptadaily*, also every seven days."

"A week, you mean?"

"A weak? A strong?"

"No, a week; a week has seven days."

"My, your world *is* bizarre. Where's the logic in 'weak'?"

Sharon shrugged and wandered out of the City Station with Apnar, in search of an appropriate hotel in which to dine and rest for the night. Apnar led Sharon down a lane which neither of them had encountered before, and which led down a slope away from the station. The lane was narrow and long, and in some places along the way were steps to ease the pain of the dramatic gradient. The lane was dark and confined, and on either side were lined rows upon rows of buildings, which looked vaguely residential, though rather dilapidated. This image of depravity should not be considered too grave, however, because despite the darkness and uninhabited look, the lane was completely clean and free from any kind of dirt or filth.

Eventually, a crossroads was met at the foot of the lane and far up ahead could be glimpsed Aylwin's upper rooms, and so the travellers chose a different route. To the left could only be seen commercial buildings and administrative properties, but to the right a great white knight stood head and shoulders above the other eastern buildings; the white stone of the 'Grand de Vere Hotel' could be seen sparkling in the radiant mid-afternoon sunlight, its golden welcoming sign regularly ushering in new guests.

Apnar walked on the outside of the wide pavement, while Sharon walked by his right, past the appealing shops and restaurants, all on upper storeys, and towards the hotel. Traffic zoomed down the road, giving the area a feeling of activity and buzz. This city was anything but dead, as one columnist had argued that day in *The Comet*, a publication which Sharon had briefly skimmed over earlier on the capsules.

Finally the grandiose edifice of the great white hotel came into view, and Apnar walked over to the main entrance jovially, eager for something to eat. As Sharon entered the high-ceilinged reception area, a sudden stillness eased her into the warm arms of such a grand hotel. Six-star luxury emanated from its very walls, and the high sense of refinement which typified the architecture of the time could be seen all around.

Apnar walked over to the reception desk at the far end of the room with Sharon, and while she admired the elaborate plasterwork of the high ceiling, he made a booking for rooms that night.

"The Celestial Suite, sir," Sharon heard the receptionist say to her guardian. It certainly sounded heavenly, but to Sharon a meal was much more important.

"I'll just have a look at the rooms before we head off to our meal," said Apnar, the keys to the suite dangling from his hands, tinkling softly as he walked.

"Right," Sharon answered.

He led her up wide red-carpeted stairs to an upper landing labelled 'South Wing', evidently lost and without a notion of where to go next.

"Are you sure we're in the right place, Apnar?" said Sharon doubtfully.

"Most definitely not, I'm afraid. We're supposed to be in the West Wing. Let's just go along here and..."

"Apnar?" Sharon said slowly, gradually raising the pitch of her voice, as if there were no more ridiculous an idea than to go to the suite now.

"Well, how about..." she began. "How about we eat?"

"Oh, very well. I seem to be being looked after again. We'll get a porter to come and show us the suite after dinner."

Sharon nodded in assent and followed Apnar back down the wide staircase past numerous gilt-framed paintings of hoteliers past and present. She found one particular portrait quite amusing, and giggled incessantly for a few seconds. The gentleman who was the object of her ridicule was one Sir Sebastian Cole, Chief Hotelier from some absurdly long date to another, completely incomprehensible to Sharon. He bore a dark moustache which curved far up his face, as if grown upside-down. He had beady brown eyes and an ineluctable smirk. His hair was long and in curls, like a barrister's wig, and he wore a deep blue coloured hat which resembled those worn by Napoleon.

Aside from this, however, there was little to laugh about. Aylwin's deadline was running short all the time, and Apnar too would have to return to work. A delicious meal beckoned in the dining suite, and Sharon could barely wait to dine there. Welcoming whiffs of food wafted delectably from the room up ahead, and the time was nearing when all could be Sharon's, doomed to the very depths of her stomach.

A steward invited the two guests into the dining room and led them to a delightful table at the far end of the room by a window. This window was draped in velvet by a pair of red curtains. The view outside was of beautiful tidy gardens, awash with colour. Many chandeliers hung from the high ceiling, glowing with radiant candlelight and illuminating the room. The table was set for two, one at either end, and was covered in a white linen tablecloth. A bouquet of glorious flowers, of assorted varieties and colours, was placed in the centre beside an array of solid silver condiment-holders. There were four of these little spice containers, each with a different pattern of holes in the top for sprinkling. These were, in the order presented then and always, waldersoupe, nonéchale, repartúi, and Dmítri's Spice. Each had a distinct flavour, as Sharon was soon to find out.

Conventional silver cutlery was arranged in a similar manner to that on Earth, and scrolls of parchment bound by red ribbons served as menus to each guest. Sharon opened hers after seeing Apnar do the same, and found to her great delight that some of the selection was in French, or 'Arvadian' as Uncle Cirrus had called it. Apnar seemed to understand it well enough, but despite her fluency in the language, Sharon found it difficult to decipher the Arvadian into anything understandable. As she well knew, food was different here, but in this particular restaurant the menu was completely unintelligible to her.

The menu ran as follows:

Starter

Le Gallinipper couronné avec des Diazingibers

Le Phytobezoar encerclé avec Fromage des Jacinthes

Main Course

Cockagrice avec des Légumes

Ninguid Ichthyarchic Arrangement

La Queue de Chameau

Pudding

La Girafe Sucreé dans une Chou-Sauce

Les Pépins Congelés

Final Course

Noisettes dans Cognac

Chapelure et Whiskey

Sharon was puzzled as to what to order, because each dish was so unusual. For her starter, she had to consult Apnar for an explanation of the unfamiliar words used in the menu.

"Le Gallinipper is a large mosquito, and Diazingiber is a type of ginger candy; the Phytobezoar is a little lump from the stomach of an animal such as a sheep or goat, mainly made of vegetable matter. All absolutely delicious!" was Apnar's explanation.

"Well I don't much fancy bluebell cheese, so I'll choose the first option," Sharon considered aloud.

"Erm, the cockagrice is the only palatable option for the main course. Pépins should be interesting, and Cognac-covered hazlenuts sounds wonderful!" she continued.

"What a superb selection!" Apnar exclaimed excitedly.

"What a weird one," Sharon added.

Just then, a waitress approached the table, dressed in black evening attire, and offering drinks. Apnar asked for red wine for himself and Bubblezibois for Sharon.

"Thank you. Have you considered your meal yet, sir and madam?" the waitress asked politely .

"We have. I shall have Le Gallinipper, followed by the Ichthyarchic Arrangement, and Pépins. Sharon?" Apnar said.

"I'll take the Gallinipper, Cockagrice, and Pépins, please," Sharon ordered.

"Thank you. May I take your menus?" the waitress replied, picking up the two menus from the table and placing them gracefully in her arms. She then walked away composedly from the table and towards the kitchens.

"This has to be one of my favourite restaurants. The whole ambience of the place is just right. You know, Sulla could do with learning from here; I mean, 'The Ritzchen' is fine if you want quality, but the selection just isn't exciting, you know what I mean?" Sharon nodded at Apnar and sat for the next angle listening to his tales of gastronomic blunders which he had encountered in Sulla and elsewhere.

Finally a different waitress arrived with the drinks, curtseying and then leaving the table. Sharon looked at her drink with caution while Apnar guzzled his red wine.

"It's all right, you know. It's the same mixture you had at the Hall," he assured Sharon.

"Good, it's just that I've got to be wary of drinks."

Sharon drank her Bubblezibois happily, and awaited her starter with fear and anticipation. It arrived in due time a little later, presented by a pristinely-clad waiter. A strong and pungent smell emanated from her starter and the sight of the mosquito slightly sickened Sharon. The dish did not appear edible, a feast for the eyes rather than the stomach. The Diazingibers were piled in a pyramidal shape on top of the mosquito, cuisine to be relished in Sullaria. Sharon studied Apnar as he lifted the silver trinket containing nonéchale and sprinkled the spice over his meal. Sharon copied this action before lifting her starter knife and fork to eat.

With a gulp of fear she inserted a small cut of the Gallinipper with a Diazingiber into her mouth. The sweet taste of the candy strangely complemented the warm steak-like mosquito wing, which was tangy and dripping with a transparent liquid poured over it to rid it of bacteria. The nonéchale tasted gentle but bitter, and the three contrasting tastes tickled almost every taste bud of Sharon's mouth. As she ate on, she occasionally sipped her bubbly drink with Apnar, and eventually, to her surprise, finished the course (except, of course, for the inedible parts of the mosquito).

When summoned, a waiter returned to the table to clear the pair's first course, to brush off crumbs into a silver dish, and to replace the napkins with larger ones for the main course which was due to arrive soon after. With this dish Sharon had less to be worried about, because she had had cockagrice in Norway with her father before, which was now bringing back happy memories. She could remember sitting in a little café in with her mother and father, one of whom was now in a distant realm, another in an even more distant one. Was she ever to see her mother again in her lifetime? After all, not much progress had been made in getting back, and time was running out all the while. Hope kept her going, and troubled as she undoubtedly was, Sharon resolved to persevere.

A waiter approached bearing Apnar's fish and Sharon's cockagrice, the scents of which tickled Sharon's nostrils.

"Would either of you like a drink?" the waiter asked politely.

"Could you possibly fill me up?" Apnar asked.

"Certainly, sir. Madam?"

"No, thank you," Sharon answered.

"Very good, thank you," the waiter said, taking leave of the table.

Apnar's plate was full of aquatic animals apparently frozen in ice. His glacial dish did not in the least look appetising, and the cold chill which came from it only reminded Sharon of the Icelandic wilderness which she had wandered for a night before being brought to Sullaria. Sharon's meal, however, was more than pleasant.

Sharon began to eat the wing of her bird before proceeding to chew at her boiled and roasted pig, a culinary treat, but unappetising to modern palates. Alongside the two animal portions were various vegetables, of all shapes and sizes, some completely unrecognisable. Sharon ate them with intrepid courage.

After this course was taken away, the puddings arrived: two servings of 'pépins congelés', frozen seeds. Apnar was obviously feeling warm, because his choice of meals seemed to be mainly polar in temperature. The pips were arranged in a circle around a sprig of some garden herb, and were eaten with small silver utensils which attached themselves like magnets when placed near the pépins. The food tasted quite disgusting at first to Sharon, before she saw Apnar add repartúi, which she then did. This was the main source of flavour, and it seemed to be flavoured like a mature and strong fungal cheese. Despite its strange taste, Sharon enjoyed the meal and could not wait to swallow something 'normal', namely the almonds promised on the menu.

The pudding was taken away and bowls of almonds and breadcrumbs dipped in alcoholic beverages arrived at Sharon's table, placed in between her and Apnar. Long telescopic spoons were provided to reach into the bowls and bring across to each guest his or her sweet course in spoonfuls. The expanding silver spoons stretched out a foot and a half in length, and a miniscule head plucked either almonds or breadcrumbs from the appropriate bowls. Two spoons were provided for each guest, one for each bowl, and Sharon ate a few spoonfuls of each before slumping, fully satisfied, into her chair. Apnar, however, carried on eating until literally the last breadcrumb was devoured. Then he too fell back into a slouch in his chair, most uncharacteristically.

After a moment or two's respite, the pair of travellers left the table to go up to their suite, this time led by a steward. Up a few flights of stairs and a long a multitude of halls and corridors, eventually the pair came to 'The Celestial Suite', a grand collection of rooms in its own high tower above the city.

"Here is your suite, sir, madam. May I?" the steward asked, gesturing to open the door.

"Please do," Apnar answered.

"The Celestial Suite comprises six rooms, two private chambers, each with en-suite lavatorial facilities, three reception/leisure rooms, and an observatory, not for the stars as one might imagine, but for the city. In fact, if I may lead you through this entrance vestibule (as you see it is decorated with heavenly symbols etc.) um… you can see Sulla straight ahead, that little glimmer of light, and to your far right, Port of Mansleigh. This suite is much famed around the world – the Marquess of New St. George was here only last septday, and other visitors of stature have included past imperial ambassadors of Arvada and Fordenia. I trust it will be to your liking. If you require any services, any at all, you are most welcome to call for a steward by using the intercom on the desk in the gentleman's chamber. Will that be all, sir, madam?"

"Certainly," said Apnar.

"Oh, yes," Sharon agreed.

"Very good. Enjoy your stay."

"Thank you," Apnar called as the steward left the suite.

Sharon looked around the rooms as did Apnar, who called a servant to bring up clothes for Sharon and him from Sulla. Until then, he said, they would have to make do, if Sharon "didn't mind". Naturally she did not; nothing seemed worse to her at that present moment than to be dragged round shops to find something to wear.

As the afternoon drew to a close and evening dawned, Sharon looked out across the empire from her window while Apnar made some important calls in the other room, which he apologised for. Sharon could not have been more pleased, however, to be alone to reflect and make sense of the situation while looking across the country at night, sunset approaching.

She opened the lower pane of the large window to feel the gentle breeze. Darkness was spreading its heavy vale over the world, and as it did so the lights slowly began to dim. Sharon could hear the clanking of dishes from the restaurant a few stories below her, alongside the chirping of swooping birds and the distant voices of citizens intermingled with the occasional horn blast from the capsules station on the hill in front of the hotel. The wind blew these sounds and others across to her window and amidst these Sharon began to consider her journey. The heavens opened a little, and gentle rain began to fall, and Sharon could not help thinking that her whole journey could be in vain. Aylwin would receive his map the next day, but what then? The oracle was the only possible next stop, and after what happened before Sharon felt reluctant to attempt to get close to it at all, and she was sure that Apnar shared her feelings.

She felt a desperate sense of isolation. Where would her mother be now? What would she think? Would Sharon be considered dead, or worse, forgotten? Had time eroded her memory on Earth?

Sharon pondered on these things thoughtfully and made the resolute decision to try her best to continue. She would not cry — that was not the strength of character which she embodied — and so, with conviction and stubborn resolve, Sharon left the observatory and went to bed.

CHAPTER SIXTEEN

The Boothcotian Girl

Sharon woke early the next morning to the sounds of the city below, which echoed throughout the room, emanating from the window she had left open the night before. She walked energetically towards the wardrobe, no longer tired, to find her clothes cleaned and hung up ready for the day. Sharon dressed herself in these, after washing in her en-suite bathroom. Opening the curtains, she could see that it was not all that early, and estimated it to be about eight o'clock by Earth time, or 120 degrees in their time.

Therefore, she left the chamber for the lounge Apnar had been sitting in the night before and, lighting the fire, sat down to read a copy of *The Artist's Handbook*, which had been deposited on a side table earlier that morning by hotel staff, along with a few other newspapers and periodicals. Inside were pages of colour pictures of top artists' newest works, most of them oil on canvas. They were classical in style, with vast landscapes and formal portraits. Sharon sat browsing through the magazine for a while, before Apnar emerged through the door fully clad in a bright white three-piece suit and robes, a shining diamond hung from his collar in the place of a tie. His hair had been flattened and waxed, and his eyes glistened through a pair of dazzling spectacles. It was the first instalment of the clothes he had ordered to be brought down from Sulla, evidently having arrived during the night.

"Good obtuse, Sharon! I should expect you've rarely seen me with these specs on. Just for detail, you know," he said, beaming.

"No, you're right, I haven't. Can we go for breakfast now?" Sharon asked him.

"Well, well, we are keen this morning! Very well, however I shan't be coming back to the room afterwards, so gather your things now."

"Right."

Sharon went back to the bedroom to take her coat while Apnar found the map to return to Aylwin. The two met in the entrance hall to the suite and, ushering Sharon out, Apnar closed the door and locked it with a heavy key, walking down to breakfast.

"Lord d'Arrawor," said Apnar to the steward at the entrance to the restaurant.

"Of course. Please follow me," the steward replied, leading Apnar and Sharon to a table near a window, not far from the one they had sat at the night before.

"Will you require light, continental, or full Sullarian breakfast?" a waiter asked, taking over from the steward who returned to his original position.

"Just light for me, please; Sharon?" Apnar ordered.

"The same, thank you."

"Thank you. It will be served shortly."

According to the waiter's word, a few pristinely cut slices of toast were served to Sharon and Apnar, along with 'purus', a natural substance served as a drink, and a butter dish with accompanying knife. The pair devoured the breakfast and left the dining room, exiting the hotel through the reception.

They then proceeded down the street they had come to the hotel by, towards the cafe they had met Aylwin in before. Eventually they reached the correct street, buzzing with pedestrians, ragged and rich. Outside the café were quite a few people, most of them begging for money, and just as Apnar was about to reprimand one for grabbing his cloak, he recognised the figure's face; without a doubt, it was Aylwin, hooded of course.

"Follow me upstairs. You have the map?" he said in the usual coarse voice.

Apnar nodded, and he and Sharon did as Aylwin had commanded, once again ascending the wrought iron staircase to the café and into the familiar lounge bar, busy as usual. The spiral staircase led them up to the next floor, and once everyone invited was in, Aylwin locked the door and sat at the worn wooden table in the centre of the room with his guests. Aylwin tapped the table nine times and the area was secure.

"Right. Let's be quick, I've got other business to be attending to. Where's the map?" Aylwin said.

"I've got it here, all bound up as you wanted," Apnar said, withdrawing the map from his inside pocket and giving it to Aylwin.

"Thank you. I trust you were successful in your quest?" Aylwin said, giving a slight laugh.

"We were, thank you. Will that be all?" Apnar asked, desperate to leave.

"Why, I was just about to ask you the same question," replied Aylwin.

"We're done if you are," said Sharon.

"Very well, then. That's settled; just remember this: everything to do with me must, I stress, be kept strictly secret. Just forget everything, if you catch my drift."

"Right," the pair agreed.

Nothing more was said; Aylwin tapped the table nine times and left the café in the opposite direction from Sharon and Apnar. Sharon was never to see him again on her journey.

"Well, what now?" Sharon asked Apnar.

"I think we're lost," Apnar concluded after some thinking.

"But we can't be — we've only just left the café."

"No, I mean our quest. We're lost. If only we knew how to get to the oracle safely."

Just then a young girl of about sixteen years jumped up, turning towards Apnar.

"The oracle?" she said in a soft voice.

"Erm, no… *The Chronicle*, today's paper. Leave us alone at once!" Apnar growled.

"It's all right, sir, I know."

"Know what?"

"A lot more than you might about… the oracle."

Sharon looked alarmed, as did Apnar.

"I told you to leave us alone!" bellowed Apnar yet again, turning a few heads on the street.

"Please," the girl pled. "Don't attract attention. I can tell you how to get to the oracle in the Tower securely, if you come with me."

"Come where?" Sharon interrupted.

"You'll see. Act inconspicuous, please, Lord d'Arrawor, and no more questions, Sharon."

Sharon and her companion were shocked at the girl's knowledge and instant recognition but too scared to ask more.

"Don't worry. The base is…" The girl cut off here and turned her head left and right to check for eavesdroppers. "Down here," she said in a whisper.

The three walked down the street before turning right into a narrow alleyway, walking along it and down a few steps to an empty square, surrounded by bleak disused storehouses. One lamp shone in the darkness due to the total eclipse of the sun caused by the storehouses' vastness.

"Here, follow me and say nothing until I ask you to speak," the girl instructed, still a little nervous about any onlookers being present, though quite confident there could not be any.

The girl pulled a sort of manhole cover off the road and stepped down into the ground, beckoning Sharon and Apnar to go with her. They followed, and once inside, the girl replaced the cover. It was a small circular room, and terribly dark. Sharon wondered what on Earth, or not on Earth, was happening, but suddenly large strips of fluorescent lighting flashed on all sides of the room revealing it to be a glass elevator, which suddenly began to move downwards, under the ground. Each floor revealed chambers manned by scores of men in black suits and white coats, huge computer screens lining the walls. This was an amazing secret operation. The elevator passed about three or four floors of these huge chambers before arriving at the bottom, in a chamber filled with scurrying intelligence agents. The elevator door slid open smoothly, and the girl walked out first.

A tall man in an all-black suit greeted her. "Welcome back. I see you have visitors."

"Yes, I'm just taking them to the Chief," the girl replied.

"The Chief? Important business, indeed. Vive la résistance!"

Overcome by all the drama, Sharon and Apnar were lost for words. The girl led them across the chamber and through a long dark tunnel, illuminated only by lights on either side of the curved roof, explaining the situation as she went.

"Welcome to the secret headquarters of the Sullarian Resistance, the agency responsible for leading the resistance against the government, supporters of the old monarchy. It is here, as you may be interested to know Lord d'Arrawor, that our schemes and espionages are formulated, unbeknownst to the government and that demon the Emperor."

Apnar was very much alarmed at this statement.

"Let me explain. When the debacle of the old regime occurred, the top officials of the kingdom escaped the wrath of the Empire by uniting to form the Resistance, contrary to what government propaganda would have you believe. As support was rallied here and abroad, agents were hired after undergoing rigorous entry examinations. I am one such agent.

"I was born in Boothcot Wells across the ocean and my family stay there. When I was recruited for the Resistance I left them behind to devote my time to working in and around Sulla. Unfortunately, as it became more dangerous, we had to move our base here to Sémento. The situation has, in the past couple of postins, escalated so much that we are being forced to disintegrate until the authorities leave us alone. The government intelligence agencies have too much information on our activities now, so it's not safe to operate inside the Empire. Each one of us has to be taken home secretly by our own methods. I'm too young to be able to do much myself; you are my only hope.

"That is why I'm offering to release highly sensitive information as to how to enter the Tower and reach the oracle unnoticed, in exchange for something."

"Money, I suppose," Apnar lamented.

"No, it's just not practical to go it alone. I want you to take me home."

"Us?!" Apnar and Sharon screamed in disbelief.

"Yes."

"But we can't," said Apnar.

"Yes, it's just not feasible," Sharon commented.

"We can't."

"I mean we can't possibly."

"Would you stop with your negativity!" the girl admonished. "I'll lead you to the oracle, and you can take me home. I'm your only chance, and you're mine. Don't you see? It's perfect. Of course I'll need the Chief's permission to do this."

"Well," Sharon considered.

"Very well," Apnar decided.

"Good. We're here."

They had arrived at his office. The girl knocked five times on the door and entered.

"Chief?"

"Yes? What is it?" the Resistance Master answered.

"I have two people to see you, and a request."

"You're the first, you know. How are you going to do it?"

The girl led the 'two people' into another dark room, with only a single lamp giving a soft light to the desk, behind which was row upon row of wall-mounted computer screens. The 'Chief' sat with the back of his chair facing his guests, staring into a screen.

"Well, well, well," said the Chief in what sounded like a deep male North American accent. "It's the raiders."

"Chief, I'd like to request to be granted to reveal some intelligence to these two, in exchange for my safe passage home."

"Do you appreciate how dangerous this is? He's a government official. I can't let you divulge…"

"But Chief, lsiten. They have no other options for their journey. They have me and I have them to look to," the girl explained.

Sharon and Apnar were equally surprised that she even knew of their journey.

"Let me talk to them. Listen up, you two. This place is so heavily guarded the Emperor's own Guard couldn't break in. We're running a highly sensitive operation here. That means no-one but Nemo, not even he, can know about us other than ourselves. Do you understand?"

The visitors both nodded. Apnar tried hard to conceal a little smile at having found the Resistance – he would be heavily rewarded by the government for this. But the girl's help could change his attitude entirely…

"Now, do you want to take one of our agents home? You do realise how dangerous this is?"

"We do and we do," said Apnar.

"Our little alliance here is top secret – that means you tell no-one about us. Do you agree to this? Do you give your word? Are you absolutely sure?"

"Yes," said Apnar.

"Yes," said Sharon.

"Very well, then. But remember, your lives will not be worth living if you divulge the slightest thing about this place. For now, you may learn one of our league's many enigmas in exchange for taking our agent to Boothcotia. I hope you realise what's at stake. Now go back to your hotel and meet her this reflex outside the capsules station. We know where you are, we're tracking your every move, now go, and remember, tell nobody anything. Good luck to you."

CHAPTER SEVENTEEN

The Plan

"We understand," Apnar consented.

The three then left the room obediently at the Boothcotian girl's command and began to walk back along the huge tunnel.

"You seem to know our names, but tell us, what's yours?" Apnar asked inquisitively.

"*My* name?" the girl answered. "Well, I can't tell you that. Just call me Pascale, that's my mother's name."

"Pascale? How can we get to the oracle?" Sharon asked.

"I think we can talk that over later. It's complicated."

"We'll go and pack up at the hotel, and be back in say, ten angles? How does that suit you?" Apnar proposed.

"Wonderfully," Pascale responded.

Pascale led the duo across the bottom chamber to the elevator and bade them farewell, telling them strictly to replace the manhole cover at the entrance. Apnar and Sharon ascended through the ground to the deserted square above, past the storeys of busy agents wandering about the underground chambers, operating complex equipment. When they had reached the top, Apnar pushed the manhole cover off, and when he and Sharon had entered the world above, he replaced it dutifully as instructed.

"Now, I think we have to go down here and along Aylwin's street. After that we should be able to return to the hotel," Apnar commented.

"Right," Sharon replied.

"No, left actually," joked Apnar, laughing with Sharon. They both turned left before they walked down Aylwin's street and arrived eventually at the hotel.

"Here we are again. It's a shame we're leaving so soon, the hospitality was excellent. Never mind, as long as we're returning to Sulla," said Apnar at the hotel doors.

"Shall we be staying at your home, all three of us?" Sharon inquired.

"Well, that depends on what Miss Bossy-Boots has to say on the matter," was the humorous reply. Sharon giggled.

The daring duo was about to become the troublesome trio; however, as long as this was not apparent to the authorities, Sharon was not worried. When they arrived at their suite, Apnar rushed to his own room to gather his things and cancel the delivery of further clothes to the hotel, while Sharon marvelled at the spectacular view from the observatory for one last time.

'Isn't it amazing,' she thought. 'I know no-one here as well as I do those on Earth, and yet, I feel at home.' But she knew that, despite the easy and relaxing homeliness of her Hinterland, she had to escape to her real home.

Out of his bedroom emerged Apnar, bearing a heavy briefcase of papers, and ready to leave the hotel.

"Are you ready?" he asked Sharon.

"I always have been," she answered.

"Then we can go to the station immediately. I'll just need to check out at reception."

Sharon followed Apnar down the grand staircase and into the reception area. She waited while Apnar talked to the receptionist and then exited the hotel with him afterwards. They walked up the steep street towards the station, Sharon taking a last look at Sémento's citizens, scurrying to and fro. The sky was clear and the day bright, and tourists made the most of the blissful weather by taking advantage of various tables lined across each side of the street.

"What a wonderful day!" Sharon heard voices echo.

"Isn't it just!" another voice carried.

Sharon could not have thought differently herself. She was going to see the oracle and know how to win her freedom from the world she was now entrapped in. The wide doors of Sémento City Station beckoned yet again, but neither Sharon nor Apnar could enter; they had yet to find Pascale. Then, out of what seemed like oblivion, she appeared outside the entrance doors.

"Hello again," greeted Apnar.

"Hello," Pascale returned.

"Hello," said Sharon.

"Shall we go in?" offered Pascale.

All three entered the station and walked straight to the familiar platform for Sulla. Apnar would just use his government pass again, to erase suspicion of Pascale's identity.

"You know, I do dread using this thing," said Apnar waiting for the capsules, referring to his pass. "I don't think it right to use it when I can quite easily afford to pay for the journey. However, I know the situation."

It seemed that payment for the service was automatic – you were tracked and the according amount payable was deducted from an account. At rural stations, as Sharon knew, there were all sorts of forms to fill in, because there weren't the facilities to track you as well as in the city.

"I'm glad you do. Now, would you mind if I stayed with you at Arrawor Hall?" Pascale asked expectantly.

"Of course not! There's no need to make up tales, though; my father's away at the moment," Apnar responded.

"Good. Thank you so much. I can't tell you what it means to be able to return to Boothcot Wells, to a free nation."

"A free nation?" said Sharon.

"It's a federal democracy with a constitutional monarchy. As long as King Edmund rules it will be free," replied Pascale.

"You mean as long as the Emperor doesn't invade. Boothcotia won't stand a chance against the Sullarian army, you know. Its only possible route to survival is to become an Empire," Apnar interrupted.

"Yes, well, King Edmund will never live to see that day. I hope I won't either."

"The Sullarian government is not oppressive, you understand, I hope," Apnar continued.

"I'm sure. Just clandestine and mendacious," was Pascale's response.

"Well, I'm sure Boothcotia is lovely, and I know Sullaria is not an oppressive nation," said Sharon, trying to cool the situation.

"Let's not make this any more difficult than it already is. We have different ideas, Lord d'Arrawor, but let's try to get along for now, while we need to, huh?" Pascale proposed.

"Indeed! And please do call me Apnar."

With the situation under control, and sufficient goodwill to make the following journey bearable, the latest string of capsules shot down the line, blowing great gushes of air all around.

Apnar led the way, naturally, to a reasonable capsule (all the aristocratic cabs were booked, much to Apnar's dismay). He opened the door and let Pascale and Sharon enter first, following behind into the capsule. Sharon sat by Pascale on one side, while Apnar sat opposite them, reading *The Proud Crier*. The well-known image of a gentleman's face flickered now on the capsule screen, and announced that the particular string was headed for Sulla directly. After this intimation, the train of cabs rocketed down the line at unbelievable speed.

As Apnar pretended to indulge himself in reading the newspaper, Pascale and Sharon sat talking together about their lives, discovering that they were like each other in many ways. Pascale, like Sharon, had lost her father and she too had a close relationship with her mother, and had been away from her for some time. It was as if Pascale's heritage was identical to Sharon's, and through this they found friendship. Sharon knew all the time that Apnar was listening to them, mainly because he was holding the newspaper upside-down. She laughed inwardly and suddenly felt the carriages grind to a halt. They had reached Sulla, the capital of the greatest Empire in the world, and a city that had let Sharon into its secrets and then run her through its legal system only to be discharged. It was like a great beast that had swallowed her whole, chewed her over, and then spat her back out again. Despite her failures there, Sharon liked the city, and she knew Apnar did.

"We have arrived at Sulla. Please gather together your belongings and prepare to depart. Thank you for choosing Motortranspo," the image on the screen intimated.

Apnar was first to step onto the platform, followed by Sharon and then finally Pascale. The three walked up the stone steps to the atrium of the station and traversed across the solid floor to the archway which led to the outside world of Sulla. This time they left by a different route out to the city, straight onto the main road where all the government buildings were based.

"Stand close to me," Apnar instructed. "It's extremely busy, remember."

Apnar was telling no lie, as hundreds of pedestrians and motorists bustled about, making a terrible commotion. Apnar led the two girls along the road safely to the great bridge which crossed the river. There were elevators down the sides of the bridge to take pedestrians wishing to sail down the river down to the water's edge. Apnar chose one of these to go down by, and all three of them descended to the river to catch a boat.

"Arrawor Hall, please," Apnar requested of a tall boatman who was offering sails up the river.

"Yep. Twenty Forden leaves, please," he replied in a heavy voice.

Apnar asked if he could pay him at the end of the journey; this, of course, was not possible, and so he paid the boatman there and then. It was, after all, a small price to pay for three passengers.

The little vessel sailed gracefully down the river past the high courts, the palace, and several private mansions until they came to the third house along from the Ruler's palace, Arrawor Hall. As usual, servants were on hand to welcome His Lordship and his guests, and even a line of trumpeters stood along the stately drive to play in the Master. With Lord d'Arrawor Senior away, Apnar was the head of the household. Apnar declined the offers of various expensive beverages and entered a black carriage with the others to take him down to the Hall. Grandeur emanated from the vast mansion which was Apnar's father's, and it was to be his residence for the next little period in Sharon's incredible quest.

"Welcome to Arrawor Hall," announced Apnar proudly to Pascale to introduce her to the manor.

"Thank you. I should like to rest for a while in my room. I've sent some people to bring my luggage so I can unpack. After dinner we can arrange a meeting in one of your splendid rooms to discuss the matter of the, eh... oracle." Pascale whispered the last word so quietly that it might as well not have been uttered.

"Good, good," said Apnar, leading Sharon and Pascale into the house. "Sharon, you don't mind taking the same room as last time, do you?"

"Of course not."

"Good, do you remember where it is?"

"I think so. I'm sure I'll find it."

"Excellent. Then let me show Pascale to her room. Just arrange things as you wish and relax for a while. I'm just going to ask the servants to prepare a nice dinner, and then I'll be in my study. Dinner will be in about ten angles, all right?" Apnar explained.

"Great," Sharon replied, walking up the staircase to her room while Apnar led Pascale across the landing to hers.

Sharon walked to her room slowly where a doorman opened the ancient door for her. It was just as she had left it many septdays before; the writing desk, the commode, the pretty chairs and the wardrobe were all still there, and there was an almost homely atmosphere to the place. The first port of call for Sharon had to be the wardrobe. She had suffered the violet pullover and brown trousers she had received from Uncle Cirrus long enough, and although she appreciated the his generosity, she was sick of the thing. With meek trepidation she pulled open the doors of the wardrobe and looked inside to discover that, to her delight, there were five new dresses, one trouser suit, a pair of hard-wearing dark trousers and a red jumper already hung up. Apnar must have ordered some of the servants to buy some new clothes for her while he was calling Sulla from the hotel room in Sémento. Sharon used her en-suite facilities to wash, and then attired herself in a beautiful light blue silk dress, which was extremely comfortable. Afterwards, she sat down to read one of the many books in the bookcase in the bedchamber. This time she scrutinised over her choice rather more, and after some deliberation, she decided upon *The History of the d'Arrawors*, a very thick book indeed, bound in red leather.

The author opened his delineation on Apnar's family with the d'Arrawors' earliest history:

'*It is unknown where exactly the Arrawor family originated from, but it is sound to suggest that a squire of that name lived in Sulla at the very beginning of that settlement in the First Ancient Age, about 600 postins ago. At this time he produced a family which inherited his land in the new settlement; all the descendants of this Arrawor thus carried the name of d'Arrawor, literally 'of Arrawor'. Several grand houses were built upon the land in the heart of the fast-developing city by the river, but it was not until Marmaduke Fritz d'Arrawor constructed the Great Palace of Arrawor, quite modest by modern-day standards though colossal at the time, that the city really began to expand. For this building, Marmaduke and his family became very well-known all around the kingdom, and as the rich squire's wealth increased through business ventures at home and abroad, so his fame grew. When the monarchy re-settled in the capital then known as Centralius, Squire d'Arrawor was awarded one of the first new peerages, a City Barony (equal to a Dukedom) becoming Lord d'Arrawor of Arrawor. All the eldest sons in his male line have been known as Lord d'Arrawor ever since.*

'*When the Great Wars plagued the area throughout AAII and III, the family moved to the safe south before returning to the re-named capital Sulla, where under the rule of Sulla the Great they remained faithful servants of the monarch and built a new seat for the family as other City Barons were doing along the banks of L'Attler. It was at this time that the family adopted the designation 'of Sulla'. Architect Sir William Henry Boyd was employed to build the magnificent Arrawor Hall by Reginald Fairbanks Winsor-Peebles d'Arrawor, and the building still stands today as an....*'

Suddenly, Sharon heard a knock at her door; it was a servant calling her to dinner in the St. John Dining Room and apologising that Apnar could not come personally as he was overseeing the preparation of the food (obviously the chef had been ordered to prepare a meal normally this time, Sharon thought.)

"Thank you. Could you take me to the dining room?" Sharon asked, puzzled by her invitation.

"Certainly. Just follow me," the servant replied.

Sharon followed closely behind the servant as he led her through corridor after corridor until finally they came to a lavish mahogany door, standing twelve feet in height, with an armorial shield positioned above it, with the inscription 'The St. John Dining Room'. The servant opened the door for Sharon and the girl walked into the large hall with windows all down the opposite side.

It was clear that she was on one of the upper floors. Seated at the huge table in front of her were Apnar and Pascale, at opposite ends.

"Sharon! So sorry I couldn't come to ask you to dinner – I was held up in the kitchens. But never mind, please take a seat," Apnar called to her.

Sharon sat at her padded chair in the middle of the table facing the main door, and replied to Apnar, "Quite all right."

"Good, good. Now, let's get the starter going, shall we?" Apnar was obviously excited about being back at home.

Servants immediately burst through the two doors at opposite ends of the hall, carrying three silver dishes and laying them before each guest.

"Oxtail soup," Apnar announced proudly.

The servants left the room and each of the three at table began eating their food from the china bowls which were laid on each silver platter. The soup was warm and strong, but more importantly, delicious.

"What a lovely dress!" exclaimed Pascale amicably.

"Ah, yes, that's one of the new dresses in your wardrobe, isn't it?" Apnar joined.

Sharon nodded.

"I had some servants order some from Marcel's. Is it a good fit?" Apnar continued.

"Yes, it's perfect. Thank you very much," Sharon at last said.

"I'm glad. Well, I'm done, Sharon, Pascale, are we ready for the next course?"

"I am," said Pascale.

"So am I," Sharon answered.

"Right, then."

Apnar snapped his fingers bringing servants to the table to clear the course. Others on table duty brought forward the main course, calf's liver. This was a truly marvellous dish, and one which Sharon was familiar with. She had had it many times before, and found it delicious every time. It was the same in Sulla.

"I feel I have to comment on this room, you know. I expect you're puzzled, Sharon, as to how you arrived on the second floor without ascending any stairs," Apnar went on.

"I was actually," Sharon answered honestly.

"Well, it's all down to a trick of the eye in the way the house was built. You don't feel as if you're going upwards, but you *are*. In fact, there are tiny inclinations all over the house which make you rise up gradually. It's all because of that brilliant architect…"

"William Henry Boyd," Sharon interrupted.

"Well, well, look who's quite the historian! How did you know that?"

"I was reading a book on the d'Arrawor family history before I came down to dinner," Sharon explained.

"Aha! You should be glad my father's not here, otherwise he'd be giving us all lectures on his heritage," said Apnar, laughing. All three were grateful he was absent.

"I've been meaning to find out a bit on my genealogy, myself, when I get the time. I'll be out of work, of course, so I should be able to study it all then," Pascale told Sharon and Apnar.

"Well, there's no need to worry now. I'm not going to bore you with family history. We're here to eat, and if you're both finished, then we can bring in the dessert."

They were, and so servants cleared the table and brought in the final course: 'flavoured ice'.

"Just a little something to cool us down, eh?" suggested Apnar, digging into his ice ferociously.

Sharon was relieved to taste something so familiar, especially as it resembled ice cream. There was no time for talking during this course, and the three had all finished within a demi-semi-angle. The servants cleared the table once more, and all three retired to the 'Westcliffe Lounge' to read and drink hot beverages.

"So, when can we have this meeting?" Sharon asked Pascale in the lounge.

"Yes, I would like to press on with this, you know," Pascale returned, aiming her talk at Apnar.

"Well, if we're all 'elegantly sufficed', then we can have the meeting now, I suppose. Do you mind, I think I'd rather have it downstairs in the Bervie Study – there's a big table in there. It would suit our purpose much better," Apnar proposed.

"Fine, but I'll have to get a little something from my room if you don't mind. It will be of great use to you, I'm sure," Pascale explained.

"Very well, so we can all meet in the Bervie Study in an angle. Does that suit you, Sharon?"

"Perfectly. Shall I just go now?" Sharon asked.

"I think I'll join you," declared Apnar.

"Good. I wouldn't know how to get there," remarked Sharon truthfully.

"A servant should take you there when you're ready, Pascale. Just ask the doorman at your room. He'll oblige, I'm certain," Apnar further directed.

Pascale left the room while Apnar led Sharon out to the study. It was just across the hall and to the right. Apnar took the head of the table while Sharon sat opposite him, waiting for Pascale to arrive.

"Do *you* know what she's gone to get?" Sharon asked.

"I've not a clue, I'm afraid. We'll soon see," answered Apnar, yawning. It seemed odd to Sharon that he should be bored at such a critical moment in the journey, but then she realised that he had the right to be tired after such a day, scurrying hither and thither to help her. Just a minute later, or a demi-semi-angle later, Pascale entered, holding two scrolls and a roll of blank parchment.

"Hello! I've got all I need," she announced as she sat at the table, herself quite excited. Sharon could not imagine where all the papers had come from, or how Pascale had brought them without her or Apnar noticing, but of course 'Pascale' was an agent for a secret anti-government alliance, so this sort of thing was to be expected.

"Let me explain everything," Pascale began, preparing to explain in meticulous detail her plan for entering the Tower safely and meeting with the oracle.

"Firstly, let me show you this document. It guarantees the authenticity of the route we shall be taking to the oracle. As you can see, it was signed by Emperor Parragon II; this is not the real copy, by the way. That is still in Imperial Vaults somewhere, probably in the G.O. But that's not very important to us; it's just to prove to you the route is real."

Pascale unfurled the other scroll.

"*This* is much more important. Here we have a map detailing the precise underground/overground route we shall be taking direct to the heart of the Tower. If you look at this point here," she explained pointing to the map, "you can observe that our little excursion begins in the grounds of St. Bartholomew's Hospital in the south-east of the city. There is a fountain there which, when operated properly, as I will require you to do, Apnar, opens to reveal a rather uninviting hole leading several hundred fournis down into the ground..."

Sharon interrupted her: "Fournis?" she said, her face blank.

"Yes, you know, about this length," replied Pascale, spreading her arms out. "Anyway, the fountain is sheltered by a walled garden; nobody there even knows it exists, and even if they did and managed to control the fountain, they'd have to be mad to fall down it. However, it is possible to throw a coin down this hole, and after about a hemi-demi-semi-angle one should hear it splash ever so faintly. That is because there is a well at the very bottom, a well which, in AAI, was used by the inhabitants of the surrounding area. Over the millennia, the city has been built over itself again and again and now the well is practically unheard of.

"This is no ordinary well, though, let me tell you. This well is in fact part of a network of such wells around the city which are connected by tunnels, and only possible for sailing a small boat on. What will happen is that you, Apnar, will open the well unnoticed, while you, Sharon, and I will be waiting at the location of another well, directly under Palace House gardens (I've got access to that). You, Apnar, will sail the small boat awaiting you along the perfectly straight route to the Palace House access point, which as you will know is near to the Tower. It should take no longer than six angles, and I assure you, it's quite safe. When you reach us, we'll get on another boat and I'll direct you through a rather complex maze of tunnels, which you can see on the map there. Once I've guided you through that we'll be under the Tower.

"All that's needed then is to ascend the ladders to the oracle's lair, directly above the well. There, now I'll write that all down for you on this parchment and let you keep a copy each for the big day. Do you have any questions?"

"When shall we be going?" Sharon asked.

"As soon as I can organise the boats and the Palace House well. The House is open to the public all postin round, but I can make sure we get through unnoticed; I have a colleague there. That won't be tonight though, so we'll have to wait until tomorrow at about midday," Pascale replied.

"How do we get back?" inquired Apnar.

"By the same route," Pascale answered.

"I see."

"If that's all, then, Apnar, you wouldn't mind me making some calls for the appropriate arrangements to be made for tomorrow?" inquired Pascale, closing her presentation.

"No, no, please do. I'll take you to my office. Sharon, I'm terribly sorry, would you mind going to your room again? I'll send up breakfast tomorrow, and we can all meet here again at, say fifteen angles before midday?"

"That's fine," Pascale conceded.

"Okay. Good night Apnar, good night Pascale."

"Good night, Sharon."

"Good night, Sharon."

CHAPTER EIGHTEEN

The Oracle

Sharon awoke to the smell of hot breakfast the next morning, the intermingled scents of tea, toast and egg wafting to her nose, invigorating her senses. It was laid by her four-poster bed, evidently quite recently, and Sharon assumed that it was the noise of her bedroom door closing that had wakened her as the servant left.

She lent over and sipped her tea, ate a corner of toast, and began to eat her fried egg with the cutlery provided. Some things were different in the new world, but others remained just the same, and just as delicious. When she had finished her breakfast, she walked over to the windows and drew the curtains to reveal the dazzling sunlight. The city was buzzing, and the 'orb' was high in the sky, so it must have been late morning. Sharon struggled to read the complicated clock on the wall, and, counting the individual angles represented, found that it was twenty angles to midday; she had five angles to organise herself for the meeting before the grand operation which was to see her come face to face with the oracle under the Tower. She selected a dark dress to wear, and set it out on a chair for after she had washed.

At twenty-two angles to midday, Sharon left the room and was guided by her doorman to the Bervie Study to meet up with Apnar and Pascale. When she arrived, the doorman found that the door to the study was locked, and so asked Sharon what she wished to do.

"Does Lord d'Arrawor usually open the doors with keys himself?" she asked the doorman.

"Oh yes, always. If you've been invited here by His Lordship, he'll open the door personally, I'm quite certain. Are you perhaps early?" the footman answered.

"I think I am. I'm supposed to be here for fifteen angles to midday."

"I see, madam. That rather explains the situation, then. You see, at present, it is fifteen angles and a quarter to midday, one demi-semi-angle early. His Lordship is never early for anything, madam, and neither is he ever late."

"Thank you. I'm sure he'll be here shortly."

"I'm sure," the doorman answered, bowing and leaving to return to his post at Sharon's bedroom. There were too doormen at the entrance to the Bervie Study, each in uniform and with sturdy appearances. Sharon smiled at them kindly, and they smiled back graciously, obviously well-trained.

Apnar did arrive that moment with the keys to the study; he opened the door and ushered Sharon in – he was serious looking and composed.

"Good morning," he said.

"Good morning," Sharon replied.

"We'll just be waiting for Pascale, now. She's a hemi-demi-semi-angle late, you know."

A hemi-demi-semi-angle did not seem as long to Sharon as Apnar portrayed it to be, and she calculated that it was, in fact, just thirty seconds. Just then Pascale arrived, with her the map all three had discussed the night before, and asking if Apnar had with him the emerald.

"Of course. It's safe here in my pocket," he answered.

"Good, good. Now, I'll just explain today's exploits. Apnar, you have your details, so you can make a head start to the hospital now. Remember – just make your way through the tunnels until you get to Palace House. We'll be waiting for you there," Pascale explained.

"Right. I'll get going." Apnar got up and left the room instantly and resolutely, making his way to the hospital.

"He should take about three angles to get there, and then his journey by boat should last another six, that's nine angles, so he'll be at Palace House at six angles to midday. That means we have to be there about an angle earlier, in case he's quick, and just to be on the safe side. It'll take a good two angles to get to Palace House, and then a further two to get organised; that's four angles, so, if we need to be there at seven angles to midday, then we'll need to leave here at eleven angles to midday, in approximately three angles. Right. Have you got that?" Pascale asked.

"I think so," Sharon answered, though she was not quite sure she had. Pascale had an annoying tendency to speak rather quickly.

"Good. So, we've a little while left. If you don't mind, I think I'd better explain about Palace House."

"Please do go on," Sharon urged.

"Thank you. Palace House is situated just north of the Tower, and is operated by a friend of mine, Mr. Lucas. Mr. Lucas runs the House for public viewing; it's owned by the Imperial Heritage Society, about the only decent branch of that infernal government. We'll come in as guests, but instead of going through all the rooms, we're going to go straight through the building and out into the garden. There's one part of the garden which is closed off because it's supposed to be too dangerous. Of course, it's not. It's just an excuse the government made up so that no-one but Nemo could find out about the fountain's mystery. Mr. Lucas will meet us in the garden at a specified time by a specified tree, and he will guide us personally to the fountain. He'll open it for us, because it's quite a task, you know, and then we can descend the ladders to the bottom and wait for Apnar. Now, do you have any questions before we leave?"

"No, I'm satisfied," Sharon replied.

"Right then, as it's twelve and a half angles to midday, I think we could get ready to go. We mustn't be early though. Really we mustn't. It'll take us an angle to get to the front door, anyway!"

Pascale and Sharon then walked side by side through the labyrinth of halls and corridors, led by a servant, to the front door, through which they left and were transported by a carriage down the long drive and out to the port.

"To the Tower, please," asked Pascale of the boatman passing by on a small vessel.

"Very well, madam. That will be twelve Forden leaves," the boatman replied.

"I beg your pardon?!" Pascale screamed in shock.

"Twelve For-den leaves, pleeeeeeese," the boatman repeated in a patronising dig at Pascale.

"Don't you think that's... Never mind, here..." Pacale presented the boatman with the cash required, because she knew she was on a tight schedule and could not afford to waste any more time.

"Thank you kindly, madam. Come aboard, ma'ams!"

Pascale and Sharon stepped aboard the boat and let it transport them down the river past a few grand and luxurious properties, then the Emperor's Palace, the High Courts, under the huge bridge joining the central road, and past a little collection of buildings to the gigantic Tower, overshadowing every other building in the city.

"Thank you for your custom, ma'ams. Have a nice day," the boatman said, floating off upstream.

"What impertinence!" Sharon burst out.

"Believe me, in my line of work, you see more impertinence than that in an angle," Pascale explained. "Well, here we are. We'll be under there in a while; but now, we'll have to walk a quarter way round the Tower and then walk straight on down Williamlebone Walk. Palace House is the first property on the street."

"Right," agreed Sharon.

She and Pascale walked round the Tower, and it dawned on Sharon how large the structure really was. Its proportions were massive, and from ground level it appeared to ascend into the sky endlessly. Eventually they came to Williamlebone Walk, as indicated by a signpost at the entrance to the road.

"Good. Now, just follow me and do as I do," Pascale instructed.

"I shall," agreed Sharon once more.

Both of them walked up to the House gates and proceeded down the drive past tourist signs.

'Welcome to Palace House, Open All Postin Round. Keep Off the Grass.'

The House was very large and ornate, about the same size as Apnar's but with a much bigger garden, and shaped more delicately. It had a grand facade, with flat columns all along the central edifice, and many windows lining the side wings. There were a few huge steps up to the front door, which was opened to a long line of visitors queuing at it. Sharon and Pascale joined the queue, and waited for no longer than a minute before they were filed through to the ticket desk.

"Two adults for the House and Gardens, please," Pascale asked the gentleman at the ticket desk.

"Certainly madam. That will be twenty-six Forden leaves, please."

Pascale paid the man and received the two tickets for the House. She and Sharon then entered the marvellous entrance vestibule, where Pascale caught sight of Mr. Lucas wandering about at the back amidst the crowds of tourists. Pascale and her confederate walked up to Mr. Lucas, asking him to take them to the fountain in the garden.

"Just follow me, and don't cause a fuss," he said in what sounded like a kind of French accent.

"Thank you," said Pascale.

"Yes, thank you," Sharon agreed.

Mr. Lucas led them down a long corridor to the gardens at the back, where he opened a large door and took them out through the private garden. He then led the pair across the garden and to a high wall, which appeared to be the edge of the property. However, opening a hidden door with a private key, Mr. Lucas entered the surreptitiously secluded walled garden where the fountain was positioned.

"If we come round this tree and past the gravestone, we come to the fountain," Mr. Lucas said quietly.

The walled garden was exceedingly dark and gloomy, unkempt and macabre. The fountain lay just where Mr. Lucas had said it would. It was a huge stone structure, rising up six feet, and with a central plume for spurting water into the circular basin round about it, with a diameter of at least ten feet. Of course, it spouted no water, and as the basin was empty, Mr. Lucas climbed into it and raised his hand high up to the top of the plume, where he turned a small knob at the top. This made the plume break away from the main body of the fountain, and Mr. Lucas lifted it, with great difficulty, off the structure and onto the garden floor. This left a small circular hole, about half a foot in diameter, leading to the vast network of tunnels below. Mr. Lucas then lifted off a part of the fountain shaped like an upside-down bowl and placed it on the garden floor by the dismounted plume. Now there was a space of at least two feet in diameter through which to enter the world below.

"There, it's done. The ladders will take you down to the port at the bottom. It should take a good angle to climb down, so be careful. There's a little lighting at the bottom, but not much, so it's very dark for a while. I'll leave it open for the remainder of the day in case you need to make use of it, but you should be able to go direct to the hospital," Mr. Lucas continued.

"Thanks, Reg," Pascale said to Mr. Lucas before she got a hold of the ladders.

"Quite all right, after all you've done for me. Good luck, Pascale. Good luck, erm… Sharon."

"Thank you," Sharon replied to the chap, who was now nervously looking all around him and walking slowly away from the fountain.

When Pascale was several rungs down the ladder, Sharon joined her and Mr. Lucas left the garden, returning to manage the House. The manager had not lied; the long passage down was incredibly dark. The Stygian gloom was so black that Sharon might have closed her eyes and not seen any difference to her surroundings. Then it suddenly occurred to Sharon that her escapades were not terribly safe or full-proof. The element of danger involved was, in fact, great; after all, she was crawling down a hole hundreds of yards deep which see could not see the bottom of.

"We're half-way," called Pascale from below, her voice booming around the echoey area, and causing the ladder to vibrate gently. Sharon felt fear grip her as she descended into the darkness, her head sweating and her nose itching; she longed to scratch her nose, but knew it was impossible for the moment. Looking up, she could see the distant light of day, high up above her and completely intangible. Below her, she could see, for the first time, what before had been pure darkness. A small circle of light could be seen far-off below, and as she got closer, it largened while the light above faded and grew weak. When three-quarters down, Sharon could just make out the image of a little patch of stone, edging the small lapping waves of the water beside. A lamp lit the scene, and it was not for another minute that Sharon heard and saw Pascale step onto the tiny port, after which she joined her in wait for Apnar.

The top of the passage could barely be seen now, and the cold stone beneath Sharon was damp but solid. Sharon could see a tunnel coming in from the left at an angle of about forty-five degrees, and one leaving the access point in the opposite direction. The tunnel to the left of her, by which Apnar was coming, was bright and lit, but the tunnel to her right was dark and gloomy like the hole she had just come down through. Occasionally, waves leapt onto the port, and the lamp nearby flickered erratically.

"Has this always been here?" Sharon asked, keen to know how old the network was, mainly to estimate how safe it might be.

"The wells pre-date AAI, but the network was only built when the Tower was, with bits added on, to Palace House and the hospital, for example. It's thought that prisoners were sentenced to a lifetime wandering the network, originally, which is why it's sort of maze-like near the Tower at the oldest section. Since then it's lain dormant, only for secret agencies to use!"

"Wow. Who else knows about this place?" Sharon inquired further.

"Some high-up government intelligence officials, the Resistance, you and Apnar, Mr. Lucas and Nemo! It's kept very secretive. Apnar should be here soon, if on schedule," Pascale replied.

Sharon thought about what her doorman had said that morning, and knew Apnar could not be late, or early. At precisely the time estimated by Pascale, Apnar came sailing round the corner to the port in triumph at having navigated the waters to arrive at the correct destination at the correct time.

"Apnar!" Sharon called out.

"Yes, it is I." He sounded profound, obviously proud of his navigating skills.

Apnar leapt out of his boat and onto the stone platform, desperate for a rest.

"Smooth journey?" said Pascale.

"It was, more or less. But where next?" asked Apnar, not having noticed the tunnel leading away to the right.

"There," said Pascale, pointing to that tunnel.

"Oh…" was Apnar's timid reply.

"Did you secure the fountain properly?" Pascale interrogated.

"Yes, yes. Everything went well."

"I just hope it continues to go that way," Sharon commented fearfully.

"Come on, there's no time to spare. Sharon, you come in this boat with me. Apnar, you sail behind. I'll navigate; the waters aren't rough, but the network is complex. It's easy to get lost, so keep close behind," instructed Pascale.

"Right," Apnar and Sharon chorused.

Apnar boarded his little ship once more, and Sharon followed Pascale into the other rowing boat which had been tied up in wait for them since they came down. It had two oars, which Pascale operated commandingly while

Sharon sat behind. Pascale lifted the oars and set off down the dark tunnel, clutching the map she had withdrawn from her pocket seconds before.

"Straight on until I say!" she shouted loudly, her voice echoing around the tunnels.

The all-encompassing darkness spread across all the travellers, and as the boats passed tunnels to the left and right, the eeriness of the place grew accumulatively.

"Now, right. Follow me!" Pascale commanded Apnar, steering the boat round with the oars.

The boats had only just turned when a new command was issued. "Second left!" Pascale screamed excitedly.

The boats turned slowly and sailed past gloomy tunnels leading to dead ends. "Left again!" was the next direction. "Right, now left ... straight on ... left then sharp right ... forward then left, right, left, left, right, left, right ... follow on ... straight ahead," the directions continued, order after order, never stopping as the maze complexified.

"Now, all ready, sharp left, go!" was the final direction.

The new tunnel was lit by several candles burning in glass cases on the walls. At the end was a raised platform, the final access point, the final port. Everything glowed in the candlelight, and a terrifying silence fell all around. Pascale tied up her boat silently, before Apnar did the same. There was a carved wooden staircase which ascended from the port to the chamber above. Pascale bravely went first, climbing the steps with courage. Sharon followed her, with Apnar bringing up the rear. This was time to confront the great mystery of Sulla, that puzzling phenomenon, the Oracle. It was not just some pagan heresy; it was a living being, a feat of artificial intelligence, programmed to answer any question posed to it, and it was steeped in obscurity.

Up above was a huge vaulted chamber, with a colossal great platform resting in the middle, upon which stood what looked like the base of a statue. But there was no statue. The ceiling was dark but for tiny lit candles all around the perimeter. Sharon approached the central object with fear. As she came closer, gentle light radiated from it, and doom felt imminent. In silence, Apnar walked forward, withdrawing the Yriadian Emerald from his inside pocket. Instantly it glowed mystically; the brightness was intense, and Pascale guided Apnar towards the Oracle's pedestal, where Apnar inserted the glowing emerald into the space provided in the monument. The stone glowed brighter and brighter as Apnar walked closer, and when he had pushed it into the pedestal, blinding light, intense as the sun's, flooded every area of the chamber. Sharon feared to look on as a great bright green ghost-like being arose from the light out of no-where. It was like a genie emerging from a bottle, but much more spectacular. It grew until its height equalled the tip of the high ceiling's, and its single feature, its mouth, began to move when fully awakened.

"I am awakened from my torpor. My dormancy is over, the Emerald Star of the Temple of Onyx has been returned to me. Who dares enter the lair of the Oracle? Who is my champion?" the Oracle boomed terrifyingly, in a strong feminine voice.

Neither Apnar nor Sharon was able to speak, because of their awe and amazement at this miraculous wonder.

"I know who you are, both of you, and your new accomplice. I cannot tell you anything until you ask me a question, but one between you all, for you have found me and returned to me my precious possession."

Sharon walked forward, trembling.

"Please tell me how I can escape this world to get back to my own," Sharon asked the Oracle, scared to tell it any more information.

"Sharon Jarls, you have asked the Oracle a question... I must accept this question as your final one. I know the answer, Sharon, and I shall tell you it today. Fear not, for you may escape this present world to return to the one you know by means of a phenomenon as mysterious as I, far north of the Imperial border. There is a portal, beyond the Omega Spires, which it is possible to enter freely, and which will take you, instantaneously, back to your world. Through this portal alone may you return to your Earth, but be warned: the portal is not open forever. It will close after a period of half a postin has elapsed since the enterer first appeared here. It is dangerous to go there, but it is the only way out.

"I have told you more than I have ever told anyone in an answer, because I am grateful for the return of the emerald. I must go now, and rest. This is the final solemn caution of the Oracle: none of you may tell anyone about what has happened here today, about this place or about me, otherwise terror will befall you, by the government and the Emperor himself, who is my protector."

The great image then fell down and died away, leaving a green mist around the gigantic hall and fear and hope in Sharon's heart. She knew the secret to returning to Earth, and she was determined to use it as quickly as possible.

Sharon could see a large solid gold door across the hall, which led undoubtedly to the Oracle's vast supply of wealth, its treasury. Apnar and Pascale backed away from the central object and returned with Sharon to the staircase down to the tunnels. It was time to return to Arrawor Hall, and to make plans to go to Boothcotia to return the girl who had helped Sharon to her place of birth. The two rowing boats were waiting for the trio to depart upon, and Pascale took up the oars of hers whilst Apnar took his; Sharon boarded Pascale's boat, and sailed down the long, lit tunnel back to the network which awaited them.

This time, Pascale did not shout orders and directions; she was too awestruck by the Oracle's mighty gaze to do so, and so Apnar just had to follow her through the maze silently.

"A portal," said Sharon to Pascale excitedly.

"It's amazing," Pascale replied. "No-one knew… there were, of course, the legends about the Omega Spires, but a portal to another world, well, that's spectacular. I've never heard a legend about that, though I expect there are some."

"What *are* the Omega Spires?" Sharon pondered outwardly.

Apnar, overhearing the discussion, gave an answer which he knew Sharon would understand.

"Do you remember the towers I showed you along the coast?" he said.

"Yes," Sharon answered.

"It's the final one of those. Omega, as being the last letter in the Accepted Alphabet," Apnar continued.

"You mean the Greek alphabet?"

"I mean the Accepted Alphabet, the writing used for formal reports and such like, and as used by writers long ago."

"As in, Motortranspo?" Sharon suggested.

"Yes, precisely," was Apnar's reply, turning a bend as he spoke.

"I still don't understand how I came here, though. There're too many questions unanswered," Sharon observed.

"Well, you've had your chance with the Oracle," joked Pascale, laughing.

"That's true. If the portal is north of the border, and I arrived south of it, in the middle of a field of all places, surely I couldn't have come through the portal. What do you think?" she asked questioningly.

"You're right – that seems strange. But I'm no wizard, I don't know about all the complex theories and spells," Pascale responded. Of course, Sharon knew she meant she was no physicist.

"Apnar, do you have any ideas?" Sharon continued to quiz.

"I'm afraid not. You obviously didn't come through the portal, or at least not that portal, but I don't know how by any other means you *could* have arrived."

With this final perplexing remark, Sharon sat silently for the remainder of the journey, until at last she and her fellow travellers arrived at the Palace House port, where they disembarked and tied up their boats.

"What should we do with my boat?" Apnar asked Pascale.

"Oh, just leave it. It'll block people from getting around from the hospital. It might be an Age before anyone else discovers this place, perhaps no-one else ever will. The government might just use it, but I'd doubt it. It'd draw too much attention to it, and to the Oracle," Pascale replied.

"Right," said Apnar, leaving his boat and following Pascale and Sharon up the huge ladder to the outside world.

The climb was arduous and tiring, but Sharon knew what she had endeavoured to know from the very beginning of her quest, and so it was definitely worth it, unquestionably necessary, and quite obviously enjoyable for Sharon, despite the difficulty. Gradually, the port below grew out of sight, and a tiny dot of light could be seen up above, in the gardens of Palace House. Sharon climbed and climbed, and as she did so that glimmer of light gradually became a spot, then a small circle, a larger circle, a still larger circle, until it became life-size, large enough for Sharon to pull herself up through and emerge out onto dry land after Pascale. She did so, and clambering down from the fountain, Apnar emerged behind her, exhausted.

"Let me just put this thing back together again," Apnar said, approaching the dismounted parts of the fountain. "Just after I get my breath back!"

After a short while of regaining his strength, Apnar re-assembled the fountain to its previous disused glory, and all three left the hidden garden, walked through the public gardens, through the grand back entrance of the house, and down the main hall to the ticket desk, when all three walked out of the house, down the drive and on their way home, or at least the most available alternative, Apnar's home.

Apnar resumed command from this point on, negotiating all the travel arrangements. The three walked round the Tower, satisfied that they had just entered its crypt without the attention of security, and boarded the nearest passing vessel.

"Seven Forden leaves, thank ye," said the old Northerner who was steering the small boat.

"A very reasonable price indeed. Here," said Apnar, paying the boatman and smiling at his unusual saving.

The boat took the trio up L'Attler, under the great bridge, past the high courts, the palace, and a few of the family seats of peers, until arriving at Arrawor Hall as Apnar directed. Apnar pointed out each stately home in turn, telling the other two about their owners.

"That's Fortescape Hall, home of the Baron Fortescape. That's Verney House, home of the Baron Verney. And that's Egsham Manor just behind it, home of the Baron Egsham. And not forgetting Wintermeath Castle..."

Here he was cut off by Sharon. "Home of the Baron Wintermeath," she suggested.

"Home of the *Baroness* Wintermeath, in fact, a great friend of my father's," was Apnar's reply.

As servants realised that His Lordship and his guests had arrived back, a few came running anxiously down the drive to the stone port to greet them.

"Your Lordship, welcome back," one said graciously.

"Thank you. It's been a terribly long haul. Could someone get me some Clarence Clemency, please? I'm famished," Apnar asked. 'Clarence Clemency' was apparently an expensive, and terribly strong, vintage of wine.

Apnar led his guests up the long drive, walking (for once) up to the glorious house which was his inheritance. All would be well; at last, Sharon could rest knowing her future was safe and that there was a glimmer of hope for her if she could reach the portal in time. Pascale's request would make that more difficult, but Sharon at last knew how to return to Earth, and need not worry over her journey; no longer lost, Sharon had come a long way in one day.

CHAPTER NINETEEN

Mentor's Folly

"But what I want to know is: how do we get to Boothcotia? I'd rather avoid Port of Mansleigh, and yet there's no other active port," thought Apnar out loud in the Grosvenor Lounge, sipping wine and talking over future plans with Sharon and Pascale as a roaring fire blazed in the background.

"Well..." considered Pascale, crunching the last morsels of some delicious ginger snaps.

"Don't tell me you've another secret to tell us!" exclaimed Apnar, laughing.

"Not so much a *secret*, as such..." Pascale continued, slowly releasing more and more information.

"Well, if it isn't a secret, then it's fine to tell; it's in the 'public domain'," added Sharon coaxingly.

"I'm not so sure. It's not in the 'public domain', and there're very few people who know about it. Neither the Government nor the Resistance have a clue," Pascale said, continuing to stall sharing the information she was apparently keeper to.

"Well I don't," said Apnar.

Pascale turned to Sharon for acknowledgment of her ignorance. "Of course I don't!" she said in answer to Pascale's inquiring stare.

"I'd better say, then, if I'm to get back, though it's not entirely safe, you know."

Sharon was not in the least surprised that it might involve danger – anything to do with Pascale usually did.

"Yes, you'd better," Apnar inveigled.

"There is a coastal tower, supposed to be uninhabited, but really active, on the south-east coast, just below Sémento of all places. There *is* a master of it, however, who owns a secret pass, an underwater pass, which crosses the ocean and joins land again at Smuggler's Point in Boothcotia. I was going to suggest it anyway, you see, because ships from Port of Mansleigh only sail to Mouthbrock Port, in Westclock. It'd take us another septday to get to Boothcot Wells; no tunnelled network exists in Zutravenstein, and the one in Boothcotia is pretty primitive. The Mentor will allow us to cross via his secret tunnel…"

"But at what price?" Apnar inquired suspiciously.

"I don't know. It *could* be monetary, or it could just be for us to keep his secret; I honestly don't know," Pascale answered, a little worried.

Sharon was a little astonished at Apnar's suspicious question, not that he had any obligation to pay for her sake or Pascale's.

"I'd better tell you, then. Part of the family-owned forests in Fordenia has been burnt; it was a spontaneous natural combustion. There seems to be no reason for it, but it just means that, until I earn more and my father investigates, I just have to be a little more careful with my investments," Apnar explained.

"I'm so sorry, Apnar. How much has gone, if you don't mind me asking?" Sharon inquired.

"That's quite all right; it's about twenty per cent of the family fortune. We'll survive, of course; there is a back-up investment in the Fordenian Bank, but that's only activated in total emergencies, and only worth around twenty per cent of the total anyway. If the branches gone can grow back quickly we'll be fine, but if the infection spreads and all our forests die, well, it could be disastrous." Apnar hung his head.

"I'm sure they'll grow back soon. Don't worry," comforted Pascale.

Apnar was still one of the wealthiest people in the whole Empire, but this 'event' was evidently still rather shocking and disturbing.

"If I might continue…?" Pascale asked, trying to pursue the original course of discussion.

"Please do," Apnar consented.

"From Smuggler's Point we can travel to Boothcot Wells by land and then return by the same route," Pascale continued.

"Are there real smugglers at that 'point'?" Sharon asked timidly, afraid of running into some old acquaintances.

"I'm afraid so, but we shan't run into any. We're underground, remember; I think we emerge over ground somewhere in the middle of a lawn improvement field," Pascale returned.

"The Boothcotians cultivate grass, they're mad about lawns. I mean, I do like a nice green lawn, but to chop it up every winter and send it to a big processing plant, well, I think it's a bit much," Apnar explained to Sharon.

"Traditionally, Boothcotians grow huge lawns which they ensure are kept luscious and green by sending them to special processing plants over winter to protect and rejuvenate them. It's just tradition, however obsessive," Pascale added.

"I understand," said Sharon.

"I'm glad somebody does. That's it – I'm going to bed now," Pascale concluded.

"So am I," said Sharon, tired.

"But it's only early evening!" Apnar exclaimed.

"We're still tired." Sharon answered for herself and Pascale.

"Well, suit yourself. I think I might sort out some files and make some calls. Good night," Apnar said finally.

"Good night, Apnar," bade Sharon.

"Good night," Pascale called, leaving the room.

The two girls asked the nearest doorman to guide them to their respective rooms, which he did.

"Thank you very much," said Sharon, bidding good night to Pascale, whose room was further away.

Sharon entered her room and fell onto the nearest chair to relax. She was not quite ready for sleep, and endlessly bored of history. Feeling adventurous, Sharon plucked a book out from the case at random, and began to read at her leisure.

'Modern Philosophic' was what it was entitled.

'A Compendious Interpretation of Knowledge and Thinking

as written by scholars of the Royal Society of Philosophy, Boothcot Wells'

Such was the frontispiece, and despite its lugubrious title, Sharon decided to read on, as she would be in Boothcot Wells soon, and she was curious Boothcotian philosophers thought.

'CHAPTER ALPHA

'It has long been considered by philosophers and thinkers of times gone by that the essential existence of matter, that is to say the being of an object as opposed to an idea formulated in the mind (including abstract cognitions), was contrary to

all that our thinking was and, to an extent, still is, and that its historic comprehension by the minds of the philosophers, especially Plutolarch, was, in their own words, 'unfound and unsound quarrellings', and that nothing existed except in the mind, this ideology being widely contested by philosophers and their learned condisciples overturning such thinking, thanks to the founding of that most esteemed establishment, the gentle flow of knowledge and enlightenment from which has long determined all conceptualisation and undesigned materialisation in the reality of the minds, as Plutolarch might have said, of 'wandering folly-makers', lost in the mists of urbanisation and, to the most unreasonable degree, empiricism, the Royal Society of Philosophy.'

This sentence was the longest Sharon had ever read or heard spoken aloud, and it convinced her exceedingly well (good philosophy *should* convince you well) to place down the book immediately! The periphrastic usage of language was ridiculous and absurd, and Sharon did not know where to begin working out the meaning in it, if indeed there was any. She placed the book back on the shelf, where it truly belonged, and changed for bed, after closing the curtains, and before lying down to sleep. Sharon was safe and sound, and well on her way to Earth.

Next morning, Sharon dressed herself in a dazzling pink dress and adorned herself with a beautiful necklace she had found in a drawer in her room. Eager to know more about the 'Mentor', she scoured the bookcase for a guide. This she found, entitled 'The Towers of Sullaria'. It was an arranged guide to each of the towers around the country, and Sharon flicked forward to 'Mentor's Folly':

'This particular Tower has lain empty and disused for an age now, as its last keeper disappeared and has never been found or even seen again. It lies on the south-west coast, and was previously the home to the Order of the Mentor members, of which there used to be many, but now remain none. They met in secret in the Folly for social and official occasions. It is not certain what the Order promoted, but it is known that the members often travelled abroad, especially to Fordenia. It has been suggested that it may have been a league of entrepreneurs who, with the help of the Mentor, bought up shares in the Fordenian forests. No trees have yet been discovered under the name of the Order, however. Several legends and mysteries surround the Folly, the most famous of which is the Mentor's connection with low-life characters from overseas, dealing with them for money to channel into the Order's financial ventures.'

Sharon thought straight away of what must have happened: the 'low-life characters' were smugglers from Boothcotia who used the Mentor's secret tunnel to travel between Sullaria and their home country in order to conduct their illegal business, and they paid the Mentor for this service, who in turn used this money to fund the Order's secret purchases. It was obvious to conclude, then, that the Mentor was not at all a law-abiding fellow, and nor was he particularly inviting or welcoming to visitors. Sharon knew she was in for an exciting day.

Just as she began looking up the Omega Spires, a knock at her door startled her and the book fell to the ground. It was Apnar, inviting her to breakfast.

"Sharon, breakfast's ready. Are you?" he asked.

"Yes, I'm just coming," Sharon replied, placing the book down on a nearby table. She opened the door and accompanied Apnar to breakfast, set for her downstairs.

"You look beautiful," Apnar complimented.

"Thank you," she replied, smiling.

"I've arranged for us to go to a little country under-tree station. I've never heard of the things, but apparently they do exist. There's one very near to Mentor's Folly, and it's possible for us to go there today to see the Mentor with Pascale. She's waiting in the dining room, and she's very excited about returning to Boothcot Wells. It must have been terrible for her living so far away from home, a bit like your ordeal, eh?" Apnar continued.

"A bit longer than mine, though, I hope."

"I hope so too, for your sake. Here we are, just the same as last time you came to the Hall."

Apnar led Sharon through the familiar doors into the same dining room Sharon had eaten in when she had last been at Sulla, where Pascale was already sitting ready to dine.

"Good morning all!" said Pascale in a sprightly manner.

"Good morning, Pascale," greeted Sharon.

"Hello again," said Apnar.

Sharon sat down at the table and began to devour her light breakfast over Apnar's conversation.

"You know, country stations are quite abundant, they tell me. Personally, I've never been to one. Have either of you?"

"I haven't," said Pascale.

"I have," Sharon revealed, munching her way through a slice of toast. "When I came from the Shanklot Corridor down to Sulla I came by a country station, I think. It was in the middle of no-where."

"I see, yes of course. Apparently, there're little minions that run them," commented Apnar.

"Well, they're not human, anyway," replied Sharon.

"Hmm. Pascale, the fact that you've never been to a country station really begs the question: have you ever been to Mentor's Folly?" Apnar continued, becoming suspicious.

"Well, no. But…" Pascale answered.

"Right, so how do you even know it exists?" Apnar's scepticism was quite off-putting.

"No, no, I'm quite sure. My mother went there, you know, when she was a girl, but can't remember much about it, I'm afraid," was Pascale's excuse.

Surprisingly, she had subdued Apnar.

"I see. I suppose I'll have to trust you, and I do," he said.

"I was reading last night, you know, from the books in the bookcase in my room. I picked up a book on the Royal Society of Philosophy, but it was incredibly confusing, so I put it down again," Sharon remarked amicably.

Pascale laughed. "That wouldn't surprise me. The RSoP's based in Boothcotia; my father's an under-lecturer. He comes out with a load of nonsense half the time."

They all laughed.

"Pascale, I was reading about Mentor's Folly this morning, and I wondered if you knew some of the things I read," Sharon continued.

"You mean its history?" Pascale inquired.

"Yes. I read that it's not used anymore, but it used to be run by the Mentor who organised a sort of group of investors as part of his 'Order'. Did you know that?"

"Well, the Folly's not quite in disuse. The Mentor didn't disappear; he just got out of public sight. And the investors, yes I did hear that once. I think the Mentor let out the underground passage to smugglers, in exchange for cash, to fund his schemes," Pascale replied.

Apnar cut in. "Cash?"

"Don't worry. The Order's dissolved, so he doesn't really need it now."

"Why would you need money if you never left your home?" Sharon asked rhetorically.

"Exactly," Pascale agreed.

"But what's all this about an Order?" asked Sharon.

"Orders are owned by each Master of the Towers, and the decoration can be awarded to anyone they please. Not all have used them, however. The Order of the Mentor's been extinct for an age, though, surely?" Apnar explained.

Pascale nodded in agreement with him, a rare occurrence indeed.

"I thought we'd leave for the Folly this obtuse, you know. Time is marching on – we'll need to be at the station soon," Pascale proposed.

"Very well, then. We'll depart immediately," announced Apnar, getting up from the table and beckoning his guests to come to the door of the room and to go back to their bedrooms to get ready to leave in an angle.

Apnar left for his own room, while Pascale and Sharon were each granted the use of a servant on-hand to lead them back to their respective bed-chambers. Sharon's bedroom was as it was, and she tried hard to think what she would need. How far would the Folly be from Sulla? It was just past Sémento, so not far by the tunnels. And so Sharon's unstoppable stream of thought continued, from idea to idea, from consideration to consideration. She picked up a matching jacket to wear in case the underground passage to Boothcotia was cold or damp, or both. It was only then, in her room alone, that she realised what a hindrance having to go abroad would be. She had a time limit for going home; the portal would soon close, and if there were to be any problems on the way there, it could potentially be disastrous for Sharon's own quest; all her work, and that of the others helping her, could be in vain. Despite the struggle ahead, Sharon held her head high above the parapet and, closing her door gracefully, walked to the front door, this time without an escort.

Apnar and Pascale were there already, waiting for her so they could all be on their way to the station.

"Come on! I've got a little private hoverer fit for three that can take us to the river, across it, and then navigate through the streets to the station. It's marvellous, brand new from Sonique's Catalogue, completely unmanned; I just hope it works well!" Apnar bellowed proudly. Evidently, the fire in Fordenia had not hit his pocket too hard.

"Let me show you this!" he continued rampantly, walking ahead round the huge house to a nearby portion of the dramatically landscaped gardens, his face beaming like an eager child's.

The 'hoverer' was like a small boat which hovered about a foot off the ground. Apnar opened a tiny side door and he let Sharon and Pascale go in first, after whom he too entered. They basked in the glorious sunlight all around and Apnar fiddled with a few buttons and levers to send the hoverer down the long drive and down the river to the bridge. The vehicle hovered silently above the busy river as it navigated independently of Apnar through the many more traditional boats which were littered all over the river. At the bridge the little craft elevated itself upwards like a helicopter to the main street above, from where it hovered down the road to the gigantic block which was the station, above the traffic below. When they had arrived at the doors, Apnar manoeuvred some switches to send the craft on its way home after he and his visitors had got down safely onto dry land.

"Right, Pascale, you take us from here, eh?" invited Apnar as the hoverer whizzed down the street and out of sight.

"Sure, we'll need to go to Countryside Departures – that should bypass the cities and stop off at several country stations instead. I've done the tiniest bit of research, and we need to get to Westerley Station," Pascale informed him, taking up Apnar's offer gladly. She obviously liked to be in charge.

All three walked into the passage which led to the main atrium, Pascale leading and Apnar bringing up the rear once again. Pascale led the party across the atrium to 'Countryside Departures', as she said she would, and down the stairs she guided them to the appropriate platform. There were only a handful of people waiting for the next string of capsules south, a rarity for a station such as Sulla.

Eventually, a train arrived, and being short it soon filled with passengers. Pascale opened the door of one capsule and entered, followed by Sharon and finally Apnar. The capsules were old and ragged, but reasonably comfortable inside. Suddenly the increasingly familiar image on the screen flashed up:

"Good day, ladies and gentlemen. This string of capsules terminates at Sryville Station, Westerleyshire, through Juntreaux, Sémento, Delftware, Carltonsimms, Upper Quire, Mid-Quire, Lower Quire, Old Trumpinghampton-on-the-Wyeming, Westerley, Dunnings, Howe and Market Raisin."

Despite the apparent lengthiness of the journey, it was surprisingly short, and the train hit a platform every thirty seconds, though thankfully not literally. It was actually rather annoying, but Westerleyshire was arrived at in no time. Sharon had little time to spare, of course, and wanted to be on her way as quickly as possible.

"Sryville Country Station. Thank you for travelling Motortranspo," saluted the image finally before the three left the capsule and walked onto the tiny platform provided.

"Up this way, and that'll be us, I should think," said Pascale, leading Sharon and Apnar up the stairway to the outside world through a small trap door. There seemed to be no-one around, but Sharon knew that was not the case. Naturally, there was a tree very nearby, which Sharon knew housed a small ticket desk. But there was nothing to pay; they had received a free ride, courtesy of Motortranspo. The little 'minion' must have been asleep, Sharon thought!

In the distance could be seen the huge tower that was Mentor's Folly, rising menacingly above the blank canvas of the countryside.

"Look, there!" shouted Sharon. "It's the Folly!"

"So I see," replied Apnar scathingly.

"It's huge," commented Sharon.

"And we're a while away, as well. Just wait until we get close up, only then can one truly appreciate the real scale of that structure," remarked Pascale intellectually.

Both Apnar and Sharon nodded in agreement and joined Pascale on a little trek over the hill ahead to the Folly. The hill was grassy and radiant in the full zenith of orblight which came streaming down from the 'orb in the sky'. The trio walked up a gentle slope before having to come right down again, only in order to clamber up a terribly steep slope! But with the blazing hope of Pascale, the journey was made simple and her determination ensured that the Folly was reached in little more than a minute.

"Behold!" said Pascale in an eerie tone, slightly mock-serious.

"How do we get in?" asked Apnar practically, ignoring the dynamic beauty of the landmark and cutting straight to the chase.

"There's a door on the other side," replied Pascale wishfully.

"I see," Sharon added.

The Folly was as majestic as the Ruler himself, and stood proudly over everything in sight. Its shape resembled that of a lighthouse with its top cut off, but it did not in any way epitomise the classic clean white structure of your typical lighthouse, because it was grey and unpainted, waiting to be blown down by some rampaging wind. But the beauty and historical importance of the building would have made it a prime picking for restoration. Why had it not been restored and transformed into a great and glorious monument to the Age, to the Empire even? Sharon knew, Pascale knew, Apnar knew, those in the Order of the Mentor knew (if there were any left), the Government herself knew, and indeed the Mentor knew: the Master of the Tower, as the title rings so grandly, was still in residence and would refuse to surrender his home to the nation.

"Look, down there," pointed out Pascale enthusiastically.

Down a small flight of old and worn stone steps to a little enclosure around the Tower itself was the entrance. It was a shabby wooden door, bolted and locked with innumerable locks, and the green paint which would once have shone brightly on its face was all but gone. Pascale went first up to the door, knocking repeatedly to no answer. After some time trying this means of entrance to no avail whatsoever, Pascale broke down in a flood of tears, the watery droplets continuing to flow from her eyes unrepentantly.

"Pascale, stop, please," Apnar consoled.

"Yes, we'll get in, and if we don't we'll get to Boothcotia anyway. Come on, calm down," added Sharon, trying desperately to soothe her new friend.

"It's over, it's over!" Pascale wailed; neither Sharon nor Apnar had ever seen her so upset.

"No, no, it's anything but over, Pascale. Come on now, let's call on the Mentor, and perhaps he'll answer us," Apnar continued, abating Pascale's tears and leading the poor girl back to the door.

"Mentor, Mentor! Master of the Tower, we want to see you!!" Apnar called to no effect.

"We know you're there; we know you own the underground passage, and we'd like to use it," Sharon shouted to the lonely inhabitant of the Folly.

"Come down, let us in! We *must* speak with you," called Pascale, finally back to her commanding self.

For a moment, there came no response, no movement, no sound, and no action. But then, with accurate ears could be heard the distinct noise of footsteps, descending a long stone staircase. Undoubtedly, this had to be the Mentor. Without a word, somebody inside the Folly could be heard unlocking and unbolting the many security locks positioned all over the door, and eventually, after a tense period of waiting, the door creaked open slowly to reveal a small and old man with a long grey beard, wearing a dark green cloak which covered him from the neck downwards. On his head was a tall hat, flopping down behind him; the whole attire was musty and grim, covered in ancient dust and languishing in the senility of the Folly and its Master.

"It is I, the Master of the Tower, the Mentor of the Folly. Follow me if you wish to do business," the Mentor said in a coarse battered voice. "But come no further if your motives are unhealthy!"

The word 'business' slightly frightened Apnar, keen to avoid any more monetary transactions between himself and any other creature. The little Mentor, with puppet-like movements, then led his visitors up a long winding spiral staircase up a side of the Folly which was cold and dark. The steps seemed to spiral up forever, only very seldom passing a window.

At the top, after an exhausting haul which must have been absolutely death-threatening to the tiny Mentor, the four people entered a large circular room with four windows positioned at the four major compass points. Most unexpectedly, this uppermost room, possibly one of the only rooms in the Tower, was decorated quite substantially and tastefully. The walls were painted white, there were dark wooden floorboards, and landscape paintings hung around the room. It was surprisingly light, and several candles helped light the area, including one on a large desk at the far end of the room. There were mahogany chairs assembled around a dying fire in the large fireplace, and cases overflowing with books. A musical instrument was hung on one wall, though Sharon could not work out what it was, or even how it was supposed to be played. Yet the most striking feature of all in the Folly did tone down the nicety of the place, and that was dust: mountains of it. As Sharon entered the room she led her finger along a nearby table to find that it was at least an inch thick in dust, settled over an unimaginable length of time.

The Mentor sat at his desk, brushing off dust from his chair, causing an irrepressible flurry of the filth to dance about the room. He coughed and spluttered exasperatingly and opened the North window wide. In silence, he opened a desk drawer, to another filthy flurry, and took out a pair of spectacles which he placed far down his Roman nose. He beckoned the three to come forward and bring up seats to his desk, and when this action was completed and all were seated, he began to speak quietly and slowly, in a kind of gruff, elderly voice.

"I - I understand you have come to use my passage?" he said inquiringly.

"Yes we have. Will you let us?" Pascale asked, electing herself spokesperson.

"W - w - w - well, that depends on wha - wha - wha - what reason you have for wanting to use it," the Mentor explained.

"I need to get home to Boothcot Wells; I assisted these people and now they would like to assist me," Pascale said.

"Understand-a-bub-ly," the Mentor added.

There was an awkward silence for a while before Pascale ventured to say something:

"Well?"

"I have decided to allow you all use of my passage. However, this comes on the condition that you tell no - no - no-one about it. It is extremely secretive, and I don't even dare to ask how *you* came to know of it. Very well; the matter is settled. Let me show you the gate to the passage."

CHAPTER TWENTY

Mentor's Tunnel

The Mentor rose from his chair most awkwardly and escorted his visitors out of the chamber to the landing, from which he took his guests down the narrow staircase to the front door. He then led them round the stone staircase to a door at the back of the tower, which had a little window in the top half, revealing further fields outside.

"Here," the Mentor instructed.

None of the three could see how this humble door, leading outside, could possibly lead them to the underground passage. The Mentor revealed the secret, however, by unlocking the door and opening it to reveal a surprising element of the Tower: instead of luscious green fields bathed in the full glory of orblight, there was an exceedingly dark little room behind the door. The window was a fake; the image behind it was a painting strapped onto the hidden side of the door. The Mentor realised the surprise of his guests and chuckled contentedly as he led them down the passage. Then, in complete darkness, he walked steadily down a massive but narrow stone staircase with the visiting trio behind. At the bottom, he waved his hands in the air above him, and instantly two wall-mounted torches, one on either side of a great wooden door, illuminated the area in eerie firelight.

"This is the gate; the passage lies beyond it. Keep going until you reach the tunnel's end."

With this final instruction, the Mentor pushed open the grand door to reveal the dark passage, lighting it in the same manner as he had just lit the torches outside the tunnel. Sharon could see a long corridor, stretching out for what looked like eternity. Then, without a word, he closed the door behind the three and walked away out of sight.

For a moment or two a scary silence ensued, when only the occasional draught could be heard along the passage. Who knew where it would end, thought Sharon? Some guessed, some thought they knew, but who really knew? Sharon felt that all she could do would be to trust in her friends and the Mentor and walk on intrepidly, as she had always done. The passage stretched out endlessly, nothing but the horizon to stop it from continuing, and this apparent perpetuity could only play on the young minds that were now held in the passage's harness.

"How long will this take, again?" Apnar ventured, hoping to avoid extreme exhaustion.

"Not long, come on!" Pascale answered, obviously in an adventurous spirit.

"Indeed," Apnar returned suspiciously.

Sharon was too busy thinking to talk. Feeling a little selfish, she thought what a waste of time it was to be going to Boothcotia, when she herself would need to speed up her quest up north, since the portal would close soon. But then she wondered what situation she would be in if Pascale had not crossed her path; what if Pascale had never set eyes on her or Apnar? What then? The answer was blatantly obvious: Sharon would never have gained access to the Oracle, she would never have known the details about the portal, and she would never have been on her way to escaping the world she was entrapped in. It was not bad fortune that Sharon had come to know Pascale; in fact, aside from meeting the Bugle-Thoms, Sophios, and Apnar, it was probably the best thing that had happened to her on her journey. This positivity strengthened Sharon, and she ploughed on through the darkness with her assistants as they made their way across the long passage of ocean through the tunnel.

"Look!" exclaimed Apnar, at last excited. Sharon and Pascale looked over to see an archway, beyond which was a steel cart on wheels, fixed to a pair of rails which led down into what appeared to be infinity.

"It's a long way down," remarked Sharon, slightly anxious, her voice echoing many times over.

"It's also the only way down. Come on," instructed Pascale, moving forward to take position in the cart.

She was soon joined by Sharon and Apnar, wondering what to do next. The three heaved their strongest to make the cart move, but it did not budge. At last, being observant, Apnar spotted a very small lever to the left of the cart, which he pulled with great difficulty towards him. As soon as his hand was back in the safety of the cart, the vehicle shot down the rails at immense speed, rocketing down like a rollercoaster. The walls whizzed by, and the three had to drop their torches before being themselves enflamed in the blazing fire. Darkness cloaked the area, making the terror more intense, and the anxiety all the greater. At first, it seemed to go down at forty-five degrees, but soon became steeper, cutting deep into the ocean. Finally, the cart came to an abrupt halt after a rather steep slope, almost catapulting its passengers into the lit corridor ahead.

The trio left the cart and walked along the short, lit hall, before turning left to be faced with a most amazing sight. This, the deepest section of the tunnel, had glass walls which curved round the travellers cylindrically, as if they were walking through a plastic bottle. What was most wonderful was that the walls revealed the various creatures alive in the ocean depths, this particular stretch of ocean illuminated by torches on either side of the pathway. All kinds of small fish could be seen making their way slowly around the depths of the ocean which bridged Sullaria and Boothcotia, none of them particularly large, none of them particularly fierce-looking, and none of them particularly interesting. Sharon was more concerned about the level of pressure on the tunnel, and how it was held up.

The three walked quickly along the long, straight tunnel, Pascale leading the way. All they could hear was an eerily quiet low-pitched humming noise, the sound of the sea. But the relative silence was soon broken by the sound of steady droplets of water drip- drip-dripping from the top of the tunnel. All three heard it, all three felt the occasional drip on their shoulders, but all three walked on in silence. But it was not about to stop. The drips grew into trickles, creating tiny puddles on the floor of the tunnel, and the walls began to shake ever so slightly.

"Pascale?" Sharon prompted.

Pascale turned round, her slightly furrowed brow lit up by the lamps either side.

"Yes? I'm sure we're quite safe, Sharon," Pascale replied, a little perturbed herself.

"Remember we're a long way down, Sharon. This sort of thing's to be expected. I'm sure it'll stop in a moment or two," Apnar said in support from behind.

Suddenly there was a giant crash against the left wall of the tunnel – an almighty bump which made the whole structure wobble uncontrollably, sending Sharon, Apnar and Pascale falling to the floor in an instant. All the lamps in the tunnel were blown out, and a great gush of water fell through the cracks in the ceiling. Sharon and Pascale let out shocked screeches, while Apnar got up sensibly and took out a lamplighter from his pocket. He picked up one of the lamps at the side of the tunnel and lit it, holding it up to the side of the tunnel which had been bumped against.

Lit up behind the glass was a gigantic, and equally horrific, fish. It had terrifying fangs which shone in the light of Apnar's lamp, and its blazing green eyes (similar to Apnar's) stared straight at all three prisoners in the tunnel, casting a vast shadow over the ocean floor beneath. Paralysed with fear, Sharon and Pascale stood still on the spot, while Apnar backed away in shock, a veil of darkness spreading over the monstrous creature.

"Wha-" Sharon began, before she was interrupted by the fish, moving away from the side of the tunnel and letting out a most peculiar, and haunting, high-pitched scream. The tunnel floor then began to quake and rock smoothly from side to side as the great beast vanished from sight, swimming under the tunnel and away to safety.

"I have no idea what that thing was…" said Pascale, fear in her eyes.

"Well, whatever it may have been, it's gone now," Apnar responded quickly, shaking himself up.

"But look at the roof!" Sharon interrupted, pointing at the leaking ceiling. "It's made the leak ten times worse!"

"Now, now, wait an angle…" Apnar began, inspecting the leakages. "It does look rather bad – I mean, we'll seriously need to get a move on if we're to get there alive."

"Get there alive?!" Pascale responded loudly.

"Well, think about it… it's only a matter of time before this place fills up with water." Apnar had a point: all three were now standing in puddles three inches deep.

"We'll have to run for it," Sharon suggested.

"I think so too. The tunnel is very long, though, so these punctures in the ceiling shouldn't cause us too much trouble if we make our way further along. Look down there," Apnar proposed, stretching out his hand with the lamp to light the way ahead. "It's dry down there."

"Not for long," Pascale added gloomily.

"That's true. But unless you want to end up wading through the tunnel, we'll have to get going. Now," replied Apnar, breaking into a jog with the others, and holding his lamp out ahead of him.

"So there's no chance of us drowning?" asked Sharon, unreservedly.

"Good gracious, no! But there's a chance we'll end up having to wade our way through here. And that's not something we should aspire to."

Sharon nodded in agreement, and just then a giant droplet of water splashed from the ceiling onto Apnar's lamp, which instantly fizzled out.

"Oh dear," Apnar lamented, fiddling for his lamplighter in his pocket. "Here we are," he said triumphantly, pulling it out and lifting three lamps from the side, lighting each in turn.

"One for each of us, all right? It seems there are a few other punctures in this tunnel's roof, but never mind. We'll just have to go a little quicker."

Pascale was now rather concerned, silently brooding over the possible outcomes of this disaster.

Sharon held out her lamp like the others and sprinted down the tunnel with them. How they were going to cross an entire ocean without being drowned seemed a mystery to her, but Apnar seemed confident enough.

"How much longer?" Sharon asked.

"How should I know?" was Apnar's less than comforting response. "Don't worry," he added, sensing Sharon's anxiety. "If the members of the Order could do it, then we can do it, flooding or no flooding."

And so they ran on. And ran on. And ran on. And… stopped, huffing and puffing, heaving and wheezing, completely out of breath. Pascale fell to her knees in an inch of water, snuffing out her lamp.

"Come – on," Apnar stumbled. "We – need – to – keep – going. We certainly won't get there by sitting here, you know."

Apnar bent down to light more lamps at the side, illuminating the tunnel once again in haunting light. The sea creatures all around seemed to snigger and scoff at these three travellers' attempts, swimming round and round the tunnel mockingly, or so it seemed to Sharon.

"Come on!" Apnar bellowed, his face now red, not with anger, but with fatigue.

Sharon helped Pascale up and walked beside her while Apnar led the way, lighting every third lamp at one side. Eventually, having traversed the tunnel for about forty angles, Apnar stopped ahead of them, a little puzzled.

"What's wrong?" Pascale asked him, a look of dread spreading across her face.

"Well, it's just…" he faltered, looking about him. "There aren't any more lamps."

"What?" said Sharon.

"They've just stopped," said Apnar, picking one up from the side and holding it ahead. About ten feet ahead of him stood a stone wall, completely blocking off the passage.

"It's a…" Sharon began.

"Wall." Pascale completed the sentence for her.

Apnar said nothing, running ahead to the wall to inspect it more closely. They were now all in two inches of water, and the depth was growing, ever so slightly, by the second. As they had moved on, they had been able to offset this, but if they could no longer go any further, the consequences could be fatal. Tiny waves lapped against the wall, while Apnar looked closely at it with his piercing eyes, his hands slowly moving over its rough surface.

Apnar pushed against the wall, and suddenly it collapsed with ease. The slightest pressure had caused it to fall through, and it fell flat onto the ground beyond.

"Look!" shouted Sharon.

All three approached the gap, holding up their lamps to see in. Beyond the gap was a capsule standing on rails which led on into what appeared to be infinity.

"Let's get in, then," suggested Apnar, opening the capsule door, which was covered in filth and grime.

"But how will it go," began Pascale, "if no-one is controlling it?"

"Perhaps we have to control it," said Sharon.

"This is a very old one," Apnar called from within the capsule.

"There's no screen, and no safety signs," he went on. "And no carpet — and these seats are all ripped."

Sharon and Pascale stood outside the capsule, looking in.

"It's obviously been well-used," suggested Pascale.

"True," Apnar agreed, waving his hand at the other two to step inside.

Once all three were inside, Apnar pulled the door shut on the capsule, and much to his surprise, it began to move slowly down the rails.

"It's moving!" Pascale pointed out, rather unnecessarily.

"And it's speeding up," said Sharon, as the capsule picked up pace and accelerated down the tunnel, making terrific clunking noises and swaying from side to side.

"How — will — we — get — out?" said Pascale questioningly, the capsule's increasing speed now affecting her ability to speak.

"It — must — stop — eventually," Apnar replied confidently, gripping the cracked leather seat he sat on with considerable vigour.

None of them could possibly speak now as the capsule rocketed down the tunnel, no longer swaying, but proceeding happily at well over six hundred miles per hour, around five times the normal speed of capsules. And it showed no sign of slowing down — indeed, for about half an hour they continued to accelerate, reaching a peak of two thousand miles per hour. Despite this, inside the capsule the passengers felt very little difference travelling at peak speed from travelling at the early six hundred mark. If they had had any idea of what speed they were travelling at, perhaps they would have thought twice about travelling to Boothcotia.

At last, however, the capsule began to decelerate, and rather more noticeably than it had accelerated. But it rattled along at around twenty miles per hour for the last five minutes, before slowing down gently to what was supposed to be a relaxed halt. Only it wasn't relaxed at all. The capsule stopped suddenly at the end of the tunnel, throwing the three passengers into each other.

"Well," said Apnar, flustered.

"What a ride!" exclaimed Sharon, having enjoyed some of this unexpected rollercoaster. Apnar rolled his eyes.

"How far have we come?" asked Pascale, more practically.

Her question was answered as Apnar pushed open the door of the capsule, revealing a very small platform, built for this single capsule. There was an archway on the wall which revealed a set of stone steps leading up out of the tunnel – this was, undoubtedly, the end of Mentor's Tunnel. Bright sunshine streamed down from the opening, illuminating the platform, and offending Sharon's unaccustomed eyes.

"Far enough," Apnar answered poignantly.

Pascale's eyes lit up with satisfaction – she had made her way home, or almost home, at least. In stunned silence she climbed out of the capsule first, walking over to the archway. Sharon followed her, but Apnar was left with a dilemma.

"But what will happen if I close the door?" he asked. "Won't it rocket off again? We'll need it to get back."

"What about the flooding, though?" Sharon pointed out quickly.

Apnar had failed to consider this slight problem; Pascale was unconcerned, now half-way up the stairway out.

"I'd forgotten about that," he replied, a little shocked. "We'll have to abandon the tunnel from hereon in, I suppose."

"But how…" began Sharon.

"I don't know," Apnar replied, his face now red. "I suppose we'll have to cross the ocean the more traditional way."

"You mean sailing?" Sharon presumed.

"Yes, of course. The Mentor won't be pleased with us, I suspect. We've ruined his passage."

"I'm sure it can be fixed…" said Sharon, doubting herself.

"Let's hope so. If not, we may be marked men again – I mean women – I mean man and woman."

"Yes," Sharon replied, laughing quietly to herself. "I mean, it wasn't our fault, was it?"

"Certainly not. And I shall see to it that the Mentor is remunerated in full, if there are any problems. But think – that wall that fell flat opened the whole capsule tunnel to the flooding, so the water will spread out very thinly indeed. It'll take days for the depth to reach a single fournis, by which time no doubt the Mentor will have it fixed. He's not stupid, and he's got a huge knowledge of magic, remember."

"I suppose so."

"I know so. Come on, Pascale's getting away…"

They laughed and Apnar slammed the capsule door shut, sending it flying off down the tunnel back to the 'pedestrian' section. There were a great deal of steps, and they were incredibly steep – Sharon counted at least three hundred before she lost count. Eventually, however, she and Apnar reached the opening, and were bathed in glorious Boothcotian sunshine.

"Isn't it wonderful?!" exclaimed Pascale, fifty feet ahead of them in a huge field of highly cared-for, pristine-condition lawn, cut in thin stripes only about an inch thick, giving it a surreal appearance.

Apnar grunted, evidently preferring the Sullarian countryside, but that was to be expected.

"It's lovely," assented Sharon. "Really nice."

"I was right, you see. We're in a lawn improvement field, quite far in from Smugglers' Point, in fact. There's the coast there, do you see?" Pascale continued.

Apnar and Sharon had now caught up with Pascale, and turned to admire the coast of the Kingdom. Open sea was all that could be seen beyond the coast – the Empire was a long, long way off.

"We'd better not stay here long, though," warned Pascale. "We really oughtn't to be here long, you know. The owner will know about the passage, but he won't want us lingering."

"We don't want to linger either," replied Apnar, for Sharon's sake.

"Very true," Sharon added. "The portal won't stay open forever, remember."

"Then let's get to Boothcot Wells immediately. It's not far from here."

"And how will we get there?" Apnar asked, still a little exhausted from all that walking earlier on.

"By a Flycraft, of course. They're banned in Sullaria, I know, and I can see why. If they became too popular they'd cause all sorts of accidents in the air, but over here they're supervised by transport officials. We can get on one at the nearest town – Stirkirk, I think."

"Stirkirk?" repeated Apnar.

"Yes, it's quite a large town just north of here, not too far from the capital. We'll be there by this evening."

"Great," said Sharon, smiling. Perhaps it would all work out, after all.

CHAPTER TWENTY-ONE

Home Sweet Home

Pascale led the way out of the 'lawn improvement field', over a wooden fence and up a little weather-beaten path.

"Stirkirk's just up here," she called back to the other two, who were straggling behind.

"Good," Sharon heard Apnar mutter under his breath.

The lane led up past the lawns to a crossroads, at which there was a neatly-labelled signpost, which indicated that Stirkirk could be reached in four angles by turning left. All signposts seemed to indicate the distance from one place to another in terms of how long it would take to get there on foot, though at Pascale's speed Stirkirk could probably be reached in half the time.

"Come on!" she shouted back at the others.

"All right, all right," Sharon called back, catching up with her.

Apnar eventually caught up with the other two and they walked blithely for a few angles before arriving at the busy town of Stirkirk.

"Here we are," said Pascale. "Now, we just need to find a Flycraft centre. Keep your eyes peeled."

Since neither Apnar nor Sharon had ever encountered a Flycraft, let alone a Flycraft centre, Pascale's instruction was rather superfluous to the say the least. Nevertheless the three entered through the town's gate and walked on up 'Wopsle Street' to the town square. The street was wide and was populated by various sorts of creatures, some being ridden on, some pulling carts, and some wandering freely, not to mention the scores of pedestrians using the road as if it were a pavement. On either side of the road were dark yellow buildings with red roofs, some shops, some restaurants, some banks. The place was abuzz with activity, though not on the scale of Sulla or Sémento, of course. But it was so much more colourful, with bright green weather vanes atop bright red spires, and fantastic yellow stone roads.

Emerging onto the town square, Sharon could see it was enclosed by pale blue-coloured buildings with white roofs, and the only entrance in was through four archways, built into the blue buildings, positioned at the four compass points. The square was full of lost tourists and trinket-sellers, though it was mainly being used as a thoroughfare for pedestrians wishing to move into another quarter of the town. On the building opposite Sharon there was a clock with a bright blue face, which showed the time to be two hundred and thirty angles, or about three o'clock.

Pascale approached the centre of the square, where there was a large signpost with signs pointing in all directions to different facilities and attractions in the town. So many signs were there that the post was at least twice Apnar's height, and there were at least forty different signs all the way from the bottom to the top.

"Look for the Flycraft centre," said Pascale to the other two, her eyes scanning the signpost carefully.

"There," said Sharon, pointing up at a sign which pointed directly towards the northern archway. In elaborate gold lettering it read 'Flycraft Centre'.

"Ah, yes," said Pascale, looking through the northern archway.

"Well done, Sharon," congratulated Apnar, leading the way out of the square.

The three walked towards a medium-sized building straight ahead of them, which had a large sign indicating its purpose in bold red lettering. Apnar pushed open the glass door to enter the grey building, and was met with scores of timetables plastered all over the walls, either side of two further glass doors leading onto the Flycraft courtyard.

"Well?" said Apnar, bombarded with timetables.

"Well, I think we should just walk out into the courtyard and ask someone about flights to Boothcot Wells. There must be one soon," Pascale replied.

So Apnar pushed open the door for Pascale and Sharon, and walked into the courtyard after them. There were no Flycraft in the courtyard, and Pascale approached a man wearing a bright red shirt with the words 'Fly Boothcotia' written across the back. He was facing the wall and paying no attention to the new passengers.

"Excuse me," began Pascale.

"Hmm?!" he grunted, startled.

"I said, excuse me, do you know when the next flight to Boothcot Wells will be in?"

"Boothcot Wells, erm, yes, of course. It should be here any moment, in fact," he replied, not turning his face away from the sheet of paper he was holding.

"Well, can we pay here?" Pascale continued, slightly annoyed.

The man turned round.

"Yes, of course."

There was a pause.

"Well?" said Pascale, with rising intonation.

"Well, you can pay at the desk. Hold on."

He then walked over to a little red desk over at the other side of the courtyard, placing down his papers with some annoyance and taking up his position behind the counter.

"That's one hundred Forden leaves each – three hundred Forden leaves in total."

Apnar was about to withdraw some money from his pocket before Pascale cut in:

"Here," she said, signing a cheque. Obviously it was impractical to pay for such things with actual leaves, so people seemed to write cheques which certified the handing over of the ownership of the leaves which were part of each person's account in Fordenia. Their account, of course, was a small tree, a few trees, a forest, or many forests depending on their wealth, and it was managed on their behalf by banks which charged their customers for the benefit.

"Thank you," the man said, his face lighting up at last.

"You can wait over…" he began, but before he could finish his sentence, a Flycraft appeared overhead, ready for its next passengers, and ruffling their collective hair.

"Oh my," said Apnar, not used to such 'contraptions'.

The Flycraft landed in the courtyard and a man in a red uniform swung open one of the three doors on one side, calling:

"All aboard for Sulla!"

The aircraft was like nothing Sharon had ever seen before. It was a cross between a helicopter and a small aeroplane, but it had no wings or rotor blades. It just seemed to glide through the air without these aids. Pascale led the way to the Flycraft, followed by Sharon and Apnar, and climbed aboard at once. The others followed on, clambering onto the craft while it hovered about a foot above the ground.

"Please take your seats," said the assistant in the red uniform, signalling to the pilot to take off.

All three sat down together in a row of three dove leather seats. The craft was spacious and very comfortable, with sheepskin rugs on the floor and screens embedded into the seats in front of them, which were surrounded by luxurious wood.

"These are really quite nice," complimented Apnar, but before Pascale could reply the assistant cut in.

"Thank you, sir. Please make yourselves comfortable and enjoy the ride. It will take about two angles to reach Boothcot Wells, equivalent to two hundred angles on foot."

Sharon, too, was impressed by the cabin, though it was nothing compared to the Nobility capsules in Sullaria. For a rather rusty machine, the interior was not too bad. There was only one other passenger on the flight, a bespectacled man with a large moustache who hid behind his newspaper for most of the journey. Sharon could make out the headline and read it aloud:

"'Mickelsonson pushes on at Torbeg.'"

It apparently referred to the Sullarian Empire's latest military campaign, which was edging ever closer to the Boothcotian border. Pascale shot Apnar a look of suspicion, but he pretended not to notice. It really had nothing to do with him, Sharon thought.

The Flycraft had no windows, so the journey's progress could not be tracked in that way. The only way to know how far you had come was by looking at your screen, on which there was a map showing the aircraft's location as it travelled across the country. Judging by the map, and by what the assistant had said earlier, it was going pretty fast. In fact, they arrived in Boothcot Wells on time, hovering down to a halt in the CFC, the Central Flycraft Centre, to see Pascale off home at last.

"Thank you," said Pascale, beaming, as she dismounted from the aircraft. Sharon and Apnar echoed her sentiment.

"Home at last," she continued, taking in the familiar surroundings with a sigh.

"Congratulations, Pascale," said Sharon comfortingly as all three made their way through the large crowded courtyard to the city beyond.

"Thank you, both of you," Pascale replied.

"It's you we've got to thank," corrected Apnar, smiling.

"Absolutely," assented Sharon.

"Well, it's good to be back home. I know my family have moved since I was last here – I'll need to go the National Embassy to find out where, though."

"My family's not moved house for a thousand postins!" said Apnar, chuckling with the others.

"Well, I think it's somewhere down here," Pascale instructed, pointing down a long and wide street called 'The Chevron'. It was apparently the city's main street, with all sorts of vehicles travelling through it, not to mention hundreds of pedestrians.

Like Stirkirk, the city was brightly coloured, with tall pale green buildings on either side of The Chevron, with elaborate roofs and spires, and countless clocks peered down at Sharon from them. Manoeuvring their way through the traffic, the three came to an abrupt bend in the street at which they had to turn ninety degrees left, though it was still the same street.

On the right hand side of the street, tightly positioned between a bank and what seemed to be some kind of post office, was a bright white building with eight or nine floors, with a highly decorative green roof and a tall flagpole on top of its entrance. The flag was pale blue with two red stripes at either side and a royal coat of arms in the centre. Directly in front of the building stood a bronze statue of a man in ancient military uniform riding a horse and holding up an arm in victory. Undoubtedly, this was the National Embassy.

"Here we are," said Pascale triumphantly, stopping outside it. "I suppose I ought to tell you my real name now," she went on. "It's Aphra. Aphra Waters."

Sharon and Apnar smiled and entered the building with Aphra, though Sharon felt she would always be Pascale to her. Inside was a large reception hall with marble floors and sepia pictures of past Presidents hung on the wallpapered walls.

"Excuse me, sir," Aphra began, walking up to the large desk.

"Can I help you, madam?" the tall man behind it replied. He had a deep voice and was wearing pinstripe trousers and a blue waistcoat.

"Yes, I've just returned from abroad, and I'd like to find out where my family are. I believe they moved house a while ago – I've been away a long time, you see," she answered.

"Right, madam. Can I have your name first, please?" he asked her.

"Waters. Aphra Waters."

"Thank you," he said, tapping away at a machine. "Can you look directly through this hole, please?" He held up a contraption with a bright hole in the front, which Aphra looked into with both eyes. There was a beep and the machine printed out a thin sheet of paper on which Sharon could make out the words, 'WATERS, Aphra St. Julian'.

"Excellent," the man continued. "Now, what is the dwelling-owner's name?"

"Fritz Waters," she replied.

"Is that his *full* name?" he persisted.

"No, it's not. That's Fritz Frederick Théodor Waters," she said. "The third."

"Ah, yes," said the man, eyeing the machine in front of him. "Yes, Calendar Grange, Beckett Drive, Fermoy, Boothcot Wells."

"Fermoy?" repeated Aphra.

"Yes, Fermoy," answered the man. "Formerly of Denhill House, Vember Road, Egsham, Boothcot Wells."

"Yes, yes, that's right," said Aphra, beaming once more. "Can I ask who else is living there at the moment?"

"Erm, Pascale Waters, wife of the above, and Persephone Waters, daughter of the above. All right?"

"Yes, yes, that's right," she repeated. "Thank you very much."

"Just the same, but they've moved to Fermoy," said Aphra to the other two as they walked out of the Embassy and stood beside the statue. "I'm so glad everyone's all right."

"I'm sure they'll be glad you're all right," said Sharon.

"Well, thank you for bringing me here. I know it was to the detriment of your own journey, Sharon, but I wish you good luck with it. And you, Apnar."

"Thank you," chorused Sharon and Apnar.

"I'll make my way to Fermoy — it's quite central, so I don't have far to go. Father always wanted to buy Calendar Grange, you know, since I was a little girl. I'll miss the old house, though, of course."

"Of course," chimed the others.

"Anyway," said Aphra, giggling. "I'll not keep you any longer — thank you again, and good luck. You can make your own way back now."

"Thank you for everything," Sharon replied, and as Aphra walked through the crowds out of sight, she felt a certain sense of loss that Miss Bossy-Boots was now gone.

Apnar broke the silence by saying:

"We'd better not hang around any longer, Sharon. We'll need to get a ship to Mansleigh. Quite how I really don't know."

"You don't?" asked Sharon, a little worried.

"Why, of course not! We'll need to ask someone here where the nearest port is. The one thing I do know is that Boothcot Wells is considerably inland."

"Oh," faltered Sharon.

"Oh, indeed. Now, let's find someone who can tell us what's what."

Apnar then proceeded to continue walking down The Chevron with Sharon until they came across a small stall set up in the middle of the road, which had a sign saying 'Information Post' hanging above it.

"Hello there, sir," said the skinny man dressed in lilac who was manning the stall.

"Hello," said Apnar. "Could you possibly tell us where the nearest port is from here?"

"The nearest port, sir? Certainly, sir."

There was a pause.

"Well?" said Apnar.

The man appeared ruffled. "Well, now, can I help you, sir?"

"Yes, could you tell us where the nearest port is from here?" Apnar repeated, dismayed with the man's incompetence.

"I certainly could, sir, I most certainly could. Why, what would I be doing here if I couldn't?!"

Again there was a pause. "Well, where is the nearest port from here??" Apnar demanded in a raised voice.

"The nearest port from this very spot, sir, that is to say The Chevron, Boothcot Wells, is Mouthbrock Port, just north-west from here."

"And how far is that?" demanded Apnar, still disgruntled.

"How far is what, sir?" asked the man, a puzzled look on his face.

"How far is Mouthbrock??"

"Mouthbrock is approximately thirty angles from here on foot, sir."

"Is there any quicker way to get there?" inquired Apnar, tired of walking.

"Certainly there is, sir. Most certainly."

The man's trick was working again.

"Well, what is the quicker way to get there?"

"Why, you can get a Flycraft — that's the quickest way, most certainly," the man replied, smiling terrifyingly.

"I see," said Apnar, walking away. Sharon was sure she heard the irritating man say in reply, "What do you see, sir?" Thankfully, it was too late.

"I should have asked Pascale all those questions. What a buffoon!!" Apnar exclaimed, calming himself down slowly.

"I think that might have been a better idea, yes!" agreed Sharon, unable to contain her laughter.

And so they walked back up The Chevron towards the CFC once again, Sharon observing all the marvels of the city, the spires and the towers and the brightly coloured buildings and statues, before it was too late – after all, it was unlikely she'd ever see Boothcotia again after today.

CHAPTER TWENTY-TWO

The Unexpected Voyage

Touching down in Mouthbrock, Sharon and Apnar debarked from the aircraft and crossed the courtyard of the Flycraft Centre, out the door and into the town. Less colourful than both Stirkirk and Boothcot Wells, Mouthbrock was a dirtier-looking town, full of people, looking out across the ocean. Outside the Centre was a wide road leading downwards towards the harbour, which is just where Sharon needed to get to, as quick as possible.

"Down here, I should think," said Apnar promisingly, looking ahead at the harbour.

"Yes, as long as it's not 'Inspection Day' today we should be all right!" Sharon replied.

All over the road were clusters of traffic, made up of vehicles being driven (or indeed driving themselves), creatures being ridden, and pedestrians. The mix of people there, too, was eclectic, some wearing peculiar headscarves and cloaks, some wearing brightly-coloured suits, some wearing grand gowns and large hats, and some heavily hooded. The variety was largely as a result of Mouthbrock's role as the major port for Boothcotia, which traded with several other nations, including Sullaria.

"Spices and spirits," said Apnar suddenly; Sharon thought this comment rather random.

"Hmm?" she said as they weaved through the traffic.

"That's what Boothcotia is good for," Apnar explained. "That's what the Empire buys from it, you see. Spices, like waldersoupe and repartúi, and spirits like Richmondy and Kaager."

"Oh," said Sharon, pretending to be intrigued. "And what does the Empire produce?" she asked.

"Oh, the Empire produces many, many things. A wonderful mix! Building materials, beautiful furniture, clothes, fine wines, vehicles, books, newspapers and periodicals, as well as perfumes and scents. The Emperor is very proud of Sullaria's economic strength, you know."

"I see," said Sharon, thinking of the many shops and boutiques she had come across in Sulla. "I suppose that doesn't leave much for other countries!"

"Well, Fordenia doesn't really produce anything at all. With all the Forden forests they have they can afford to import everything, and it's really not a problem. Though they do, of course, control the banking system, which is rather profitable."

Apnar paused for a moment.

"Arvada makes a wide selection of things, like us, from machinery to clothing and good food, and then there are all the smaller states in the north-east, too. The Emperor is very keen to expand into that territory – there's a lot of natural wealth there that isn't being used, a lot of scarce resources."

Sharon could see he was referring to the military campaign in the north led by General Mickelsonson.

"Really, Sharon, the Empire is expanding for the good of everyone, and if only people like Pascale – I mean Aphra – would see sense they'd see all the benefits it would bring and welcome it with open arms. But never mind that now, here we are."

They had reached the harbour side, which was lined with ship-merchants' offices, advertising crossings. The harbour was full of ships and boats of all sizes, from huge galleys and yachts to tiny rowing boats.

"Well, it looks like we've got a wide choice of ship-merchants," pointed out Sharon as they walked down the promenade.

"Good, good, let's make inquiries immediately," proposed Apnar, eyeing the particular merchants' offices named 'Baron & Baron Crossings' with considerable suspicion. "We'd best avoid that one, though."

Sharon laughed and they walked passed 'Baron & Baron' onto 'Quintus, Quintus, Quintus and Quintus'.

"It's a shame there aren't five of them," said Sharon, walking through the green doors of the establishment. Apnar chuckled characteristically.

"How can I help you today, sir?" began one of the Quintuses when Apnar had approached the desk.

"When is your next crossing to Mansleigh?" asked Apnar.

"Next crrrrrossing to MANSLEIGH, Charles?!!" he screeched, calling to another of the Quintuses who was in the next room.

"Three angles time, precisely!" called the hidden Quintus from behind.

"Three angles time, precisely," repeated Quintus number one, with a cough.

"I believe it's in the dock at this very moment!" called Quintus number two again.

"We believe, sir, it is in the dock at this very moment," Quintus the first repeated politely.

"Very good. I'll take two tickets, please," requested Apnar, fiddling in his inside pocket for a book of cheques.

"TWO tickets to MANSLEIGH!!!" roared the man at the desk annoyingly.

"How many??!" called Quintus the second, infuriatingly.

"TWO, Charles, TWO. ONE AND ONE, Charles, ONE AND ONE!!!" the original Quintus bellowed, getting annoyed himself. "Useless oaf, is Charles," he said quietly to Sharon and Apnar.

"I heard that!" called Charles, still hidden.

Eventually a pair of blue tickets dropped from a tube on the front desk, and the man checked them carefully before presenting them to Apnar.

"One thousand, two hundred and seventy-six Forden leaves and a half, sir," said the man, smiling most disturbingly, but before Apnar could write the cheque he spoke again. "Which, including the recently-introduced shipping tax, comes to — let me see — one thousand, nine hundred and thirty-three Forden leaves exactly."

Apnar was about to put quill to paper before he was interrupted again.

"Which, including the even more recently-introduced surcharge on private transport, comes to — ah, yes — three thousand, six hundred and twelve Forden leaves, and a half, and a stalk, and a half of a stalk, and a quarter of a stalk."

Apnar rolled his eyes and waited for the next interruption, but it didn't come.

"Could you say that again, sorry?" he asked, still bemused as to how the ticket prices had almost tripled in price, and at such peculiar intervals.

"I said, three thousand, seven hundred and twelve Forden leaves, and a half, and a quarter, and an eighth, and a stalk, and a half of a stalk, and a quarter of a stalk." Again he smiled, this time even more annoyingly. Sharon was sure he had inflated the price again.

Apnar wrote down the amount on the cheque, which took up the entire length of the paper, and handed it over.

"Thank you, sir, and I wish you all the very best for your voyage with us today," said the man finally, quickly filing away the cheque. "Our ship is the galley *Victory*, sir, the tallest in the port at present," he explained, before disappearing into the back of the offices.

Sure enough, *Victory* had anchored at the docks, a very tall wooden galley with bright white sails which seemed to sparkle in the sunlight. It was the tallest in the port, just, but it was certainly not the biggest.

"Don't you think we should have tried other ship-merchants first?" asked Sharon, surprised at the cost of the trip, and a little suspicious of both Quintuses they had heard.

"Oh, nonsense, nonsense. Come now, it's time that matters, not cost," Apnar replied, approaching the galley.

Aboard the vessel were about twelve others, standing around the deck with bored expressions. Their rather wretched apparel and dirty faces suggested rather strongly that they would not be able to pay the four thousand Forden leaves for the trip, and they were grouped in three or four huddles, shooting suspicious glances at Sharon and Apnar as they toured the deck. Sharon assumed they must be part of the crew, but struggled to find any other passengers.

"Are we the only passengers?" she asked Apnar quietly as they looked out to sea.

"Sorry?" he said, dreaming.

"Are we the only passengers on board?" she repeated.

"I haven't seen any others – have you?" he said, still looking out across the ocean.

"No, not one. Who were all those men standing around?"

"Well, I think they must be part of the crew. Either that or they're travelling third class, or something."

"I didn't hear the ship-merchant say anything about classes, Apnar. It all seems a bit strange."

"Really? I must admit I've never been on a public ship – but if I was to get the yacht sent over from St. Ludi it would have taken even longer. St. Ludi's on the other side of Sullaria, you know."

Sharon looked behind her at the galley and said:

"Why don't we go inside and have a look?" she suggested.

"Good idea," agreed Apnar, walking beside her towards the raised block in the centre of the deck, which was actually quite large.

There was a small wooden door with gold bolts leading into a spacious room all set with six or seven tables and chairs. The room was light and airy, with windows all the way along the two walls, and sitting at the tables were about twenty other passengers, fashionably dressed (in the Sullarian sense) and dining on roast duck. They were chatting quietly when Apnar opened the door and walked in with Sharon, sitting at the nearest table on the left. It was set with a repulsive floral tablecloth and a silver candlestick, with only two of the four spice jars customary on dining tables which Sharon had seen earlier in the hotel at

Port of Mansleigh. Sharon recognised them to be waldersoupe and nonéchale, and sat staring at them inquisitively.

"I'm glad we've found the right place!" said Apnar loudly, chuckling.

"Yes," said Sharon much more softly. "It seems we aren't the only passengers, after all. But look, they've only got two spice jars."

"Oh, yes, so they have. Well, those are the two most commonly-used ones, you see. And it's only the finer places which have all four," Apnar explained, eyeing a man dressed in white who was approaching their table from the opposite door from which they had entered.

"Good day, sir, madam. Delighted to have you aboard. Would you like something to drink?" said the man, holding a notebook fiercely.

"Oh yes, thank you," said Apnar. "I'll have a small Richmondy, please. Sharon, would you like a Bubblezibois?"

Sharon was about to nod in agreement before the man replied gruffly, "Oh! We don't have that sort of stuff here, sir! No, no, no!"

Apnar was rather taken aback. "Oh..." He was lost for words, "right."

"Well, I'm terribly sorry, sir. Can I get you a Gizmond, a Piedmonty, or, er, some Villiards, p'r'aps?"

"Well, I suppose I'll have to stomach some Villiards. Sharon, would you..."

"I'll just have some water, thank you," she said, interrupting him.

"Right," grunted the man, stomping off to the kitchen.

"Villiards is such nasty stuff, you know," said Apnar, making faces which were intended to convey his disgust but only resulted in him being stared at by about a quarter of the other diners.

"What is it?" asked Sharon, curious.

"Well, it's wine, of course, if it deserves the title," said Apnar, ignoring the stares. "I really needed a Richmondy just now. But never mind."

The man in white returned to the table promptly with a grotty silver tray which he threw, rather than lay, down on the table with the announcement:

"Eighty leaves," he grunted, "sir."

Apnar took out his book of cheques again and signed the parchment with his pocket quill in red ink.

"Thankee, sir. Now, today's speciality is the duck, roasted. Would you like some?"

"Oh, yes," answered Apnar quickly. "Sharon?"

"Yes, please," Sharon replied, pleased to be eating at last.

"Right, then, it'll be along in a moment." With this final statement, the man left the room and slammed the kitchen door shut.

Apnar sighed. "I'll tell you something, Sharon, this country has the worst service I have *ever* seen. Honestly."

"You're probably right," agreed Sharon, laughing.

"I know I am. Sullaria puts everywhere else to shame every time."

But he was biased, thought Sharon. But then again, he was right.

About an angle later, the same burly man appeared through the kitchen door, struggling with two plates of roast duck and two drinks. He looked as though he was immersed in immense concentration, and eventually flung down the plates on Apnar and Sharon's table.

"Viola, as they say in Arvada," he said, grinning madly.

"I think you mean *voilà*," corrected Apnar, replicating the man's grin mockingly.

The man stopped grinning but said nothing.

"Enjoy your meal, and your voyage," he said finally, turning around and stomping back to the kitchen.

One aged couple got up from their table and stumbled out of the dining room to the deck. One half of the couple was a wrinkled man with a high forehead and a long, grey beard. The other half was an equally old woman wearing a pale pink dress and a matching hat with a broad rim. Sharon saw them walk past their window and then turned to her duck. It was delicate and succulent, and although it was delicious, Sharon was disappointed by the lack of anything else on the plate. Aside from the breast of duck itself, the large plate was completely empty.

Apnar lifted his glass of Villiards to his mouth and, smelling it carefully, made a terrifying grimace. Reluctantly, he sipped the wine and Sharon could see it was not as bad as he had made out. Considering a single glass had cost him about seventy Forden leaves, it certainly wasn't the cheapest of the cheap, though it could never match up to the richness of Richmondy. Tearing into his duck, Apnar began to look around at the other diners. Another table of them got up and left the room, and again Sharon saw them pass by her window. This sequence repeated itself, indeed it seemed to speed up, as Sharon and Apnar's duck disappeared from their plates, until all the other passengers had got up, and had passed by Sharon and Apnar's window.

"Let's have a look outside," said Apnar as soon as Sharon had finished her duck.

"Right," she said, getting up from the table and exiting through the door they had come through.

Strangely, the other passengers were no-where to be seen. Sharon and Apnar walked round the entire ship, but no-one else was on deck, not even the dirty-faced men they had seen hanging around when they had boarded.

"Where is everyone?" asked Sharon once she and Apnar had completed a lap of the deck.

"I don't know. They all seem to have disappeared. Let's check out our cabins below deck – they've probably all gone to bed!" replied Apnar. "They certainly looked as though they needed the sleep."

As they walked round to a door leading down to the lower decks, Sharon asked Apnar about something that had been troubling her ever since the idea of getting on a ship to Mansleigh had been put to her.

"Apnar, how long will this voyage take?" she asked.

"Well, at least three hundred angles, I should think," he answered. "You thought it would be shorter?"

"Well, I didn't know. If we're crossing an entire ocean, then I'd expect it to take much longer than that."

"Ah, but the ship speeds up considerably during the night, I believe. No-one's allowed on deck, I don't think."

"I see," said Sharon, following Apnar through the little wooden door which led down a very steep staircase.

Apnar went down first, beckoning Sharon to follow him. At the foot of the stairs was a narrow corridor with numbered doors leading off either side; Apnar checked his ticket and found the number '4' stamped on his, and '7' stamped on Sharon's. He approached cabin number four and turned the doorknob – it was unlocked, and he pushed the door open and went inside. It was a tiny, dark room with no windows, and nothing but a low single bed and a rickety chest of drawers.

"Well," said Apnar, disappointed. "Not exactly first-class, is it?" he said, showing Sharon the room. So small was the cabin that Sharon could hardly squeeze in beside Apnar and had to look through the doorway.

"Have a look at yours," he said, pointing down the corridor.

"Identical," Sharon called from her cabin when she had entered it.

"I suppose we shall have to make do during the night, then," said Apnar, pulling on the top drawer of his chest of drawers. He put all his strength into forcing it open, but it just would not budge. Apnar let out an undignified grunt, and gave up.

It was only a few moments later when Sharon called back from her cabin, "The drawers won't open!"

But before Apnar could reply, a door further down the corridor was shoved open and one of the gruff men Sharon had seen standing around earlier emerged from the cabin wearing a dark hooded cloak. He glanced at Sharon, standing in her doorway, and marched out the opposite door, slamming it shut. He was soon followed by all the others, filing out of the cabins in silence through the mysterious door, before it was slammed shut for the last time.

"What's going on?" asked Sharon, bewildered.

Apnar walked down the corridor to the mysterious door and turned the doorknob slowly before opening the door ever so slightly to make a thin slat through which he could see what was going on beyond.

"Sharon," he whispered, beckoning her to come closer. "Look."

Beyond the door was a large room, heavily lit up with candles, and crowded full with the men, who looked as though they were standing in a circle, facing inwards and staring at something or someone (Sharon couldn't see what) in the centre of the circle.

There was a low murmuring of voices, before a man began to address the others. Sharon thought he must be the one standing in the centre of the circle, transfixing the others.

"And so," he began, pausing. "And so we are nearly ready to carry it out."

He spoke in a quiet, deep voice, and when he stopped speaking the murmuring resumed, this time with renewed enthusiasm. It stopped instantly when he began to speak again. Sharon looked anxiously at Apnar. It seemed that, try as they might, they just could not avoid trouble.

"Tonight, I will signal to Charles when we have sailed out of Boothcotian waters, and he will close down the tracking facility in Mouthbrock. From that point onwards, my friends, we cease to exist, as far as the government is concerned. And at that point, we plot our course to true victory!"

There were hushed cheers and murmurings before the ringleader continued:

"We shall use the co-ordinates of *HIMS Sulla* to form a blockade around that ship, when we are joined with the *Triumph* and the *Jubilant*. Both are now headed that way already. At precisely three hundred and twenty angles tonight, you will storm the passenger cabins and retain the Sullarians in this room, awaiting further instruction. Is that quite clear?"

There were murmurings of assent.

"Then make sure it's all done without any trouble. When that 'task force' is surrounded by our ships, they'll soon pay up, let me tell you."

Again there were hushed cheers before the ringleader disbanded the circle and the men stood about in huddles talking quietly. Apnar closed the door quickly and ran down the corridor when he saw the ringleader, a tall, sultry figure, approach the door.

"Aha!" he bellowed, smiling at Apnar. He had not yet had time to reach his cabin. "I see you found our briefing rather interesting. Why, it's Lord d'Arrawor, is it not?!! I thought that dunderhead of a cook was wittering on, again!"

Apnar stood in silence while Sharon pressed her ear against her cabin door, feeling more grateful than ever that she had made it to her cabin.

"Well, we'll soon see what your government thinks of this!" he continued, dragging Apnar down the corridor and into the room in which the men had been assembled.

"What?!" Sharon heard Apnar cry. "Leave me alone!" he cried again, before the door was slammed shut.

Apnar was the first hostage to be taken. Sharon had read in the papers that Sullaria was sending a 'task force' to carry out talks with the Boothcotians about collaboration with the Empire, and could see these low-lives were prepared to take hostages for personal monetary gain – they had no political aims. She stood, leaning against her door, deliberating over what to do, before deciding on a plan of action. She would alert the other passengers and try to come up with a way of dealing with the situation. Should they go along with the hostage plan? Or should they try to thwart it?

Her heart throbbing wildly, Sharon opened her cabin door, which creaked terribly, and knocked quietly on the door of cabin number five, next to hers. A lady's voice answered her knocking from within:

"Yes? Who is it?" she said in a clipped accent.

"I'm another passenger," said Sharon, whispering. "I need to talk to you, now."

The cabin door was opened, and the woman, in a bright orange dress, replied:

"Whatever for?" She was not amused at being disturbed in this way.

"The crew," began Sharon. "The crew want to make us hostages. They're going to lock us up at three hundred and twenty angles and demand money from the task force aboard *HIMS Sulla.*"

The woman stared at her blankly.

"Is that all?" she said, getting ready to close the door.

"But," said Sharon hopelessly.

"Don't tell me you didn't know," replied the woman with an air of infinite superiority.

"Did you?" asked Sharon.

"Well, of course! We were all marched round to the bow to have it explained to us after dinner. Terrible, terrible, terrible!" the woman despaired.

"But they took my fellow passenger away because he heard," Sharon explained, still confused.

"They probably took him away so he wouldn't start ranting on like you are, trying to convince us to resist them. That's it, isn't it?" said the woman, bending down to Sharon's level.

"So you're going along with it?"

"Well, of course I am! What else can I do?!" exclaimed the woman. "No, no, no, don't even begin to answer that."

"Right then, I'll go along with it, if you're sure."

"I'm sure I value my life, dear. And I'm sure the Emperor won't betray us."

Sharon really wasn't quite so sure about this last assertion, and she wandered back to her cabin in shock, her mind in complete disarray. She sat on her stiff bed in silence, thinking about what could happen. Should she go along with the hostage plan like the lady had suggested? Would that really offer the best solution to her crisis? Sharon had doubts.

For what seemed like an age, Sharon sat there on that bed, thinking and pondering and wondering and worrying, the sound of the boat sailing on through the ocean her only comfort. Until it was too late. Sharon heard the door at the end of the corridor burst open, a few burly men stomping their way down the corridor. All she could hear were doors being flung open and passengers being rounded up. Within seconds her door was thrown open, and a gruesome figure stood before her.

"OUT!" he growled, grabbing Sharon by the arm and man-handling her out of the tiny cabin. Not wanting to risk anything, Sharon stayed silent.

When she was tossed into the main room she looked all around for Apnar. The other passengers were chattering amongst themselves, and the hostage-takers were keeping close watch over them all. Finally she caught sight of him, tied up tightly to a rickety wooden chair in the farthest away corner of the room. She started walking over to him before she was stopped in her path by the ringleader.

"Well, well," he said loudly, drawing the attention of everyone else in the room. "Look who it is!"

The other passengers stared at Sharon.

"Is it not the Sulla Vandals?!" he exclaimed to loud roars of laughter. "Our fellow freedom-fighters! What will His Imperial Majesty have to say about his loyal servant this time, getting all mixed up in all sorts of crime?! Why don't we ask him?"

The ringleader's men cheered and he left the room, presumably to make communication with the *Jubilant*. Of course he could not ask the Emperor his opinion of Apnar, but he could ask his representatives with the 'task force'.

Sharon was growing concerned about Apnar's reputation, but his face was as placid and unflinching as ever. As she stood against the wall of the room, outside any of the other huddles of passengers which had formed all around it, she stared at him, trying to make eye contact with him. Not once did he look round at her, instead remaining facing the opposite wall. If negotiations went smoothly enough, they would all be free to continue to Sullaria – if they didn't…

Sharon stopped thinking – it was no use turning things over a thousand times in her head, and it was pointless to contemplate the fate that awaited her if the task force held out. However the negotiations were going, they were going slowly. Incredibly slowly. So slowly that Sharon was almost asleep by the time the ringleader re-entered the room.

Silence ensued as soon as the Captain's door was opened, and everyone in the room looked round at the ringleader, Quintus number three, gaping.

"They want proof!" he growled. "Proof! Proof! How dare they?!"

This remark was met with growls of acclamation on the part of the other hostage-takers.

"Bring him in!" he continued, pointing his fat finger at Apnar.

Four of the men took a leg of Apnar's chair each, and paraded him above their heads through the room and into the Captain's room beyond. Apnar simply scowled darkly. The Captain's door was slammed shut again, and the room fell silent as everyone tried eagerly to overhear the proceedings.

But all they could hear were faint shouts, completely unintelligible and almost entirely blocked out by the sound of the waves crashing against the ship's sides. The galley rocked slowly from side to side once or twice, but apart from a few concerned faces belonging to the Sullarians, nothing was made of it.

It seemed to Sharon as though the whole thing would never end, until Apnar was brought back in, safe and well, albeit rather wet, followed by the ringleader, whom Sharon had by now nicknamed Quintus the Great, though her opinion of him was quite the opposite.

"My friends," said Quintus the Great, a gigantic smile spread across his dirty face. "We have," he paused, "an agreement!!"

It had taken him over four hours, but the entrapped hostages and the Boothcotian criminals were as attentive as they could ever have been.

"A *handsome* agreement!" he proclaimed, relishing the moment, and exploiting it for all it was worth.

"All the might of the Sullarian Empire," he said, rolling the 'r' in Sullarian with great relish, "has been reduced to nothing by a couple of pirate ships!"

The hostages looked alarmed while the others cheered and bellowed their various exclamations, ranging from 'Aha!' to 'Long live the King!'

"All the might of the Sullarian Empire," he repeated, "has failed to stand up to four Quintuses! Victory, gentlemen, victory indeed!"

Again the shouts went up.

"Victory, my friends, in the form of a Forden forest! In the form of a Forden forest!!" The ringleader could hardly get out the repeat of this exclamation, so loud were the cheers that went up at this point.

The shock displayed in the hostage-takers' faces was only met with the greedy joy in their eyes. Instantly they began to talk and cheer and laugh with each other, and in the commotion Sharon managed to steal across the room to Apnar.

"Apnar!" she called to him, having to shout to get above all the raucous noise.

"Sharon, everything's all right," he said, smiling.

"But…"

"No, no, everything's all right. The task force wanted to see me and eventually they offered a forest of Forden trees for the safe release of all the Sullarian citizens."

"But what about you?" Sharon persisted.

"Me? I'm fine, I'm fine! I look fine, don't I?" Apnar had a fatherliness about him sometimes which radiated calm.

"What now, though?" said Sharon.

"We're headed straight on to Mansleigh now. The task force was allowed to proceed and they're on their way to Boothcot Wells. I know the leader of the force quite well, and everything will be fine," Apnar explained.

Sharon couldn't say anything more – she was so tired she could have fallen asleep there and then, had it not been for the ringleader's announcement:

"All right, now, I hate to bring this rejoicing to an end, but in order to make it to Mansleigh on time we'll have to really get a move on. So we'll be on Full Ahead for the next hundred and eighty angles. Understand?"

The man paused and then went on:

"So take our passengers to their cabins and lock the doors. Then you can go to bed, too. Come on, then, hurry up!"

The ringleader waved his arms in the air to motion to the assembled men to disband, before himself disappearing into the Captain's room.

The man who had taken Sharon away from her cabin grabbed her by the arm again and took her to her cabin, while Apnar was ushered to his in the same way.

Sharon was exhausted, and it did not take much to send her to sleep. She collapsed on the bed, fully clothed, and gently closed her eyes. The last thing she heard was the turning of a large key in the lock of her cabin door, and with this valedictory sound she fell sound asleep.

CHAPTER TWENTY-THREE

Northward

It was not until late morning that Sharon's eyelids finally slid back to reveal her cramped, and dark, cabin. She rubbed her eyes and sat upright on her bed, wondering if she was allowed out yet, but no sooner had she done this than Apnar knocked at her cabin door.

"Sharon?" he whispered, knocking. "Sharon? Are you up yet?"

Sharon made the very short walk over to the door and opened it to reveal Apnar standing behind it, beaming at her.

"Oh you are!" he said. "Come on then, it's time to get off, you know."

"Oh, is it? I only just got up," Sharon replied.

"Well, come on, there's nothing to pack, after all."

And so they walked down the corridor to the steep set of steps which led up to the open deck. Having ascended these, Sharon took in the now familiar sounds and smells of the harbour – the sound of bids squawking and chirping, of boats bobbing up and down, of the gentle waves, and the unforgettable smell of the sea air.

"Back on dry land, at last," said Apnar as they walked off the boat, Apnar giving crew members piercing dirty looks.

As they touched Sullarian soil, Sharon knew it was now up to her to fulfil her quest – there were no other distractions to stop her now. She would travel northward, say goodbye to everybody, and then disappear back home through the portal. It was as simple as that, she thought.

"Off to the station straight away, I think," said Apnar.

"Can we get to the Shanklot Stead from here?" asked Sharon hopefully.

"Now there's a question. I wouldn't really have thought so, Sharon. It is pretty remote."

Sharon sighed, knowing that if the Shanklot Corridor could not be reached directly from Mansleigh, they would have to go via Sulla.

"Can you remember the name of the little station up there?" asked Apnar, testing Sharon's memory.

"Erm… Rastinun, I think. Yes, Rastinun."

"Right," said Apnar, leading Sharon away from the bay and up Toobalt Close to the archway which led onto Stokechapel Square.

"Here we are," he said, looking ahead at an entrance to the station.

Sharon and Apnar entered through the small door and descended the stone staircase to the main hall of the station from where many different streets of Mansleigh and all the different platforms could be accessed. The place was buzzing with people, as Sharon had expected, and both she and Apnar looked around for a notice above a platform access reading something like 'Far North'. To her surprise, Sharon found a sign which read 'Direct Northward', just what they were looking for.

"Look, Apnar," she said, pointing at the archway.

"Well, well! The network is extending all the time, of course! Let's have a closer look," Apnar replied, walking over to the archway.

To the right of it was a board detailing all the different stations this platform would take you to. In fact, it would only stop at a station if a passenger specifically requested it, and Sharon scanned the list for 'Rastinun'. Right at the bottom of the last column, in tiny lettering, was the word she had been looking for. She pointed it out to Apnar and he nodded, as if he knew it would be there all along, and both of them descended the narrow stone staircase to the dusty platform.

There was no-one else waiting on the platform at all, and it took about an angle before there was any sign of life down there. Eventually, however, a string of not more than eight rusty capsules came clinking down the track, slowing to a halt at the platform, and one elderly gentleman got out of one and brushed past Sharon and Apnar. Every capsule was now vacant, and so every capsule door slid open. Apnar chose the capsule second from the front and let Sharon board it before him.

Inside, these were just like the capsules Sharon had first encountered – light grey leather seats, a small, flickering screen above the door, and a copy of *The Chronicle*. It appeared to Sharon that *The Chronicle* was a business newspaper, which carried the headline 'Tunnels to be privatised', but before Sharon could pick it up the image of a man sitting at a desk in a pointed hat appeared on the screen, saying:

"Welcome aboard the capsules Direct Northward. Capsule number two – you are our only passengers aboard this string at the moment. Please select a destination – these capsules will only stop off at pre-selected stations."

Sharon looked around for a button or another screen, but things were simpler here.

"Rastinun Tunnel Station, please," said Apnar, talking directly to the screen.

Instantly the capsules shot off like a bullet down the line.

"Thank you. These capsules terminate at Rastinun Tunnel Station. Please bear in mind that the route may alter slightly to accommodate other passengers' requests, and remember that in the unlikely event of an emergency you are to stay within the capsule and not perform any magic whatsoever. Enjoy your trip and have a good day."

The man was then replaced by the following message on the screen:

'DIRECT NORTHWARD – Long Haul

Refreshments served at your disposal'

Apnar picked up *The Chronicle* and began reading – he was evidently quite intrigued by the leading article, and was lost in it for some time before he said:

"Oh, sorry Sharon, would you like something to read?"

"I'd like something to drink," she said, and before Apnar could answer a glass of Bubblezibois appeared on the arm of Sharon's seat. "Ah!"

"Refreshments served at your disposal, remember," reminded Apnar, pointing up at the screen.

"Oh yes, I had forgotten about that!"

"Take your pick," said Apnar, conjuring up a pile of newspapers and magazines. This time Sharon went for *Musical Monthly* which was a lighter read than many of the others, and moderately interesting. Sharon had learnt to play the piano reasonably well, but the instruments featured in the magazine were all weird and wonderful, at least to her.

The leading article was about a new craze for bell-ringing, which was about the most conventional form of musical instrument featured. It read:

'All over the country a movement is gathering ground which will transform the bell-ringing world. 'Mega-ringing', as it has been dubbed, involves ringing a huge bell, at least forty fournis in diameter, by means of swinging on a large rope from one side to the other. Seen by many as more of an extreme sport than a form of music-making, the craze now has over a thousand dedicated players, who have set up a music school and governing body for the art, which was rejected as a legitimate musical pursuit by the Imperial Board of Music Colleges, which refused to teach it in its institutions last postin. Now, however, cathedrals and steeples across the country are opening up their belfries to players, who are proving themselves equal to any form of mechanised ringing.

'Saquinay Lizarde, President of the Board of Mega-Ringers, says the past-time is more fun than playing any other instrument. "The thing about mega-ringing

is that it's daring and it's dangerous to do – that's a thrill conventional instruments can't offer. And the sound they produce, though simple, is spectacularly beautiful."

'Lord Romsey, a keen Mega-ringer, says the IBMC should seriously re-consider its position on the art, which he says is "the greatest musical revolution in a century". Indeed, the Board of Mega-Ringers is organising a concert in Sulla in which Mega-Ringers from all over the country will ring all the bells of the city together to make a "tuneful clamour."'

Sharon was so engrossed in reading the magazine that she did not even notice when the capsules came to a halt at Leminghurst, where a hunchback of an old woman, dressed bizarrely from head to toe, hobbled onto another capsule in the string with her little dog.

Apnar had by now moved onto the *Sulla Herald* which he was studying with great determination, and Sharon placed down her magazine to pick up *The Chronicle.* As she went to pick the paper up, a bright yellow supplement fell from the inside of it to the floor. Sharon picked it up and found it was 'The Chronicle Rich List'. On the front cover was a picture of a tall, thin, pale man with round glasses, with the headline, 'Ark tops list again'. Opening the supplement, Sharon found a full list, extending to a thousand people, which detailed the estimated assets of each one and arranged them in order of size. Top of the list was Dennis Ark, the owner of Clement Maurice and Marcel's, with 7,860 Forden forests to his name. Apparently this was his third time at the top, a spot which had previously been filled by the Duke of Barrych, who was now relegated to fifth place. The supplement explained that the Emperor and Ruler was not included in the list, because technically he owned everything in the Sullarian Empire. It did note, however, that his personal wealth, irrespective of this rule, totalled more than 470,000 Forden forests anyway, putting him firmly in the number one spot. The supplement also pointed out that the average wealth of a Sullarian was 7,800 Forden leaves, or 0.0078 forests, the highest it had ever been. It didn't seem very high to Sharon when she considered the Emperor's wealth.

Scanning the list, Sharon saw that most of those in the Top 100 were Chief Executives or private investors or people who had inherited fortunes, like the Duke. The present Duke of Wilfredshire, who owned the famous bookstores, came in at number eight, with 2,910 forests. Just above him was a 'Professor Kellnor-Bowman', the inventor of Hoverers. There was a large article about Will and Annabelle Polonius, who rented out capsules to Motortranspo, and who were now in talks with the government about privatising some of the network, which would make their fortune soar instantly. But after about number fifteen, the fortunes dwindled, falling to only a hundred forests by number thirty-four. Sharon continued to guide her eye down the page and, to her surprise, there at number one hundred and twelve was Apnar's family's entry:

'Lord d'Arrawor & Family – 42 forests – Inheritance, land, property'

The newspaper had clearly not heard about some of Apnar's forests burning down, Sharon thought. Nevertheless, he was still one of the richest in the world, and one of the best companions Sharon could have chosen, she thought. She put down the supplement and looked out of the capsule window – endless lengths of tunnel zoomed by while Apnar continued to read the *Herald*, and it was about three angles later that they began to slowly judder to a halt at a small platform which Sharon didn't recognise.

The little old lady who had got on at Leminghurst got out of her capsule and Sharon saw her walk off the platform into the waiting room. A small, worn-out sign read, 'Jamestown Tunnel Station'. Sharon thought it must have been another rural station.

"Almost there, I believe," said Apnar, looking up at the screen, which now read:

'DIRECT NORTHWARD – Approaching Rastinun TS'

Sharon gave a sigh of relief and it suddenly dawned on her how close she was to the end of her journey, were she to succeed. She might never see Sulla again, or any of the other cities, she might never see Apnar's father again, or Pascale, or the Mentor, or, or, or…

Her train of thought was interrupted harshly, however, when the capsules slowed to a halt at Rastinun. The capsule door slid open, and Sophios and the Bugle-Thoms lay not for beyond it. Apnar gestured to Sharon to disembark, and having done so they both walked over towards the glass elevator which would take them up to the field above. The glass doors slid open for them as they entered the lift, which slowly ascended through the ground. Sharon caught her last glimmer of the Tunnelled Network before the roof of the elevator broke up and she and Apnar were left to climb out into the field. Apnar got out first and helped Sharon pull herself out after him – it was not the easiest of systems.

At last, however, Sharon was outside, and there before her stood the great chestnut tree which was the entrance to the tunnel station. The place had not changed at all since Sharon was last there – the birds continued to twitter in the trees and the skies were as blue as ever they had been. The only difference she could see was the absence of the bandy-legged man who had sat beneath a tree playing the lyre the last time.

"This is beautiful," remarked Apnar, walking off in the wrong direction. "Really quite beautiful!"

"It is," Sharon replied. "Is this your first time here?" she asked.

"Yes, of course. I'm very rarely in the countryside, and I've never been this far north before," he said.

Sharon found it odd how, in her short stay in Sullaria, she had been to places even people who had lived there all their lives, like Apnar, had never been to before.

"I think it's this way," said Sharon, eyeing the stone bridge.

"Oh, yes, of course it is," was Apnar's reply.

The pair walked on until they came to John Harolder's bridge, which they 'crossed in haste' like the poem said they should, and then followed the riverbank through the next field. Apnar didn't say a word while he enjoyed the fresh country air and the gentle breeze, but Sharon was concerned.

"How will I get to the Omega Spires?" she asked Apnar.

"Oh, wait an angle, Sharon. We'll discuss all that when we get to Sophios' house. You'll be just fine, I know it," he said encouragingly.

Eventually Sharon found the weather-beaten path which led to the church in the village. She was getting close now, she thought.

"So this is the village up ahead, is it?" said Apnar curiously.

"Yes, Sophios lives in... what is it... Halsworth Square, that's it," replied Sharon, directing Apnar onto the cobbled street in front of the church.

"Right then," said Apnar. "You lead the way."

Sharon wasn't sure if she would be able to lead the way, but the village was small, and the square could not be far away.

"Down here, I think," she said, walking with Apnar down the street.

A moment later, a man wearing a green velvet robe turned a corner farther up the road and came riding down it on his bicycle. Sharon recognised him at once to be Mr. Tolliery. He seemed to recognise her, too, though, and promptly fell off his bike, landing with a thud on the cobbles. Sharon and Apnar ran up to him.

"Miss Jarls?" he said, lifting his head up.

"Hello, Roland," said Sharon. "This is Apnar."

"A — Apnar?" he said, a look of shock on his face. "As in..."

"Yes, as in Lord d'Arrawor," said Apnar, smiling at his fellow nobleman.

"Well, it gives me great, I mean it gives me the warmest, the greatest pleasure to, to make your noble acquaintance, sir," said Mr. Tolliery, picking himself up from the ground.

"How do you do?" said Apnar.

"This is Lord Tolliery, Apnar," said Sharon, taking control of the situation. "He runs the local transport service."

"Ah, Lord Tolliery, what are you doing here?" said Apnar, confused.

"That's a long story," he said, mounting his bicycle.

"Well, perhaps you could enlighten us on our way to Sophios' house. Halsworth Square, I think you said, Sharon," proposed Apnar.

"I'd be delighted," said Lord T. "Hop aboard!"

Apnar and Sharon mounted the other two seats on the contraption and Tolliery about-turned and rode off down the way he had just come, explaining to Apnar all about his family history, which Sharon had heard before. At last they came to the Viennese square in which Sophios resided – Sharon recognised the yellow paving and the beautiful buildings straight away, and they called back memories of the time she had first encountered them, seventy days before.

"Here we are!" said Tolliery excitedly. "Good luck, Sharon."

"Thank you, Roland," replied Sharon, dismounting the vehicle with Apnar.

"Yes, thank you," added Apnar.

They both waved as the bicycle went off on its way down the road, and Sharon led Apnar to Sophios' house, number three Halsworth Square. Apnar climbed the narrow steps the front door and rang the brass bell, whose tones resounded in the square from the belfry above. Not quite big enough for Mega-ringing, thought Sharon.

Yet when the huge oak door was opened, it was not Sophios standing behind it, but a tall, thin man dressed in a white uniform, armed with a sword. Sharon need not have been as disturbed as she was at that moment, because of what followed:

"Yes?" the man said in a militaristic voice.

"Er, we're here to see The Honourable Sophios of Sulla, please," said Apnar, a little confused.

"It's not… it is… it's not Lord d'Arrawor, is it?" said the man.

"It is indeed, sir," Apnar replied, smiling.

"Well, do come in, sir, do come in," answered the man, bowing. "I am Guard on Duty for Sophios of Sulla, Emperor's Fifth Armed Regiment. Sophios is in his study."

The guard, who Sharon now realised was the one who had been off sick when she had visited Sophios before, was now acting like more of a butler than a policeman. He ushered Sharon and Apnar into the drawing room while he went to alert Sophios in his study. A moment later, Sharon heard the sound of footsteps bounding towards the drawing room – it was Sophios, of course.

"Sharon!" he exclaimed, his face lit up. "How nice it is to see you again, dear. And Apnar, how are you?"

"I'm very well, thank you, Sophios," replied Apnar, surveying the room.

"Oh, do sit down! Come, come!" said Sophios, waving his arms in the air. Sharon and Apnar followed his request.

"This is a beautiful house," commented Apnar.

"Well, thank you. Of course, it's nothing like the Sullarian mansions!" Sophios replied. "But tell me, were you successful?"

"Yes, we were. I need to cross the border," explained Sharon.

"You do?" said Sophios more quietly. "And why is that?"

"The Oracle said there was a portal, beyond the Omega Spires north of the border, which should take me home," Sharon went on.

"Ah! So the legends were true," said Sophios, scratching his chin.

"It's been an incredible journey," said Apnar.

"But it's not over yet," corrected Sophios. "But Sharon, do stay a few nights before you go. Tell us all about everything that's happened – the Bugle-Thoms are hanging on your every word, I assure you!"

"But we can't, Sophios," said Sharon. "I'm sorry – I'd love to. But I have to get back home – everyone will be so worried. I need to get there as soon as possible."

Sophios looked alarmed.

"And another thing," said Apnar. "I... I need to return to Sulla, Sharon."

"What?" said Sharon, confused.

"I should have told you earlier. But I... I got a letter – you know, at Uncle Cirrus's, and I need to return to the city by tonight in order to attend a meeting. It's terribly important," Apnar explained.

"But what about..."

"I'm sorry, Sharon. I really am. If only I could see you to the portal, and say goodbye properly. But if I don't go down... well, it's very serious, and I can't say what it's about. All I can tell you is that if I'm not there tonight, I may be discharged."

"Oh dear, dear, dear," remarked Sophios, his eyebrows twitching. "How can this be? Don't worry, Sharon, I'll lead you to the border. Apnar, you make sure you get to Sulla – you've been more of a help to Sharon than anyone else, heaven knows."

"Oh, Apnar," sobbed Sharon, now shedding a few tears. "How can I ever thank you for everything?"

"Now, now, I never said I wanted thanks. I've only done what I had to, for your sake, and I'm more glad than you know that I have. It's been great," consoled Apnar.

"Yes, it has," said Sharon. "Thank you, Apnar, for everything."

"All right then," said Sophios, standing up from his chair. "Apnar, do you need to leave now?"

"Oh no, Sophios, I can stay a little longer," he replied.

"Excellent. Then I'll invite the Bugle-Thoms round and you can both tell us all about all you've done, if you don't mind," proposed Sophios.

"Of course not," agreed Apnar, walking over to the huge bay window. "I do love the countryside."

Sophios left the room and went to notify the Bugle-Thoms from his study, leaving Apnar and Sharon to talk over her present situation. They hadn't had much of an opportunity, however, before Sophios came bounding back into the room with a huge smile on his face.

"They're on their way over now," he said, lighting the fire. "Would you like anything to drink, Apnar, Sharon?"

"Do you have any Richmondy?" asked Apnar hopefully.

"Richmondy – why, yes of course. I'm rather partial to it myself," replied Sophios.

"Could I just have water?" asked Sharon.

"Certainly," said Sophios.

Within seconds, these drinks had appeared beside Apnar and Sharon, not to mention a large bottle of '22' which had appeared next to Sophios. Sharon recognised it at once as the drink that had knocked her out last time.

Sharon took a sip of her water and began explaining what had happened since she last contacted Sophios on Yriad a few days ago. As she now realised, a lot had happened in those few days, and she was just in the middle of relating her experiences in the Temple of Onyx when the bell above rang out loudly, intimating that a guest had arrived.

"Let them in!" shouted Sophios to the guard.

Moments later, the Bugle-Thoms entered the room, Jock in his best suit and Martha in a pink frock which could not have suited her less.

"Sharrin!" she exclaimed.

"Martha! It's good to see you again," said Sharon, beaming. "And you, Jock. I've got so much to tell you both."

"She certainly has," verified Sophios.

Apnar rose from his chair to greet the couple, whom he told firmly to call him Apnar.

"It is a pleasure indeed to meet such an est-ee-med gentleman as yourself be," said Martha. "A pleasure indeed."

Apnar told them the pleasure was all his.

And so for the next thirty angles or so Sharon and Apnar told the assembled party their entire story over a fantastic feast laid on by Sophios. The stags' heads on the wall of the dining room gave disapproving looks while they munched on venison, and Sharon felt, strangely, at home.

At the end of the meal, and once Sharon had finished her tales, Apnar rose from the table and said he had to leave for Sulla, at which point Sophios said:

"Then we'll leave, too. There's no time to lose anymore, eh Sharon?"

Sharon agreed and, saying final farewells to Jock and Martha, left Sophios' house for good, waving Apnar off as he went down the road the other way towards the station. Her faithful companion was now gone forever.

CHAPTER TWENTY-FOUR

The Omega Spires

Sophios led Sharon to the end of the road leading north out of the little village. The cobbled road ended suddenly, leading onto battered grass which covered the riverbank. The clear river was just a few feet ahead of Sharon, and it bubbled soothingly, leading Sophios and Sharon upstream, towards the northern border.

"This is the true Shanklot corridor," said Sophios gravely, leading Sharon by the river.

"How far is the border?" asked Sharon.

"Oh, not too far. Only a few angles away. The village is one of the most northerly in the Empire," explained Sophios. "You see, this river comes down from Mount Gleddock, over there."

Sophios pointed to a distant mountain, the only one Sharon had ever seen in this new world, from which the river seemed to run down.

"No-one knows where the river leads ultimately," said Sophios. "But it certainly runs well past the border, right to the very edge of that map I gave you. Do you have it with you now?" he asked.

"Erm," fumbled Sharon. "No, I don't."

"Well, nerver mind. But as I said, the river runs off the map," Sophios continued.

The countryside in this untouched area was truly the most beautiful Sharon had ever seen, either in this world or her own – it was so bright, and the sunlight sparkled through the branches of ancient trees, a few butterflies flying around the bright plant life on Sharon's left, fish swimming through the river on Sharon's right. There was not a bee or wasp in sight, to Sharon's relief, and despite the season, it seemed as though it were the middle of summer.

"What do you know about the portal?" Sharon asked Sophios, still taking in the picturesque surroundings.

"Not a great deal, I'm afraid," said Sophios. "I had suspected there might be some kind of portal north of the border – the Forbidden Portal, as some legends put it. Only country folk tend to remember these things, and I only learnt about it from some locals here. No Emperor has ever been able to breach the forest beyond the border, you know, so it was always suspected there must be something stopping them. That's why it was known as the Forbidden Portal, because it would not let anybody use it."

Sharon looked alarmed.

"Oh, but it'll let you use it. Certainly it will, if the Oracle said so. Because of course you need to use it – you don't belong here, Sharon."

This was something Sharon knew indefinitely already.

"What does it look like?" she asked, looking up at Sophios.

"Well, I don't know, my dear. Nobody does. But you soon will, I hope," he replied, smiling.

"And you, surely?" corrected Sharon.

"Oh, no, my dear, not I. I will lead you to an acquaintance of mine, who lives beyond the border here. He's the only one to live here now, and I'm about the only person who knows about him. Windar's his name – just Windar. He lives in the heart of the forest, and he will show you to the Omega Spires. You see, Sharon, I've been thinking about you every waking moment since we last talked. And I wondered, if it is the portal, then how could you get there? And then the idea popped into my head: Windar knows about the Omega Spires, and the portal is rumoured to be near there!"

"So you're not seeing me off, either?" replied Sharon desperately.

"I'm afraid I'd be no use – no use at all, Sharon. I don't know the forest one bit. All I can do is follow the river, and that's no use."

"Oh, Sophios! How much longer is it to Windar's house?"

Sophios burst with laughter.

"My dear, don't apply such a grand term to Windar's residence! 'It's a hut', as he says, 'no more and no less'. He really is very friendly, though."

"But how far?" Sharon persisted.

"Oh, not long now. Look, beyond here is the border," Sophios replied, pointing beyond a tree up ahead whose branches blocked the view of what was behind it.

When they walked round the tree, the most glorious sight Sharon had ever seen stood before her – all of Sulla's majesty, all of Asher's treasures, and all of Fordenia's wealth was nothing in comparison. It was the most beautiful sight Sharon had ever set her sparkling blue eyes on.

"Amelia's Falls," said Sophios, presenting the feature to Sharon.

It was at this point that the river widened hugely, from only a few feet wide to hundreds of feet wide, and the bubbling waters cascaded vertically down a gigantic waterfall which Sharon was standing at the top of. There was a hazy mist of steam in the air, and as Sharon started walking towards the edge of the waterfall to get a look at the drop Sophios stopped her:

"Careful now! Don't go any further – it's called Amelia's *Falls* for a reason, you know."

Sharon wasn't quite sure if Sophios had intended this a joke, so she took it as deadly serious, and backed away from the edge.

"You'll see it in its full splendour once we get down," Sophios explained. "Now, you just come over here with me and we'll climb down beside the falls."

Sophios led Sharon past the top of the waterfall to the other side, where there was a steep grassy slope.

"I often used to come up here in my youth," explained Sophios. "When we went on holiday from Sulla."

Sharon could now survey the long, very long, drop down from where she was standing, and struggled to imagine a youthful Sophios.

"You'd be pardoned for not knowing this was the northern border," said Sophios, still smiling.

"Where?" said Sharon, looking all around her.

"The falls, of course!" explained Sophios.

There was not a signpost, a fence, or a line or warning of any kind that this marked the northern frontier of the greatest Empire in the world, even though it had been like that for centuries.

"So you've left the country!" joked Sharon as Sophios examined the slope down.

"Back again," he said as he jumped back no more than a metre. "I think you ought to go down first – it's quite a long way down, but it's safer than it looks. All right then, on you go."

Sharon went forward towards the grassy slope and turned round the other way, slowly making her way down the slope while grasping onto the ground with her hands. The steam from the waterfall was now all around her and she could see that by the time she would get back onto flat land she would be around fifty feet from the falls.

"Here I come!" shouted Sophios from up above, following Sharon down. "Just keep going – that's it!"

Eventually she reached the foot of the slope and, giving a sigh of relief, stepped back to take a good look at the waterfall. She was in the perfect position to appreciate the vastness and glory of this natural phenomenon, water crashing down into the river below, which was very wide on this side. Then, as if nothing had happened, the water simply flowed on gently down the river, just as it had done on the other side. Turning back again to look forward into the forest, Sharon could see a maze of huge trees all ahead of her, with no indication of human intervention. The river narrowed and meandered away through the forest, beyond some trees to the right of where Sharon was standing, and just as she was surveying the forest's natural beauty and wondering how Windar could possibly live there, she was interrupted by a giant thud behind her. It seemed Sophios had lost his grip and had submitted to sliding down the slope backwards, reaching the bottom with a most unceremonious tumble.

Sophios picked himself up and dusted off his cloak, saying:

"Well, that wasn't quite how I planned it. But never mind – come on!"

He pointed ahead with his bony forefinger towards the forest.

"Windar's hut is just beyond those trees," he continued, leading Sharon towards the forest.

As they entered the forest Sharon felt a sudden chill, a haunting breeze which seemed as though it were the breath of a giant, and for a moment, it spooked her.

"What's the matter?" said Sophios, turning to Sharon.

"It's just…"

"The cold, yes? The forest can be terribly cold, ruthlessly cold, my dear. Windar will give you a scarf, I'm sure."

"Good," replied Sharon. It was too cold to make idle conversation.

As she walked on it became darker and darker, and when Windar's wooden hut came into view it was almost pitch black. The only thing stopping Sharon and Sophios from repeatedly bumping into each other was a small fire burning outside the hut, which crackled eerily.

"That is Windar's hut," declared Sophios, his long arm outstretched towards the meagre building. "He built it himself using trees from the forest."

Suddenly, and out of nowhere, a huge great bearded man appeared from behind the hut, wearing a long dark cloak. He was bald, and Sharon thought at first he resembled a monk in his habit.

"Windar!" called Sophios to the man, whose deep brown eyes glinted in the light of the fire. "Windar!"

The man remained silent, pounding the earth beneath him as he walked closer to Sharon and Sophios.

"Who goes there?" he said in a hoarse, tired voice.

"Sophios – only Sophios and a friend," bellowed Sophios, taking his gold medallion from his pocket and lifting it towards Windar.

"Sophios!" Windar repeated, now forcing his coarse features into a smile.

"Windar, how good to see you again!" said Sophios, shaking Windar's great hand heartily.

Windar was a man of no less than eight feet tall, warm-hearted but simple, and he looked as though he could fell every tree in the forest with only his left hand.

"And good to see you, too, Sophios," he replied in a very low voice which seemed to boom and cause even the tallest tree to judder. "Come with me to the fire."

"Windar, I must ask you a favour," began Sophios as they all took a seat on the boulders assembled round the pyre. "Sharon, who arrived in the Shanklot Corridor a couple of months ago, needs to get to the Omega Spires, as soon as possible." Sophios emphasised the last clause by hissing every letter 's' as though he were a python.

"Why?" was Windar's simple but profound reply.

"Because she must get to the portal, which has been opened…"

"By who?" grunted Windar ungrammatically.

"By Sharon herself," Sophios answered, pausing. "She is from another world, if you will."

"Another… Another world, you say?" repeated Windar, astounded. "Say no more, Sophios, I'll take her to the Spires. The portal must be protected."

"Indeed," agreed Sophios. "Then you will take her tonight?"

"I'll take 'er now," Windar replied, standing up tall.

"Excellent."

"Thank you, Windar, and thank you, Sophios. You've done so much for me…" Sharon began before it would be too late to thank Sophios.

"I consider it a duty," interrupted Sophios, "to help others."

Windar nodded gravely.

"Farewell, Sharon, and good luck!" With this final statement Sophios got up from his seat and marched off through the forest towards his home.

"Thank you, Sophios. Goodbye!" Sharon called to him, but he was out of sight within seconds.

Windar stared down at Sharon from his elevated position, examining her face with great scrutiny.

"Sharon," he said. "I will take you to the Spires tonight. And you will go home tonight."

"Thank you," replied Sharon, looking up at him.

The giant man turned around and went into his hut for a moment, reappearing with a pair of long woollen scarves.

"Put this on," he said. "The forest can be cruel."

Sharon did as he said, wrapping the scarf tightly around her neck – it would be perfect for when she returned to Iceland, she thought, if she would return.

"Now, be careful and follow me. The way is not far, but it's terrible dark. Terrible dark," Windar repeated, shaking his head so vigorously Sharon thought it might just fly off his neck.

He lit a large lamp with a stick from the fire and held it out in front of him to guide the way, wrapping his giant scarf around his giant neck.

"What do you know about the portal?" asked Sharon as they walked, quite slowly, through the forest.

"Oh, I know that it takes people from place to place, always so different from one another. I never have seen it, mind. Never," said Windar, again with a shake of the head. "But it must be protected – if it were to be used by someone often, for whatever reason, it could have 'dee-sas-ter-ous cons-quences' as the legend says."

"What else does the legend say?" asked Sharon, feeling safe under Windar's direction, despite the darkness, the coldness and the shrieking winds which sometimes blew through the trees, making them shake as though they were little dandelions in the breeze.

"Why, that's about the lot of it. Only written down once, you see, 'undreds of postins ago. But no-one has ever been able to use the thing as the legend says, for many a King and Emperor has tried and failed to recapture this land beyond the border."

"Why's that?"

"Nobody knows. The portal is 'forbidden', and that's that. I think that's why. This place is 'forbidden'."

"I heard the Omega Spires were the last in all the towers around Sulla," said Sharon.

"Yes, that's right. And it's the only one not by the coast. It's the largest, too, to be sure. Only been there twice myself, mind, only twice."

"When was that?"

"Once, when I was a lad, when I lived inside the Kingdom as it was then, I went explorin' and saw it from a distance. Puts the fear of death into you, that sight, 'specially at the age of six!"

At this point Windar made a gruff splutter intermingled with a cough intermingled with a shout which Sharon assumed to be his way of laughing.

"I ran and ran!" he shouted. "Ran and *ran*! And then when I came to live here I went out to find it again. That time I went closer – right to the door. The great door! And I opened it and looked inside – it was like a great cathedral, without any candles or pews or pulpits or anything! It was bare, real bare, I mean. Just stone, with a huge window at the north end. The portal is just beyond it, they say."

"Will I have to go in?" Sharon asked, looking up at Windar.

"Well, that will depend upon whether or not you need to. Per'aps you could walk round it and the portal will be there afore you. Per'aps you will 'ave to go through the building itself. We'll see."

"What does it look like?" was Sharon's next question.

"You'll soon see, my dear. I'm no good with dee-scriptions. No good at all!"

Windar was right on both counts – within a few angles Sharon could see an immense building of gargantuan proportions, rising up out of the forest. It looked to her like Westminster Abbey, only with a hugely extended pair of towers, the spires tapering off at the very top. Beyond this frontage, hundreds of spires, each a different size, rose up from the rooftop like organ pipes, in a random and disorganised manner. It was every inch a gothic cathedral, more of a monster than a monstrosity, and it towered over everything for many miles.

"Behold!!" boomed Windar, holding out his great arms towards the Omega Spires.

Sharon could see why the building had 'put the fear of death' into Windar – it was at this moment having the same effect on her.

With renewed enthusiasm, Windar held up the lamp and marched forward towards the Spires. Sharon walked by his side, struggling to keep up with his huge paces, and approached the Spires. In silence, Windar looked right up at the face of the structure, taking in the full height and magnitude of the building, before looking forward at the giant oak door in front. It was arched at the top, and gargoyles in every possible kind of grimace stared down at the entrant from above the door. Sharon was even sure she saw one move, but dismissed it as nerves.

Windar took the wrought iron handle with his huge right hand and pushed with all his might at the door. Slowly it began to open, offering Sharon glimpses of the terrifyingly barren interior. With an expression of anguish on his face, Windar made one last shove at the door, and it flew fully open, rebounding off the inside wall with an almighty crash. The bang sent scores of bats diving down from the rafters, screeching unbearably, and heading straight for the forest. Sharon had to move out the way of the door immediately to ensure she was not knocked over by the flight of the bats. They burst through the doorway like lava bursts forth from a volcano at the beginning of a great eruption, and they terrified Sharon, who was now holding her face in her hands.

Still in silence, Windar put his forearm around Sharon and brought her back to the door, taking her hands away from her face, pale with terror. As she looked in, what she saw was a stone hall, leading up to the magnificent window at the other side, and flanked by huge, thick stone columns. The place was completely bare, and the huge north window, though it was completely dark outside, let in huge shafts of light as if by a miracle. But the most frightening thing about it was its silence – it truly deafened Sharon.

"I'll go now," said Windar. Sharon looked worried. "You will find the portal if you are meant to. I cannot approach it – *I* am not meant to approach it, and I won't. Look through the Spires, and if you find nothing, look outside and it will appear, if only in the corner of your eye, I'm sure. If all fails, stay here in the Spires and I will come for you later. Good luck, and goodbye."

Sharon could not speak. She swallowed hard and smiled at Windar, before he turned around and started making his way back. She managed to say, "Thank you!" but Windar did not hear her. He was out of sight in no time.

Sharon turned back round to face the Spires, and walked in. It was even colder in here than outside, and as soon as she had walked a few slow paces the giant door, which had taken so much effort to open, crashed shut behind her with a harsh swoosh of wind. The event made her jump, and her heart began to throb inside her. She had never been in a more tense situation before in her life, and she doubted if she ever would be again.

Suddenly she heard a distant door slam shut, a much smaller door than the monumental one she had come through, but a door all the same. This was followed by the gentle sound of distant footsteps on a stone floor – footsteps that were determined and meant.

Sharon could not think what to do. Her heart was already racing, and she made a dash for one of the columns, hiding behind it and holding her breath.

The footsteps got louder.

And louder.

And louder.

Suddenly they stopped, decidedly, and Sharon peered out from behind her hiding place. There, standing beneath the north window, was a tall figure, cloaked in a very long, black cloak which completely covered his body, and wearing a heavy hood over his head, preventing Sharon from seeing his face. He cut a frightening pose, illuminated only by the powerful shaft of light which shone through the north window, and his silhouette was captured, and stretched out, down the hall as a tall shadow. The head of his shadow almost reached where Sharon was standing, and she saw it move as he looked left and right.

Sharon thought she would faint, if not die on the spot.

After a maddening silence, the man shouted out across the hall:

"Sharon!"

This was the only word he said, and yet Sharon seemed to hear it a thousand times as it echoed constantly for a while throughout the vast hall. Sharon felt she recognised the voice – she knew it was somehow familiar. Then it hit her: it was Apnar.

CHAPTER TWENTY-FIVE

The Portal

Sharon cowered behind the column, utterly confused – Apnar had said he was leaving – more than that, she *saw* him leave. It didn't make any sense at all.

"Sharon!" he repeated. "Yes, it's me," he added, walking slowly down the hall, his footsteps echoing.

Sharon dared not look at him – instead, she fixed her eyes on his huge shadow, which moved up the wall as he came closer. Eventually he stopped and Sharon got up from behind the column to face him in the middle of the hall. She looked straight at him, with a blank expression on her face. He was smiling, revealing snow white teeth which glinted, his green eyes staring straight at Sharon.

"Hello again," he said, in a tone Sharon had never heard him speak in before.

"Why are you here?" asked Sharon gently, looking up at Apnar.

He gave a sort of quasi-laugh and replied, "I shall explain."

Sharon doubted whether he was telling the truth as a deadening silence ensued for a few seconds.

"Sharon, I am here to find the portal with you," he said.

"But I thought you had to return…"

"No, Sharon. You thought wrongly. I will return to Sulla as soon as I have found the portal."

Apnar maintained his smile and had his hands on his hips.

"Well, thank you for," Sharon began to thank him, in spite of his peculiar tone.

"No, no, no, Sharon. It is I who has to thank you – truly!"

"What d'you mean?"

"What do I mean! I mean that you will show me where the portal is, and you will return home, and…"

Apnar paused again, apparently for effect.

"And I shall live happily ever after."

Sharon was baffled. What he was saying was music to her ears, but he carried it off with such a cruel attitude. In the end, she said nothing.

"Because, Sharon, I shall use the portal – extensively. I shall use it and use it until it closes. Sharon, this is my quest we have been on. This is *my* journey, and this is *my* happy ending."

His smile grew slowly to its full extent, and then dropped back down to a scowl.

"What?" was all Sharon could muster.

"What indeed! Sharon, many postins ago I read a book. Half of a book, to be precise. I found it, tattered and grubby, in my father's library, right at the end of a shelf of old tomes. I must have read it a thousand times! It is an ancient book, many hundreds of postins old, and it is long forgotten. Yet this book is what has guided my entire life – this book is my greatest treasure."

Sharon stood still silently, watching intently as Apnar went on.

"This book was called *Beyond the Mist*, Sharon, and *you* are the main character. Yes, you," he repeated as Sharon frowned in disbelief. She had heard of the book before; yes, she had seen it at the Shanklot Stead, the one which glittered in the sunlight.

"You will be surprised to know that it charts the entire first half of your journey, and it has been invaluable to me, and, of course, to you. I knew of the portal, and I saw it mentioned in the book. I read my name and saw that I would help you, saw that I would lead you, eventually, to the portal. This was four postins ago, Sharon, when I had just started working for the government, and I kept the whole thing to myself for the whole time, waiting and waiting.

"Until it started to happen. First when father received the message from Sophios about you, and he suggested I should be your guide in Sulla. It was happening just like in the book, and my waiting was nearly over, Sharon. I met you in Sulla wearing exactly what the book specified, and I tried so hard to do everything just as it was written. Eventually, Sharon, I found I didn't even need to try. Everything just fell into place and happened just as the book said – I said just what the book said I did, without even thinking about it. When we got to Yriad, Cirrus told me the Arvadians were looking for the portal too, and I admit I was shocked. I had forgotten he would tell me that! But I knew it wouldn't matter. The whole process was going to be so much easier than I had thought!"

"Uncle Cirrus knew?" said Sharon, surprised.

"Everybody knew, Sharon! The whole family knew. Mother knew, and it cost her dearly."

"What do you mean?"

"There is no 'Act 22', Sharon. Really, I had doubts you would ever believe that one, but you did. Mother didn't agree with the rest of us – she tried to tell the Boothcotians about the plan, but we stopped her."

Sharon gasped in disgust.

"Whoever made up this whole plan was sailing pretty close to the wind some of the time – but then, I don't know if anyone did make it up. The whole sequence of events just materialised out of no-where, didn't it?! Your story was recorded in the book because you had lived it, but you had only lived it since I had read the book."

"But you only had half the..." said Sharon, interrupting him.

"Book, yes. But the second half, well, I didn't need it, did I? I'm sure I've done everything it says, too. As I said, everything just comes naturally. You see, Sharon, the book could not have been written if you do not return to your home, so I knew you would, I knew you would find the portal. I just did what I thought I should do, I did everything in my power to make this work, Sharon, and it has."

"Not yet," she corrected him. "What do you want with the portal? You can't come with me!" she shouted, her voice booming all around the ancient building.

"I never said I would. Sharon, do you appreciate what the portal IS?" Apnar demanded, coming closer.

"Well, no..."

"Do you really believe you are in some other world?" he demanded again.

"Of course," said Sharon. "This is no dream."

"Certainly not! But you are in no different a world from that which you left."

Sharon was silent – all this information had left her in the deepest puzzlement.

"You have simply... moved on a little."

"Moved on a ..." Sharon repeated in a whisper, still trying to piece together what was going on.

"Yes, moved on – in time. More than a little, in fact. You have moved on hundreds of postins, at the very least. Probably a thousand. I don't know, but you're here, and that's all that matters to me."

"You mean I'm in... the future?" asked Sharon, astonished.

"Well, it is future to you, I'm sure. But to me, this is the present – you are a gift from the past."

"But it's so different…"

"Sharon, hundreds of postins ago something terrible happened, something incredible and awful. No-one knows what, but it caused the complete break-up of the world as you know it. Then came Ancient Age One, when the people of the world were scattered across the world and began to rebuild what they had lost. Their main aim was only to survive, and this remained the case for their children, their grandchildren, their great-grandchildren, for around four hundred postins. After this time, people began to explore and pioneer again. They tried to recover knowledge that was lost, and they progressed and developed, and eventually, well, here we are today."

Sharon was amazed. The future of the world had just been revealed to her in a matter of seconds. She was living the future.

"The portal was developed, in great secrecy, using ancient documents and remnants of the knowledge possessed before the first Ancient Age, at about this time. It was originally called the Foramen Vermis, the hole of the worm. Why it was called this, I don't know. I doubt if anyone knows, but that doesn't matter to me.

"What matters is that you are here and you must lead me to the portal."

"What do you want with it, though?" insisted Sharon.

"I want to use it to travel through time, of course. I want to use it to give me wealth and power, and the government wants it to plan battles and see ahead. You see?"

"But… why?" she continued. Apnar was already tremendously rich and powerful, and abusing the portal could only have disastrous consequences, she thought.

"Why? Why? I've had enough of this, Sharon. I really have. I've put up with you this far, and I'm not prepared to do it any longer. Now go and find the portal – you need to get home and 'tell your story'."

"But," she said.

"But?!! But?!! If I did not need you to get through that portal I swear I would kill you right this instant. All your questions, your ignorance, your stupidity. It's enough to warrant murder."

Sharon felt the hair on the back of her neck stand up as Apnar toyed with a silver sword he had just withdrawn, brandishing it in front of her madly.

"Go on then!" he shrieked ferociously, turning round and holding up the sword to the north window.

"Stop at once!" boomed an ancient voice from behind Sharon. It was unmistakable – it belonged to Sophios.

"Sophi—" Apnar began, swivelling round on the spot and almost chopping Sharon's head clear off with his sword.

"Stand back!" he thundered. "Stand back!!"

Apnar took a few hesitant steps backward, lowering his sword.

"Get out, Sophios!" he shouted gruffly. "Before I kill you."

Sophios shoved Sharon to the side and held his palms up to the ceiling. Sharon ran behind another column as sparks began to fly forth from his hands. Apnar looked unconcerned, but then an enormous lightning bolt flew out from his right hand at Apnar, striking him in the chest and knocking him down to the floor. His sword went flying threw the air and landed with a crash at the side of the hall. Apnar let out a scream of pain – his eyes were no longer green, but burning red as the lightning bolt still connected him to Sophios.

Sophios raised up his hand, and as he did so Apnar was lifted into the air, still connected to Sophios by the bolt, right up to the full height of the ceiling. Sharon could only look on in fear. Sophios pushed his hand through the air, as though he were pushing open an imaginary door with great power. As he did this, Apnar was flung through the air, as the lightning bolt stretched out across the hall, and crashed through the north window, shattering the glass in an instant and disappearing from sight. He was well and truly dead.

It had all happened too fast for Sharon – she was terrified and relieved, confused and desperate.

"Sharon," said Sophios in a soothing voice, walking over to her. "It's all right, now. It's all right."

"But Apnar… he was… he told me…"

"I heard it all, Sharon. I was standing at the door."

"But how did you…?"

"When I was returning through the forest I saw him, running through the forest with that great cloak on. I knew something was wrong," Sophios explained, his hand on Sharon's shoulder.

"But he did so much for me…" she insisted.

"No, Sharon. Now we know he was only doing it for himself. The Arvadians will be looking for this place, but I will guard it with my life. I will *ensure* that this portal is kept completely safe from abuse, Sharon – you can be sure of that. But now; now you must go home. It has been an ordeal, and it has come to a sour end, I confess. But Apnar's gone now, and he won't be able to bother anyone anymore. And as for Noggard, well, I thought I could trust him…"

"But I'll always remember Apnar as he was… before tonight, I mean," protested Sharon, fighting back tears.

"I wouldn't think too fondly of him, my dear. Remember what he meant by it all – but I don't want you to feel this experience has been a bad one…"

"I'll take plenty of good memories home with me, I'm sure," replied Sharon, getting up.

"Good, good," said Sophios slowly and softly. "I wish you luck – everyone here is so pleased you came. You've made a great impression on us all, you know."

Sharon laughed a little, and then said, resolutely:

"So where's the portal?"

"That's the spirit, Sharon! That's the spirit! Now, let's have a look, shall we…"

The pair walked down the hall towards the shattered north window. Shards of clear glass were strewn all over the stone floor, and Sharon was afraid of going outside, of confronting Apnar again.

"Here, look!" said Sophios, smiling effusively.

To the far left of the window was a little wooden door, only three quarters the size of Sharon, which led outside. Sharon followed Sophios towards it, and Sophios pulled it open easily to reveal the forest outside. Sharon swallowed as she thought of how Apnar's dead body was only a few metres to the right.

"Come out through here," said Sophios. "The portal can't be far away."

Reluctantly, Sharon followed him out, not daring to look right, though it was too dark to see far ahead of you anyway.

"There's a path," said Sharon, observing a weather-beaten track leading away through the trees up ahead. It was only about a foot wide, and was so coarse and rough that it could have been easily missed.

"Well done! Well done indeed, dear!" exclaimed Sophios loudly, eyeing up the track.

Sharon walked down it slowly, every step taking her that little bit closer to home, and began to think over her journey. It had been an incredibly journey – she could not have hoped for a better companion, despite his alterior motives, and she was cared for and looked after in the best possible way. Most of all, it had been an adventure, and one she would never forget. She had been to places the average citizen would never see in his or her lifetime, she had explored the unknown and the forbidden, and she had taken risks which, more often than not, had landed her in a mess. She had had nothing to lose, of course, while all the others around her risked everything for her sake, or so it had seemed.

The track was becoming rougher as she and Sophios went on, and there was nothing to light their way. Eventually, the track tapered off in the most unlikely of places. They were still in the middle of the forest, and there was no portal to be seen. Sharon looked all around her, and Sophios began to explore the surroundings.

Then, suddenly, something caught Sharon's eye. It was over to her right up ahead, just between two trees, but it was too dark to make it out properly. She walked on a little further and shouted, "There!" to Sophios, who quickly caught up with her.

"What is it?" he said, wondering.

Even more slowly than before, they approached the 'something' and within a few seconds Sharon could make out that it was a door, a blue door. Two narrow blue doors, in fact. It was the most battered and ragged door Sharon had ever seen, and it was bolted on the outside. It looked quite out of place in the forest – it was obvious there was nothing behind it, or either side of it, and yet it stood freely of itself, unapologetically.

"What?" whispered Sharon characteristically.

Sophios stared at the thing in bafflement.

"This can't be it?" Sharon said dismissively. "What's it doing here?"

"Well, one can always try opening it…" suggested Sophios, himself confused.

Sharon took his advice and, unbolting the bolt without any trouble, opened the double doors towards her. What happened next took her by complete surprise. A jet of cold air blew straight towards her, and she stumbled, almost falling flat on her back before Sophios caught her and set her straight. Sharon could not quite believe her eyes – beyond the door was nothing but the colour white, contrasting starkly with the blackness of the forest. Sophios looked equally as surprised as he felt himself shiver with the cold air that was being blown onto him from the door.

"What is it?" asked Sharon. It could have been a white sheet of paper strapped onto the back of the door for all she could make out.

"Is it…" began Sophios slowly in a soft voice. "I mean, is that… your home?"

"No!" replied Sharon, shaking her head vigorously. "But… no, it couldn't possibly…"

"Yes?"

"Iceland?" she said, so softly that she hardly heard herself say it.

"Ice-land??" repeated Sophios more loudly. "It looks icy!"

Sharon stepped forward and put her hand through the door. It went straight through, and Sharon felt her fingers tingle in the icy cold.

"It is!" she shouted. "It's Iceland!"

Sophios looked amazed. Sharon stuck her head through the opening and felt the cool breezes whip the back of her neck.

"This is where you left?" asked Sophios.

"Yes, yes!" she replied, recalling the desolate wilderness of the icy plains. "But they must have given up searching by now."

"By now?"

"I've been away so long – they'll think I'm dead," she panicked.

"Now, now, Sharon. Don't say such things. Since it seems to have taken you back to the *place* you left, perhaps it will take you back to the *time* you left, too," Sophios suggested logically.

"I hope so," said Sharon, looking out through the opening.

"Well, you can't go back now," said Sophios rather darkly.

"No," Sharon consented, still staring out into the wilderness.

"We'll all miss you, Sharon, you know," said Sophios finally. "Very much."

"And I'll miss this place, and you, Sophios, and everyone," Sharon replied. "Thank you, Sophios, and pass on my thanks to the Bugle-Thoms when you get back."

"Oh, I will. I will. On you go, then – no stopping you now. Good luck, and thank *you*."

Hearing these parting words, Sharon took one last look at Sophios, smiled, and walked through the door, the portal. At long last, she was **home**.

Epilogue

Sharon turned round, expecting to see Sophios standing there for her in the forest, but there was nothing there. Nothing but harsh miles of Icelandic terrain, all stretched out around her.

She stood thinking for a moment before she caught sight of her travelling bag, lying in a heap in the snow, her lilac scarf draped over it. Suddenly she realised Windar's scarf was missing – she was wearing it when she had walked through the door, but now there was no trace of it. It was gone forever, like Sullaria, and Sophios, and Apnar, and the Bugle-Thoms, and Aphra, and... everything. And her clothes – they were just as they were when she had left, her new ones left behind. But there was something to take comfort from – if the bag was still there, and it hadn't been blown away, or covered in snow, surely no time could have passed on Earth, or as Sharon corrected herself, *in the present.*

She picked up her bag, wrapped her scarf round her neck, and started walking towards the coast.

~

Sharon was soon picked up by a member of the search party, who took her to her mother in Reykjavik, before they flew home together. Sharon could not help thinking of the Flycrafts as the plane glided over the north Atlantic, but of course she never said anything about them to her mother. She never told anyone about what had happened, but she could not possibly hold it all in forever. And so, some years later, she wrote it all down, sealed it in an envelope, and hid it. She didn't give it a title, or try to hide the identities of those she met along the way. All she was concerned about was getting it out of her system, and it was a terrific relief when she did.

And so her story lay hidden for some time, known only to her. But she couldn't keep it a secret – she couldn't sleep knowing what was hidden under her bed. So her story got out, gradually, and you're holding it in your hands right now...

The End

Printed in the United States
65649LVS00006B/88